THE CHILDREN'S TRAIN

A NOVEL

ESCAPE ON THE KINDERTRANSPORT

JANA ZINSER

BQB

Georgia

Published in the United States by BQB Publishing
(Boutique of Quality Books Publishing Company)
www.bqbpublishing.com

Printed in the United States of America

978-1-939371-85-0 (p)
978-1-939371-86-7 (e)

Library of Congress Control Number: 2015940363

Book design by Robin Krauss, www.bookformatters.com
Cover design by Ellis Dixon

I could not put this book down. These children's stories take an unbelievable journey through gut-wrenching sorrow and horrifying pain, yet explode with their raw courage and brute determination to survive and hang on to hope. This book is inspirational, informative, interesting, and should be read by all ages.

—Charles J. Weber,
Weber Communications, Los Angeles

The Children's Train takes the reader on a wide-eyed, unflinching ride through hell. Like *The Boy in the Striped Pajamas*, the novel reenacts the atrocities suffered by innocent victims of Hitler's Germany, through the eyes of its youngest casualties. You'll weep, you'll cheer, you'll stay up all night reading. This book will give you a deeper understanding of the scope of one of history's most egregious horrors.

—Suzy Vitello,
author of *The Moment Before* and *The Empress Chronicles*

CONTENTS

DEDICATION

It is with great passion that I tell the story of these children who lived in a time of tremendous evil and had to be bold just to stay alive. Although the children in my story are fictional, they represent both the many children who rode the Kindertransport and those who were not lucky enough to get a seat on the train. Since the moment I heard their historic tale, they have not left my mind. The Kindertransport children came to live in my conscience and would not leave until I told their story.

The Nazis killed six million Jews. One-and-a-half million of those Jews were children. Peter and Becca represent two of the more than ten thousand children who safely escaped to England on the Kindertransport. Most of the Kindertransport children never saw their parents again. All of them survived in their own ways and found their own paths in the world. If their tragedy taught them anything, it was that as long as there is life, there is hope, and sometimes, if you're lucky, love.

The children who survived these times are now in the twilight of their lives. But, in each, I imagine the heart of a child still lives and remembers what it was like to face the fear and sorrow that no child should ever know. They have shown us how valuable life is—and how hope can push us to survive beyond anything we thought we could bear. If we have learned anything from the struggles of their young lives, we will not be silent and stand by when evil comes calling. We will fight back.

AUTHOR'S NOTES

Although *The Children's Train: Escape on the Kindertransport* is inspired by actual historical figures, events, and places, this is a work of fiction. Names, characters, businesses, places, events, and incidents are either the products of the author's imagination or used in a fictitious manner. Any resemblance to actual persons, living or dead, or actual events is purely coincidental or incorporated in a fictitious way. The camps, ghettos, and many towns in the book are fictional, but are representative of real places.

For more information on the real events and children of the Kindertransport, contact The Kindertransport Association at www.kindertransport.org.

ACKNOWLEDGMENTS

It is with enormous gratitude that I acknowledge the support and encouragement that has allowed me to write this story. I want to thank Lisa Zinser, Lee Zinser, Jill Davidson, Celia Zinser, Branden Fox, Josh Fox, Conner Fox, Lanae Fox, Leslie Fox, Billie Evans, Christin and Buddy Lynn, Rabbi Aryeh Azriel, Dianna Gordon, Marc MacYoung, Amy Stephens Photography, Eric Woolson, and Robert Gosnell (author of *The Blue Collar Screenwriter*).

CHAPTER 1

HIS MUSIC WILL SAVE THE JEWS

(November 1938)

Peter Weinberg, with the gray, piercing eyes, was eleven when he had to face the truth that the world was filled with evil, and there was nothing he could do about it. The Nazi monster, Adolf Hitler, had risen to power in Germany, and he didn't like Jews, not even the small ones.

That day in November, 1938, Peter pushed back his sun-streaked blondish-brown hair and swept the butcher shop floor, chasing down even the tiniest speck of dust. "A clean floor shows German pride," his father Henry said. "If you work hard, you can make your own luck."

"Yes, Father," Peter said as he put the broom away. But Peter wasn't sure luck could be made. Not in Germany anyway.

Peter lived with his father, mother, and two younger sisters in a small cozy apartment above their butcher shop in Berlin. Peter's father, Henry Weinberg, a tall handsome man who walked with a cane, was a good butcher who only sold the best cuts of meat in his downstairs shop and cared for his customers like his family.

"Watch, Peter. It's all in the motion and the sharpness of the blade," his father said. He showed him how to wield the meat cleaver and make perfect cuts of meat, the sharp metal slicing through meat and bone in one swift, precise cut. "Set your mind and focus only on the cut."

"And keep your fingers out of the way," Peter teased.

His father smiled. "Yes, a butcher's first lesson. You will be a fine butcher some day."

Peter cringed inside but practiced his cleaver technique to please his father. He had become remarkably good. However, he preferred to line up the pieces of meat neatly in the display case to make a symmetrical design. Peter thought quality and presentation were a butcher's focus.

Peter felt comforted by the order of the meat lined up in precise rows in the spotless glass case, waiting to be sold. He loved the consistency of routine, and although he would much rather be listening to music, he enjoyed being with his father in the butcher shop. He could name the cuts of meats before he was four, and he often quietly recited them to calm himself.

Although the Jewish way of slaughtering animals was banned in Germany back in 1933, Peter knew his father continued to use the shechita method. His father told him that he would rather have Hitler mad at him than God.

The door swung open. Frank Soleman, the balding policeman, walked into the shop. The bell on the shop door tinkled right before Bruno, Frank's German Shepherd, trotted in behind him and barked at the small swinging bell, like he did every week.

"Good morning, Frank," Henry called out from behind the counter.

"Hello, Henry," Frank said, smiling.

Peter walked over to pet Bruno, whose bushy tail swung wildly with anticipation. The big dog nuzzled Peter, almost knocking him over. Bruno was tan, with a black face and a patch of black on his back that made him look like he was wearing a dog-size dinner jacket. "Guten Tag, Bruno," Peter said and laughed, scratching behind the dog's pointed ears. "Did you come for your bone today?"

Frank smiled at Peter. "Bruno comes to see you. The bone is just a bonus."

Peter liked Bruno. The dog didn't care that Peter was Jewish. To the dog, religion was irrelevant. Peter wasn't allowed to have a dog in the small apartment with his mother's oversized furniture, or in his father's shop filled with meat. So he loved it when Frank brought Bruno with him each week. Peter would play with the good-natured, big dog and pretend Bruno was his pet.

Sylvia Weinberg, Peter's mother, tucked a loose strand of hair into her swept-up do and hurried over to the meat counter. "Frank, Henry saved you a nice beef loin roast. I'll get it," she said, smiling and nodding. It was hard not to be happy around Sylvia. Although Henry was the butcher, the customers were really Sylvia's.

"Danke, Sylvia. I was hoping you'd say that," Frank said.

"Of course. We're only the best butcher shop in Berlin," Henry said.

"That's why I come here, and also because I live close by." Frank laughed.

Peter got a big meaty bone for Bruno, threw in some scraps of meat and fat, and wrapped it in shiny white butcher paper he ripped from the huge roll. He tied it closed with a string and handed the package to Frank. "Here is Bruno's bone, and a little something extra."

"Thank you, Peter, and Bruno thanks you," Frank said. "So, how about a song today?"

Six-year-old Becca, Peter's sister, skipped around the meat counter, carrying Gina, her doll. A dark-haired girl, Becca had defiant eyes and a sassy walk. As much as Peter sought refuge inside himself, Becca was outgoing, spirited, and unbridled. She rolled her eyes. "All he cares about is his stupid violin, and Bruno."

"Well, all you care about is your stupid doll," Peter shot back.

"Violins are stupider." Becca flipped back her curly hair.

"Play him a song, Peter," Sylvia coaxed. Baby Lilly, Peter's rosy-cheeked one-year-old sister, sat in a play area in the corner. The butcher shop was truly a family business.

Peter went into the back of the shop and came back with his beloved violin. Once he placed it under his chin, he felt transformed into another person, a bold person of great confidence and emotion. He could imagine doing great and daring things when he played the violin. His small hands orchestrated the melodies that were born from wood, string, and the depths of his soul. The music gave him a feeling of unfettered freedom and unsurpassed bravery, neither of which he felt like he had in real life.

He played a tune called "You Are Not Alone." It was a song his mother sang to him at night. It helped him go to sleep, kept away his nightmares of the monsters hiding in the corners, and banished that terrifying feeling of hurtling through darkness with no direction and the fear of what would happen when it stopped.

Sylvia smiled and nodded. "That's my Peter. His music will change the world someday," she bragged to Frank.

Peter turned away, hiding his face as he continued to play. His face flushed with embarrassment, but he couldn't hide his smile or the dance of his nimble fingers over the strings.

Frank nodded at the small maestro. Bruno, entranced, thumped down on his hind legs, with his huge tongue hanging out, and watched Peter's bow seesaw across the violin. The dog's ears, which always looked like they were saluting, twitched. He was a dog in a dinner jacket that appreciated good music and meaty bones.

Henry, in his white butcher's apron, leaned on his meat counter. "Maybe your music will save the Jews from Hitler," he said, smiling at Peter.

A shadow crossed the storefront window where the weekly meat specials were advertised. Frank looked over.

Policeman Karl Radley stood looming in the store window, blocking the sun as he glared at them. Radley, a tall man, about the same age as Henry and Frank, had short blond hair and a very small, thin, turned-up nose that always made him look like he smelled something foul.

As Radley stared through the window, he pointed at Henry and made a slashing gesture across his throat. He turned abruptly and stomped away.

Frank stiffened. He quickly paid for his meat and hustled Bruno out, without waiting for the song to end. Peter, who swayed with the music seeping from his pores, didn't even notice their abrupt departure. The door bounced shut from Frank's hasty retreat, and the bell tinkled. Peter kept on playing, locked in his own world where he was in control.

"You shouldn't have mentioned Hitler," Sylvia scolded Henry.

Henry waved his hand at her. "Ah, I've known Frank for years."

"I know, but Hitler doesn't care if you served in the Great War together," Sylvia pointed out.

Peter's father was a veteran of the Great War, when the Central Powers of Germany, Austria-Hungary, Turkey, and Bulgaria had fought the Allies of France, Russia, Italy, the British Empire, Belgium, Japan, and the United States, ending in 1918. Shrapnel from a land mine during the war had left Henry's strong athletic legs scarred and weak. He had told Peter that wars were started by people in offices and ended by soldiers on the front lines.

Henry was a German hero, but his wobbly legs had drained his spirit. Peter could sense his father's growing fear of the bold, abusive German soldiers, the same ones he had fought beside as patriots for Germany.

Peter had often heard his parents and their friends discussing the dark and devious tales of Adolf Hitler and the Nazi regime. Adolf Hitler, Chancellor of Germany, had appointed himself Fuhrer. All the armed forces now answered to him. As a dictator, his power had grown, along with his hatred of Jews. His laws had taken rights away from the Jewish people. Hitler was a name whispered when the lights went out, like stories of the Bogeyman: something dark and scary, yet so enormously cruel it could not be real. But Policeman Karl Radley was part of Hitler's force and Peter could not ignore that Radley was real, and to Peter, much scarier.

Radley was a man of high ambition, but from a loving family of low means. His career options had always been limited, because he wanted power without having to work for it. Although he was strong and determined, he had been refused admittance to the military because one of his legs was a tiny bit longer than the other, and he walked with a slight limp. He had the cobbler make special shoes to hide his imperfection.

Radley's father had finally helped him secure a job in a bank where his father's childhood friend was the president, and Jewish. Radley swept, mopped, and emptied the trash. To the arrogant Radley, this was a humiliation he had not been able to accept. In order to compensate for the insult, Radley had done as little work as possible, just to even things out.

One day, before the war had made his legs not work, Henry had entered the bank in his military uniform. The bank president had been confronting Radley, who had been leaning on his mop and bucket instead of cleaning up the snow melted from customers' shoes. "You do not seem to want to give the effort this job requires. Perhaps you would be happier at another job," the president had quietly suggested to Radley.

Radley's slightly trembling hands had balled up in fists. With all the fury and power he had held in for so long, he had attacked the bank president. Henry had defended the bank president, taking a few blows from Radley, but eventually knocking a bloodied Radley to the floor. "Go, before you are arrested," Henry had ordered.

Radley had wiped the blood from his mouth, and looked at all the customers staring at him. He had kicked the bucket of water and thrown the mop, then stomped out of the bank, promising himself that a Jewish man would never again determine his fate.

A few months later he had taken a job as a messenger for the police, who did not know about the slight difference in his legs because of his special shoes. It had paid less money than the bank job, but Radley had seen an opportunity for advancement and power, something he strongly desired. Radley had been willing to sacrifice anything to move up the ranks.

He had found his first opportunity when he had discovered two high-ranking on-duty officers smoking cigarettes and drinking with women who were not their wives late at night in the police station basement, where the important records were kept. Soon after, those same officers had gladly helped him gain a position as an officer, in exchange for his silence. His special shoes thudded heavily as he walked, and he used it to intimidate. In this manner, he had stomped his way to the top over many years. His proclivity to hatred was primed for the rise of Hitler, and he had eagerly become a Nazi as soon as the opportunity had presented itself.

—〰—

Peter's father had known Karl Radley would never be his customer, but he had never imagined that Radley's grudge against him would last a long time and cause so much trouble.

In the butcher shop that day, Peter put Radley out of his mind, and concentrated on making the music flow from his violin. The violin was his best friend, his escape. When he played the violin, he was happy, and the world was safe. When the music burst into the air, he felt his worries about this man named Hitler, and about Radley, his father's enemy, melt away, as the melody surrounded him, soothing his fears. He was lost in the songs of his Germany, his home.

CHAPTER 2

THE FUHRER IS HERE

(November 1938)

The trees in nearby Edelweiss Park were ablaze with the red and gold of fall. The birds, as always, were squawking and singing. German weather was unpredictable, but this was one of the last warm days of the year, "altweibersommer" or "old woman summer," as they called it.

Peter's school was a large brick building near the center of Berlin by the business district, not too far from his father's butcher shop and their apartment. Peter and most of the neighborhood children walked to school.

Inside the school, Peter hurried down the hall, swinging his violin. He had come from the music room. As always, he had been reluctant to stop playing, and now he was late for his homeroom check-in before school ended.

Wolfgang, a brutish boy with thick eyebrows and cruel eyes that a cunning smile couldn't hide, stepped out of the hall bathroom. He snatched Peter's violin and tossed it to Kurt, the tall, sweaty boy who was his unquestioning sidekick. The boys were older and much taller than Peter and easily played catch with his precious violin, as he repeatedly jumped for it. Wolfgang dangled it, and then threw it over Peter's head to Kurt.

The bell suddenly shrilled, announcing the end of school. Done with their keep-away game, Wolfgang tossed the violin above Peter's head. It twisted in the air, beyond Peter's frantic grasp. Wolfgang and Kurt laughed at Peter's clumsy attempts to grab his somersaulting instrument.

Wolfgang swept his leg out and hit Peter's legs, knocking him off his feet. As Peter fell, his long delicate hands reached for his falling violin. Wolfgang and Kurt laughed and pointed as Peter hit the ground.

When Peter's uncoordinated, flying body came to rest, he held the violin safely above him, a prized trophy. Peter was as surprised as Wolfgang that he had rescued the treasured violin from the taunting assault. As Peter realized he'd won, his mouth couldn't help but curl into a smile of triumph and that made Wolfgang mad.

Wolfgang snarled as he quickly advanced toward Peter, kicked him with a black leather boot, and turned away. "Jew rat!"

Peter couldn't hear what he said. All he heard was the loud beating of his own frightened heart and his pounding thoughts. At least his violin was safe.

Then Wolfgang gave a Nazi salute, his arm extended.

"Heil Hitler!" Kurt said in response.

Then Peter understood. They hated him, not his violin, which, oddly, was a relief. He was used to people hating Jews and had come to expect it, but there was little hope of redemption for anyone who hated music.

Wolfgang sauntered down the hall with his self-satisfied swagger, never looking back. Kurt, his ruffian shadow, ran after him.

Peter knew that Wolfgang had been born into a family of hate. Wolfgang's father, Wilbur, had been fired from his button factory job for stealing tools. He had blamed his years of making small buttons with the machines for his arthritic hands and had felt entitled to supplement his income with the factory's tools. His family had lost their home and had to move in with Wolfgang's grandparents. Wolfgang's father hadn't been able to find another job, because nobody wanted to hire a tool thief with gnarled hands. He had started drinking, and soon he had no hope left. The factory owner who had fired him had been Jewish. Wolfgang's father's hatred of Jews had grown from his own thievery, misplaced blame, and painful arthritis. He had eagerly passed that hate on to his son.

In the school hall, Peter pulled his violin to him in a protective hug, breathing heavily, still curled up on the floor.

The classroom doors flew open, and children stampeded down the hall, somehow avoiding the small boy curled around his violin like a musical cocoon.

"Peter, what are you doing down there? You're going to get trampled."

Peter looked up. Eva Rosenberg, eleven, with black hair, towered over him. Her friend, Olga Schmidt, was standing beside her. Olga tossed back her long blonde hair. She was pretty, and she knew it.

Eva reached down and grabbed Peter's skinny arm, which was still locked tightly around the violin. She unexpectedly pulled him up off the floor, like a ribbon of horsehair snapped from the violin's bow.

Peter shot to his feet. He nodded, still clutching his violin. "Danke. Thank you."

He didn't move, because he did not want Eva to release her touch. He knew everyone thought Olga was the prettiest girl in the school, but all Peter could see were her cold empty eyes and her bad attitude, and he was not impressed. Eva was obviously the most beautiful girl in the world, and one day he wished she would be his girlfriend. Who was he kidding? That was never going to happen. She was already taller and braver than him. Peter didn't stand a chance.

Olga sneered at the disheveled Peter. "You look like you almost got run over by a train. No one is going to take your violin."

Eva let go of Peter's arm. He looked down the hall where Wolfgang and Kurt strutted, and he nodded. "Not today."

"Is your mother meeting you?" Eva asked him.

Peter shook his head. Eva was so pretty that it was hard for him to respond when she talked to him. "No, she had to take Becca to see Dr. Levy." Peter looked down and straightened his clothes.

"What's wrong with my favorite little spitfire?" Eva asked, smiling.

"She talks too much, but the doctor can't fix that."

Eva laughed.

"She got a blister from roller skating, and it's infected," Peter explained.

"Come on then, you can walk with us." Eva smiled at him again.

"Okay."

"Behind us. You can walk behind us," Olga corrected. Peter shrugged, but Eva reached over and pulled Peter beside her.

Outside the school, the German children poured out the front door. Charlie Beckman, a slight seven-year-old, ran to his father Arnold, who waited for him at the corner like he did every day. Charlie ran into his arms, and Arnold picked him up and swung him around. Charlie threw his head back and laughed at something his father said. Peter wondered if his father would have done that, if he hadn't been in the way of a land mine in the war.

Gripping his violin, Peter walked with Olga and Eva as they hurried down the steps. Olga was not as well dressed as Eva, but she had a confident, almost flippant, attitude that made her stand out in an attention-getting, superior way. However, Peter's eyes were on Eva.

Hans Vogner and Stephen Levy came up to the girls and Peter. "Hey, Peter, are you ready to play football?" Hans asked.

Peter shook his head. He was terrified when the ball came hurtling toward him, and all he wanted to do was avoid it. To him, the game of football seemed to be pointless and extremely injury-prone.

"Real heroes of Germany play football," Stephen said, smiling.

Peter shrugged. "I don't want to be a hero." His father was a hero. What good had it done him?

Hans and Stephen laughed. "Are you going to the park today?" Hans asked.

Eva nodded. Olga flipped her long blonde hair back and scoffed, "You're not allowed there."

"They haven't caught us yet!" Stephen said, sending out the weekly challenge before their race to the park.

"What about you, Peter? Are you coming?" Hans asked.

"No, I have violin lessons."

"Too bad," Stephen replied.

"Not really." Peter knew he would much rather play the violin than have a ball kicked at him by Stephen and Hans, embarrassing him in front of Eva.

"Last one there loves Hitler!" Hans teased. Stephen and Hans laughed and jogged away, disappearing into the crowd of students.

Olga and Eva left the schoolyard and hurried through the crowded downtown streets, with their school knapsacks over their shoulders. They could barely move through the surging crowd that was shifting and murmuring in anticipation. Peter followed the girls, swept up in the frantic motion of the nervous people.

"Oh no, we're going to be late. The boys will get there first," Eva said.

Olga pointed as the crowd's excitement rose. "What is this? What's going on?"

The girls stood on their tiptoes, straining to see through the sidewalk crowd. Peter pulled his violin in closely and bent down to peer through the moving throng of people. The crowd squished him as he looked for Eva. He saw her right in front of him, as she bounced up to see over a hulking man with gnarled arthritic hands and a frazzled, fair-haired woman. Peter tried to squeeze in closer to the girls.

"What is it? What's everyone looking at?" Eva asked.

Olga shrugged. "I don't know."

The woman in front of them turned around. She smiled, her face flushed. "It's the Fuhrer! Herr Hitler is coming!"

Peter's eyes grew big with fright. The Bogeyman was coming here, right in front of him. Peter's heart pounded, his hands shook, and he was ready to run.

As the woman turned back around, the crowd lurched forward, surrounding them. There was no escape.

Olga bumped into the man with crooked fingers in front of her. He turned around and glared at her. It was Wilbur, Wolfgang's father, the tool thief, come to pay his respects to his hero.

Peter didn't even notice the sweat beading on his forehead, as he watched the motorcade of dark cars draped with swastika banners approach. Following the escort, Adolf Hitler stood up in his open car, his face drawn in seriousness, as if smiling was undignified. His eyes were pinched into slits of dull arrogance. Peter thought he looked like the hungry rats on their hunt for prey in Vogner's nearby fastener factory. The crowd cheered, beside itself with awe and excitement. Peter shivered.

Hitler raised his right arm, holding his hand straight. "Sieg heil!" he shouted.

The people in the crowd responded by raising their arms in the Nazi salute. "Sieg heil! Sieg heil!" they yelled in unison. "Hail to victory!"

Eva and Olga stared, but they did not raise their arms. Peter gripped his violin, as his eyes darted around the crowd. He wished he could get out his violin and disappear into his music, so all this would vanish. This was too real for the magic of his violin, and he was worried about Eva.

Wilbur whipped around and glared at them. "Salute! Show your respect," he ordered, as he pointed his crooked fingers at them. He spied Peter. "You too, you little worm!"

Peter could smell Wilbur's alcohol-soaked breath. He turned away, hiding behind Olga.

Olga looked at Wilbur's snarling face, then at the agitated crowd around her. She glanced at Eva. Then she quickly looked down, unable to look her friend in the eyes, as she slowly raised her arm in a salute.

Peter's eyes widened as he watched Olga's arm creep upward. He peeked out at Eva, who clenched her arms at her side, her face contorted into defiant lines of anger. Peter's knuckles turned white, as he gripped the violin as if it were the only thing that could save him.

"Heil Hitler!" the crowd shouted in impassioned unison.

Wilbur stepped in front of Eva. His breath hissed out; Peter could smell the foul odors of alcohol. He cringed and hid back behind the temporary protection of Olga.

"Raise your arm! You must be a dirty Jew," Wilbur shouted at Eva. She looked at Olga, who was frozen with fear. There would be no help there. Peter stayed hidden behind Olga with only the end of his violin visible.

Eva turned and faced the ugly Wilbur, with her hands balled into fists, unable to move.

Peter carefully released one side of the violin and reached out to Eva from behind Olga. He wanted to save her, but he wasn't brave or fast enough.

Wilbur swung his huge gnarled hand at Eva with great force. Peter pulled his outstretched hand back, as the man hit Eva on the side of her head. She fell down, slamming her head on the sidewalk.

Wilbur kicked her and turned back around, as if he assaulted young girls every day.

Wolfgang's mother looked back with concern at Eva sprawled on the sidewalk, but Wilbur jerked her back around. "Pay attention! The Fuhrer is here!" he ordered.

"Heil Hitler!" the crowd shouted in political unison.

The motorcade passed by Peter, who saw the Fuhrer from between the surging bodies. Adolf Hitler, the great leader of Germany, was not a cartoon after all; he was real. Peter pulled back his violin to protect it, then vomited on the ground. No one noticed.

After Hitler passed, the crowd dispersed, stepping around Eva lying dazed on the sidewalk. She reached up, touched her head, and groaned. Her school knapsack lay beside her.

Peter wiped his mouth on his sleeve and watched, as Olga knelt beside Eva and looked up at the hurriedly passing people. Tears ran down her face. Then she stood up and ran into the crowd, leaving Eva on the ground.

Peter crept up cautiously to Eva, reached out his hand, and pulled her up. He had missed his chance to save her, and he saw in her eyes that she knew it.

CHAPTER 3

TIMES HAVE CHANGED

(November 1938)

Eva lived several blocks from Peter in a well-kept house with a manicured yard. Olga's family rented the tiny house next door. Later that day, Olga peeked out of her modest bedroom. Her breath misted the window as she watched the white lace curtains being closed in Eva's bedroom across the yard. She absently dragged her finger against the pane of glass, bowed her head, and disappeared from the window, leaving the outline of an X over Eva's house on the windowpane.

―⁓―

Dr. Jacob Levy stood beside Eva's lacy bed. Though her head was bandaged with gauze, she was awake.

Eva's mother Helga wore a dark drab dress despite the fact that she was a seamstress. With her hair severely pulled back in a bun, she watched them from across the room, her arms crossed against her heavy chest. Eva's father Bert, a well-dressed, slightly pudgy man, sat on the bed and patted Eva's hand.

Peter stood in the doorway and peered in tentatively. Bert motioned to him. "Peter, come in."

"I'm late for music lessons." Peter hesitated. "I just wanted to make sure she was okay."

Bert nodded and smiled. "Thank you, Peter."

Dr. Levy looked at Peter. "I was just with your mother and sister." He turned to Bert. "Two patients in one day is unusual, since Hitler won't let me practice on non-Jews."

"I know. Hitler's boys still sneak in the back door of my shop to get their clothes, but soon they'll be too scared to do even that," Bert said.

The doctor patted Eva's shoulder. "Don't worry, Eva. You're going to be fine."

"What about next time?" Bert frowned. "No one's safe anymore. Thirty-two countries met in France to discuss Jewish refugee policies, and almost all of them just gave excuses why they can't take any Jews."

"There's no place for us anymore," Jacob said.

Bert patted Eva. "And now our children. Is there nothing left for us? Will no one stand up for a young girl?"

Peter hung his head and slipped out of the room.

He walked slowly down the sidewalk, carrying his violin by its handle. His feet dragged, as if he struggled against extraordinarily heavy shoes.

As he approached the entrance to Edelweiss Park, he spotted Hans and Stephen near the indoor pool building next door, chasing each other around. "Do you think the girls are there yet?" he heard Hans ask Stephen.

"Yes, they will be waiting for us, the true German heroes," Stephen said. He flexed his muscles, dancing backward.

Hans stopped chasing him and stared at the door to the pool.

"What?" Stephen asked.

Hans pointed. Stephen turned around to see a sign on the door to the indoor pool reading: "JEWS NOT WANTED IN THIS PLACE."

"I don't understand how we would hurt the water," Hans said, sighing.

"We would just show them up anyway," Stephen said.

"But I like to swim."

Peter walked up to them. "The girls won't be coming today. Something . . . came up."

Before Hans and Stephen could say anything, Peter turned away. Clutching his violin, he ran up the impressive flight of stairs of the large stone building across the street, at the German Music Academy.

—ɱ—

Adeline, a slender woman with braided blonde hair, quickly ushered Peter into her music room. He set his violin case down gently and opened it.

Adeline reached out and slowly closed the lid. As it snapped shut, she sighed and smiled, the kind of smile that is forced and fades quickly. "Not now, Peter." She pointed to a chair. "Sit down. I have something to tell you."

Peter picked up his violin and held it to his small, heaving chest, but didn't sit. He stared at her.

Adeline took a deep breath, looking down at the floor as she did. When she looked up at Peter, her eyes brimmed with tears. Peter had never seen an adult cry before. Seeing her so distraught was frightening.

"I'm afraid your lessons here must end. I'm very sorry, Peter."

Peter stepped back, feeling cold with shock. "I'll practice harder. I really will. Please, Frau Adeline, don't—"

Adeline placed her hand on his shaking shoulder. "Peter, it's not your practicing. You're very good, really quite extraordinary, but times have changed." She cleared her throat. "Someone has reported that I was teaching Jews."

"Why? Music can't hurt anyone."

"You're right. Many of us wish we could change things, but—"

"Then, why can't you?" Peter asked.

"I'm sorry, Peter. I could lose my job." Adeline sighed. "This is Hitler's Germany. There's nothing I can do."

Peter carefully snapped the latch on his violin case. "Yes, I understand."

But he didn't.

CHAPTER 4

THE WORLD TURNED OUT ITS LIGHT

(November 1938)

A few days later, Eva played checkers with Olga on the floor of her room. Her bandage was gone, the wound was healing, but the damage to her soul felt unfixable. Eva's fluffy white cat, Snowflake, watched them, rubbing against Eva.

The cat meowed. Eva laughed. "Snowflake wants to play checkers."

Olga laughed. She looked around Eva's beautiful room with the big lacy bed. "I wish I had a room like this."

Eva's brother William burst into her room. He was eighteen, a handsome boy with a confident swagger and the twinkle of a daredevil in his eyes.

"Hey, ugly sister, I need money." He ran his hand through his hair.

"No, you never paid me back last time," Eva said. "Get a job."

"I don't have time to work." He tossed his head, jerked open the drawer to her bedside table, and grabbed a few reichsmarks. "This is all you have?"

Eva nodded.

"It's not enough. I need more," William said, as he tucked the stolen money into his pocket. As he walked by the girls, he kicked their checkerboard. The checkers flew, and Olga glared at him.

"Get out of here, William!" Eva threw her shoe at him, hitting him in the back before he slammed the door.

"I wish I had a bigger shoe." Eva shrugged at Olga. Then she put her finger to her mouth and motioned Olga over to her dresser drawer. She pulled out a fat sock, reached into it, and pulled out a small roll of reichsmarks. She smiled slyly. "He's not as smart as he thinks. Hey, let's go to the candy store."

Olga nodded and followed Eva out of the house. They skipped, linking arms, as they approached the candy store. They sang a children's chant:

Best friends, best friends
The best days are when we're together.
Best friends, best friends
Best friends forever and ever.

—ᴍ—

Peter walked back from delivering a beef loin roast to Herr Frank, who hadn't been back to the shop since he had left in such a hurry during Peter's last serenade. Instead, he had called to have his meat delivered to 435 Edelweiss Street, a few blocks away. Peter didn't mind. Herr Frank usually let him take Bruno for a walk after he delivered the meat. Bruno loved to scamper up the steps to the bandstand at the edge of the park, as Peter pretended he was playing his violin to a crowd, waiting anxiously to hear him. He dreamed that he would be the talk of Berlin someday: Peter Weinberg, the famous musician.

That day, Herr Frank had said both he and Bruno were sick, and asked Peter to leave the meat on the table. Peter had done what he was asked, but neither one had looked sick to him.

Outside, Peter walked slowly with his head down until he was almost in front of the candy store. He heard Eva and Olga's voices and looked up.

"Let's get chocolate-covered cherries," Eva was saying to Olga.

"Yes, lots," Olga said.

Then Eva and Olga stopped suddenly. Painted in yellow and black across the candy store window were six-pointed stars of David and the words: "DON'T SELL TO JEWS. THE JEWS ARE OUR MISFORTUNE."

A Nazi officer stood outside with his arms crossed. He looked at Olga, and then nodded sideways at Eva. "What are you doing with that girl?" he asked.

"She's my friend," Olga said, but she let go of Eva and backed up.

The officer shook his head. "Is she a Jew? Didn't you see the sign? The Jews are our misfortune. Jews cannot be our friends."

Peter peered out from behind a tree. His heart pounded. His feet felt like they were made of lead, and he couldn't run away. He was too scared to do anything but watch.

Another Nazi officer down the street whistled loudly and motioned. "Come on, Boris."

"All right, Thomas." Boris waved his hand. "Be a good German girl and leave the Jews alone." He turned away from the girls and headed toward the other officer.

As the Nazis headed off down the street, Eva hesitated, and then ran to the candy store steps. She motioned for Olga to come with her.

Olga shook her head. "I don't think they'll let you in."

"Come on. They won't know I'm Jewish."

Eva paused on the candy store steps as movement and raised voices from down the sidewalk reached her ears. The girls turned to see Boris and Thomas harassing Rabbi Mosel, who nervously stroked his gray-streaked beard.

"Step off the sidewalk when you see us coming!" Thomas shouted at the old man.

Peter watched the confrontation unfold from behind his tree bunker.

Boris pushed Mosel's shoulder. "Show respect, old man." He pulled a standard issue Nazi dagger from his belt with one hand, and knocked Mosel's kippah off his head.

Mosel looked down at the ground. The children could hear him praying in Yiddish: "God, look down on me now."

"Shut up, old Jew man!" Boris swung the dagger close to Mosel's neck, then roughly grabbed Mosel's beard and cut it off. Blood oozed from the old man's injured face. As the whiskers fell to the ground, Boris and Thomas laughed and pushed the rabbi.

Peter's eyes grew big and his mouth hung open. Rabbi Mosel was a powerful man of God, but the soldiers were controlling him.

"Next time, step off the sidewalk when you see a German officer coming, or you'll end up like your beard," Boris said. The two Nazis turned on their heels and continued down the street.

Peter looked over to where Olga had been standing, but she was no longer there. He could see her running down the street toward her home. Eva stood still, as if frozen, on the candy store steps.

Mosel picked up his kippah and walked away. Eva shook herself a little, and then ran after him. "Rabbi Mosel! Are you all right?"

"They're robbing our souls, and the world has turned out its light and gone to sleep," Mosel said sadly.

Eva looked up at the wise man. "The world can't sleep forever."

"This I hope and this I pray. Go home where it is safe, Eva." Mosel hobbled down the sidewalk, cloaked in humiliation, his beard cut, and his spirit crushed but not broken.

Peter warbled his usual three shrill whistles to get Eva's attention, then stepped out from behind the tree and ran to her. "Are you okay?" he asked.

Eva ran over to him. "They cut Rabbi Mosel's beard," she said, still in shock.

"I know. Come with me, I want to show you something." Peter thought that maybe he could distract her from the rabbi's attack.

Eva followed more from numbing shock than really wanting to go.

Peter led her down the block to a fleet of red-and-green garbage trucks parked in neat rows, waiting their turn to negotiate the city streets and pick up the remnants of trash no one wanted.

"This? This is it?" Eva asked, when she saw the tidy line of garbage trucks.

Peter nodded, as he climbed into the cab of a truck and motioned Eva to follow. He reached out his hand and helped her up. Her hand was smooth, soft, and warm.

She sat beside him, as he pretended to drive the powerful truck. Then she pointed to the ignition. "There's no key."

"I wasn't really going to—"

"It's no good without the key," Eva said seriously, suddenly very interested.

"I know where the keys are." Peter smiled. "Wait here."

Peter jumped down from the cab and walked over to the tiny building that served as the office. He knew the schedule of the trucks and that no one would be in the office for a little while. He carefully pried open the office window and reached in to the board of hooks that held each truck's key on its painted number. He counted down three from the front, matching the position of the truck in the parking lot, and pulled the key off the pegboard.

Peter smiled and warbled three short, shrill whistles as he walked back to the truck, holding his prized key aloft like a trophy for Eva to admire. He climbed back into the cab, reached down, and put the key in the ignition. He had often driven his father's meat truck on their delivery route, while sitting on his father's lap, substituting for his father's legs.

He turned the key. As the garbage truck started up, he hollered like he had seen his father do at a football game. Eva clapped.

Peter felt powerful. "Look at this." He leaned out the window and pretended to steer the wheel with his feet. "Don't worry, I'm a good driver. I don't even need my hands." Someday, he would be a remarkable driver. People would stare as he drove by with a beautiful girl, hopefully Eva, he thought. "Someday, I'll take you for a real ride in one of these," he promised.

"Okay, but don't drive with your feet," she said. They both laughed, the constricting fear from watching the rabbi's humiliation temporarily forgotten.

Peter knew the drivers would be arriving soon, so he turned off the motor. They both jumped down, before the fleet of trucks took off on their bold journeys across the city, seeking the perpetual rubbish. He put the key back on the pegboard. "I'd better get back to the shop. My father has some lamb chops and a roast for me to take to the Vogners."

"Okay."

Eva followed Peter back toward their block. Peter turned toward the shop to get the meat packages for his next delivery, and Eva headed toward home.

Eva turned back. "Peter?" she called.

Peter stopped and turned around.

"Someday, you will drive that truck."

"And you will ride with me." Peter smiled. "I'm a good driver."

Eva laughed and waved. "Tell my favorite little spitfire 'hello'!"

Peter ran down the street toward his father's shop, jubilant that he had sat so close to Eva and that she thought him capable of driving the massive truck.

As he turned the corner, he saw William, Eva's brother, opening up his father's tailor shop that was closed for the day. Bert was a tailor, and Helga was a seamstress. William let a well-dressed man, with a scar across his eye, slip inside.

Curious, Peter detoured across the street to the shop. He reached up to the windowsill to peer in, but lost his grip and slid back down. He wedged the toe of his shoe into a crevice in the bricks and pulled himself up again to see into the window.

Inside the tailor shop, William held out his hand, wiggling his fingers. "Hurry up! Did you get all my documents?"

The man nodded and handed William an ink-smudged envelope.

William opened the envelope and looked inside. He nodded. Then he pulled a key from his pocket, opened the store's money drawer, and handed the man some money. "You'll have to find someone else to be your connection. With these papers, I'm out of here."

William shoved the papers inside his shirt and turned quickly. Peter ducked down, his foot trapped in the crevice, and fell to the ground. His foot was freed by the fall. He jumped up as William opened the door.

"Peter? What are you doing here? Get out of my way when you see me coming." William pushed Peter out of his way.

Peter limped down the sidewalk, hurrying away from William, who clutched his secret documents that would get him out of Germany inside his shirt.

CHAPTER 5

FEARLESS GERMAN HERO

(November 1938)

Later that day, Peter set off to deliver the lamb chops and roast to the Vogners. He approached the large house, which was fronted by an ornate iron gate. In the yard, Hans and Stephen played football against Otto, seventeen, a strong, friendly boy. Since he was so much older, they looked up to him and his superior football skills.

Eddie Vogner, Hans's eight-year-old brother, was sitting on the porch with his mother, cheering the other boys on. He was short and stocky, with small hands and feet, his eyes were almond shaped, and his tongue was a little too large for his mouth. He wore a hat that hung down to cover his face, hiding his slight differences from the hatred Hitler had for anyone with a disability. Peter knew that doctors called Eddie a "mongoloid." But Eddie's mother never let anyone use that word. He also knew that people like Eddie were often institutionalized, even before Hitler had come to power. But Eddie continued living a relatively normal life with his family, due to his mother's insistence, Dr. Levy's medical support, and the fact that Eddie was protected by seldom leaving home.

"Go, Otto!" Eddie called, and then let out a squeaking cheer.

Peter gave the meat to Hans's mother, who took it inside. He sat down on the porch next to Eddie, out of the way of the ball.

"Go, Otto!" Eddie shouted over and over.

Peter watched the boys play a sport he would never understand. Why would anyone want to run back and forth while kicking a ball? The perpetual uselessness and potential for facial injury made no sense to him. Peter took his yo-yo from his pocket, made it zip down the string, and snapped it back up. A yo-yo was something you could control, he thought. A yo-yo took real skill.

Otto maneuvered the ball down the yard, pushing Hans and Stephen out of the way. Stephen chased after him and jumped onto Otto's back. Laughing, Otto threw him off and continued down the front yard. He jumped into the air, kicking his leg out in an explosive side-kick, and scored. Then he cupped his hand to his ear.

"I can hear the crowd cheering. Otto! Otto! They love me. I am a fearless German hero!" Otto yelled and emitted his boisterous cheer.

Peter laughed at the competitive nonsense of which he would never be capable. He did not like any game that involved pain. He made his yo-yo leap out and twist around the front porch post, and then snapped it back. No one paid attention to his extraordinary yo-yo talent. They were focused on the football match.

Eddie clapped and cheered. "Otto! Otto! I love Otto!"

Otto bowed to Eddie. "Thank you, Eddie. You are my best friend because you appreciate superior talent."

Eddie beamed.

"What about you, Peter?" Otto asked.

Peter couldn't help but smile at Otto's enthusiasm. "You are a fearless German hero," Peter admitted.

Otto turned to Hans and Stephen. "It's officially been confirmed!" He smiled. "I'll see you at the school field tomorrow. You better practice your side-kicks." He jumped into the air, kicking his leg out to the side.

They waved. Eddie stood up and waved enthusiastically. "Bye, Otto. Remember, I'm your best friend. You and I have superior talent."

Hans and Stephen laughed, and Peter smiled.

"That's right, Eddie. That's right." Otto waved and strode off.

Otto's father, Martin, was waiting for him outside the gate. Peter knew Martin; he was a burly red-faced police officer who was perpetually in a foul mood.

Martin grabbed Otto's ear and pulled him away. He smacked Otto's head as the four boys watched.

"What do you think you're doing?" Martin yelled at Otto.

Otto shrugged. "Just playing football."

Martin looked at the other boys with narrowed eyes and a pinched mouth. "With them?" Martin hit him again.

Otto raised his hand to protect his head from repeated hits. "They're my friends."

"I've taught you better than that." Martin sneered.

Anna was watching from the porch window, her mouth open. She frantically waved the boys inside, motioning directly at Eddie.

Peter saw her and wanted to run inside to the safety of their big house, but he could not pull away from the terror of what he was seeing. He had the urge to throw his yo-yo at Martin with full speed. Maybe it would wrap tightly around the man's neck, as if it were a porch post, he thought. But Peter's violent shaking and all-encompassing fear made it impossible.

The next day, Peter hurried up the school steps with Becca close behind. Olga walked a few steps away. Eva waved, but Olga hurried on, pretending she didn't see her.

Hans and Stephen approached Otto, as he strode up the stairs. "You won't win today, even if we both have to hang on your back," Stephen said, laughing.

"And Eddie, the traitor, isn't here to cheer you on," Hans said, as he slapped Otto on the back.

Otto looked down at the ground. "I can't play today."

"Why? Did we hurt you yesterday?" Stephen teased.

Peter paused and pulled Becca back, so he could hear what Stephen and Hans were saying, but Becca wasn't paying attention. She was watching a defiant butterfly dance on the cooling fall wind.

"What happened to your superior talent?" Hans asked. Stephen laughed, as he exaggeratedly mocked Otto's football side-kick.

Otto didn't laugh. "I won't be able to play with you anymore."

Stephen and Hans looked at each other. "Ever?" Hans asked.

Otto looked down, unable to meet his friends' eyes. He slowly shook his head. "My father says I can't even talk to you."

"Why?" Stephen asked.

"You're Jews." Otto's voice cracked.

"We know," Hans said, trying to make a joke.

"We've always been Jews," Stephen said.

"It's different now. Now, there's Hitler." Otto paused again. "My father has become a Nazi." Otto shrugged. "I'm a kid, and he's my father."

Otto's eyes filled with tears. Pursing his lips, he finally looked up. He had a black eye and a swollen lip. He quickly turned and walked away.

Becca looked at Peter. "Why don't you play football?"

"Hush, Becca. Don't you know when to be quiet?" Peter grabbed Becca's hand and pulled her toward the school, frightened that a father would do that to his son.

"But why? Why don't you want to play football? All the boys play."

"Because it's stupid. I don't care about football. Now, hush up, Becca."

Later that day, Otto and Wolfgang, the same boys had who taunted Peter over his violin, played football with the other boys on the school field. Hans, Eva, Peter, and Stephen stood against the fence, watching them, unofficially banned from playground games.

Peter didn't care. The fence was where he usually spent his time, watching the other children play while making music in his head, wishing he could spend this useless time instead in the music room with his violin.

Otto brought the ball down the yard, as Wolfgang tried to take it away. Otto twisted the ball around with his foot and faked out Wolfgang. He side-kicked the ball, shooting his leg into the air and falling to the ground, but he scored.

Hans and Stephen cheered and clapped. "Goal!" Stephen yelled. Peter smiled.

Wolfgang suddenly whipped around and unexpectedly hurled the ball at them. It hit Stephen in the face, and blood gushed from his nose.

Otto instinctively took a step toward Stephen to help him, but Wolfgang held him back, laughing. "Look, they do bleed!"

Stephen wiped the blood from his face. Peter looked away, as if he didn't see it, but he didn't know what was worse, the fact that no one stood up for Stephen or the bloody injury.

The bell rang, and the football players all rushed past, intentionally pushing and knocking into Stephen, Hans, Eva, and Peter. Otto stopped uncertainly, and waited, caught between allegiances.

As they entered the school lunchroom, the Wehrmacht marching music, so popular with the Third Reich, played from a phonograph in the corner.

A thick plain teacher clapped her hands loudly. "Quiet down! Eat your food, and enjoy the music!"

Hans, Stephen, Peter, and Eva sat at one table. Olga sat behind Eva at another table. Eva turned around and leaned toward Olga. "Olga, what's wrong? Why won't you play with me?"

"Things have changed," Olga said.

"But—"

The teacher hit Eva's injured head with a book, and Eva cried out.

"I said shut up, and eat your food!" The teacher loomed over the children, the book ready to strike Eva again.

Footsteps stomped in the hall outside the lunchroom, and then the door burst open.

Karl Radley strode in, wearing his police uniform. He stomped into the lunchroom. The nauseating aroma of his cologne swirled around him.

Radley's boots clicked to the front. "Attention, kinder! I have an announcement from the mayor of Berlin. Jewish children are no longer welcome in this school. They must leave, immediately!"

All the children turned and stared at Hans, Stephen, Peter, and Eva.

Radley turned on his heels and glared at them. "Now!"

The four banished children stood up. Otto looked at them, his eyes wide like a frightened animal not knowing which way to run from danger. Olga kept her eyes on her food.

"You may take nothing with you. Go," Radley shouted. "Schnell!"

The Jewish children walked toward the door, looking back at the children who used to be their friends.

Otto suddenly stood up. Hans, Stephen, Peter, and Eva stopped and stared at him.

"Why do they have to go?" Otto said, his voice wavering. "They're students here. We have known them all our lives."

Radley glared at Otto and marched over to stand in front of him. "Because they are contaminating this school. Sit down, you idiot!" Radley spat out each word.

Otto glanced at his friends, and then slowly sat down, his allegiance chosen reluctantly by an unspoken threat of force.

The three boys, and Eva with tears in her eyes, turned back around. Their football friend could not help them today. With their heads down and shoulders slumped, they shuffled to the door, exiled from their school.

As they passed by, Wolfgang stuck out his foot. With the same leg sweep he'd used to get the violin, he pulled Peter's legs out from under him. Peter stumbled and fell, his arms and legs flopping as he tried to hang on to his violin.

The students laughed, mostly from nervousness, but Radley laughed the loudest, with real ridicule. "Well, look, it's the butcher's boy."

Otto unknowingly grunted, as he clenched his fists and gritted his teeth. His face turned red, but he did not speak.

Splayed out on the floor, Peter could see all the children's feet under the lunch table. Their feet look no different from mine, he thought. He pulled himself up, but refused to look at Wolfgang. He wouldn't give Wolfgang the satisfaction of acknowledging his humiliating fall.

Eva swallowed hard to force back her tears. She quickly glanced at Olga, who sat still, not breathing, and stared at the table.

The children turned and walked out. The door clanged shut behind them. Peter lingered and could still hear the others through the door.

"Thank goodness, they're gone. I can breathe fresh air again," the teacher said, sighing.

"Continue your lunch, please, kinder." Radley paused. "You, Otto, isn't it? Watch yourself, Jew lover. I know your father."

The four rejected students walked out of the school they had attended since they were small. Peter looked for Becca. He warbled three shrill whistles, the way he always did.

Becca, her friend Charlie Beckman, whose father would not be waiting for him this early, and a few other younger Jewish children ran out of the other school door and joined them in the group of ejected kinder.

Becca looked up at Eva, her eyes wide. "They don't want us here."

Eva wrapped her arms around Becca, something Peter would not do in front of his friends. "Don't worry, little spitfire. We will be okay." She kissed Becca's head.

The school's librarian, dressed in a tailored suit and heels, held her head high as she marched out the school door.

Becca looked at Peter. "Oh, Peter, what will we do now?" Tears started to spill from her eyes.

"I don't know. Don't cry, Becca, because then they win," Peter said.

"They always win," Charlie said.

"Why do they hate us?" Becca asked, as she wiped the tears away furiously.

Hans flipped his hand. "Because we're Jews."

"Why don't we ever fight back?" Becca asked.

Eva nodded. "We should."

"If you want to die. There are too many of them, and not enough of us. You know that, and they have guns," Peter said.

Eva touched her injured head and looked away.

"I don't want to be a Jew anymore," Becca said.

"Shhh," Peter hissed, as the school librarian marched toward them. Her eyes were red and puffy from crying.

"Go home, kinder," she said. "Go home. This is not a good place for you anymore." She quickly scurried on.

"She isn't even Jewish," Eva whispered.

"Her husband is," Stephen said. "That's enough."

Slowly, the group of children moved away, down the street toward their homes.

As they turned the corner, they spotted a crowd gathered around a fire raging in a barrel in front of the city library. Policemen were feeding books into it.

Peter thought of the book burnings when he had been only six. He wondered: How are there even any Jewish books left to burn?

A policeman threw more books onto the fire, and the small crowd watched and cheered.

The school librarian screamed and ran to the flames. She knocked over the barrel, kicked the burning books out, and stomped on the flames, trying to put them out. "No! No! Not the books!"

The policeman grabbed her arm and tried to pull her away from the burning pile of books. "They are only a few Jewish books. Stop!"

She continued to kick the books from the fire. Peter turned away and spotted Karl Radley. He must have followed them from the school. Now he stared at them as they watched the books burn.

Becca gripped Peter's arm. "Peter, that mean man from school is watching us."

"I know."

"What does he want?" Becca asked. "We already left."

"Shut up, Becca, he might hear you," he said, as Radley walked toward them.

The police officer burning the books held up his hands, his palms toward the irate woman. "Stop, lady, what do you care?"

"I am a librarian! Literature should not be a part of politics!"

The policeman gripped her arm more roughly and yanked her away. "Stop for your own safety, or I'll have to—"

"You'll have to answer to God for the things you destroy!" the librarian shouted, spit flying from her mouth.

Radley pulled the librarian away. "Arrest her!" he shouted. He pulled out his gun and pointed it at her head, until she was dragged away by the policeman, as she still clutched a smoking book.

Radley turned to the children. "Go home, or you will be next."

He turned back, as if a distasteful chore was completed.

Eva lurched forward, and Hans and Stephen grabbed her, preventing her from running to the woman. Peter shook his head and held on to Becca, as she jumped up and down.

"I hate the Hitler men," Becca said, quietly. "They're not nice."

Without a word or as much as a hiss, Radley spun around to Becca and slapped her face, knocking her to the ground. He stomped off.

Becca looked up at Peter with tears in her eyes and a red handprint across her face from the impact of Radley's hand. "Why did he do that?" she whispered, gasping.

Radley turned, glaring back at her. "I wanted you to remember me," he answered, with a tip of his head. "Little Jews should keep their mouths shut." He smiled, looking quite pleased with himself.

CHAPTER 6

A NAZI IS A NAZI

(November 1938)

Marla Kincaid, twenty, with shoulder-length brown hair twisted up on the sides, and blue eyes that could not hide her fiery passion for life, walked with Sebastian Rounde, a brawny Englishman wearing an overcoat with a fur collar and a hat.

"I'm sorry about your brother, Marla," Sebastian said, as he patted his friend's shoulder. "Such a shame."

"I know. I couldn't save him," Marla said.

"No one could."

"It's hard, because he's all I think about."

—m—

The Berlin skies were cloudy and gray. The cold winds of fall had finally arrived.

A young Jewish teacher was now teaching all the Jewish children in the neighborhood in the back room of the Vogner Fastener Factory. Hans's grandfather, Oma Greta's husband, had started the factory after he and Oma arrived from Poland when they were young.

"What is today's date?" the teacher asked the children, who sat at a makeshift table in the corner. Machines and scraps of metal surrounded them.

"November 9, 1938," Hans said. "Just another dark day in Hitler's hateful world."

"No political notation is needed. Write today's date and your name at the top of your paper and hand it in, please," the teacher said.

"I've never had a teacher say please to me," Peter whispered to Hans.

"Don't get used to it. Next week Hitler will ban us from thinking," Hans whispered back. "Things are bound to get worse."

"Why do you say that?" Eva asked.

"Because my father took all his money out of the bank and hid it in our house," Hans said.

That night, Hans and his family sat in the kitchen at their house. They gathered around their big wooden Volksempfanger tabletop radio. Oma Greta, Hans's grandmother, an elderly woman with bad knees and a bent back, was knitting, her angry hands flying with every stitch. Anna Vogner paced behind her.

Eddie shot marbles in the middle of the room on the braided rug. Vincent, Hans' father, a scholarly man with glasses, read the paper. One headline read: "JEW MURDERS GERMAN EMBASSY OFFICIAL IN PARIS."

Oma Greta turned up the radio volume. The voice of Joseph Goebbels, Hitler's Minister of Propaganda, blasted forth, his hatred surging out of the radio's speaker.

"The Fuhrer has decided that demonstrations should not be prepared or organized by the Party, but—" Goebbels shouted.

Eddie stopped playing marbles. "That man has a bad temper!"

"Hush, Eddie," Anna said, gently.

"—insofar as they erupt spontaneously, they are not to be stopped," Goebbels's voice continued.

In Peter's apartment, his mother and father sat in front of the radio. Peter stood at his father's shoulder.

"What does that mean?" Peter asked.

"We shall see," Henry said, rubbing his injured leg.

Sylvia grabbed Henry's hand. "Can no one see what they're doing?"

"What are they doing?" Peter asked.

"They're ruining Germany," Henry said sadly. He pulled Peter to him and hugged him. "How about a song, Peter? I could use a little music to lift my spirits."

At Hans's house, Oma Greta turned the radio off. "I've heard enough of that lunatic. Hitler and his henchmen are evil in the flesh!"

"Shhh, Oma Greta, they'll arrest you for such words," Anna said.

"So, what does it matter? You can't turn around without getting arrested these days. They've already sent all the Polish Jews back to Poland, but somehow they missed me. But it won't be long before they find me, too."

"We will have to wait him out." Vincent sighed. "There are good people in this world who will stop him."

"Why can't we leave?" Hans asked. "Hitler wants us to leave, doesn't he?"

Vincent put down the paper and looked at Hans. "Yes, Hitler wants us to leave, but it's not that easy. Arnold Beckman has relatives in the United States, and even he can't get out."

"Why?" Hans asked.

"Papers, the documents. The other country has to want you, and they don't. Many are afraid we will take the jobs they need. But you need to get a quota number, someone to sponsor you, and permission and the documents to leave all at the same time before one of them runs out. It's almost impossible," Vincent explained.

Eddie moved the marbles back and forth between his hands, making a loud clacking sound. "Why does everyone do what Hitler says?"

Vincent put the paper down and got up. He patted Eddie. "They're afraid. We're all afraid," he said. "Times are changing." He paced nervously and then turned quickly to Anna. "I need to check on the factory."

"Please be careful," Anna said.

"Don't worry, I'll hurry back. I want some of Oma's delicious cobbler." Vincent smiled, but it was forced, and everyone could feel the air was thick with untethered fear.

"Hitler and his friends are bad, bad men," Eddie said. All his colorful marbles fell through his hands to the floor.

CHAPTER 7

THE NIGHT OF BROKEN GLASS

(November 1938)

Peter and his family had gone to sleep in their cozy apartment over the butcher shop. Becca slept in her bed, holding onto her doll, Gina. The doll's untied but well-brushed hair spread out like a fan on the pillow. Peter, in the bed on the other side of the small room, watched Becca sleep while he rested his hand on his violin.

His parents slept in their room. Baby Lilly was in her crib beside them, wrapped in her pink blanket with bunnies on it.

The night was unusually quiet, and that disturbed Peter. He fidgeted in his bed, straining to hear through the silence. Something seemed amiss, like when the wind calmed down right before the thunder crashed. He couldn't figure out what it was.

Suddenly, glass shattered in the butcher shop below. Footsteps stomped. More glass crashed.

Peter jumped from his bed and looked out the window to the street below. Becca sat up suddenly. "What's happening?"

Peter grabbed her and pulled her out into the hall. "Someone's breaking into the shop."

There was a loud pounding as something rammed the door to the butcher shop.

Henry limped out of the other bedroom, cane in hand. Sylvia followed, clutching Baby Lilly. She handed the baby to Peter. "Take your sisters and hide in the big wardrobe. Don't say a word, Peter. I'm counting on you."

"Please don't," Peter said. He'd never liked being the older brother, particularly to Becca, who was so headstrong.

Becca stared at her mother, eyes huge and round. "But Mama, I'm scared. I want to stay with you."

"No, you must go with Peter," Sylvia said. "Hurry!"

"I don't want to go with Peter," Becca whined.

"Not now, Becca!" Sylvia pleaded.

Peter grabbed Becca's arm and pushed her into the big wardrobe in the living room. Sometimes, she was just too much. He climbed in after her.

Inside the wardrobe, Peter patted Baby Lilly and rocked her slightly. Becca shook with fear. Peter reluctantly put his arm around Becca in the cramped wardrobe, but his hand shook as well.

Suddenly, Peter remembered his violin. He opened the wardrobe.

"Peter!" Sylvia scolded, when she saw him emerge from his hiding place.

"My violin!" Peter ran to his room, still carrying Baby Lilly, as the pounding continued below. With a splintering crash, the wood broke, and the shop door crashed in. Footsteps thundered through the rooms underneath them.

Henry watched Peter tear across the room and shook his head. "Hurry, son!"

As Peter grabbed his violin and yo-yo off his chest of drawers, something hit the apartment door with a loud thud.

Peter stepped back into the wardrobe and carefully shut the door, until it clicked. Becca looked at the yo-yo. "Why'd you bring that?"

"It's a weapon," Peter whispered. "I'll twist it around Hitler's neck. Now, be quiet."

"Hitler's not coming. He'll send his tin soldiers," Becca said.

A huge thud, and the apartment door crashed open.

Becca grabbed Peter, digging her little sharp nails into his arm. Peter trembled and grimaced in pain. What did his mother expect him to do?

Protect two little girls? He was barely able to not wet his pants in fear. He put his eye to the keyhole in the wardrobe door.

Two Nazi policemen charged into the apartment. Henry with his cane, and Sylvia with her arm around her husband, stood frozen with silent fear as Hitler's men invaded their home.

Inside the wardrobe, Baby Lilly's face scrunched up. Startled by the sound, she was ready to cry. Peter put his finger in her mouth. She sucked, suddenly soothed and oblivious to the reign of terror that had entered their living room.

One of the Nazis searched the apartment, passing so close to the wardrobe that Peter could smell his sickening cologne. It was Karl Radley, the vindictive officer from his old school, who'd taken the opportunity of the night's hysteria to exact his revenge.

Then the other Nazi turned. It was Frank Soleman, Bruno's master and the loin roast lover. Peter relaxed and nodded at Becca. Peter was relieved. Maybe everything will be okay if Herr Frank is here, he thought.

Frank faced Peter's father. "Are you Henry Weinberg?"

Henry looked at him with furrowed eyebrows and a frown. He looked questioningly at Sylvia, and then at Radley and Frank. "Frank, you know who I am."

Radley glared at Frank. Frank swallowed hard, but he stared straight at Henry. "I said, are you Henry Weinberg, the butcher?" He took a breath. "The Jew."

Peter's forehead wrinkled as he squinted to look out the keyhole. He could make no sense of Herr Frank's question.

Henry sighed. "Yes, of course, Frank. I am Henry Weinberg, the butcher. Perhaps, it is I who doesn't know you."

Radley quickly stepped in front of Frank and backhanded Henry hard across the face. The blow knocked Henry off balance, and he crashed to the floor, dropping his cane.

Radley kicked him. "Get up, you Jew swine. Your meat is as rotten and as foul as you are. It's time to even up the score." He turned to Frank. "Arrest him," he ordered.

Frank didn't move.

"Now!" Radley ordered.

Henry scrambled to get his cane and wobbled to a standing position. Frank grabbed his arm to help him up.

Radley shook his head at Frank. "Let go of him. Don't help the crippled Jew."

"He's a veteran from the Great War," Frank said weakly. "I served with him."

"This is a new war, a war to take back Germany." Radley glared at Frank. "And he is the enemy."

"What has he done?" Sylvia asked, her eyes filled with fear.

"He is a Jew," Radley said, as if that explained it all.

Sylvia pulled at Frank's arms, pleading. "Frank, you know us. You live down the block. You come in every Saturday. You like a beef loin roast with the fat trimmed."

"Let go of him. He is a policeman. Let go, I say, or you'll be arrested, too," Radley threatened.

Sylvia slowly let go of Frank, staring at him. "Frank?" Her voice sounded as if she was trying to identify someone in the dark.

Frank looked at Radley, unable to meet Sylvia's eyes.

Radley waved his arms at Henry and Sylvia. "Evacuate this building. It belongs to the German people now!"

"Our butcher shop?" Sylvia asked.

"And your apartment. It is ours now," Radley said. "Be gone by morning."

Sylvia dropped her arms to her sides.

Radley and Frank dragged Henry toward the exit, his wobbly legs and cane trying to keep up. Henry looked back at Sylvia as they stepped out the door. He mouthed, "I love you."

Then they were gone.

Sylvia waited till the Nazis' footsteps could no longer be heard. Then, with trembling hands, she opened the wardrobe. The children unfolded themselves from their compact hiding spot and stepped out.

"Mama, what happened?" Becca asked.

"They took Papa away," Sylvia said, as she took Baby Lilly from Peter.

Peter shook his tingling arms, released from the tension of holding his sister.

"Why?" Becca asked.

Sylvia hugged Becca against her side. "I don't know. Nothing makes sense anymore."

"What are we going to do without Papa?" Tears began streaming down Becca's face.

Sylvia looked sadly at the smashed apartment door. "I don't know. They took the butcher shop and our apartment, too."

"How can they do that?" Peter snapped. "It's ours."

"A Nazi is a Nazi," Sylvia said. She glanced at the window, and then did a double take. The sky outside was glowing red.

Sylvia ran over and looked out at the sky. "The synagogue's on fire!" she cried.

They stared out the window and down the street. Nazi storm troopers were making a bonfire out of Torahs, holy scrolls, and prayer books next to the blazing old majestic synagogue. They could see Rabbi Mosel trying to stop them, pulling at them, but the officers struck him and pushed him to the ground.

"There's no hope now. The world has gone mad," Sylvia said, her voice trembling, "and I am nearly there."

The children wrapped their arms around their mother. The burning synagogue reflected in Peter's eyes, and he feared the music inside him had died.

CHAPTER 8

THEY'RE HUNTING JEWS TONIGHT

(November 1938)

That night as Vincent neared the Vogner Fastener Factory, he saw the building ablaze before he even got there. Vincent froze in his tracks, staring at the factory his father had built, watching his livelihood burning down. The flames taunted the dark sky, and smoke billowed from the broken windows.

A group of Nazi storm troopers watched the fire from across the street, a safe distance from the deliberate destruction. They laughed and cheered, as if they were at a bonfire.

"I could cook a bratwurst or two on that fire," a storm trooper said. Then he turned and saw Vincent standing there, stricken with horror.

He pointed accusingly at Vincent, as if he was to blame, and then the others rushed toward him. Vincent turned to run, but the storm trooper quickly overpowered and restrained him, dragging him off. Nazi terrorism had taken his business and his freedom, all in the same night, the night of broken glass.

—⟋⟍⟍—

The ringing of the phone in the Rosenbergs' house woke Eva. The telephone was seldom used. When it rang, it usually meant important news. Her father answered it in the living room, and she could hear the fear in his voice.

"Yes, are you sure? Yes, we will. Thank you, Jacob," Bert said. "You are a good friend."

Eva sat up in bed as she heard her father's footsteps hurry up the stairs, shuffling in his slippers. Bert burst into her room. "Eva! Eva, you must do as I say, right now. Put on your shoes and grab your coat. We must go to the root cellar. Now."

Eva jumped out of bed. "The root cellar? Now?"

"Now! No questions!" Bert said, sternly.

Eva heard the firmness in her father's usually gentle voice and understood it was a time to obey. She put on her shoes, although it took her longer than usual because her hands shook. She grabbed her coat, and then searched frantically under her bed and in her closet. "I can't find Snowflake, Papa."

Bert patted his daughter's shoulder. "She'll be fine. No time to look now."

"If they find her, they'll—"

"Come now, Eva," Bert's voice shook. "We must be quick."

Eva and her parents ran across their backyard and pulled open the heavy door to the cellar. They climbed carefully down into the cold, damp root cellar, feeling for each step with their feet before moving down into the darkness.

"What's the reason for this nonsense in the middle of the night?" Helga hissed.

"Jacob called. They're hunting Jews tonight," Bert said, as the cellar door slammed shut.

Even with the door shut, they could still hear the Nazis kicking in the Rosenbergs' front door and storming into the house, breaking furniture, smashing dishes, and ransacking the family's valuables.

Under the ground in the dark cellar, Eva trembled, sweating despite the cold, damp cellar air. She heard the horrifying screeching of her cat Snowflake, somewhere inside her invaded home, and then a gunshot.

"Not Snowflake! No! No! Papa! No!" she whispered.

Bert put his arms around his little girl. "Shhh. Not now. At least we are safe."

Then there was only silence, and that was even worse. Eva dissolved into quiet sobs of grief for the loss of her snowy white cat.

Helga looked at Bert over Eva's head. "Tonight, the line was crossed," she whispered. "There is no going back to our old life."

—∿—

A few blocks away, Jacob, Nora, and Stephen Levy ran across dark backyards, to the small house of their friends Klaus and Clara. Klaus, an elderly man still in his nightclothes with a huge sweater wrapped hastily around him, hurried them inside. "Dr. Levy, please come in," Klaus said, as if ushering him in for a drink.

Klaus led the Levys down the hall and directly to the attic stairs. Clara shuffled behind them in her nightgown and rose-colored chenille robe, carrying a plate piled with roast beef sandwiches and a bottle of cold milk. She huffed as she hurried, her body nearly as wide as the narrow attic stairs.

Mattresses and blankets were piled on the floor of the dusty attic, with only two small windows, one on each side. Stephen flopped down on one of the mattresses, and a cloud of dust billowed up. He coughed.

Jacob grabbed Klaus's shoulder and shook his hand. "We are very grateful to you and Clara."

"You're a great doctor. You've saved our lives many times," Klaus said. "We're not all Nazis."

Clara put her arm around Nora. "I'm sorry it's not more comfortable, dear."

Nora hugged Clara. "It's beautiful, Clara, really perfect. Thank you."

Stephen picked up a sandwich from the plate and took a bite. "I hope this doesn't last long."

—∿—

Miles away, at the border between Germany and Holland, William Rosenberg presented his forged papers to the bulky, intimidating German border guard. The guard looked at the papers, and back at William. "Where are you going tonight? It is late."

"To visit my uncle in Amsterdam. He's sick."

The guard studied William's papers again. "Ah, I see." He looked up at William.

William gave the Hitler salute. "Heil Hitler!"

The guard returned the salute. "Heil Hitler!" He paused, glancing at William from the side, and nodded. "You may pass."

William held his breath and continued purposefully to the gate, as it slowly rose.

The guard yelled a few Yiddish words he had memorized, meaning, "Look out, duck your head!"

William reflexively ducked his head and spun around. A moment later, he realized what giving away that he knew Yiddish would mean to the guards. His heart sank.

The guard pointed his gun at William's head and raised his bushy eyebrows. "Looks like you picked the wrong night to be a Jew."

—✖—

As Berlin's brutal night faded away, Frank Soleman walked home, past the smoldering synagogue. He stopped and stared at the broken windows and doors of the demolished butcher shop. There was a light on in the Weinbergs' apartment. Frank's eyes became vacant as he shuffled on to his apartment building a few blocks away.

He trudged up the stairs to his apartment, his heavy steps reverberating in the quiet after the storm. He opened the door and entered. Bruno slept by the window, unaware that his favorite butcher shop had been destroyed. A big bone lay next to him—a bone Peter had given him, Frank thought.

Frank leaned down and petted the big German Shepherd. Bruno looked up with his big, sleepy, adoring eyes. Frank opened the front door and snapped his fingers, motioning for Bruno to go out like they did every day when they went for a walk.

Dawn was breaking and a small sliver of light peeked over the city's horizon. Bruno yawned and lumbered out the door, obeying his master despite the cold, smoky air. Frank suddenly shut the door behind his loyal dog, as he remained inside.

As he let go of the doorknob that didn't quite latch, Frank saw dried blood smeared on his hands. He went to the sink, turned on the water, and scrubbed his hands, watching the red blood swirl in the white porcelain sink and disappear down the drain.

When he stood up, he caught a glimpse of himself in the mirror. He bent toward the mirror, staring blankly at his reflection. He took his uniform hat off and ran his hand over his mostly bald head. He put the hat back on and adjusted his uniform collar. He sat down on the worn couch, where he had spent many nights reading his paper and waiting for his loin roast to cook.

He stared straight ahead for a long moment. Then he removed his official police-issued pistol from its stiff leather holster.

Frank took a deep jagged breath, raised the gun to his head, and pulled the trigger.

CHAPTER 9

BRUNO THE DOG

(November 1938)

As Peter watched from his bedroom window and saw the destruction of his neighborhood, he understood Goebbels's radio threat had successfully been carried out. Peter knew there was more than glass broken that night. The massive attack on Jews had changed everything. But despite the devastation and mayhem, the morning still came. He thought of the song he liked to play: "You Are Not Alone." He sang the words to himself in a hushed voice, remembering the way his mother used to sing it.

> The night is dark until the sunrise.
> Your heart is lonely until I answer your cries.
> Your path is steep and filled with stone,
> But I will walk beside you,
> You are not alone.

He wished his father were there. He would have known what to do, but he had been snatched away by the Nazis. The rest of his family was left to clean up the wreckage of their lives.

Peter carefully wrapped his ball and jacks, his yo-yo, and his father's sharpest butcher shop meat cleaver in a cloth and put them in a dented tin box. He closed the bent lid and buried it under the shop's back steps, like a ceremonial funeral for his old life.

He returned to the front of the shop, where Sylvia was cleaning up the vandalism. Becca sat on the bottom step of the stairs, playing with her doll. Suitcases and bundles rested next to her, surrounding a sleeping Baby Lilly to keep her out of the wreckage.

"They did this to all of us, didn't they?" Peter said to his mother.

Sylvia nodded sadly.

Becca picked up her doll and held it close to her worried face. "Gina, I told you to be quiet in the wardrobe. You must not say a word," she whispered to her doll, "or they will take away your sweet Papa."

Peter grabbed the other broom and began helping his mother. "I don't understand why we're cleaning it up," he said. "It's their mess now."

"Hitler demands it," Sylvia said. "Anyway, your father always kept a tidy shop."

From around the corner, Bruno appeared, wagging his bushy tail. The tan-and-black dog ambled over to Peter. "Bruno?" he asked. "Look, Mutti, it's Bruno!"

Sylvia sighed. "Hurry up and take him back to Herr Frank's apartment. But don't go in. It's too dangerous, and we've got to finish up," she said. "Herr Frank has changed. He is no longer our friend."

"Herr Frank is a Nazi," Becca said, her eyes wide. "He took Papa."

"It's not Bruno's fault," Peter said. He slapped his hip. "Come on, boy. Let's get you home."

Bruno trotted beside Peter as they walked the short way to Herr Frank's apartment. It was a trip Peter had taken many times to deliver meat packages, but this time he had to dodge the destruction of the Nazis Storm Troopers, the SA paramilitary forces—policemen who stood by and watched and sometimes participated—and other vandals.

Peter hesitated outside the apartment building. "Go on, Bruno. You're home." Bruno wouldn't budge. He pushed his nose into Peter's leg, and Peter sighed. "Okay, okay, I'll walk you up."

Bruno followed Peter up the stairs to Herr Frank's apartment. They stopped outside the door, which was open. Peter looked at Bruno. "You weren't lost, were you? You came to get me."

Bruno nudged Peter through the apartment door. Peter stepped around the corner to see what was wrong. "Herr Frank?" Peter called, his voice shaking. He was in direct defiance of his mother and terrified of his friend turned Nazi. His foot slipped. Peter stared, his gray eyes filled with fear and confusion. Herr Frank was splayed out on the floor.

Bruno growled and backed away. It took Peter a second to comprehend the disturbing scene. He had slipped on the slimy remains of blood, flesh, and brains on the floor. When he finally realized that he was seeing Herr Frank's exploded head, he turned and vomited. Bruno barked.

Peter looked around in a panic. "Come on, Bruno, you can't stay here."

Bruno barked again. Peter grabbed Bruno's collar and pulled him out the door. He didn't stop running until he reached the butcher shop.

"Mutti!" he cried as soon as he spotted his mother.

Sylvia stopped sweeping when she saw the horrified look on Peter's pale face. She put the broom down and straightened up. "What is it? Peter, what happened? Why is Bruno still with you? I told you to take him back to Herr Frank's apartment."

Breathing heavily, Peter spit as he talked. "Herr Frank is dead," he whispered. "I think he killed himself."

"Are you sure?"

Peter nodded. "His fingers were still wrapped around the gun, but his head was gone."

Sylvia hugged Peter, clutching him to her as if the tighter she held him, the more it would protect him. "I told you not to go in. I told you it was too dangerous."

"I'm sorry." Peter couldn't believe that Herr Frank had arrested his father, or taken his life and left Bruno alone. He had seemed like such a good man. "I couldn't leave Bruno there with him, the way he was, you know. There's no one left to take care of him."

"Peter, I'm so sorry, but we can't take care of Bruno. We need to go. This is all too much." Sylvia looked up at the building that had been her home, her livelihood, and sighed. "We have to move on. I don't know just where yet."

Sylvia picked up the suitcase and rested Baby Lilly on her hip. She, Becca, and Peter walked down the street of their neighborhood. Peter carried his violin and a suitcase. Becca held her doll and a small bundle tied with a rope.

"What's Bruno doing here?" Becca asked.

Peter looked at his mother.

"Herr Frank is dead, Becca," Sylvia explained.

"I'm glad he's dead. He used to be nice, and then he wasn't. He took Papa away."

"It's hard to judge a person trapped in fear and desperation," Sylvia said.

They walked slowly, maneuvering around broken glass. Peter looked at Bruno. "You can't go with us." He turned away, following his mother. Bruno trotted after him. He had nowhere to go either.

"Where are we going?" Becca asked her mother.

"Away from here," Sylvia said, as she stared vacantly into the distance. "Somewhere."

———※———

After a sleepless night in Klaus and Clara's attic, Stephen Levy and his parents were walking back to check on their house. Stephen spotted familiar people walking up the street ahead of them: a woman and some children. One carried a violin case.

He tapped his mother's arm. "Mutti, there's Peter and Becca."

"Henry's not with them," Jacob noticed.

Nora looked at Jacob, and he nodded. Nora called out, "Sylvia!"

Sylvia spun around at the sound of her name. Nora held out her arms, and Sylvia stumbled into her embrace.

"They took him, Nora," Sylvia said.

"They took Henry?" Nora asked.

Sylvia nodded, as tears rolled down her face.

"Do you need a place to stay?" Nora asked.

Sylvia nodded again. "They've taken everything."

"You're welcome to stay with us, if we still have a house," Jacob said.

"Thank you, yes," Sylvia said. "Yes, I would be so grateful. With Henry gone, and the children—" Her voice trembled with emotion.

"It's okay," Nora said, taking Baby Lilly from Sylvia's arms.

Jacob put his hands on Peter's shoulder, noticing the big dog following him. "You know we can't take care of a dog."

"I know, but he's got nobody but me." Peter looked up at Jacob. "You wouldn't leave one of your patients if he needed you, would you, Dr. Levy? Even if he wasn't Jewish?"

Jacob clicked his teeth. "Quite right. Bring the dog. He can stay in the back room."

Peter smiled and patted Bruno. Then he ran to catch up to Stephen, with Bruno right on his heels.

———

At a café in London, Sebastian and Marla sipped their tea and ate biscuits.

"Are you sure this is something you want to do?" Sebastian asked. "It's a huge job and it could be dangerous."

"We've got to get the Jewish children out of Germany."

He nodded. "They're getting the Quakers and the Christian and Jewish leaders to work together, which is really quite remarkable. We'll guarantee to pay for each child's care and education through private funds."

"I hope it's soon. The children need to get out, and so do I."

———

After the "Night of Broken Glass," all Jewish children in Germany were expelled from the schools. Peter's school had been a foreshadowing of the nightmare to come. Nothing of normal life was left.

In Berlin, Stephen and Peter knocked on the front door of the Vogners' house. Hans opened the door.

"Have you heard anything about your father?" Stephen asked.

Hans shook his head. "No."

"My mother says you can come live with us, if you want," Stephen said, nodding at Peter. "Peter and his mother and sisters are already with us."

They sat on the front porch steps.

"Someone cut off our electricity, but Mutti wants to stay, so my father can find us when he comes back," Hans said.

Peter pointed to the empty spot where the beautiful wrought iron fence had been. "Hey, what happened to your fence?"

"The Nazis took it," Hans said.

"Why?" Peter asked.

"To make guns to kill Jews," Hans said.

A short distance away, they spotted Martin storming up the walk toward them. The three boys hurried toward the front door, to avoid a confrontation with Otto's rigid and brutal father.

"Stop!" Martin said. The boys froze in their tracks. "I have an official letter for Anna Vogner."

Hans turned around slowly. "She's inside." He pointed, reluctantly.

Martin handed the letter to him. "This is to inform her that Vincent Vogner died while in custody at the Sothausen Concentration Camp." His voice was monotone, as if he was announcing the weather.

Hans staggered back, as if hit by a blow to the stomach, and gasped for air. Stephen grabbed him, preventing him from falling, and helped steady him.

Martin turned on his heels and hurried away.

—⁂—

Marla pulled her coat closed against the cold London wind and ran up the stairs of Bloomsbury House, a massive stone building in London's West End. "So, it really is true?" she called, as Sebastian came toward her from his office. He seemed to fill the entire hall.

Sebastian smiled. "Yes, the Prime Minister and House of Commons have agreed to relax the immigration laws. The Jewish children can come to England. It's official!"

Marla jumped up and down, dancing. "It took the horror of the pogrom to do it, but we'll get the children out." She grabbed his arm. "What about the States? Will the Yanks be with us? Will they take children, too?"

"We'll see. Hopefully the U.S. Congress will do something soon.

Come on, we've got work to do. We've got to get foster homes, and set up offices in Germany, and find the donations to sponsor the children. There are a lot of things to set up." Sebastian sighed. "I'm tired already."

"For the first time in a long time, I'm not tired," Marla said. "The Kindertransport has begun. I better brush up on my German."

Marla was only twenty, just a few years older than some of the children she was helping to escape the Nazis. She'd grown up privileged, not wanting for anything, but instead of being spoiled, Marla and her older brother Dwight had been raised to be daring. "It doesn't take money to be bold, only boundless determination," her father used to say.

Marla and Sebastian hustled along the crowded halls of Bloomsbury House. Phones rang constantly. "Be quiet, everyone, please," Sebastian shouted. "It should be coming on."

Sebastian went to the nearest radio and turned up the volume, so everyone there could hear the radio announcement.

" . . . we need you to open your homes and your hearts to help these children before it is too late. Get them out. There are six hundred thousand of them calling to you for rescue. They must be rescued quickly. Either that, or abandon them finally to the fate from which a speedy death will be the most merciful release. Please contribute to the refugee fund today," the radio announcer pleaded.

Marla and the other refugee workers cheered. Marla twirled around in celebration. "We did it!"

"We haven't done anything, yet," Sebastian said. "Now comes the hard part." But he smiled.

CHAPTER 10

A PLEA FOR A FATHER

(December 1938)

Peter walked into the crowded Berlin police station next to Edelweiss Park. He hesitated. He didn't want to be there, but his mother had made him come. She had insisted he enter enemy territory and demand his father back. She had instructed him to find the police officer with the big nose, who had served in the war with Henry.

Peter was scared of the German police officers, but he was more scared of his mother's disappointment if he failed. He took a deep breath.

It was easy to spot the older police officer with the big nose. Peter had seen his father talking and laughing with him many times in their butcher shop, as they had discussed their days together in the Great War.

As the man wrote a report, Peter stood right in front of him and cleared his throat. "Excuse me, sir."

The police officer looked up from his writing. "What do you want, boy?"

"My mother sent me. She wanted me to tell you that there's been a mistake. You arrested my father," Peter said.

"Is he a Jew?" the officer asked.

Peter nodded. "Yes."

"Then there was no mistake," the big-nosed police officer said. Some of the officers nearby laughed. The man shook his head and went back to writing.

Peter's hands shook, but he didn't move from his spot. "He's a veteran of the Great War. He received the Iron Cross for bravery. He's disabled. He walks with a cane and everything. He shouldn't have been arrested. He did nothing wrong. Please, can you check? You know him," Peter said, quietly.

The man looked up. "What's his name?"

"Henry Weinberg."

"Henry Weinberg? The butcher?" the officer asked.

"That's him," Peter said, although he knew the police officer was well aware of his father.

"I'll look into it if I have time." The officer waved his hand, shooing Peter away. "Go on now."

Peter left the police station and hurried down the street. He trotted around the corner but stopped abruptly when he saw an even longer line outside the Red Cross building. A woman in a brown wool coat, with a scarf over her head, stood at the top of the stairs, ushering the next family inside.

"Next in line, please!" she called out in German.

The line of mostly women and children inched forward. Peter walked up to a curly-headed boy, who was playing with a yo-yo in the back of the line. "What are you waiting for?" Peter asked.

"It's for the Kindertransport to England," the boy said. "For Jewish children."

"A train to England? Why would Jewish children go there?" Peter asked.

"To get away from Hitler," the boy said.

"Hmmm. Do they let you take violins?" Peter asked.

"You can take two cases," the boy said.

Peter motioned to the boy's yo-yo. "Want me to show you something?"

The boy nodded and handed Peter his yo-yo.

Peter flicked the yo-yo. It shot out, twirled back on the string, and then danced along the ground.

The boy laughed. "I wish I could do that."

"It's all in the spin and the snap back." Peter smiled. "Let me show you."

The English Kindertransport woman came back out. A Nazi officer walked up to her. "So, are you the English do-gooder?" he snarled.

"I am helping to transport Jewish children out of Germany. We have Fuhrer Hitler's permission," the woman answered.

"What's your name?"

"Marla."

Peter smiled at how unafraid the woman seemed.

"I'll be watching you, Marla. No monkey business. Jews are very tricky." The officer grinned. "My advice? Just kill them. It's a much easier way out of Germany."

Peter's eyes widened. He quickly gave the boy his yo-yo back and ran off.

Later that night at Stephen's house, Sylvia and Nora sat with Peter and peppered him with nonstop questions. Bruno sat at his feet, thumping his tail.

Stephen listened to them from the table, where he was eating thick slabs of rye bread with strawberry jam and drinking a big mug of hot cocoa.

"Are you sure that's what they said? A Kindertransport to England?" Nora asked. "Are you sure?"

Peter nodded. "You go down to the Red Cross building by the police station and sign up. There's this pretty English lady there. They called her Marla."

Stephen stuffed the last piece of rye bread in his mouth. "Count me out. I'm not leaving Germany."

There was a knock on the front door. Nora looked startled. She got up and slowly moved to the window, then carefully pulled back the corner of the curtain and peered out.

"Who is it?" Sylvia whispered behind her.

Nora quickly let the curtain fall back down. "A dirty man. He looks like a beggar."

The man knocked again, this time louder.

"Can I help you?" Nora called nervously through the door.

"Nora?" the man said in a quivering, scratchy voice. "Do you know where Sylvia is?"

Sylvia stepped back in fear.

"Why do you want her?" Nora asked, cautiously.

Peter peered around Nora and looked out the window. The man was dirty and bald and clad in rags, leaning on a stick.

"Peter?" the man called, his voice cracking with emotion. "Peter, let me in!"

"It's Henry!" Sylvia ran to the door and threw it open. "He's back!"

Henry teetered uncertainly. Peter stepped up to him and grabbed his now thinner arm to steady him.

Henry leaned on Peter, sobbing, his whole body shaking. Peter stared at the weeping man who used to command his butcher shop. The man who knew all the cuts of meat. The man Peter relied on. The war hero. All that was gone, and Henry stood diminished, a shell of a man leaning on his son, a boy of eleven. The Nazis had taken his father and sent back a weak and broken stranger. Peter hugged his father and held up the frail man, realizing his head was bald because it had been shaved. But all Peter could say was, "They took our shop!"

Henry nodded. "I know, son, I know."

Becca ran down the stairs and flew into Henry's arms, nearly knocking him over. "Oh, Papa, is that you? We missed you."

With a few solid shoves from Bruno's paws, the door to the back room flew open, and Bruno bounded out. He barked with excitement.

"Bruno? What are you doing here?" Henry laughed, and Peter finally recognized his father.

Baby Lilly tottered to Henry with her little fingers opening and closing. "Papa! Papa!"

"Baby Lilly, my girl," Henry said, as he picked her up.

"God brought you home!" Sylvia said, hugging her husband. "God gave you back to us!"

"Yes, it was God's wish, but I was told it was my son's request that brought me home," Henry said, smiling at Peter. "I was released because of my war record. You saved me, Peter."

Peter smiled, but he knew it had really happened because of his mother, who had sent a reluctant boy to ask after his father. Sylvia had gambled that a fellow war veteran, even a Nazi, might not be able to turn away from a child's request. As always, she had been right.

Sylvia embraced her husband tightly. His butcher's girth from a diet of good meat was gone. He groaned and flinched in pain.

"What did they do to you, my husband?" she asked.

Henry slowly shook his head and gently rubbed Sylvia's cheek. "It's the beginning of the end. May God save our people," he said, as he wiped his wet cheeks.

The next morning, Peter ran into the room where his parents slept. He could hear his mother singing to herself in the Levys' kitchen.

He smiled when he saw that his father was still asleep. Good, it hadn't been a dream. He walked over and gently touched his father's arm. "Vati?" he whispered.

Then Peter recoiled and gasped. His father's pasty skin was cold. He shook him. "Vati!"

Henry didn't move. Peter jumped away, his mouth open. His father, one of Germany's bravest war heroes, was dead. He was finally free from the clutches of the Nazis, but dead nonetheless.

Peter stroked his father's expressionless face and cried. "No! No! Not now!" He looked up at the ceiling. "Not when we just got him back." He looked down at his once handsome father. "Poor Vati, God has taken you when we needed you most."

He bowed his head. "May God remember the soul of Henry Weinberg, who has gone to his eternal home. May God not forget those of us who are still here."

Then, he collapsed on the floor beside the bed, his last hope destroyed.

CHAPTER 11

THE PACKING OF A LIFE

(December 1938)

Sylvia, Anna, Nora, and Bert waited in the long line outside the Jewish organization offices in Berlin to put their children's names on the Kindertransport list. Peter stood beside them and pointed to Marla, as she came out the door of the Red Cross Building. "That's her. That's the lady from England."

Marla stood at the door beside Jules Whitmore, a German Jewish organization worker, and looked at the unending line of people wanting to get their children out of Germany. "The queue never ends," she said. "I think it goes around the block. We'll keep the office open until everyone is registered."

"I had no idea there would be so many," Jules said.

Marla smiled. "We're going to do this, Jules. We're going to get the children out, all of them."

A policeman walked by, and glared at Peter. The officer tapped his gun, then held his index finger out and his thumb up in the shape of a gun. He pointed his finger and jerked it up, like it was responding from the kick of a gunshot. Peter jumped back. The officer laughed at Peter's fear. It was all a cruel game to him.

Jules watched the officer intimidate Peter. "You need to get them out of here fast," he said to Marla.

"How many children will a train car hold?" she asked.

"A hundred or so," Jules said.

"We'll need many trains. I'll escort one train, and you do the next until we get them all out." Marla grabbed Jules's arm, like a child set on getting what she wants. "I wish you could remain in England with us."

"If I don't return, they'll stop the transports," Jules said. "Only those who have nothing to lose can be rebels. The rest of us are too scared to risk our families and friends."

Marla smiled. "Maybe I'll smuggle you out."

"Don't say that too loudly," Jules said. "They will have you arrested, too."

The next night, the light shone in the upstairs bedrooms of Stephen's house. Nora packed her son's things, as he sat on the bed, refusing to look at her. "Why are you doing this?" Stephen snapped, gesturing to the suitcase.

"So when you get approval for the Kindertransport, you'll be ready. It could be at any time."

"Why do I have to leave? Germany is my home," Stephen said.

"There may be little left of it soon."

Stephen sighed and crossed his arms. Nora patiently ignored his youthful defiance, continuing to fold his clothes lovingly and put them in the suitcase.

In another room of the house, Sylvia helped Becca and Peter pack what little they had left. Bruno watched from his prone position, taking up most of the floor.

Baby Lilly wasn't going on the train because his mother said she wasn't old enough to be without her. But Peter thought it was because his mother couldn't live without someone to love. Surely, a baby would be safe from the cruelty of the Nazis, his mother had said.

"Pack only what you can carry. There won't be anyone to help you." Sylvia's eyes teared up. She looked at Peter. "You'll have to help Becca."

"I don't . . ."

Sylvia slipped a picture of the family in front of the butcher shop inside Peter's violin case. "If you have your music, you'll never be lonely."

Peter picked up his violin and put it under his chin. He pulled the bow across the strings, making a lonely, howling sound.

"Don't, Peter. Don't make that horrible wolf sound. Only happy songs, please." Sylvia frowned. "Your music will save us some day."

Peter sighed. The sound was exactly like he felt. There were no happy songs inside him. He put the violin back in the case, shut the lid, and set it next to his small suitcase on the bed.

"I don't know if I can go," Peter said.

"What does that mean? Of course, you'll go."

"Who will take care of Bruno?"

"I will take care of Bruno, and you will be in charge of Becca," Sylvia said firmly. "Remember, you are the lucky ones."

Peter reached out and held his mother's hand. He knew his music could not save anyone. He also knew his mother was wrong. He could never be in charge of Becca. But he could not admit either to his mother.

Becca, in her nightgown, gently set her doll on top of her clothes in the suitcase. Sylvia bent down and kissed the top of Becca's head. As she closed Becca's suitcase, Becca's eyes teared up. She jumped out of bed, opened the suitcase, and pulled Gina back out.

She kissed the top of her doll's head. "What will I do without you, Gina?" Becca asked the doll, but she was looking at her mother.

At the Rosenbergs' house, Eva placed her well-loved teddy bear in her suitcase. She was too old to care about a silly shabby, old teddy bear, but it was the only comfort she had. She sadly sang a children's song called "The Sleepy Moon."

> The Moon, the Moon
> The big sleepy Moon says
> Goodnight to you
> He'll see you soon.
> Close your eyes
> Make believe and
> Float away on the tune

Of the big sleepy Moon.
The Moon, the Moon.

She closed the lid of her suitcase, leaving the bear's leg hanging out.

———∞———

A few days later, Jacob and Nora found Stephen and Peter playing the card game Watten in the window seat at Stephen's house.

"My son, we have news!" Jacob cried. Stephen looked up, frowning.

His mother smiled. "It's good news. We received the letter. You're going on the Kindertransport. Becca and Peter are going, too, and hopefully Hans." Nora nodded and smiled at Peter.

Stephen shook his head and scattered the cards as he jumped up. "No! I'm not going. I will live and die with Germany!"

Jacob put his hand on Stephen's shoulder. "Stephen, things are bad here, very bad, and they're going to get worse. This is your chance to get out while you can."

"To go to school, to live a regular life," Nora said, "away from here, away from the Nazis."

"A regular life?" Stephen flailed his arms. "With strangers in England? No, I choose to stay. I won't go."

"You will go. We'll be right behind you. We'll come to England soon," Jacob said, firmly. "Anna hopes to hear that Hans will go, too."

"What about Eddie?"

"Anna doesn't want to let Eddie go. How would he survive without her? It's amazing that she's been able to protect him this long. He needs her. Do you understand?"

Stephen nodded.

Nora held her arms out and pulled him into her embrace. "We love you and—"

Stephen pushed away from his mother's hug and ran out of the room.

"Stephen!" Nora scolded. "Oh, Stephen."

Peter gathered the cards left from the unfinished game of Watten, and looked up at Nora. "He's just scared."

—ɱ—

Candles lit the Vogners' house. The electricity was still cut off, in an attempt, they thought, to run them out, but it would take more than darkness and cold, much more.

Anna hugged Hans. "You'll leave for England in a few days. That doesn't give us much time."

"I can't go, Mutti. Who will take care of you, and Oma Greta, and Eddie?" Hans asked.

Anna patted his face. "You're a good boy. You always have been. I will take care of both of them. This is your chance, and you must take it. Sometimes you don't get another one."

Hans hugged his mother. "I wish Father were here."

"Me, too. We must use his strength to get us through. We must not give up, no matter what. We are Jews, the chosen ones. We must be strong," Anna said.

Hans nodded. "Sometimes, I wish the Jews weren't always the ones chosen to suffer."

—ɱ—

Eva's father climbed the porch steps two at a time. He ran into the kitchen, out of breath, waving a letter.

Eva was helping her mother peel potatoes, cutting out the rotten parts. Potatoes had become the main staple of their meals. Meat was hard to come by since the Weinbergs' butcher shop had been destroyed.

"Eva, you are approved! You have a seat on the train! You leave next Saturday!" Bert said, out of breath.

Eva jumped up and hugged her father. "Oh, Papa! Thank you! Thank you!"

Helga threw down her potato. "She can't travel on Saturday. That's Shabbat."

"Surely, God will understand," Bert said.

Helga grunted her objection to her husband's disregard for God's laws and turned back to the potatoes.

Bert looked at Eva. "We must think about packing. You can take one suitcase and one hand luggage, and we must make you a new coat for the English winter. You're in luck! I happen to be the best tailor in all of Berlin."

"No, in all of Germany! Oh, Papa. It's like an adventure you read about in books. Only it won't be fun, because I won't have you. What will I do?" Eva asked.

"It can't last long. All the good people of the world will end Hitler's madness soon. You will be where he can't touch you. England will keep you safe," Bert said, hugging her. "And we will come soon."

Eva danced over and hugged her mother, but Helga shrugged her away.

"What about William?" Helga said. "What about your son?"

"William is eighteen. He's too old to go. He hasn't been home in weeks, and he's made his choice," Bert said.

"I'm going to England!" Eva said, dancing out of the kitchen.

"Why are you doing this?" Helga asked Bert.

"Don't you understand, Helga? If the children live, our people will survive."

Helga rolled her eyes and swished her hand through the air. "Oh, Bert, don't be foolish. No one's going to kill all the Jews."

CHAPTER 12

THE BETRAYAL

(January 1939)

In the Vogners' house, Hans pulled a book from the bookshelf. He opened it to a secret compartment cut into the pages that contained a few reichsmarks.

Hans took the remaining money inside the book and slipped quietly out the back door of the house.

He hurried through the dark Berlin streets, flinching at every shadow and footstep. He ducked behind the Rosenbergs' tailor shop. William's old document forger waited in the shadows with a package of food.

"Do you have the items?" Hans asked, still looking over his shoulder.

"Sausages, sugar, and butter," the man said, opening the bundle to show Hans. These were items that were difficult to get, because stores did not want to sell to Jewish people, and the stores run by Jewish people had been destroyed.

Hans examined the items and nodded, then gave the man the money.

"Okay, I need some cooking oil next time. And some chocolate for my brother."

He shrugged. "It'll cost you. Chocolate is hard to come by."

"I've got to go. My family will be worried if they find me gone."

Footsteps shuffling on the sidewalk in front of the tailor shop distracted Hans for a second. When he looked back, the man was gone.

As Hans crept down the streets clutching his food bundle, two Nazis banged on the door of the Vogners' house. They paused to take a breath, exhaling smoky fog in the cold air, and then kicked the door open.

They tried to turn on the lights, but the electric wires had been cut. The terrifying intruders flicked on their flashlights. They knocked over furniture and destroyed anything that would break.

One of the officers crept into Anna's bedroom and shined the light in her face as she huddled in the corner. "You are all under arrest! Get dressed and come immediately!"

"What? What is happening?"

He pushed her out to the hall, where Oma Greta and Eddie cowered in their nightclothes. Anna looked around for Hans, but the flashlights shone in their faces, making it hard to see.

One of the officers pointed at Eddie. "How did this one slip by?"

The other officer shrugged. "Get dressed. Polish Jews were deported to Poland, but somehow you were missed. We will make up for that now."

Oma Greta hugged Anna.

"They're sending me back," Oma Greta whispered. "They found me."

"We are sending you all back," the officer said, overhearing her.

"But I'm the only one from Poland. They are Germans. Let them stay."

"My orders are for all of you. Deportation to Poland, it says. There should be four Vogners."

"My son Hans is not here," Anna said.

Eddie clung to his mother. "Mutti, why do we have to leave? We didn't do anything wrong."

Anna patted Eddie and gently pried his hands from around her arms. "I know, dear. Now, get dressed. Wear something warm. Everything will be okay."

Eddie shook his head. "Mutti, the rabbi says God doesn't like it when you lie."

"That's enough, Eddie. Do what I say," Anna said, sternly.

"Is there a problem?" the Nazi asked.

"Yes, there is a problem, a big problem," Eddie said, nodding.

Anna grabbed Eddie's arm and steered him toward his room.

Eddie whispered angrily. "The problem is Herr A. Dolf Hitler."

Anna shook her head and gave him her scrunched-eyes-of-mother-disapproval. "Hush, Eddie. Hush, now. Do you want to get us killed?"

Eddie shook his head. "No, Mutti. I don't want to get us killed. That would be bad."

—◊◊—

Peter, Stephen, and Becca ate apple strudel at the kitchen table. Nora had used up the last of her baking supplies to make them a goodbye treat.

"Are you ready to go tomorrow?" Peter asked Stephen, as he took a big bite of the pastry.

"The only reason I'm going is because Hans is going," Stephen snarled.

"Maybe, you can get placed together with a nice family," Becca said, "like Peter and me."

Stephen shrugged. "I hope there's a swimming pool we can use."

"I hope they have apple strudel," Peter said, as he ate another bite.

Despite his foul mood, Stephen laughed.

—◊◊—

Hans slipped in the back door of his dark house with his bundle of food purchases. He was used to the house being dark, but a few steps into the kitchen, he fell over something and hit the floor hard. He sat up and felt what had tripped him: one of the kitchen chairs, splintered into pieces.

As he looked around in the shadowy gloom, he realized all the furniture was knocked over and smashed. His shoes crunched on the broken china littering the kitchen floor as he walked into the next room.

He negotiated around the debris and quietly tiptoed up the stairs. He stepped into Anna's bedroom, but no one was there.

"Mutti? Oma? Eddie?" he called in a whisper.

No answer.

He hurried out and into Oma Greta's bedroom. Oma was gone, too.

Panicking, he dashed into Eddie's bedroom, no longer careful about making noise. Eddie's bed was tossed. His dresser drawers were pulled out. His pajamas lay on the floor, as if he had just stepped out of them.

Hans stood there, staring around him in disbelief. The Nazis had come for his family, while he was scrounging for food, leaving them unprotected.

Hans, still carrying his food package, felt around in the dark till he found his carefully packed Kindertransport rucksack. It had been knocked into a corner. He grabbed the letter telling him what time the train left the next day, which still waited on the top of his chest of drawers.

There was nothing else he could do. The house was no longer safe.

He fled back out onto the dark streets.

—ɯ—

At Eva's house, there was a sudden, insistent knocking on the door.

Bert slowly opened the door. Eva and Helga watched from behind him.

The Schmidts were on the front steps. Olga's father stood nearest the door, his fist raised to pound the door again. Olga, dressed in a League of German Girls' brown uniform with a red kerchief and a swastika on her armband, stood smiling beside him and her mother.

"This house is now ours," Olga's father said, almost shouting.

"No," Bert said, staring at his neighbors of fifteen years. He tried to close the door, but Olga's father held it open with his foot.

"We don't need your approval. Evacuate the premises, immediately," Olga's father said.

"No!"

"Haven't you heard? Tonight is our revenge. You have ten minutes to get out, or I call the police and tell them you are a thief. And tonight they will be not be on your side. They will finally see things my way. So unless you and your family want to be arrested, you should leave quickly," Olga's father snarled. "There is no reason for you to have such a nice house."

Eva stared at Olga, who giggled into her hand. Eva scrunched up her fists, ready for a fight. Bert gripped her shoulders.

Olga suddenly sprinted past Eva and up the stairs. Eva broke free of her father's restraining grasp and chased her. Bert ran after them.

Eva ran into her room after Olga, who flopped onto the big lacy bed. As Eva threw herself at her old friend and pulled her long blonde hair, Olga screamed.

Bert pulled Eva off the flailing Olga. He pointed to her Kindertransport bag standing by the door. "Eva, get your things. It's time to leave." The calm in his voice was forced.

Eva jerked up her suitcase and glared at Olga. Glancing at Eva's sock drawer, Olga leaped across the bed, her feet sinking into the soft mattress. Eva dropped the suitcase, and dove for the sock drawer, but Olga got there first and grabbed the sock containing Eva's secret stockpile of reichsmarks.

Bert put his arm around Eva and pulled her to him. He spoke in a firm, hushed tone. "It's over, Eva. Let it go. There are more important things now."

Olga's father's footsteps clomped, as he quickly climbed the stairs.

Eva stopped, breathing heavily. Her shoulders slumped in defeat, as she glanced over at Olga, who clicked her heels together and gave the Nazi salute.

"Sieg heil!" Olga said.

Eva's eyes opened wide. She gritted her teeth and lunged for Olga, but Bert was faster. He grabbed Eva and her Kindertransport bag with the reluctant teddy bear inside, and pulled her out the door.

—⁓—

Peter, Becca, and Stephen sat down with their parents for their last dinner in Germany. No one spoke. Peter looked around the table. Stephen's family was kind. At least his mother would have a comfortable place to live, and Nora would help her take care of Baby Lilly. "Be grateful for small things," he remembered his father telling him. "If you work hard, you can make your own luck." His father's luck had run out.

After dinner, Peter took out his violin and, at his mother's urging, played "With God by Our Side." The grownups sang, the impending loss of their children weighing heavily on their hearts. Peter's penetrating notes chased the sullen Stephen out of the room.

> We are marching forward with God by our side.
> We will not leave our path, for He will be our guide.
> Hold my hand, lift our voices in prayer across the land.
> For we have made our choices, and together we will stand.

—⁓—

Hans walked the dark, empty Berlin streets, trying not to be seen as he made his way toward the Levys' house. He planned to stay there until the Kindertransport left.

As he rounded a corner, he came face to face with a policeman. Hans jumped back, his heart pounding.

"What are you doing out here?" the officer demanded.

Hans looked around. The Levys' house was within view, but he could not put them in jeopardy. The large brick building down the block was the Jewish Children's Orphanage. He pointed to it. "I'm late. They will beat me and make me scrub the floors."

The officer slapped him hard on the back of his head. "Good! Jew scum! I'll give you one minute before I start shooting."

Hans sprinted down the street and up the steps to the orphanage. He banged on the door, glancing over his shoulder at the Nazi officer, until the door opened a crack. "Please let me in!" he begged. "My family's been arrested, and I don't know where to go. The policeman across the street is watching me. In a few seconds he's going to start shooting!"

A mousy man looked out through the open door. A small boy, about nine years old, with unruly hair and freckles, peered around him.

"Herr Benny, you better let him in, or we'll have to clean the blood off the steps," the boy pointed out reasonably.

Herr Benny still hesitated. The boy quickly pointed at the package in Hans's hands. Hans looked down and then back at the boy, who nodded. Hans held out his food package to the man. "I have sausages, sugar, and butter."

The man opened the door and beckoned Hans in. Hans nodded and quickly stepped inside. He smiled at the little boy with an aversion to cleaning and a keen sense of bribery. "Thanks for the help."

"I like sausages," the boy said. "I'm Noah. Come on, I'll show you a cot where you can sleep."

———※———

At Stephen's house, Peter wasn't feeling well. He lay on his pallet on the floor, next to the bed where Sylvia and Becca slept. A drawer, removed from the dresser, sat on the floor next to Sylvia's bed. It was lined with Lilly's pink bunny blanket and used as a bed. A drawer-bed in the Levys' beautiful house wasn't bad, compared to where other people were living. Peter had seen many families were homeless and wandering the streets, begging for food and hiding from Hitler's men.

Still, Peter couldn't help but wish they were back in their tiny apartment above the butcher shop, and that he could hear the clacking of his father's cane across the floor. All of that was gone, and now, even this would be gone. Tomorrow, when the Kindertransport left the station, Peter would leave behind everything familiar. The thought made his stomach churn.

———※———

Bert, Helga, and Eva made their way to Bert's tailor shop. It had been boarded up since the attack.

When they got there, they saw that the bottom board had been pried off the door. Bert cautiously looked around, ducked under, and went in, followed by Helga and Eva.

They were startled to find a man asleep on the floor. At the sound of them entering, the man turned over and glared at them for disturbing his trespassing sleep. It was William, Eva's brother, his shaved hair barely grown in.

Helga ran to him and knelt down beside him, hugging him. "William! Oh, my sweet, sweet boy!"

Bert put his arm around him. "Where have you been, son?"

"They arrested me and sent me to Sothausen," William said.

Helga grabbed her head. "Oh, dear God!"

"What did they do to you?" Eva asked, giving her brother a hug.

Helga glared at Eva. "Let's not talk about that now. He's safe, and that's all that matters."

"I've got to get out of Germany, now," William said. "This is my last chance."

"You can take Eva's seat on the train tomorrow!" Helga blurted out.

Eva gasped and grabbed her father. "No, Mama!"

"Helga, no! That's not fair," Bert stared at his wife. "It's Eva's seat!"

"Oh, Bert. They're not going to hurt a little girl," Helga said. "William's the one in real danger. He's lucky he escaped."

Eva looked up at Bert. "Papa?"

William hugged his mother and turned his back to Eva and his father. He smiled. "Where's the train going?"

"England," Helga replied.

"That'll do," William said.

At the German organization office in Berlin, Marla and Jules combed through the piles of paperwork. They had lists, timelines, and documents for each child. Marla yawned and rubbed her red eyes.

"When was the last time you slept?" Jules asked her.

"November," Marla said. "How about you?"

"Years ago, before Hitler kicked the Jews out of the military," Jules said.

"You were in the German military?"

"I was a soldier. A good one. I don't really have any other skills."

"Yes, you do. Organizing and transporting children."

"And that's almost as hazardous," Jules said, laughing.

The night crept in moonless and cold, with a sharp wind blowing through the streets of Berlin.

Sleeping on the floor of his mother's room at the Levys' house, Peter was awakened by Bruno nudging him with his wet nose. "How did you get in here?"

The black dinner-jacket-wearing German Shepherd nudged him again.

"Now? Really? You need to go outside now?"

The dog whined.

Peter sleepily got up and slipped on his shoes. He staggered out the door, thumping his leg for the dog to follow. "Come on, then. Let's go and get it over with." He walked to the back door and opened it. Bruno trotted out into the dark night.

"It's cold out here, Bruno. Hurry up!"

Bruno heard something move in the bushes next door and bounded away. "Come back, Bruno!" Peter called, as he ran after him.

Bruno was buried deep in the bushes, hunting some rodent, by the time Peter got to him. He grabbed Bruno's collar and tugged, but Bruno was a determined hunter. "Bruno!" Peter pulled again, trying to make the big dog come out.

A gunshot rang out, cutting the cold brisk air. Bruno no longer tugged. The friendly German Shepherd slumped to the ground. Blood seeped out of a small hole ripped in his side. Bruno was dead.

Peter fell to the ground, terrified. He moved backward on his hands and feet, away from the unseen, cowardly dog murderer. Who would do such a thing? Bruno didn't do anything.

A deep man's voice spoke from the darkness. "I know you, Jew boy. Go home or you're next."

Peter's eviction from school, the arrest and death of his father, the destruction of his apartment and butcher shop, and the frightening, cheering Nazi crowds, all came together in his mind for one confusing, angry moment. The injustice welled up inside him.

"Why did you do that? My dog's not a Jew!" he shouted at the hidden killer.

Another shot rang out, barely missing Peter. He jumped to his feet and tore down the block. He quickly climbed the nearest tree and hid in its dark branches, as the footsteps stomped by looking for him.

He stayed, shivering in the tree all night, silently crying for the dog inherited from a Nazi man, who had killed himself in shame.

CHAPTER 13

BOARDING THE TRAIN

(January 1939)

Peter waited through the dark night, cold and scared. When at last the sun rose over Berlin, he climbed down from the tree and struggled to pick up the lifeless Bruno. Bent over, he dragged the heavy dog, weighing nearly as much as he did, back to Stephen's house.

He gently laid the best dog in the world under the large rosebush and covered him with leaves. This was an unfitting burial for such a loyal friend, but it was the best Peter could do. He would just tell them that he had found a new home for Bruno, and in a way, that was true.

All Peter could think about was Bruno and his cruel murder. Nothing was the same in Germany. When cowardly hidden assassins could gun down dogs and shoot at eleven-year-old boys, it was time to go, he thought.

The train would leave that day. There was no avoiding it. At least now he had something to do: leave Germany.

He was washed, dressed, and ready to leave by the time everyone else awoke.

—⁓—

Hans stepped outside the Jewish Children's Orphanage, carrying the rucksack his mother had so carefully packed for him to take to England. He ran down the steps, headed for the train station.

Noah slipped out the door behind him, following him.

The train station was overflowing with children carrying suitcases and parents saying their last goodbyes, words a parent should never have to say. The parents sent their children on a train to strangers with the faith they would see them again, a faith that got thinner with each passing day.

Marla and Jules checked the children in at the station as their breath steamed in the frigid Berlin air. Marla rubbed her hands together, trying to keep them warm. "I can't believe they won't let the parents on the platform," she said. "Kept behind a gate? Not only are they giving up their children, they are not even allowed proper goodbyes."

"The Nazis don't like displays of affection. They have no hearts," Jules said. "It's a scientific fact."

Mothers sobbed and clung to their husbands, who gritted their teeth trying to keep the tears back themselves as the children were sent to the platform alone to board the train. Many of the smaller children struggled to reach the step onto the train car. The children wore numbered cardboard tags on strings around their necks. An identical numbered tag was tied to their suitcases.

As Hans waited in the check-in line with his rucksack, Noah from the orphanage edged past him and mingled with the crowd watching the children entering the train. Noah's parents had once taken him by train to Amsterdam on holiday, but now they were dead.

Noah stood listening to the sound of the powerful train that would command the right-of-way as it barreled across Germany. He would bide his time for the right moment. Life was all about timing, and Noah's time was running out.

Marla checked off Eva's name and put a cardboard number on a string around Eva's neck.

Helga shook her finger. "No, there's been a change. William is going to take Eva's place." She pulled the grinning William up beside her.

Marla looked down at Eva, who held her father's arm tightly. "You don't want to go?" Marla asked the pretty girl.

Eva's eyes filled with tears. "I do." She clutched the number hanging around her neck. Marla looked at William, standing beside Eva with a smirk on his handsome face. He wore a hat to hide his shaved head from the concentration camp.

"I think Eva should go, because it's her name on the list," Marla said.

"No, it's been decided. I am their mother." Helga scowled.

"He must be under seventeen," Marla said firmly, eyeing William's thick, manly build.

"He's still sixteen. I should know, I gave him birth," Helga said.

Eva opened her mouth, but her mother pinched her. Eva gasped. She looked at her father, whose face was one of stony shock.

"Let me see his papers," Marla said. Helga handed them over. Marla looked at the hastily faked documents, but could not detect the forgery. "Okay, then, if you're sure."

Helga nodded vigorously. "Yes, I am."

As Marla quickly moved on to another child, Helga reached down and grabbed Eva's number.

"No, Mutti!" Eva held the cardboard identification number tightly. "It's mine!"

"You selfish girl! It's your brother's now." Helga roughly pulled Eva's number off her head and placed it around William's neck.

William smiled broadly. "Sorry, Eva," he said flippantly. "Trains make you sick. I'm doing you a favor."

Eva looked away.

William, with his escape assured, walked toward the train with a short dismissive wave at his parents and his little sister, whose seat he had stolen.

The train waited on the track, chugging gently. Some children waved out the windows to their families, still behind the fence several feet away.

Peter and Becca hugged Sylvia. She grabbed Peter's shoulders. "Peter, remember valuable things are not allowed, so don't put your violin in the luggage compartment where they can see it. Don't give them a reason to kick you off the train. I want you to take care of your sister. Be obedient to your new family, and write to me. Remember, no matter what, don't ever let go of who you are. Now, promise me you'll stay together." Peter nodded. "I will come to you soon."

Peter and Becca hugged Baby Lilly, kissing her face.

"Be a good girl, my Baby Lilly," Becca cooed. She kissed her sister, and tears ran down her face. "I love you very, very much. More than the moon and stars."

Peter rubbed Lilly's chubby cheeks, but he could not say anything. His throat was choked with despair and the fear that he might vomit. Finally, he swallowed, and a space opened up. He looked up at his mother. "I don't really want to go."

Sylvia shook her head. "You will be in my heart when you are in England, and I will come and find you as soon as I can. I will tell Baby Lilly every day about her wonderful brother and sister. Now, go, before the train leaves without you. I love you forever, no matter what."

Becca gripped her mother. "I love you. You are the best mother."

Peter pulled Becca away and fulfilled his older brother duties of getting her on the train bound for England.

—⅏—

Jacob and Nora hugged and kissed Stephen, who shrugged them off. "We will see you shortly. Things will improve," Jacob said, encouragingly.

"Don't have such an attitude with your new family. Be grateful, be good." Nora's voice was shaky.

"Of course. Goodbye!" Stephen said, as he quickly hugged them and turned away. He lumbered off toward the train and an unknown future in England.

As he approached the train, Hans strode quickly past him. Stephen reached out and grabbed him. "Hans, finally! You are here!"

They walked together to the train platform. "I thought I was going to have to go to England by myself," Stephen said. "Where have you been?"

"I've been hiding at the orphanage down the street. They destroyed my house and arrested my family," Hans said.

"Even Eddie?" Stephen asked.

Hans nodded. "I was headed to your house when the Nazis caught me."

"Somebody needs to kill Hitler," Stephen said. "It's the only way to stop him."

—⁓—

Peter, carrying a suitcase and his violin case, and Becca, with the other suitcase and the bundle tied with a rope, walked to the train.

Hans turned around. "Peter! You and Becca stay with us, okay?"

Peter nodded.

Becca cried, and Peter put his arm around her.

"I don't want to go," Becca said. "I don't want to be one of the lucky ones."

"I don't either," Peter said, "but I don't want to stay here. Do you remember what Papa looked like when he came back?"

Becca nodded and sniffled.

"I don't want that to happen to us," Peter said.

"What about Mutti and Baby Lilly?"

"Time to get on the train," Peter said, avoiding answering the same question he was thinking. "Just follow me."

Hans, Stephen, Becca, and Peter boarded the train. As they walked down the aisle, a pair of eyes looked out from amongst the cases and bundles in the luggage rack. It was little Noah, from the orphanage, hiding in a small cramped space among the luggage. Noah pressed his finger to his lips and smiled. Hans gave a short nod and moved on.

Peter looked back and pointed. "Was that—"

"Shhh. He's from the orphanage," Hans whispered.

"Oh," Peter said. He thought, The orphanage? How would Hans know that? What would it be like to have no one left?

The train was packed with almost one hundred children, ages sixteen and younger, plus one lying eighteen-year-old, and one hidden, resourceful orphan boy.

Some children were quiet, showing no emotion. Some chattered happily, as if the journey was an adventure. Others wept quietly, staring out the window with the grief only a child separated from a parent can know. They were filled with both the joy of a train ride and the hollow knowledge that the world was an empty place, and nothing would ever make it right again, but most believed their parents would soon follow them to England.

Peter nudged Becca. "Look, it's Charlie." Becca and Peter waved to Charlie Beckman, seated by the window. Charlie waved back, smiling.

"Charlie, you're going to England, too?" Becca asked her old classmate.

"Yes. I'm on holiday," Charlie smiled and waved out the window to his parents. "My parents are going to come later. I'll see them in a few days."

"Should we tell him?" Becca whispered to Peter.

Peter shook his head. "No, he'll find out soon enough."

Hans and Stephen helped Peter and Becca put their suitcases in the luggage compartment above their heads. Hans reached for Peter's violin, but Peter quickly pulled it to him. "Not the violin."

Hans and Stephen found seats and sat down next to each other. Peter slid into the seat behind them, and Becca scooted into the seat beside Peter. He set the violin on the seat between them and laid his coat over it so it was hidden.

William, the Kindertransport interloper, slumped in a seat down the aisle. Stephen and Hans waved to him. William raised his chin in a reluctant jerk in reply.

Peter looked around. "Hey, where's Eva?"

Hans turned around in his seat. "William, where's Eva?"

William tilted his head to the side. "She didn't want to go. You know what she's like." He shrugged, then yawned and closed his eyes, acting like this day was nothing special, like he fled Germany all the time.

Peter looked frantically out the window and saw Eva standing on the platform, with her arms crossed in defiance and her father's protective arm around her. Peter could tell she was mad. "He stole her seat!" Peter whispered.

Stephen and Hans joined Peter in looking out the window at Eva.

She saw them and gave a half-hearted wave. Peter's heart pounded. He'd thought she was coming on the train. He hadn't even said goodbye.

"If William wasn't Jewish, he'd be a Nazi," Peter said. He worried about what would happen to the prettiest girl in Berlin, trumped by her selfish brother.

CHAPTER 14

THE TRAIN WHISTLE BLEW

(January 1939)

A Nazi officer with narrow dark eyes stomped onto the train filled with frightened children. The nametag on his uniform read Becker. He swung his club randomly, pounding the seats and the walls. The children started and froze with the tension of terror infused in the very air they breathed when a Nazi officer was nearby.

The club landed hard against a suitcase and hit Noah, hidden amongst the baggage. A startled, muffled groan erupted.

Becker slowly stepped back. The silence of the train amplified his footsteps. He glanced around the luggage. Then he reached up and yanked Noah out from behind the bags. "Sneaky Jew, huh? Can't be trusted. You're off this train!"

As the children watched, Becker dragged Noah down the aisle by his collar. Marla, who had stepped onto the train, ran over. "What's wrong? What happened?"

"Tried to stow away," Becker said, holding Noah out like a wayward dog caught in a spilled garbage bin.

Marla reached for Noah. "I'll take care of him."

"No, this little swine needs to be taught a lesson," Becker said.

Marla panicked. She looked over at Noah, so tiny, but standing so straight, his eyes clear and brimming with defiance. He was a boy with nothing left but his courage.

"This one's mine." Becker grabbed Noah's wiry little arm and marched him off the train. "Stowaway! Arrest him!" he yelled to the police at the station.

Marla stretched out her hand to Noah as he was thrown off the train. She let her breath out, and with it came a groan. Her body went limp as Noah's little body thudded against the ground.

The train whistle blew, pulling the children back into the reality of their own sorrows. They hung out the windows waving, pushing to get one last look at their families still corralled behind the fence. Parents bravely smiled and waved, as if they were seeing their children off for the first day of school. Some jumped up to see over the crowd and get one final glimpse of their children before the train took them beyond their reach.

Marla and Jules checked everything on board one last time. The train whistle blew again, warning of its impending departure.

Jules stepped off the train and waved to Marla. "Good luck, Marla. I will be on the next train."

"Goodbye, Jules. All these children will thank you someday."

—⚊⚊—

Anna, Oma Greta, and Eddie waited in a crowded room at the police station across from Edelweiss Park for a train out of Germany, headed for the unwelcoming Poland. Anna hoped Hans had made the Kindertransport and was on his way out of Germany.

—⚊⚊—

The Kindertransport was finally about to leave. A woman suddenly climbed over the gate and bolted to the train, carrying someone's forgotten basket, which she held up to the open window.

She shoved the basket gently through Hans's window, and whistled softly to him. "Here, young man, take this, careful. Please, be very careful."

Gingerly handling the surprisingly heavy basket, Hans pulled it inside. Stephen, sitting beside him, leaned over for a look. "Who's it for?" Hans asked the urgent woman standing outside his window on her tiptoes.

"My sister will pick it up in Holland. Bless you."

A Nazi officer ran over and pulled the woman away from the train, but the basket was already safely inside with Hans. The woman's shoulders hunched, as if she was exhausted from the weight she had carried in that small basket.

Inside the train, Stephen and Hans stared at the basket. It was covered with a red-checkered cloth, like a picnic basket. "What is it?" Stephen wondered.

"Food, I hope. I'm hungry," Hans said. "I think we're rightfully entitled to part of it for the trouble of transporting it."

Hans flipped off the cloth, prepared to see chicken and potato salad. But it was not a picnic basket filled with food. It held a baby girl.

Hans leaned out the window. "Wait!" he called, but the Nazi officer was dragging the woman roughly away behind the fence.

Hans looked at Stephen. "What do we do with it?"

Stephen read the note pinned to the baby's clothes: "'Karla Blinker will be picked up at the Holland train station.'"

"How will we keep her quiet until Holland?" Stephen asked.

Hans shrugged.

Peter leaned forward from the seat behind them. "I'm used to babies. I'll help you."

"Thanks, Peter," Hans said.

Becca leaned over and played with the baby's fingers. "I miss my Baby Lilly," she whispered.

Outside the train, Arnold Beckman, Charlie's father, nicely dressed, pushed through the crowd behind the fence. Arnold didn't even let Charlie walk home from school by himself, and here he was, letting him go to England alone. Evelyn Beckman, a thin woman with a kind face, held on tightly to Arnold's arm.

Suddenly, Arnold's agony burst through his contorted face. "No!" he yelled. He shook loose of Evelyn's loving restraint, jumped over the fence, and ran toward the train.

"Arnold, don't!" Evelyn called to her grief-stricken husband.

Arnold ran up to Charlie's window as if desperate for one final goodbye, but instead he reached into the window and grabbed his little boy's hands. Charlie stared wide-eyed at his crazed father. "Papa!"

"My son, I can't live without you!" With an anguished cry, Arnold pulled little Charlie through the train window and hugged him tightly to his chest.

Evelyn pushed through the crowd, but she was restrained at the fence. "No! No!"

The police pushed Arnold and Charlie away from the train, and Evelyn pointed helplessly to the train, sobbing uncontrollably.

Peter leaned out the train window, watching Charlie's horrified face, as he was suddenly back where he started and without his holiday train ride to England.

Peter pulled back into the train car as Becca looked at him with big scared eyes. "Where did Charlie go?"

"His father pulled him out," Peter said.

"Why?"

"Heartbreak, I guess."

"Looks like Charlie's holiday is over." Becca shook her head.

—⚊⚊—

Charlie stared up at his frantic father. "I thought I was going on the train, Papa," he said, his eyes wide with confusion.

"Charlie! Charlie! What have I done? Wait! Wait!" Arnold shouted, suddenly regretting his impulsive action. He picked Charlie up and ran with him alongside the train. But the police grabbed him and escorted him back. Arnold couldn't undo his spontaneous rescue of Charlie from the freedom train.

He hugged Charlie and ran back into the crowd of parents, who wailed as the train readied to pull away, free at last to express their deep sorrow.

Evelyn hugged Charlie, her son, saved from being saved. "Oh, Charlie. I guess we were meant to stay together." She put her arms around her husband. "Let's go home, Arnie."

The policemen began prodding the parents with billy clubs. "Go home!" they shouted. "They are ready to leave the station."

The parents began moving slowly toward the exits, now openly grieving for the children they had lost, children they didn't know if they would ever see again, children who would have a new life in England without them.

Jacob and Nora wept, clinging to each other in their sorrow. "Stephen is gone," Nora murmured.

—〰—

Stephen looked out the window and saw his parents' despair, but it was too late to make things right for his bad behavior.

Becker strutted through the packed train compartment. "Your parents aren't here now. You are to make no noise!" He struck the seats with his billy club. "No trouble, do you understand? At the border, your bags will be checked. If anything of value is found, it will be confiscated, and you will be sent back to Germany!"

Becker thumped through the train, glaring menacingly at the children, as he entered the next compartment.

Marla followed him, holding the children's travel papers and passports. "What did you do with the little stowaway?"

"He was arrested," Becker said, menacingly.

"He's just a boy."

"He is a criminal."

The door between the cars slammed shut. Then the train doors were locked with the children inside. Becker swung off the train and was gone. The children let out their breath.

The wheels began to move as the train pulled away from the station platform, and slowly the children's train left Berlin. The city and suburbs outside gave way to woods, lakes, rivers, distant mountains, small towns, and villages.

It rained. Lightning flashed, and thunder shook, as the train traveled across Germany. The train cars were crowded with the sounds of children talking, laughing, crying, and shouting. It was hard to tell which was louder, the children inside or the raging storm outside.

Peter remembered his nightmare of that terrifying feeling of hurtling through the darkness, with no direction and the horrifying fear of what would happen when it stopped. Now he was living it.

Stephen and Hans slumped in their seats, with the baby in the basket beside them. Peter stared out the window, with Becca wedged against him and the hidden violin.

CHAPTER 15

TO THE HOLLAND BORDER

(January 1939)

Back at Stephen's house, Nora, Jacob, and Sylvia slumped on the couches in the living room. Baby Lilly fidgeted, arching her back, throwing herself against the couch in an uncontrolled baby rebellion.

"Did we do the right thing?" Nora asked.

"We did the right thing, for right now." Jacob sighed.

Sylvia snuggled with the wiggling baby. "I feel like I gave away my soul. Without Baby Lilly, I would give up."

"If you give up, they win," Jacob said.

"I think they've won anyway," Sylvia responded. "They've divided our families. Our children are gone, our businesses ruined, our friends taken away in the middle of the night. What is left to take?"

"Our lives," Jacob said.

"They break us apart little by little." Nora sighed. "The house seems so empty. It will never be filled again."

—ʍ—

The Kindertransport chugged to a stop. "What's happening? Why did we stop?" Peter asked, gripping Hans's seat.

Hans looked out the window, but could see nothing but darkness. He handed the baby basket to Stephen, and then opened the window. Rain poured in. He leaned out briefly, looking ahead. "Looks like the track is flooded."

The baby woke up and cried. Stephen quickly handed the baby basket back to Hans. "What do we do with the baby now?"

"How should I know?" Hans turned to the seat behind him. "Peter!"

Peter took the basket on his lap. He put his little finger in the baby's mouth and gently rocked the basket. The baby quieted and sucked.

As the rain pelted the ground, the train workers dug a ditch to drain the water.

The children shifted restlessly inside the locked train. Too nervous to sit, William got up and paced in the aisle. "Come on! Come on!"

"You got somewhere to be, William?" Hans teased.

"Yes, out of Germany, you idiot!" William hissed, turning on Hans.

—〰—

In Berlin, Arnold, Charlie, and Evelyn walked down the street on their way home. The police had already stopped them twice.

From the shadows, someone threw a bottle at them. It crashed in the street, barely missing Charlie. Startled, they jumped and looked around, searching for the assailant. There was laughter from the behind the corner of the nearest building.

Arnold picked up Charlie and put his arm around Evelyn. They hurried on.

"I wish we all could have gone on that train," Charlie said.

"Maybe we will, Charlie," Arnold said. "Maybe we will. Uncle Ernst lives in America, and he is trying to help us."

"I hope the other kids have a nice holiday," Charlie said quietly.

Arnold let out a shaking gasp. His wife put her arm around his waist and pulled him forward, toward the relative safety of their newly evacuated apartment.

—〰—

At the Berlin police station next to Edelweiss Park, Noah was curled up in a ball in a crowded jail cell with wall-to-wall Jewish men. He didn't cry. He had become accustomed to being alone and afraid. In another section filled with women and some children, Oma Greta, Anna, and Eddie still waited.

—⚏—

The Kindertransport finally rumbled to a stop at the last German station before the train crossed over the Dutch border. A Nazi border guard with close-cropped hair and suspicious eyes barked orders. "Schnell! Schnell! The Jew train has arrived!"

All along the length of the train, German border guards banged on the train doors and unlocked them for one last inspection. The door swung open. Two guards stepped into Peter's car. One of the guards tapped the other guard's shoulder. "Now comes the fun, huh, Gregory? I'll take the next car."

Gregory smiled. "Luggage inspection!" he called.

Hans quickly took the sleeping baby from Peter, put her back in the basket, and hid the basket behind his rucksack on the floor.

Gregory, holding Marla's list of names, stomped down the aisle. "This train reeks of Jews!" he shouted.

The children sat up straight against their seats, their faces forward. No one spoke. No one dared look at the Nazi tormentor. The children barely breathed. Hans glanced at the baby, blocked by the rucksack and covered with the red-checkered cloth. His forehead broke out in sweat beads.

Gregory checked off the names on the list. He approached William. "What is your name?"

"William Rosenberg."

"You took your sister's place? Yes? You look too old to be on this train," Gregory said.

"I'm big for my age," William said, flippantly.

Gregory leaned in closer to William. "Remember, you're still in Germany. I can send you . . ." He snatched off William's hat, revealing his shaved head. "Ah ha! Back to the concentration camp, you filthy Jew!" Gregory yanked William onto his feet.

William pulled back, glaring at him. "I won't go back."

"You're right. You won't make it past this stop." Gregory pulled his gun from its holster, held it against William's head, and pulled him down the aisle. The children watched in fear, motionless in their seats, as Gregory opened the train door and shoved William out.

Peter searched out the window to see what Gregory would do. It was dark, and the shadowy movement made it hard to see what was happening.

A gunshot rang out. A body fell with a thud in the dark, and disappeared underneath the train.

Becca pulled on Peter's shirt. "Did he kill William?"

Peter put his finger to his mouth, glaring at her to be quiet, but he knew she wouldn't listen. She never did.

"I just want to know," Becca whispered.

The door between the cars opened. Becca and Peter looked at each other with wide eyes.

Gregory strutted in, acting like nothing had happened. He randomly opened suitcases and searched through them. When he found nothing but children's clothes and toys, he dumped them on the floor of the train.

Becca dropped her doll, and Peter bent down to pick it up, glancing at the basket under Hans's seat. The checkered cloth had moved off the baby's wiggling head, and her eyes opened, but Hans could not see her. The baby's face scrunched, ready to cry.

Peter fidgeted nervously, afraid the baby would be found, and Hans would be kicked off the train. He got back up and gave Becca her doll.

Gregory walked to Hans and Stephen's seat. He pointed to the edge of the basket under their seat. "What is that?"

Panicking, Peter pushed the violin off the seat to distract him. It clattered to the floor and slid into the aisle.

Gregory stopped his advance on the basket baby. He stooped and picked up the violin. "Ah, whose is this?" he asked.

No one said anything. Becca, clutching her doll, grabbed Peter's arm. Gregory turned over the cardboard number attached to the violin.

"I can find out. Number 1—" Gregory said.

"It's mine," Hans said, jumping up.

Peter froze as he realized Hans would be blamed. Protect me, he prayed to God, as he slowly stood up. "No, he's mistaken. It's mine."

Becca pulled on Peter's shirt, trying to get him to sit back down.

Gregory advanced on Peter until he was right in front of him. Peter closed his eyes for a second, but didn't move, not from bravery, but out of mind-numbing fear. "What is this? Are you smuggling valuables to England to sell?" Gregory accused.

Peter shook his head. "No, it's my violin."

Hans sank back down in his seat. He bent down and glanced quickly at the baby and rocked the basket with his foot. The baby fluttered her eyelids and went back to sleep. Hans let out a heavy sigh.

Gregory threw the violin case at Peter. "Open it. Quickly! Schnell! Schnell!"

Peter opened the case and showed Gregory the violin. Gregory examined it. "This must be very valuable. You could sell it for a large sum of money in England, couldn't you?"

"No. It's old and very out of tune."

"What do you plan to do with it then?" Gregory asked.

Peter shrugged. "Play it."

"Play it? You?" Gregory sneered, cocking his head back. "You are a tiny bit of a boy. You are nothing. This is yours?"

Peter nodded.

Gregory shoved the violin at him. "Then play it."

"I haven't played in a long time," Peter said, thinking it was a trick.

"I said play it!" Gregory ordered.

Peter, hesitatingly, tucked the instrument under his chin. He clumsily dropped the bow. It clattered to the floor. He picked it up and took a breath. All eyes were on him. Not a sound was heard in the train car. Marla watched from the front of the car, her brow sweating, her hands shaking.

Peter moved the bow, and the violin strings howled like a wolf. He looked around. Becca's face was red, and Peter realized she was holding her breath. He gripped his bow and made it dance slowly on the violin, playing the song that reminded him of Becca. He played "Schmetterling," a song about a butterfly, but instead of the normal lively flitting of notes, he played it slowly, like a funeral march. Becca released her breath.

The flawless notes from the tiny minstrel reverberated in the train car. When the swaying music of the distorted children's song ended, some of the children's faces were streaked with tears from the memories of the homes they had left, but no sound was heard.

Gregory looked around, his faced pinched with anger. "It's out of tune! Better get it fixed! Sit down. You will never be a good musician."

Peter carried the violin to his seat. His hands shook. Hans looked at the baby, and her eyes fluttered open.

Gregory stomped through the car, knocking the remaining suitcases down. He spat on the floor. "Don't come back to Germany, you godless scum! May England rot with your stench!" He climbed down the train stairs and slammed the door.

"Go ahead and take the Jews! Let them infect England!" he shouted from outside the train.

No one moved inside the train. The baby cried as the whistle blew, and the train slowly inched forward.

William appeared at the door between the cars. He swaggered in, filthy but gloating, with his usual arrogance and spite.

"William? How did—" Stephen sputtered.

"You didn't think the Nazis got rid of me that easily, did you?" William flopped down on the seat. "I dodged the bullet and played dead till the man left. Then I climbed back in through the window of the next car."

The children were quiet. The wheels on the train turned, and it slowly crossed the border into Holland. The children on the Kindertransport were finally out of Germany and beyond Hitler's reach.

As the train rolled onto Dutch soil, Peter stared out the window and breathed deeply for the first time since he'd boarded the train. The wheels of the train screeched, and the train stopped again on the other side of the Dutch border.

The Dutch border guard stepped on board. He looked at the frightened faces of the children, then smiled and opened his arms. "The Nazis are gone! Welcome to Holland, my German friends!"

The smiling children cheered and clapped, the noise deafening in the car's small space.

Peter tucked his violin under his chin, rose to his feet, and played

"Schmetterling" the way it was meant to be, happy, fluttering, and joyous. When the children heard the change in the tune, they laughed and smiled. Some danced in the aisles. They all joined in loudly singing:

> On a bright and sunny afternoon
> Out of its dark and lonely cocoon
> Crawled a beautiful schmetterling.
> Flitter-fly, passing by
> Dancing on the air with new wings
> Flying magic everywhere.
> Hovering above my milking pail.
> The swishing of the cow's tail
> It's an old German tale
> That the Butterfly is a witch's scheme
> To try to steal the cow's cream.

A plump woman with her hair in a bun, and a friendly teenage girl with braids, brought trays of hot cocoa and cookies on board the train. The woman offered the cookies to Becca, who slowly reached out and tentatively took one.

"Take two, my little sunshine," the woman said.

Becca looked at Peter. "Is she talking to me?"

Peter nodded. Becca smiled and quickly took two. "Danke."

Peter also took two cookies. He and Becca ate them quickly, as if they might magically disappear.

The border guard checked off the children's names on his sheets. Hans and Stephen looked out the window, but it was dark.

A woman in a hood ran onto the train car behind them. She ran down the aisle, looking in each seat. "I'm looking for my sister's baby, Karla Blinker. Please," she said, frantically. "Someone, please! She's got to be here!"

Hans and Stephen stood up and gestured, pointing to the baby. "Shhh. She's sleeping," Stephen said.

"Ah!" the woman said, relieved to find the baby. She lovingly took the basket with the sleeping child and gently kissed the little girl. At ease, she looked at Hans and Stephen and bowed her head to them. "Thank you. God put this child in the right hands. Your parents are very lucky to have you for sons."

Hans pointed to Peter. "He's the one who knows babies. He's the one who kept her quiet."

The woman smiled at Peter. "May God be with you on your journey. You will save the Jews." She hurried down the train aisle with the basket in her arms, and disappeared into the night with the baby, who had escaped Hitler through a train window.

Peter looked at Becca. "I wish everyone would stop saying that."

CHAPTER 16

ARE WE ALLOWED IN?

(January 1939)

The Kindertransport started up again and traveled on through Holland. The children laughed and talked. When weariness overtook them, the train grew quiet, and the constant rhythm of the wheels on the track rocked the little ones to sleep at last.

Stephen and Hans stared out the dark windows. Stephen turned back in his seat to look at William over Peter's seat.

"Eva should be here," Stephen whispered.

"William doesn't deserve to take her place," Hans said.

Becca shifted in the seat next to him. "I hate William. He's not a good brother. A good brother helps you out." She rested her head on Peter's shoulder. "I love Eva. Peter does, too."

The spunky little spitfire didn't see her brother's glare, because she closed her eyes and drifted off to sleep, knowing that the responsibility to keep her safe was now Peter's.

—◆—

At the Rosenbergs' tailor shop in Berlin, Eva, dirty and disheveled, slept fitfully on the hard cold floor. When she awoke, her eyes darted around the dark room.

A rat lurked in the corner, its two calculating eyes staring at Eva, who froze at the sight of it. The filthy vermin scooted out from the corner and moved toward her, its rodent claws scratching. She bit her lip to prevent herself from screaming.

Suddenly, the back door crashed in, smashing the rat. Eva jumped back. Startled, Helga sat up as two men barged in.

Bert jumped up and faced them: Simon and Burl, two local young men the family knew. "What do you boys want?"

"Where's William?" Simon was a rough-looking young man, spitting with anger.

"He's not here," Bert answered.

"He's on a train to England!" Helga said, haughtily. "Long gone."

"I doubt that," Burl huffed. "Search this place."

Simon searched the shop as Burl, a chubby young man with an unusually large head, kept a gun trained on the Rosenbergs. Slowly, Eva crept behind Bert, holding his waist, as she dared to peek around him to stare at the intimidating intruders.

Simon came back and shook his head. "He's not here."

Burl put down his gun.

"What's he done?" Bert's voice sounded exhausted.

"He stole food and blamed it on Vincent Vogner," Burl said.

Helga shook her head vigorously. "No, that can't be true. William would never do that."

"The Nazis killed Herr Vogner and let William out of Sothausen because he promised to emigrate," Simon said. "He told them he had the needed documents and that he'd be gone in a week."

Eva gripped her father's arm tightly. Bert buried his face in his hands as the men stomped out.

Peter looked out the window of the train, as Becca slept, resting on his shoulder. The Holland air smelled different, cleaner somehow, and he filled his lungs.

William stretched his feet onto the train seat beside him, pushing a little boy against the window.

The train passed Rotterdam and pulled into a dimly lit station at

Hook Van Holland on the English Channel, directly across from Harwich, a small English fishing town.

The children, carrying their belongings, streamed out of the train as a bone-chilling dampness greeted them. Peter's breath blew smoky in the chill. He wondered if Jewish people were allowed to play music in Holland.

Marla escorted the sleepy children into a building at the Harbor House. Hans, Peter, Stephen, and Becca shuffled into line with the rest of the disheveled, hungry children. Becca and Peter stopped at the door, reluctant to enter.

Marla motioned them in. "What's the matter?"

"Are we allowed in?" Peter asked, quietly, as if someone might overhear his impertinent question.

"Yes, of course. This is all for you," Marla said.

Becca smiled up at Peter. "They knew we were coming, and it's still open."

"Then we better go in while we can," Peter said.

Inside the Harbor House, a table was laid with hard-boiled eggs, sandwiches, and milk. Becca slipped a couple of eggs into her coat pockets. Around them, the children laughed, ate, and ran around, acting like youngsters again.

Peter nudged Becca next to him. "We're one boat ride away from England and our new English family."

—⟋⟍—

In Bert's tailor shop, the morning light streamed in through the windows, waking Eva before the others. She sat up and looked around at the destruction. The door the men had kicked in was propped back up against the doorway. Reams of colorful cloth and spools of thread were tossed about, and the sewing machines were bashed in. It was such a contrast from the neat shop her father had run for over twenty years. He had sewn clothes for many of the most powerful leaders of Germany. Now, he was secretly sleeping among the ruins of his profession.

A man's face suddenly appeared in the window, staring at Eva. She recognized him; she'd seen him around the neighborhood many times since the Nazis had come to power. His name was Grundy. He was a young Nazi officer with a misshapen face, and an apparent need to make up for his lack of attractiveness by proving himself a loyal tormentor.

Eva reached over and grabbed Bert's arm. As Grundy kicked the broken door aside and stormed in, Bert jumped to his feet.

"You are trespassing!" Grundy shouted.

"It is my shop," Bert answered, motioning to all his equipment and materials. "I am Bert Rosenberg, the tailor."

"You used to be the tailor, but not anymore. Get up! You are all under arrest! Your son William used this shop to run a document forging business."

Bert helped Helga up. He looked at Eva, his eyes filled with sadness and regret. "I'm sorry, Eva. That seat on the train was rightfully yours."

"No talking! Get out!" Grundy shouted.

As Grundy marched them out the door, Eva looked back. She saw her Kindertransport suitcase, the last bit of comfort she owned, propped against a broken sewing machine, the teddy bear's leg still hanging out.

At Harbor House, the adults began calling the children into a line as a ferryboat steamed slowly into the port. Peter carried his violin and pushed Becca toward the group. She dragged her feet as she pulled one more hard-boiled egg from her pocket, peeled it, and stuffed half of it in her mouth.

"Hurry up, Becca."

"Do you think Charlie's mad that he's not on holiday anymore?" Becca asked, as bits of egg popped out of her mouth.

"No, at least he's home," Peter said. "You and I will live with strangers who don't even speak our language."

"But we know English," Becca said happily through a mouthful of egg. "And we'll be together."

A dog barked somewhere nearby.

"That sounded like Bruno," Becca said, tilting her head to listen like Bruno had.

"It's not Bruno," Peter snapped. He thought of how Bruno had been murdered and placed under a bush in Stephen's backyard, an utter humiliation for a dog in a dinner jacket. "Let's go, Becca! England's not going to wait for you."

Then they boarded the boat bound for Harwich.

CHAPTER 17

WE SUFFER FOR GOD

(January 1939)

A rundown Berlin house, made into apartments with broken windows and no electricity, stood as a hollow reminder of the power Nazis held over Germany and the Jewish people.

Inside his ransacked apartment, Arnold Beckman, wrapped in a tattered blanket, sat on the side of the couch where Charlie slept. Evelyn, wearing an oversized robe with a coat over it and well-worn boots, walked into the room and rested her hands gently on her husband's shoulders. "Have you been in here all night?"

Arnold reached up and patted Evelyn's hands. His eyes were puffy and red, and his cheeks were wet from tears. He nodded. "Evelyn, I have been sitting here wondering if God will forgive me my selfishness for taking Charlie off the train."

Evelyn shook her head. "They will arrest us if they find us living in our own apartment. I don't think God is even watching us anymore."

"Don't say that. Don't ever say that. We suffer for God," Arnold said, as his breath blew smoky in the cold air.

"Perhaps, then, suffering together is better than suffering apart. Forgive yourself, Arnie." Evelyn wrapped her arms around her husband. "Charlie has."

—ᴍ—

After many days of waiting at the police station for deportation, Anna, Oma Greta, and Eddie were packed into a crowded train and returned with a vengeance to Poland. Greta slumped asleep on Anna's shoulder.

Eddie tapped Anna's other shoulder. "But we didn't do anything wrong."

"I know. I know," Anna said. "Eddie, please stop saying that. Just for now, okay?"

Eddie patted his grandma's head. "Is my Oma okay?"

"She is fine. Just very tired."

"And old, right?" Eddie said. "Where's Hans? I wish he was here."

"I don't know, Eddie, but he's a smart boy."

"Yes, he's a smart boy," Eddie said, sadly.

The train that held Anna, Oma Greta, and Eddie, along with a few other Polish Jews who had somehow escaped the initial deportations in October, slowed. Anna could hear the two policemen on board, near the front of the car, discussing the passengers' fate.

"What are we supposed to do with them?" one said. "Poland doesn't want them either."

"We will force them across the border. Then they will be Poland's problem," the other policeman said.

—∿—

High winds and swelling waves rocked the boat that took the children across the English Channel that morning. Peter, whose stomach was always a little sensitive, was seasick from the rocking and swaying of the rollicking boat on rough waters, and the smell of the black exhaust smoke puffing from its engine. As they pulled into Harwich Port, he held onto the side of the boat and leaned his head over.

Becca wistfully watched the water. "I miss the butterflies. Where do they go in the winter?"

Peter didn't care about butterflies; all he cared about was stopping the rocking boat.

The boat horn bellowed, announcing its arrival. Becca grabbed Peter's arm. "We're here, Peter! We're in England! Our new family is waiting!"

"My stomach's still back in Holland. Give me a minute." The rolling boat lurched to its side as the gangplank was lowered. Peter swayed with it and vomited off the side of the boat.

He straightened back up, feeling somewhat better. "Okay, I think I can walk now."

"That was a waste of some good eggs," Becca said.

Peter glared at her. "Be quiet, Becca."

Marla waved her arms and smiled. "Come on, children, gather your things. We need to get off the boat." She patted Peter's shoulder. "You'll feel better when you're on solid ground."

Peter nodded, but he wasn't so sure. He and Becca gripped the sides of the gangplank and made their unsteady way onto English soil.

There were crowds of people waiting for the children: foster parents, local curiosity seekers, English refugee worker volunteers, and reporters with big cameras.

A reporter, wearing a fedora hat tipped slightly to the side, stepped in front of them. His camera bulb flashed. "So what do you think of England, children?" he shouted at Peter and Becca.

Becca looked in his direction, unable to focus after the blinding flashbulb.

"At least it's not a boat!" Peter looked back at the dreaded boat. It looked so steady now as it stood almost empty, obviously mocking him.

"What do you think about Hitler?" the reporter asked, talking quickly and loudly.

"Someone should do something," Peter answered.

The reporter smiled and nodded.

"My papa is dead," Becca said. Tears welled up in her eyes.

The camera bulb flashed, and Becca stumbled back. Peter pulled her away, so the reporter could not assault them again with questions about home and the man they were fleeing. He moved Becca along, not knowing where to go, but following the line of German children leading to Sebastian, the London refugee official.

Sebastian checked off the children's names from his list as they entered Harwich Port. Peter and Becca waited until they were finally next in line.

"Name?" Sebastian said in a businesslike tone, his face showing no emotion. He was not even looking at him.

Peter looked up at the big man, and his voice left him. All he could think of was Karl Radley, the policeman who kicked him out of his school. The one who thought it was amusing when Wolfgang tripped him. The one who slapped Becca. The one who took his father away and stole their home and shop.

"I'm Sebastian. What's your name, lad?" Sebastian asked again, this time smiling at Peter.

This man Sebastian isn't Karl Radley, Peter thought. We're in England now. People aren't like that here. He swallowed hard and stuttered, "Peter Weinberg. This is my sister, Rebecca."

Sebastian searched his list. "Peter, you're on the bus to Dovercourt, over there." Sebastian pointed to a red double-decker bus waiting in the road. A few of the older boys were boarding the bus. "Rebecca, you have a family waiting for you at the Liverpool Street Station in London. You go over there." He pointed in the opposite direction to a group of refugee volunteers, waiting to take the children to the train station.

Peter and Becca looked at each other. Becca wrapped her little arms around Peter's waist. "Tell him," she said to Peter.

Peter gestured to Sebastian. "No, no, I'm sorry, maybe my English isn't very good. We're together, she's my sister."

Sebastian pointed in two different directions. "Your sister goes to London. You go to Dovercourt. I'm sorry, mate."

"No! That's not what we agreed to." Peter stared at Sebastian. "That wasn't the arrangement. My mother is expecting us to stay together. She will demand it."

Sebastian shook his head, cleared his throat, and looked away. Then he quickly motioned to Marla, who walked over and took Becca by the hand. "Come on, love, only one more train ride."

Peter ran up beside them and grabbed Becca's other hand. "I'll go with her then."

Marla shook her head at Peter. "No, no, the family only has room for

Rebecca. You go over there. Your name's Peter, right? See that big bus. It'll take you to your camp."

Peter grabbed Becca. "I'm in charge of Becca. I'm her brother. We need to stay together!"

Marla pried Peter's arms away. "I know, but this is the best I can do." She scooped Becca up and walked away.

Becca kicked and screamed. "He's my brother! I need him! He's my Peter! Don't take him away from me! Peter!"

"Becca!" Peter called, as he ran after her.

Sebastian left the line of children and hurried over. He stood in Peter's way, preventing him from going after his sister. "Not today," Sebastian said.

I was wrong, Peter thought, as he glared at Sebastian. You are just like Karl Radley. Why does everyone keep taking my family away?

In Marla's arms, Becca reached out for Peter, crying. "Peter, don't leave me! Peter, you promised Mutti!"

Peter struggled to get to her, but Sebastian, an imposing figure, steered him toward the red double-decker bus with a firm hand. "Be a good bloke and get on the bus, now," he said, quietly, his voice cracking with emotion. "Please."

"Do something!" Becca commanded Peter, her quiet, but always reliable, brother.

Peter was only eleven, in a foreign country, and didn't even fully understand the language. What was a Dovercourt, anyway? His shoulders slumped, and his head bowed. He had lost his last connection to love, his sister Becca, and his mother's trust that he would take care of her.

He turned away and covered his ears, so he couldn't hear his sister calling for him, as he walked toward the bus that would take him away from Becca.

Marla deposited Becca in the line for the London train and turned back toward the children streaming off the boat. She looked back at the anguished Becca, as Peter was led away.

Marla grimaced. She knew what it was like to lose a brother. Her older brother Dwight, the dashing light of her world, had taken a job at her father's tavern to learn the business. He took advantage of being the owner's son and drank his weight in scotch. Two months earlier, while trying to find his way home in the middle of a moonless night, he'd teetered across a dangerously high seawall, like a drunken tightrope walker, and fallen into the sea. He'd drowned, a few feet from shore within sight of his father's tavern. It had changed her life forever.

There were more children coming off the boat, clamoring to be placed, so she wiped her tears away, pushing her own grief aside.

—◊—

In Berlin, Grundy, the Nazi officer who had pulled Helga, Bert, and Eva from the tailor shop, forced the Rosenbergs into the back of a truck already filled with people.

Eva held onto Bert's arm to steady herself. "Where are we going, Papa?"

An old man in an expensive, but very dirty and ripped, suit motioned to them. "I heard them say that they are taking us to the Bockenburg work camp near Munich. From there, it is only God who knows."

Meanwhile, Noah, the daring stowaway from the orphanage, was squished in a group of men being herded out of the police station next to Edelweiss Park and onto a transport bus. Their hands were tied together with rope, because there were not enough handcuffs since the mass arrests.

A group of schoolchildren passed by them. Noah wiggled his small hands out of the rope knots made for adults and pushed his way out of the crowd of new Jewish prisoners. He slipped into the group of schoolchildren; although a bit disheveled, he blended in with them, as the rest of the inmates were loaded roughly onto a huge military truck. No one noticed his quick escape.

He walked with the German schoolchildren for a few blocks. They stared at his dirty clothes, but ignored him. Noah slowly made his way to the back of the group, letting the other children pass him. At an alleyway between buildings, he ducked out of the line and hurried off, ditching his clever school group camouflage.

Noah ran down the street and up the steps of the Jewish Children's Orphanage. He opened the big double doors, smiling at the man he saw in the foyer. "Herr Benny, I'm home!"

Then he stopped short. It was not Herr Benny, but a large scowling Nazi officer.

"You do not live here. The orphanage is closed." The officer pushed Noah out and slammed the door shut.

Noah, with nowhere to go, ran down the steps and out into the dark and uncaring streets of Berlin.

CHAPTER 18

MUTTI STILL REMEMBERS YOU

(January 1939)

Peter climbed inside the double-decker bus with his suitcase and violin. He'd overheard the volunteers saying they were headed to Dovercourt, a summer holiday camp in Essex about sixty-four kilometers south of London. The only problem with this arrangement was that it was winter.

Peter quickly wiped a tear away and looked around to check if anyone had seen him crying, but no one had noticed.

Hans and Stephen were already seated in the bus. They waved to Peter.

"Peter!" Hans called. "That boat was rough, eh?"

"Where's Becca?" Stephen asked, looking behind Peter.

Peter looked at Hans and Stephen, eyes hollow with grief. "On a train to London."

"What?" Hans asked.

Peter walked on past them, unwilling to discuss "the best the English could do."

Hans and Stephen looked at each other. "Maybe the holiday camp won't be such a holiday," Stephen said.

"At least it's not a Nazi camp." Hans shrugged.

Peter passed William, who had his feet lounging over the seat in front of him. Peter didn't look at him. He could not forgive him for taking Eva's seat. He went to the back of the bus and plopped into a seat all by himself, stewing in the painful knowledge that hope always leads to disappointment and heartbreak, and there was nothing he could do about it.

The big red bus started up and pulled away. Peter looked out the window as they passed the train station. He saw Becca walking into the station with the other little children.

He turned his face away from the window and buried it in his arm, leaning forward on the seat in front of him. He recited the cuts of meats in his mind: loin, shoulder, porterhouse, rack, shank, but that only made him think of his father. He remembered how his father would say Maybe your music will save us from Hitler, and that made him sad, because he knew he couldn't even save his sister.

—ɯ—

The train bound for Liverpool Street Station was loud and disorganized. Becca refused to sit in her seat. She planted her feet in the aisle and refused to budge. "I've changed my mind. I want to go home. I want to go back to Germany. I don't like this place."

As the whistle blew and the train started up, Becca was thrown back into the seat behind her. She hit her head on the window and screamed, kicking the seat in front of her. "How could you take Peter away from me? He's my brother! He'll come for me! Watch and see! He'll find me!"

The other Kindertransport children, in their own excitement and quiet grief, gazed out the windows at the gently rolling hills of the English countryside, the fields, woods, farmhouses, and smoke drifting gently from the chimneys, trying to ignore the rantings of the small, disgruntled passenger.

Becca gasped heavily, and then broke out into a howl of raw agony. After losing her father, her mother, and Baby Lilly, she was not prepared to lose Peter, too. She was in a strange country, and no one knew her. For the first time in her life, she was alone, unloved, nobody's darling, and nobody's little spitfire.

—ɯ—

Anna, Oma Greta, and Eddie were herded off the train on the German side of the Polish border. Then, at gunpoint, they were forced across the border near Zbaszyn. It was a small town of about four thousand people on the main railroad between Frankfurt on the Oder and Poznan. Now it was overrun with Jewish people who had nowhere to go, and who were not allowed to return to Germany.

Anna looked around. "Where are we?" she asked.

Oma Greta heaved a great sigh of resignation. "Near Zbaszyn, Poland."

"Where is Poland?" Eddie asked.

"Poland is where I was born," Oma Greta said. "We all left Poland a long time ago. I know no one here anymore."

"Why did you leave?"

"To find a better life in Germany."

"Did you find it?" Eddie asked.

"No." Oma Greta said sadly. "Hitler made sure of that."

—m—

Becca got out of a sleek black sedan at the long driveway in front of a wide expanse of lawn. It led to a beautiful large home, surrounded by a thick grove of trees and bushes.

This was 16 Poppleton Circle, the home of the Cohens.

Harry Cohen, a well-dressed, reserved man, and Doris Cohen, a precise woman, pushed Priscilla, their eight-year-old daughter, up the drive in a wheelchair. Becca walked with her disheveled curly head down, dragging her feet, exhausted from her tirade against the English.

Mrs. Daniels, their no-nonsense Welsh housekeeper, adjusted her crisp white apron and opened the door. When she saw the little unglued refugee, she gasped. "Blimey! You look like death warmed up, lass!" She waved them in, her great flabby arms swinging with enthusiasm.

"Mrs. Daniels, please," Harry said, slightly shaking his head. "Rebecca has had a very difficult trip."

"She's been screaming about her brother Peter since we got her," Priscilla said. "My ears are ringing."

"We need to welcome her," Doris said to Mrs. Daniels.

"Welcome," Mrs. Daniels said, half-heartedly. "I hope you're done crying, Rebecca."

Becca looked up. "It's Becca, and I'll never be done crying. I hate all of England!"

"That's a lot to hate for one little girl," Mrs. Daniels said.

"I'd hate Germany, too, but my mother and sister are still there." Becca stomped down the hall.

"Well, she's a right beauty, eh?" Mrs. Daniels said, her hands resting on her ample hips. "I'll have my work cut out for me with two cheeky girls."

—⁓—

The truck carrying Eva and her parents slowed and then stopped at the Bockenburg Camp near Munich. A moment later, the huge door of the truck opened, and light streamed in.

Grundy pointed a gun at them. "Out! All of you! You have arrived at the Bockenburg work camp, where you can no longer be lazy and a drain on German society."

—⁓—

At the Dovercourt Holiday Summer Camp, the boys and girls formed a long line, leading into the main hall of the camp. The refugee committee volunteers greeted the children and began leading them in groups to the small wooden cabins built for summer camp.

A volunteer escorted Stephen, Hans, Peter, and a boy named Ralph, a chubby child who always spoke loudly, to a cabin. Peter opened the door and cautiously walked in. Hans, Stephen, and Ralph followed.

Inside the cold cabin, there were small beds with one woolen blanket each and small, misshapen, stained pillows, several small windows, and a sink. The boys set their suitcases down. Peter carefully placed his violin case on his bed.

Stephen patted the thin mattress. "All right, I want to go home now. What do you think, Peter?"

"Home doesn't exist anymore," Peter said.

That night, the boys slept with all their clothes on under their single wool blankets, for protection against the cold. Peter lay awake in his bed, his fingers playing the chords of a pretend violin, and his other hand guiding an invisible bow. He fell asleep to a rather difficult Mozart melody running through his mind.

—ɷ—

Back in Berlin, Noah crept in among the rubble of broken glass and the splintered boards in a looted Jewish watch shop. He made a barricade with the shelves to hide from intruders, and for protection from the wind and snow that blew through the shattered windows. He didn't clean up the room. That would make it too obvious someone was hiding here if anyone looked in. He slept fitfully among the broken remnants of the timepieces and the Nazis' fear of all things Jewish.

—ɷ—

At the Cohens' luxurious house in London, Becca lay awake in her beautiful new room, in a big feather bed under a down comforter. Gina, the doll she'd brought from home, lay beside her. In the hall outside, she could hear Priscilla and Mrs. Daniels talking about her.

"She doesn't belong here," Priscilla whined.

"Hush, now. She might hear you and start that incessant crying again."

Lying on her back, Becca stared up at the ceiling. Her face was stone, blank and emotionless. She turned and hugged her doll. Taking the edge of the bedsheet, she pretended to wipe tears off its face. "Don't worry, Little Gina," she whispered. "Mutti still remembers you."

CHAPTER 19

DO SOMETHING

(January/February 1939)

In Stephen's old house in Berlin, where Sylvia and Baby Lilly still lived with Nora and Jacob, Sylvia dusted her bedroom with a feather duster. She reached around and dusted the dresser.

She accidentally hit a picture frame, which dropped to the floor, breaking the glass. Sighing, she bent down and carefully picked it up.

It was a picture of her family. They stood in front of the butcher shop, smiling, so proud and happy. Sylvia stared at the picture, as drops of despair ran down her face and splattered onto the picture of her children whom only England could protect.

The Bockenburg work camp was surrounded by a ditch and a wall with seven police guard towers.

Eva and her mother were housed in the small women's barracks. Not many women or children were sent to work camps. Her father was housed with the men, which made up most of the camp. Each morning the prisoners, including Helga and Eva, were marched to the work areas where they built roads, worked in the gravel pits, and drained the marshes.

That first cold day, Eva pulled boards along the ground, leveling out a roadbed. Her father traded places with the man beside Eva, so he could help her pull.

"How long will we stay in this horrid place, Papa?" she asked.

"Hitler's power is growing. It may take a lot to stop him. It may take a war."

"I thought my life would be different," Eva said, sadly.

Bert put his arm around her. "So did I."

———

At Dovercourt Camp, the huge dining hall was like a large army mess hall. Holes in the roof had allowed snow to fall inside. The children brushed the snow off their chairs and ate with their gloves and coats on.

Stephen, Hans, Ralph, and Peter waddled in, rounded out by wearing every item of clothing they owned against the cold. They sat down with their food trays at the crowded table, and stared at the watery soup and thin meat paste sandwiches.

"I'm not hungry anymore," Peter said.

"Where's the rye bread?" Stephen asked, looking around. "I thought England was a civilized country."

Hans opened up the bread, examining the meat paste in the sandwich. "What is this?"

Tellis, a boy with big ears who was sitting next to them, leaned over. "It's horse meat."

"You're kidding, right?" Hans asked, making a puckered face.

Tellis shook his head. "No, it's horse."

"Horse, as in Muhamed." Stephen made a whinnying sound and he pawed the ground, tapping with his foot.

Tellis nodded and laughed.

"Peter?" Hans asked.

Peter, the butcher's son, lifted up the bread and examined the meat. He smelled it. "It's horse, ground shank, about seven days old."

"The old gray mare ain't what she used to be," Hans said. The boys laughed.

Stephen pushed the sandwich away. He spooned the watery light brown soup, making a small brown waterfall. "Looks like dirty dishwater."

"This is going to be a long few weeks," Peter said.

"Weeks? More like months, maybe years. If we're not little and cute, we never get picked for a family," Tellis said.

Stephen and Hans looked at each other. "We're goners for sure," Hans said.

"I've already been rejected," Peter said. "Becca's family didn't want me."

"Guess they don't know your music will save the Jews," Hans said, teasing Peter.

"If there's any music left by then," Peter said.

Stephen looked at his food. "I'd kill for some hot cocoa and pastries."

—m—

In the Beckmans' vandalized Berlin apartment, Arnold and Evelyn sat at their kitchen table, while Charlie slept on the couch.

"What if Uncle Ernst can't help us? America takes so few. What if no country will take us?" Evelyn asked.

"They'll take us." Arnold nodded his head. "You'll see."

"It better be soon. We're running out of time." Evelyn sighed. "If the Nazis find us here, we'll be on the streets, or worse."

—m—

The wind blew through the trees and bushes near the street that almost blocked the view in front of the Cohens' huge London house on 16 Poppleton Circle.

In the dining room, Becca sat with her arms folded and her mouth shut tight. Mrs. Daniels held kippers up to Becca's mouth. "Open your gob, lass!" she ordered, but Becca turned away, determined to starve before surrendering to the nasty English fish. Priscilla glared at her from across the table.

"Eat your toast and kippers, dearie. You're too skinny," Mrs. Daniels coaxed.

Becca, with her little arms folded across her chest, glared at Mrs. Daniels. "It tastes like wood and rubber boots, and you're too fat."

"Listen here, young missy," Mrs. Daniels scolded.

"See what I mean? She doesn't belong here," Priscilla said, loudly. "She's cheeky."

"And you're mean!" Becca retorted.

"That's quite enough, both of you!" Mrs. Daniels snapped.

Priscilla rolled her wheelchair out of the dining room, bumping into the doorframe as she fled. Becca got up and ran out the door. Both plates of food sat uneaten on the table.

Mrs. Daniels shook her head. "Why do I even bother?" she muttered. "You're both off your trolley!" she shouted after them.

—⁓⁓—

At the Dovercourt dining hall, Peter stared at Tellis as he loudly slurped his soup. Hans and Stephen pushed food around on their plates.

Suddenly, the dining hall door opened, and a crowd of children tumbled in. "That must be the children from the Kindertransport that is already two days late," Tellis said.

The new Kindertransport children mixed into the crowd in the mess hall. They were all talking amongst themselves. Some children let loose tears and howling cries. The girl sobbing next to Tellis said something to him.

"What's going on?" Peter asked.

"They say Hitler sentenced five hundred Jews to death, and no one is safe in Germany!" Tellis shouted.

The crying and wailing in the hall intensified as the news spread.

"Do something!" Tellis called to Peter.

"Me? Why me?" Peter said. "I can't do anything but play the violin." He covered his ears and ran out of the dining hall.

The room erupted into chaos. The refugee volunteers tried to calm the children down, but nothing worked.

Peter ran outside, gulping the fresh air, feeling as if he had been choking on the emotion in the hall. He slowed down and walked toward the football fields outside his cabin. His head felt like it would explode. *Are Mother and Baby Lilly, are they . . .?* No, he couldn't think of it. Could life get any worse?

He remembered the day his father gave a huge roast to Yenta Moss.

Peter had asked his father why he had given her such a gift when they themselves had eaten fatty meat scraps and potatoes the night before. His father had said that when life was at its worst, there was always someone who needed something you could give.

Peter hurried off the football field and into his cabin. He quickly returned to the mess hall. Peter swung open the door and rushed in carrying his violin.

He held his bow up, took a deep breath, and played "You Are Not Alone." Peter swayed with the music as his bow caressed the strings.

Infused with courage from the violin, Peter moved among the children, as he played the song. As he passed, the children hushed. Hans and Stephen rose from their table and sang the words. Their voices were uncertain at first, but grew in strength with the power of each word.

> The night is dark until the sunrise.
> Your heart is lonely until I answer your cries.
> Your path is steep and filled with stone,
> But I will walk beside you,
> You are not alone.
> Although the heavy pain you carry is your own,
> You are not alone.
> You are not alone.
> I am God. Follow the way I have shown, and
> I will help you find your way home.

Soon, the soul-wrenching cries and screams were replaced by the hopeful music that swirled around the hall. Peter closed his eyes and became part of his music. For a moment, he forgot he was at Dovercourt and that Becca had been kidnapped by the English. He remembered his home above the butcher shop and how his parents had said God must surely know who they were, since the synagogue was across the street.

The music in the massive dining hall seemed to float to the ceiling, out the holes in the roof, up to God, who was watching Peter, and would help him find his way home to Becca, his mother, and Baby Lilly.

—∿—

Forced by threat of death into Poland, Anna, Oma Greta, and Eddie arrived at the area called no man's land in Zbaszyn. They had nowhere else to go, and even if they had, Oma Greta would not have the strength to walk there.

In a desperate city of tents, makeshift shelters, and hopeless desolation, the unwanted people waited for the two countries to decide their fate. The ones who still had relatives in Poland had made their way into the cities, but many had nowhere to go. Other Polish Jews across the country were contributing what they could in terms of food, blankets, temporary shelter, and even schools for the children. But the need was overwhelming.

"What will they do with us now?" Oma Greta asked.

"Who knows? Neither Poland or Germany wants us," Anna said.

Eddie shook his head vigorously. "Tell them I don't want them either."

In fact, shortly after the Vogners had arrived, both countries had agreed not to deport each other's citizens. But that was no comfort to the thousands already there and trying to survive in no man's land.

—✳—

A few days later at Dovercourt, Stephen and Hans hung around in front of their cabin, kicking a rock around like a football with the sides of their feet. Although there was still a thin layer of snow on the ground, it was never too cold to think of playing football, and being cooped up in the tiny cabin was unbearable.

Peter sat on a stump, reading *A Tale of Two Cities* by Charles Dickens. It was a story about poverty, injustice, and violence due to the irresponsibility and cruelty of the ruling elite. He could relate.

Hans kicked the rock back and forth between his feet. "I miss Otto."

"He was a good striker," Stephen said.

"I liked his side-kick," Peter added, looking up from his book and smiling. "He looked like a crazy acrobat."

"He made us laugh," Hans said.

"Not so much when they kicked us out of school," Peter said.

"Yes." Hans sighed. "But at least he said something."

Tellis walked up to them, carrying a football. "Are you tired of that rock? Do you want to really play?"

Hans and Stephen smiled and nodded.

"Well, then, the English boys are here," Tellis said.

Hans motioned to Peter. "Come on, Peter, you can watch us lose."

Hans, Stephen, and Tellis played football with the local English boys. Peter sat nearby, reading, occasionally looking up from the daring Dickens story of revolutionary France. He thought of how, in the book, England became a safe haven for those escaping the violence. Although he'd read the story before, this time it had a whole new meaning.

Lennie, a tall, athletic English boy, kicked a goal just as the bell sounded at the dining hall.

"What's that?" Hans asked.

"Time for the cattle market. The families come, look us over, and decide who they want to take home," Tellis said. "Moo."

Peter shook his head. "I don't like cows, unless they're displayed in a meat case."

"You're required to go," Tellis said.

"It's too stressful to try to look cute," Peter complained.

"At least you still have a chance. You look sort of English," Stephen pointed out. "They seem to like that."

"We've got to go, Lennie!" Tellis yelled.

Lennie picked up the ball and ran over. "See you tomorrow."

"You want to play with us again?" Hans asked.

"Sure, why not?" Lennie said.

Hans and Stephen looked at each other. "We're Jewish," Stephen said.

"So?" Lennie said. "You're good football players."

Hans and Peter laughed.

"Then, I'll see you tomorrow," Lennie said.

"Okay," Hans said. Stephen nodded.

Lennie ran across the field with the other local boys, waving.

"The people here are kind of odd," Stephen said.

Hans nodded. "I like it."

Bert, Helga, and Eva trudged in a crowded line, surrounded by the police guarding the Bockenburg Camp. Grundy watched Eva, as she waited in line for whatever food was available.

Eva held out her cup, and a kitchen worker poured in a splash of milk. She waited for more.

The woman pushed her away. "That's all you get. This isn't a fancy cafe!"

Helga and Bert followed Eva. They took their splash of milk and moved down the line, to get dried-out sausages and stale bread.

Helga snarled, "A work camp, they call it. That's a lie. They round us up and force us to live like animals with bad food, bad plumbing, and bad manners. It is a prison of the worst kind."

"At least we're still together," Bert countered. He glanced at Eva as he poured his milk into her cup.

"Sometimes, you die suddenly, and sometimes you're killed little by little," Helga said, "but it's all the same in the end."

—〰—

Peter and the other Jewish refugees filed into the great room of the Dovercourt dining hall. The volunteers lined them up like they were preparing for an auction of children.

Peter stood awkwardly behind Stephen and Hans, trying to avoid the onslaught of eager foster parents hunting for a child to take home. Their stares made him feel uncomfortable. It was as if they were examining him for imperfections, and he knew he had many. He was sure they could see them all. It was too much to endure, so he hid.

Peter didn't really want to leave Dovercourt. Although it was often cold and the food wasn't very good, he enjoyed watching the boys play football. Dovercourt wasn't bad. He had Hans and Stephen, and they made him laugh. His plan was to stay at Dovercourt until he could rescue Becca. Then they would find a place together.

The foster parents cruised the crowd and picked the smallest children, as Peter peered from his hiding place behind Hans and Stephen. He wanted this to be over, so he could go back to his cabin and read *A*

Tale of Two Cities. He'd reached the part about the Defarges leading a band of revolutionaries using the code name of Jacques, or in German, Johan. That would be his code name, his new identity in England, Peter thought, Johan. Maybe he could leave the old Peter behind. There wasn't much left of him anyway.

A squat, crusty man in farmer's clothes hurried across the dining hall. He was wiping his rough hands on his pants, making a dust trail behind him. A plump woman scuttled and huffed behind him, her weathered cheeks rosy. They made a beeline for Hans and Stephen.

Peter's stomach clenched tighter. Hans and Stephen couldn't leave. What would he do without the entertainment of their football matches with the English boys? They were all he had left of his connection to home.

The man pointed his short, stubby finger at Hans and said, "You!" His voice sounded raspy and deep, like a storyteller mimicking a troll in a children's fairy tale.

"Me?" Hans replied with a face of horror.

"No! The other one!" the man said.

"Me?" Stephen asked, as he gripped Hans's elbow.

The woman stepped up. "No! The little one. You two couldn't fit in the attic." Her voice was shrill and grating.

Hans and Peter stepped aside, and Peter was fully exposed.

"Not me," Peter said. "I'm going to stay here until I can find my sister."

"Nonsense," the man said. "I'm Emil, boy, and this is Maude. We've got a farm in Coventry. You'll love it."

He grabbed Peter's thin arm and marched him over to Marla. "We'll take this one," the troll farmer said. Peter wondered if it was the same voice the man used when buying livestock. He looked back over his shoulder to Hans and Stephen, who stood ramrod stiff with panic.

"He doesn't look too Jewish," Emil observed.

Peter turned to Marla, shook his head, and mouthed, "No."

Marla placed her hand gently on his shoulder. She looked as pained as he did at the farmer's proposition. "Peter, you can't stay here. We have to make room for the other kids. We have another trainload coming in tomorrow." Her voice was quiet, and her smile looked forced. "You'll love the countryside."

Peter was not fooled. "I'm used to the city."

"I'm sorry. It's the best I can do." Marla hesitated, meeting Emil's eyes, looking for reassurance but finding none. "Go get your things," Marla said, quietly, her eyes moist. She cleared her throat.

Peter stared at Marla, pleading with his piercing gray eyes. His head shook his request not to be sentenced to these two farmers.

Marla forced another smile. "It'll be okay." She turned to Emil and Maude. "Peter is quite a little musician."

"Music is complete nonsense," Emil spat.

Peter walked back over to Hans and Stephen. "I guess I'm going home with the Brothers Grimm couple," he said quietly.

"I'm sorry, Peter," Hans said. "Maybe it won't be so bad."

"The old man said music is complete nonsense," Peter said.

"If we get to London, we'll look for Becca," Stephen reassured him.

"Tell her I'm in Coventry, and as soon as I can, I'll come for her," Peter declared, trying to sound brave.

"We will," Hans said.

"London's really big, isn't it?" asked Peter.

Stephen nodded, his confidence fading by the minute.

They hugged Peter. He collected his things from the cabin. Then he trudged off to serve out his time in a farmhouse attic with his agrarian captors.

—⁂—

Late that night, at Bloomsbury House in London, which housed the children's refugee offices, Marla paced as Sebastian sat in a ripped leather chair behind a desk. Marla threw an old January *London Times* down on the desk. On the front page was a photo of a horrified Becca and a seasick Peter, wobbling down the gangplank, as they disembarked at Harwich.

"I know I shouldn't have let Peter go off with those people, but I have no other options. We have over a hundred more children coming in tomorrow," she said.

"There was nothing you could do." Sebastian looked at her sympathetically.

"You should have seen his face," she said. "It was not a good match."

"But they chose him," Sebastian reasoned.

"Because he could fit into their God-forsaken attic!" Marla gestured wildly with her hands, her blue eyes alive with anguish.

"He'll be safe and well fed in the countryside, which is more than I can say for the children still remaining in Germany."

"I know. I have to tell myself that to sleep at night, although I don't do much of that anyway. I understand England is a small country, and we're limited in the number of children we can bring in. But America is big, and I hope they'll stand beside us and take in the Jewish children."

"Well, unfortunately, they won't." Sebastian handed Marla a letter. "I didn't want to tell you. It's from America."

Marla, her hands shaking, pulled the letter out of the envelope.

"Go ahead and read it," Sebastian said.

Marla read the letter, and her hands shook from anger this time. "The Wagner-Rogers Bill to authorize the admission into the United States of a limited number of German refugee children has failed in committee with the fear it would overburden new social programs . . ."

Marla paused. "But it was supported by private funds."

She read the letter again, " . . . and take American jobs."

Marla stared at the page in disbelief. "They're children." She kept reading. "Accepting children as refugees without their parents is contrary to the laws of God."

She threw the letter down on the desk. "The U.S. senators think God wants the children to remain in Germany with Hitler? It's over. No help from the Yanks. Cowards!" She crumpled up the letter and threw it across the office. "And Peter Weinberg will be milking cows, instead of playing music. Nothing makes sense anymore!"

"England had some of the same concerns at first, and the Americans did allow some children in."

"Yes, but their State Department made it almost impossible to get visas."

"We are not America. We are England." Sebastian handed her a long list of names. "And here's the list of children arriving tomorrow. Peter's predicament will have to wait."

— ∿ —

At the Coventry farmhouse, Peter slept on a mattress on the floor, next to his violin. He was in the small attic room with the slanted roof and one tiny window, overlooking the barn and fields.

Emil stomped up the stairs to the attic, each step creaking under his heavy farm boots. He walked over to Peter and vigorously rang a cowbell near his ear. "Get up, German boy!"

Peter jumped defensively to his feet, uncertain of where he was.

"You're in Coventry, plank," Emil said. "We've got work to do. The cows won't milk themselves."

Peter rubbed his eyes. "I don't know how to milk a cow."

"You'll learn," Emil said.

Peter tucked his violin safely under his thin ragged blanket and put on a shirt. Through the small attic window, he could see it was still dark outside.

At the kitchen table, Maude set a bowl of lumpy porridge in front of him. Peter looked at it and stirred it around. "No, thanks. I'm not hungry."

"You will be after your chores." Maude laughed mockingly. "Not used to hard work, are you now?"

"I work hard," Peter contradicted.

"With that ridiculous musical instrument?" Maude asked in her high-pitched, screechy voice.

"No, I am a butcher," Peter said, defiantly.

"No use for a butcher here. We milk our cows," Emil growled.

Peter spent the day at farm work. He milked the cows, as the evil one with a white face sneered and kicked at him. Then he fed the chickens, cleaned the stables, and chopped the firewood.

When he came in that night, he ate every unpleasant thing on his plate.

Maude sat back in her chair and smiled. "We'll make an Englishman out of you yet."

"I am German," Peter said. "I don't want to be English."

Emil's face wrinkled in anger. "Germany didn't want you. You best take what you're offered."

That night, in the small attic room where he could see his breath in the cold, Peter looked at his raw, blistered English farmer's hands. He angrily shoved the violin away and fell asleep, only to dream tortured visions of being trapped inside a burning wardrobe.

CHAPTER 20

NO BREAD

(March 1939)

At Stephen's old house in Berlin, Sylvia rocked Baby Lilly and patted her back. Nora sat still as her husband carefully unfolded a letter from Stephen. They all huddled together as he read it aloud.

"Dearest Mutti and Vati, Hans is here with me at Dovercourt."

Nora jumped up, clapped, and danced. "They made it! Praise be to God!"

Jacob smiled and continued to read. "It's a summer holiday camp. The beds are hard. The food is bad, but we are fine."

Sylvia leaned over and grabbed Jacob's arm. "Where are Becca and Peter? Does he say?"

Jacob read again. "We wait for families to pick us. They want the little ones, like Becca. A family chose her right away, and she is living in London. Peter was with us for a while, but he was recently chosen by a farm couple in Coventry."

"Becca and Peter are not together?" Sylvia asked incredulously. Shaking, she pressed her face into Lilly's little body for the comfort of knowing she at least still had her baby.

Nora hugged Sylvia. "At least they are safe."

Jacob went back to reading the letter. "We play football with the local boys who are our friends, now. Sometimes we win. The English boys don't seem to mind that we are Jews. I think they might actually like us."

Jacob's voice quivered, and he stopped reading. "God bless the English children."

He cleared his throat and took a deep breath, then kept reading. "Please, don't worry about us. We hope all is fine at home and that you will have good news for us soon. I am sorry I was not a good son to you. Now I know that you sent me here to keep me safe, and I was not grateful. Please forgive my selfishness. Your loving son, Stephen."

Jacob quickly wiped away a tear and folded up the letter. He looked at Nora sadly. "Our son is becoming a man without us."

—w—

Bert, Helga, and Eva ate pieces of moldy bread outside overcrowded barracks at the Bockenburg Camp. A rat ran across the yard.

Eva screamed and dropped her bread. The rat grabbed it in its whiskery mouth. Bert chased the rodent away and slipped Eva the rest of his bread, while Helga gobbled up her remaining crust.

Later that night they heard rumors spreading among the prisoners that all of Czechoslovakia was now occupied by Germany. Hitler was on the move, and Eva could feel her life squeezing shut.

—w—

Noah, ragged and dirty, stared into the window of a Berlin bakery. It was filled with the most delicious rye breads, rum cherry cakes, marzipan cakes, apple strudel, pretzels, cookies, and pastries.

In the reflection of the window, he saw a policeman approaching behind him. Noah quickly hid in the shadows at the side of the building, as the officer passed by.

A frog sitting in the rocks nearby stared at him, emitting a ribbit every now and then. Noah thought of how he'd loved to catch frogs with his father down at the pond in Edelweiss Park. He shook the memory away. That was a long time ago, last summer, before the "Night of Broken Glass," when he was just a kid.

Noah emerged from his urban camouflage and was entranced again by the delicious breads and baked goods in his favorite bakery's display window. He stood and stared at the food. His tongue seemed to swell as he viewed the temptations. It had been three days since he had eaten. There were sores in his mouth, and his saliva had almost dried up. Noah returned to the side of the building, bent down, and scooped up the complaining frog. He slid it in his pocket.

He went back to the front of the bakery, hesitated at the door, and then stepped inside. He reached into his pocket and carefully pulled out the wiggling frog.

He held his hand on the counter and let the frog jump to freedom. The frog croaked, then hopped toward the display of delicious strudel.

A portly lady with a braided bun, and her plump arms filled with baked goods, screamed at the sight of the hopping frog. She tossed her bundles of tasty pastries and breads into the air. The baker cupped his flour-sprinkled hands and awkwardly scooped at the frog, missing him every time.

During the frog chaos, Noah grabbed a loaf of brown rye bread from the counter and ran out of the bakery. The baker, whose protruding stomach proved he enjoyed his own creations, stopped chasing the elusive frog and chased the boy instead, but he was not successful at catching Noah either. He slowed his running when his breathing became labored and his heart pounded. He was not used to any exertion except opening and closing the ovens. With his last breath he called, "Stop him! That dirty Jew boy stole my bread again!"

Noah ran down the street past the police officer, who heard the breathless cries of the baker, and took up the chase.

Marla, on her way to the Kindertransport office, saw Noah dodging the officer's pursuit with the baker trailing behind. She recognized Noah as the Kindertransport stowaway.

"Hey! I know you!" she shouted, as he passed. He glanced back and gave a slight wave, not losing a step.

The baker stopped chasing Noah and bent over, his hands resting on his big knees and his heart pounding in his chest. Marla ran to him. He was breathing heavily from his pursuit. "What happened? What did the little boy do?" she asked.

"He stole bread," the baker heaved.

"That's it?"

"It was a whole loaf!"

Marla took out some money and slapped it in the baker's hand. "Here. For the whole loaf. Perhaps, he was just hungry."

"You're from England, aren't you?"

"Yes."

"Stay out of Germany's business." The baker stuffed the money in his pocket and thumped back toward the bakery and the doomed frog.

Noah, the little sprite of a runner, quickly ducked through a gap in the boarded-up door of his new home, the broken and looted Jewish watch shop. The officer stopped running. He looked around, but Noah had disappeared.

Inside his watch shop shelter, Noah looked through an empty knothole as the policeman stomped, flailed his arms, and angrily walked away.

Noah sighed. He had done it, outsmarted them again. He smelled the rye bread. His stomach growled. He tore a piece from the end of the loaf and quickly stuffed the spongy dark bread into his mouth.

A shadow passed by the shop, but Noah didn't see it because the partially boarded windows blocked the view. He was happy as he chewed the soft dark bread, the greatest banquet a homeless, hungry boy in Germany could ever ask for. The shadow slowly crept behind him.

"Drop the stolen property, you thieving Jew boy!" the police officer snarled.

Noah, startled, dropped the bread onto the broken glass. With the taste of the bread still in his mouth, he instinctively reached for it.

The officer hit Noah's arm with a billy club. "No! You are done now."

Noah grabbed his injured arm that surged with pain. He eyed the crust and the dark spongy bread he had worked so hard to get.

"Bread is too good for you!" the officer said, spitting his venom at the little boy who had risked his life for rye.

—w—

In the park in London, Priscilla watched from her wheelchair as Becca played hopscotch with other children.

Becca hopped and reached for the white rock in the corner of the shakily drawn chalk box. Upside down and looking between her legs, she looked at Priscilla in her wheelchair all by herself, watching her hop. She picked up the rock and walked over to Priscilla. "Do you want to play?" she offered. "You could throw the rock, and I—"

"You can do everything, can't you?" Priscilla spun her wheelchair and rolled away. "Why would I want to play with you?"

"I didn't want to play with you anyway!" Becca shouted back. "I just felt sorry for you." She turned and ran back to the hopscotch game.

Priscilla's rolling escape was interrupted when her wheel hit a crack in the pavement, tipping over her chair, and sending her sprawling to the ground.

The children nearby righted the wheelchair and helped Priscilla back in. All the while she huffed and glared at Becca's back, as Becca deftly hopped on one foot, ignoring Priscilla's crash.

Priscilla had been born as nimble and quick as any fairy sprite in the stories she liked to read. When she was little and her legs worked, she'd loved to run, jump, and pretend she was flying like the pigeons at Trafalgar Square, looking down on the poor people below who only had feet and no wings. Her imaginary flights had come crashing down at five, when she'd mysteriously contracted the polio virus, which rendered her legs useless. All the money her parents had could not buy her recovery, and Priscilla, the beautiful and lively fairy sprite, was paralyzed.

She had a clear memory of the light and carefree feeling of legs that worked, and that made it even worse. With Becca living with her, Priscilla had a constant reminder of what she'd lost, her ability to soar over the commoners.

—⁓—

At Stephen's old Berlin house, Otto, Stephen's old football school friend, now wearing a policeman's uniform, stomped up the porch. He knocked loudly and rapidly.

Nora looked out the window.

"Open up immediately!" Otto yelled, looking displeased.

Nora opened the door. Otto quickly stepped in and slammed the door closed. His demeanor quickly changed. He stood awkwardly shifting back and forth, glancing around.

Nora stared at him. "Otto, you're a Nazi?"

"Yes, ma'am. You know my father. He'd kill me faster than Hitler if I refused."

Jacob walked into the room. He stopped in his tracks when he saw Otto dressed in his uniform. "Otto, is that you?" Jacob asked, staring at the transformation created by the uniform of hate.

Otto nodded. "Hello, Dr. Levy."

"Have we done something wrong?" Jacob asked.

"I only have a moment. I've come to tell you that you must leave, immediately. They are arresting Jews tonight. You must go, quickly." Now Otto sounded more like his old self. "Wait for nothing."

"Thank you, Otto. You were always a good boy," Nora said, hugging him.

"There is no room for good anymore." Otto clicked the heels of his black Nazi boots, turned abruptly, and marched out with the wide stride of a young man on his way to trouble, instead of a football game.

As fast as they could, Jacob and Nora packed what little they could throw together. They stepped out the back door of their house, carrying suitcases and Jacob's doctor's bag. "What about Sylvia and Baby Lilly?" Nora asked.

"They went to the postal office. We can't wait for them. Hurry, go back in, and pull the curtains open. She'll understand the message," Jacob said.

—ɯ—

Sylvia walked up to the postal office, pushing Baby Lilly and two small packages in a buggy.

Inside the postal office, Sylvia gave Mildred, the stylish lady behind the counter, the two packages from the buggy. Mildred smiled. "Hello, Sylvia."

"Hello, Mildred. I need to send these to Becca and Peter in England."

Mildred nodded and accepted them. She spoke to Sylvia in a quiet voice, all the while busily processing the packages. She glanced around to make sure no one was listening. "So, how are your kinder doing?"

"They're safe, thank God," Sylvia said.

Mildred nodded and smiled. She looked at the addresses on the packages.

"They're not together?"

Sylvia's eyes teared up, as she shook her head. "No, and I miss them, and Henry, and the butcher shop."

"Why didn't you send the baby?" Mildred asked.

"She can't be without me."

Baby Lilly reached her arms out to Sylvia. "Mutti!" she squealed.

"Or maybe I can't be without her. She's the only thing that keeps me going," Sylvia said. "God sent me my children for a reason. Without them, I would have no hope."

—⁂—

Jacob, with a hat pulled down low, and Nora, with a scarf wrapped around her head, hid their suitcases and his doctor's bag behind the bare but thick branches of the lilac bushes on the side of Klaus and Clara's house. They walked briskly up the steps.

Klaus opened the door before they even reached the top. Jacob took off his hat and nodded to Klaus, as if it were an everyday greeting. "Our things are hidden behind the lilac bushes."

"Don't worry, Doctor. We'll get them. Hurry upstairs now," Klaus said. "Clara is waiting for you."

—⁂—

Sylvia pushed the buggy to the front of the Levys' house and turned up the sidewalk. She stopped, abruptly, when she saw the curtains spread wide open. No one left the curtains open anymore, unless . . .

She whipped the buggy around and hurried back down the sidewalk.

A door opened in a black vehicle parked across the street, and Karl Radley jumped out. Sylvia grabbed Baby Lilly out of the buggy and ran.

Baby Lilly, startled from being jerked around, flung her little body backward. Sylvia lost her grip and juggled the falling child. She slowed down and pulled Baby Lilly up into her arms.

Gripping Lilly tightly, she turned sharply, and headed up the lawn between the houses, trying to avoid Radley. Baby Lilly cried. Sylvia had lost precious time, and Radley had the advantage. Within a few powerful strides, he was only a breath behind her.

"Stop, or I'll take you both down!" he yelled.

Sylvia stopped. She pulled the crying baby into her arms, as tightly as she could, and turned to face him.

Radley gripped her arm tightly. "Are you Sylvia Weinberg?"

Sylvia looked at him and nodded, realizing there was no escaping this man.

Radley reached over and pinched Baby Lilly. She screamed.

"What was that for?" Sylvia demanded, her motherly protection overcoming her fear for a moment.

"For your impertinence."

Sylvia patted Baby Lilly and made a shushing sound to calm her. She could see a red welt where he had pinched the child. "What have we done wrong? Why are you arresting us?" Sylvia asked as Radley pulled her back across the lawn.

"For not paying for the repairs to the butcher shop. Keep that little howling pig quiet!" Radley barked, as he pushed Sylvia into the back seat of his car. "Where are the other girl and the boy?"

Sylvia watched as the empty baby buggy rolled backward down the sidewalk and into the ditch, finally tipping over. Lilly's pink blanket with the bunnies on it flew into the street, and a new, smaller Volkswagen ran over it. "They are safe in England."

In Coventry, Peter tried to balance on the three-legged milking stool. As he moved to pat the agitated white-faced cow, the unstable stool teetered.

Peter tried to right the off-balance stool, but his leg jerked out, and the milking can tipped over. All the creamy white milk that Peter had worked so hard to get spilled onto the straw-strewn floor of the old barn.

Peter buried his face in his hands for a second. Then he glared at the animal. "You are a cantankerous cow. I'm going to call you Olga, because you remind me of her. You're mean and nasty, and you like to swish your tail."

He laughed and righted the milking can. He patted the restless and snooty cow he'd nicknamed after Eva's cruel friend. He didn't want to milk the cows, but he didn't have a choice. Emil expected him to do all the farm chores in exchange for his staying there. Peter thought Emil was getting the better deal, but he had no other options, so he milked the cows, even the ones with bad attitudes.

A lone butterfly, a schmetterling, circled over Olga's head and fluttered down, hovering over the milk bucket. Peter thought of an old German tale that said butterflies were witches trying to steal the cream. It reminded him of how butterflies used to hover around Becca.

Olga's tail swished across Peter's face, and he laughed, "Stop it. Okay? Okay?"

The butterfly flitted away.

"How about I trade you a song for your milk?" he asked the haughty cow. Olga rolled her big cow eyes and mooed a reluctant acquiescence.

Peter sang "Schmetterling." Olga stood still, listening, and Peter milked her until the bucket was full again. Peter had earned his meager keep for another day.

CHAPTER 21

THE FIRST ONE TO KILL HITLER WINS

(April 1939)

Eva sat down on her bunk in the Bockenburg Camp barracks. She grimaced and bit her lip as she pulled off her shoe. Her foot was bloody and blistered. Pus oozed out of open sores. She wrapped a dirty strip of cloth around her foot and lay back on her bunk. She was asleep before the blood seeped through her unsanitary makeshift bandage.

Jacob and Nora sat on the mattress on the floor of Klaus and Clara's attic. The doctor read a newspaper with the headline "MASSIVE ARRESTS OF JEWS." Nora crocheted lace doilies, not a very useful hobby, but beautiful nonetheless. It helped her pass the empty, agonizing time. The only bright spot in their lives was the knowledge that Stephen was safe in England.

They left the house in disguise from time to time, to visit consulates, embassies, and government agencies to complete the necessary paperwork to emigrate. Although England was their goal, they were willing to temporarily go anywhere that would take them. But they knew Jewish doctors and other professionals were Nazi targets. It was safest, they felt, to stay hidden in their friends' attic as much as possible, until they could get out of Germany and find Stephen.

—ww—

The sunrise in Coventry reflected off the attic windows of the small farmhouse, as the cows chewed the grass in the field. The horses pawed at the ground right underneath Peter's attic window. The rooster sat on the barn roof and crowed a complaint against the crotchety old farmer and his ugly wife, and from his thin mattress in the attic, Peter silently agreed.

From the bottom of the stairs, Emil pounded on the wall. "Peter! The cows need milking, and the wood needs chopping. This isn't like Germany. We work hard in England!"

Peter put his hands around his throat and pretended to strangle himself, until he flopped his tongue out, closed his eyes, and tilted his head down. Sometimes, it was hard to tell if England was an improvement over Germany. But Becca was here, so he would put up with the farmer trolls, until he could develop a plan to rescue her.

—ww—

Hans stood with his rucksack outside the main hall in Dovercourt. Stephen fidgeted beside him.

"Since we're obviously not cute enough to get a family, I figured we'd stay together here," Stephen said.

"I could refuse to go," Hans said.

Stephen shook his head. "Good luck with that. It didn't work for Peter. Be glad you're getting out of here."

"What's a hostel anyway?" Hans asked.

"I don't know, but if it has heat and no horse meat, it's better than this place," Stephen said, and Hans laughed.

William arrogantly strutted by and nodded curtly to Hans and Stephen. They gave each other a surprised look, shrugged, and ran after him.

"William! Hey, where are you going?" Hans asked.

"Did they find you a family?" Stephen asked, unbelievingly.

"Me? No, I don't do family very well. I'm almost nineteen. I've got my own business to attend to," William said. "I'm taking the train out of here before they try to put me in a hostel." He pulled a cap down on his head and walked away.

Hans and Stephen looked at each other.

Marla pulled up in her two-seater car, a 1934 MG PB Airline Coupe. It was a two-toned blue sleek car that only the rich could afford. She honked and waved at Hans and Stephen, waiting for her in front of Dovercourt, an unsuitable place to call home.

They were startled, but then, they waved back. "Here comes the great kinder boss," Hans said.

Marla got out of the car and smiled at them. "Who wants to get out of here?"

Hans and Stephen looked at each other. "All of us!" Stephen answered.

Hans walked over and picked up his rucksack. "Keep practicing your strikes," he told Stephen.

"The English boys might win, now that you're gone," Stephen said.

"We're fierce, because we have one thing they don't have," Hans said.

"What's that?" Stephen asked.

"Nothing to live for!" Hans said. The boys laughed.

"You boys will find your way home again, I promise," Marla said.

"If there's anything left," Stephen said.

"How's Peter? Does he like the farm?" Stephen asked.

"Coventry is a beautiful place," Marla said, avoiding a direct answer about Peter's farm accommodations.

"Good," Stephen said.

"He's so orderly. I wouldn't think the mess of farming would suit him," Hans said.

"Well, now, it's time for you to go, Hans," Marla said, trying to avoid the topic of Peter, the gentle musician chosen because he was small enough to fit into the farmhouse attic.

"Neither one of you forget me," Stephen said. "You know where to find me here at the fabulous Dovercourt Inn!"

"If a spot opens up, I'll save it for you. We'll go swimming." Hans smiled.

Stephen nodded. Hans turned to Marla. "London has swimming pools, right?"

"Yes, and they're filled with water, too," Marla said, teasing them.

"Don't forget to find me a fraulein, Hans," Stephen said.

"The German gents need some English dames," Hans said, imitating an English accent.

They said goodbye with great German back slaps. "The first one to kill Hitler wins!" Hans called to Stephen, as he got into Marla's car.

The door shut, and Marla pulled away in her fancy car with Hans. Stephen remained in front of the Dovercourt Summer Camp. Thank goodness summer is coming soon, he thought.

—⁓—

As Marla drove Hans to the London hostel, Hans ran his hand across the blue leather of the two-seater car. "This sure is a nice car. Are you rich or something?" he asked.

Marla smiled. "No, but my father is. I spend his money and his friends' money bringing Jewish children to England."

"Jolly good! Jolly good!" Hans said, with an exaggerated British accent.

Marla laughed. She came from a wealthy family, not the lucky kind of wealth that was handed down through generations, but the hard-working wealth that was earned.

Her father, Barnaby Kincaid, had grown up poor, but starting small and working hard, he opened restaurants and pubs across England and Wales. Then, he started buying buildings, and soon he was rich. He once confided to Marla that he never forgot the feeling of being taunted by other children for not being good enough. He had always taught Marla and her brother Dwight to reach out to those with less. Marla absorbed the lesson. Dwight had more of Barnaby's father, the drunken sailor, in him, and the call of liquor was stronger.

Now, Marla's ambition was fueled by her father's legacy of giving back and her guilt over not being able to save her brother, but she found that saving people was not as easy as she thought. Many times, like today, she found herself having to do things she didn't want to do. Many nights she cried herself to sleep, not only for the children still in Germany, but also for the ones she brought to England.

—∽∞∽—

Hans watched the countryside pass by outside. Nearly two hours passed before they pulled up in front of a rundown row house in an urban residential neighborhood of London. Marla turned and looked at Hans.

"Well, Hans, this is it. They're expecting you, so you can go on in."

"Yes . . ." Hans didn't move.

"What's wrong?"

"Nothing. If Peter and Becca can do it, then I can, too."

Hans took a deep breath and got out of the car. He waved half-heartedly to Marla, and then walked up alone to the row house that would be his new home.

Inside, it was cozy and clean, if still in need of repairs. In the kitchen, other teenagers were busily cleaning up after dinner or doing their homework.

A chubby German boy shook Hans's hand. "Guten Tag! Come on, I'll show you around."

The boy led Hans past a central bathroom in the hall and into a room with rows of beds. "It's no Hotel Adlon, but it's not bad," he said, smiling.

—∽∞∽—

In April at Zbaszyn, although the camp had dwindled, there were still many people stuck there. Anna heard Germany was forcing Jewish people to move into designated areas in German cities called Jewish Residential Districts. Although she feared she might regret it, Eddie's lung congestion, Oma's frailty, and the deplorable living conditions forced Anna to seek better conditions.

She had nowhere to go in Poland, and even if she had, she didn't think Oma and Eddie would make it, so they left Zbaszyn in the dark of night. Without authorization, they crossed the border back into Germany on foot. They walked several miles, headed for the closest Jewish Residential District in Dinsdorf, hoping no one would recognize them as escaping no-man's-land people.

When Anna, Oma Greta, and Eddie arrived at the overcrowded, unsanitary designated area of Dinsdorf, Germany, they were cold, hungry, sick, and completely demoralized. Anna had heard that, although there were no walls or fences containing them in the district, the police marched the Jewish residents out of the district every day and forced them to work for Germany. But at least it was dry and there was food.

In the faint morning light, Anna, Oma Greta, and Eddie shuffled along the hall of an apartment building and climbed the stairs, continuing to look for an empty apartment. It wasn't until they reached the top floor at the end of the hall that they saw a door cracked open.

Anna nodded to the door. "This is our last chance."

She pushed the door open, and a foul, repugnant smell burned their noses.

"No wonder this one is left," Eddie said. "It smells worse than the rat that died in our chimney."

"That is exactly what it is," Oma Greta said. "The death of trapped rats."

They pulled their sleeves over their noses and went into the putrid apartment. Inside were two dead people in advanced stages of decay. Maggots crawled on the bodies, and flies buzzed in swarms like in the back of the old Berlin garbage trucks parked by Peter's house. But Anna decided death could be dealt with and the apartment could be their home.

Anna and Eddie awkwardly carried the bodies, wrapped in old rugs, down the stairs one at a time.

Once outside the building with the second body, they were intercepted by a police officer. "Drop them. Now," he said, covering his nose from the decaying stench.

"They need to be buried," Anna said. "I will be glad to—"

"They will be taken care of," he said.

"But they are very dead," Eddie said.

"You must be new here," the officer said. "Do what you're told or you will end up like them."

CHAPTER 22

FAR AWAY FROM GERMANY

(June 1939)

The summer had finally arrived. Now, Peter's freezing cold attic was stifling hot. He struggled to open his small window, as a horse neighed quietly in the pasture nearby. Then he picked up the opened package he'd received from his mother several months ago. Inside the box were chocolates that had melted into their wrappers, sheet music, and a letter.

He licked a bit of chocolate left in a corner of a wrapper and read the letter again: *Dear Peter, Baby Lilly and I miss you and Becca so much, but I am so grateful you are safe in England, even if you aren't together. Things here seem to be getting worse, but I know if we wait it out, someone will do something, and things will eventually improve and we will be able to join you. Hopefully, we can be together again soon. Please find Becca and play your beautiful music. No matter what happens, I will love you forever. Mutti.*

"No matter what happens," Peter repeated to himself, as he took one of his new sheets of music and spread it on his thin dirty mattress. The song was called "God Save the King," Britain's national anthem.

He studied the music, memorizing the notes. His fingers moved in the air to make the soundless tune that only he could hear inside his head.

He blew the dust off his violin, and, carefully, pulled it out of the case. He wiggled his fingers and grabbed the bow, holding it poised in the air and hesitating. Then, he played a few notes.

His blistered fingers fumbled on the strings. Mad that his fingers could no longer summon the melody, he gripped the bow and intentionally made the screeching strings howl like a lonely wolf. The startled horses in the field neighed loudly and bolted wildly, frightened by the violin's harsh, reverberating sound.

Peter's fingers were thick and slow, and their dance of music was gone, sucked into the chores of a farmhand. His angry music scared horses. His beautiful melodies had been reduced to the terrifying wolf sounds his mother used to hate.

He hung his head and gently put the violin back in its case, like a dead body in a casket.

He looked at his hands, turning them over. "I am a butcher," he said to himself.

—◊◊◊—

Arnold crept through the shadows of his damaged Berlin apartment in the ransacked house. When no one was looking, he ran up the stairs to his dark apartment. He burst through the door waving a piece of paper. "Come here! Come here!"

Evelyn and Charlie ran to him. "What is it, Arnold?" Evelyn asked.

"Did we win something?" Charlie whispered.

"Yes, my son. We won freedom! We're going to America on a boat! Uncle Ernst did it! God has provided a safe passage out of here. We are saved. We'll leave from the Port of Wilhelmshaven. I knew we'd make it! I knew it!" Arnold laughed. "I'm so glad I pulled you from that train window. Something good is finally happening. I told you all we needed was faith."

They danced and hugged each other. "I can have us packed in no time," Evelyn said, laughing, "because we have so little left!"

Arnold hugged Charlie and swung him around like he used to when he picked him up from school.

"Where is America, Papa?" Charlie asked.

"Across the sea, far away from Germany, and that's all that matters!"

Charlie looked into his father's eyes and patted his face. "You won't change your mind this time, will you, Papa?"

"No, not this time, Charlie. Nothing can stop us now."

—⚬—

It was late summer, and the weather had grown warm and rainy in London.

One afternoon, there was a knock at the hostel door. Hans opened the door to see Stephen standing on the doorstep with a suitcase.

"Telegram for Hans Vogner!" Stephen pretended to read a telegram in front of him, as Hans stared. "Hitler's a sissy boy. Stop. Must destroy. Stop. Send bombs. Stop."

"Get in here, right now! We've been waiting for you. I've told everyone about you," Hans said.

"I'm doomed, then," Stephen said.

Hans pulled him in and hugged him. "What took you so long?"

"I couldn't leave the horse meat sandwiches," Stephen said, laughing.

That afternoon, the boys went down to the neighborhood swimming pool. They stood outside in their suits, holding their towels.

"You sure it's okay?" Stephen asked.

"It's England," Hans said, nodding.

"When Hitler invades England, then where will we go swimming?" Stephen asked.

"If that happens, we'll have bigger problems. Come on!" Hans snapped his towel at Stephen.

—⚬—

In the Cohens' London living room, Priscilla played with paper dolls. Becca handed Mrs. Daniels a returned letter she had sent to her mother. It was stamped: Nicht Lieferbar.

"What does that mean?" Becca asked, pointing to the word.

"Undeliverable, I guess. It's been returned. It means she's no longer at that address, but she's probably fine," Mrs. Daniels said. "She moved. That's all."

"But she has no place to go," Becca countered.

"Come on now, love. Let's go have a bit to eat," Mrs. Daniels said. "You, too, Priscilla."

Priscilla shook her head. "I don't want to eat with her. She has to go. Hitler didn't want her, and I don't either."

Becca's face grew red, and she turned on Priscilla, the pampered invalid. "Hitler doesn't like people whose legs don't work, either. He thinks they're weak and not perfect." Becca shook with anger. "I know why your parents wanted me to live here, not because they wanted to help me, but because you needed a friend. No one likes you, but it's not because of your legs. It's because you're a brat, Priscilla. You think you're better than everyone. You make everyone miserable around you."

Priscilla wheeled toward her. "You don't know what it's like to sit in this wheelchair on the playground and not play hopscotch. I used to be able to fly before I got polio. I hate my legs, and I hate you!"

Becca stomped her feet. "Well, my Papa's dead, and I'm afraid my mother and baby sister will never get here. I had my brother, but your family didn't want him, so I lost him, too. I hate you, and I don't want to live here anymore! I don't care about your stupid legs!" Becca grabbed the handles of Priscilla's wheelchair and spun it in a circle.

Then she ran out, leaving Priscilla shrieking: "Send the little Kraut back to Germany!"

—⟋⟍—

After returning from the pool, Hans and Stephen sat on their beds in the hostel. Stephen folded a letter back up after reading it out loud.

"Where did you get the letter?" Hans asked.

"Marla brought it to me."

"What does it mean?"

"I don't know," Stephen answered.

Hans motioned to Stephen. "Read it again."

Stephen unfolded the letter again. "We've had a lovely visit with your parents and have persuaded them to stay. They send their love. We will stay in touch. Yours always, Klaus and Clara."

"They're in the attic again," Hans said.

"How long can they last?"

"Klaus is a brave man. He will protect them."

Stephen nodded. "If he can."

That night, Priscilla's wheelchair rolled to a stop just inside Becca's door. Becca lay on her bed with her face to the wall.

"Becca? You know what you said about me being mean?" Priscilla asked.

Becca suddenly turned over and sat up. "I'm sorry. I'll be good. Don't let your mother send me back to Germany."

"I wanted to say, without my legs, I'm not special anymore. I feel mad all the time."

"But legs don't really matter. My Papa's legs didn't work either," Becca said, "and he was very special."

"Really?" Priscilla paused. "I don't actually want you to go."

"Danke. Thank you," Becca whispered, air escaping as if she had been holding her breath.

"Maybe we could be friends," Priscilla offered.

Becca looked at the girl who had made her life in England miserable and saw her for what she really was: a sad, lonely little girl, a lot like herself. Becca nodded.

"Good, then," Priscilla said, smiling.

At the Bockenburg Camp, Eva dipped her cup into the large barrel filled with rainwater and flicked the bugs out before she drank. She filled it up again and gave it to her father. "Remember when we used to make big mugs of cocoa and eat the delicious apple strudel from the bakery?"

Bert nodded. His slight pudginess was disappearing. "Yes, my pants no longer fit me."

"Do you think we'll we ever have cocoa and apple strudel again?" Eva asked.

Bert gripped the cup Eva had given him like a mug and blew on the pretend hot chocolate. "You can be sure of it, my little mouse. When we are free, we will gorge ourselves on all our favorites. We will celebrate that we have survived, and I will proudly be your plump papa again."

CHAPTER 23

THE RIGHT TO BE DIFFERENT

(August 1939)

Sebastian sat at his desk in Bloomsbury House, surrounded by files, each with a child's name on it. They were piled high, appearing to reach to the ceiling like a tall, unstable tower. He grabbed his head in frustration.

Marla stood beside him. "Sebastian, what's wrong?"

"It's strange, I think, that freedom depends on money. Don't get me wrong. It's timing, politics, bravery, and luck, but mostly money, and that is something we're running short of." He patted the side of a file stack. "There are so many more children."

"I'll talk to some people before I head to Germany for the next train. I'll get you the money," Marla said. "Somehow."

Sebastian looked up and smiled. "Marla, I know the children don't really know, yet, how much your gift means to them, but one day they will. Maybe, after they have their own children, they will fully understand what you have given them."

"What we have given them," Marla corrected him. "Sometimes, I think about Peter, sent to that couple that use him like a farmhand. His sister Becca lives in luxury, and both of them are alone and miserable. Have we really done such a great job?"

"They're alive," Sebastian pointed out.

"So it seems."

—⚶—

Peter lay on his bed in the farmhouse attic, looking at a picture of his family standing proudly in front of the butcher shop. Henry rested his hand on Peter's shoulder. Sylvia held a tiny Baby Lilly in her arms. Becca was looking up at Peter, instead of at the camera as instructed. Peter smiled, despite the tears welling up in his eyes. He knew he would give anything to have the luxury of complaining about his annoying, demanding little sister.

Suddenly, Emil's shouting pierced his sadness.

"Air raid! Under the stairs, Peter!" Emil yelled in his booming troll voice, as he and Maude thumped across the floor beneath him. But Peter heard no siren.

If the Germans bombed the farmhouse, he would be the first to die, here in the tallest part of the house. Maybe that would be a blessing, Peter thought. He slid the family picture under his violin and closed the case.

He carried the violin with him down the low-ceilinged attic stairs. "Under the stairs! Don't dawdle!" Maude yelled to Peter from the stairwell.

"Why would they bomb Coventry?" Peter asked.

"Munitions factories," Emil said.

Peter crawled under the supports and sat down, his violin resting in his lap.

"There's no room for your violin!" Emil scolded, as he huddled in a corner.

"It's small," Peter said. "It doesn't take up any room."

"No," Maude said gruffly.

Peter sighed and crawled back out from under the stairs. He thought he'd rather die than be without the violin his father gave him. It was his last connection to music and all joy, and to his father.

He sat outside the stairs, under the kitchen table, still clutching his violin. He could hear Emil and Maude talking about him.

"He's very peculiar, that little German boy," Maude said.

"How did a butcher's boy end up with a violin anyway?" Emil wondered. "It isn't right."

Peter leaned his head back against the table leg and pulled his knees up, thinking of his father. Henry had given Peter a football for his birthday when he was little, but Peter hadn't been interested in balls. He'd sat on the ball, like a round chair, in front of the radio as he listened to music. His little body swayed back and forth until the football rolled out from under him and he fell onto the floor.

At Edelweiss Park, his father would throw the ball to him and shout, "Kick it! Kick it!" However, Peter would shy away from the hurtling ball.

"Don't be scared of the ball, Peter. Use your legs. Jump and kick it! Kick your leg out! You can do it," his father would yell.

Peter shook his head. Henry put his arm around his child. "Son, before my legs were crippled, I was one of the best football players in Berlin. I had an unbeatable side-kick. I know it's hard to believe, but it's true. You can do it, too. You're my son. I was the shortest one in my class, like you, until I was fifteen. Then I shot up. We Weinbergs are late bloomers."

"But I don't like balls," Peter said.

Henry had been a strong, fearless young man who never backed away from a fight. He was a good soldier, a decorated war hero, and proud to have defended his country.

Peter was Peter. He shied away from confrontation, felt uncomfortable in physical challenges, and was deathly afraid of injury, ridicule, and defeat. He was most at home listening to music, reading books, and avoiding trouble.

"What do you like then, Peter?" Henry asked, confused to find his son was not like him.

"I like music. I like violins."

"Violins?" Henry repeated. "I know nothing about violins. I'm a butcher, and you will be, too. It will grow on you."

Peter remembered that the next day, Henry had delivered meat orders in the truck. Peter sat on his father's lap and drove the meat truck, his legs pressing the pedals because Henry could not.

As they had walked down the sidewalk with a delivery, a police officer strutted toward them. He'd intentionally bumped Henry as he passed, knocking him to the ground.

"Worthless, crippled Jew!" the police officer sneered.

Henry huffed as he tried to get back up and defend himself, but he twisted helplessly on the sidewalk. "Help me up, Peter."

The boy reached down and struggled to get his father back on his feet. They stared at the police officer, who was laughing as he sauntered on down the sidewalk.

Peter handed Henry back his cane and looked at him. "Why do they want us to be exactly like them? Why aren't we allowed to be different?"

Henry had looked at Peter and nodded. "You're right, son. We all have the right to be different. You may play the violin, and I will dance to your music, the best I can." Henry tapped his cane against his wobbly legs. But that seemed so long ago.

At the Coventry farm, Emil and Maude emerged from under the stairs. Emil stood up and looked at Peter, still huddled under the table. "What are you doing, boy? It was just practice. We wanted to see if you were prepared, but you would have been dead if it was real."

"A drill?" Peter asked.

"We must be prepared in case the Jerrys are brave enough to attack," Emil said.

"It's not all Germans, it's just the Nazis," Peter corrected him.

"What's the difference?" Emil snorted.

—⁓—

It was the last day of August in 1939. Hans and Stephen rode a bus into the countryside outside the city. The sun was hot, and they opened the bus windows to let the breeze blow in. Hans clutched the piece of paper that Marla had given them, with the name and address of someone who might be able to help them bring Stephen's parents to England.

They got off the bus at the town written on the paper, and walked along the road until they came to an imposing English estate.

"Is this the right place?" Stephen asked. Hans looked at the piece of paper in his hand and nodded.

"This is bigger than our school in Berlin," Stephen said in amazement at the expansive estate.

"Let's hope they don't kick us out of here like they did at school," Hans teased. "Are you ready?"

Stephen nodded.

The boys opened the huge metal gate, with its curlicues surrounding the letter K. They walked up the long, wide, bricked driveway to the mansion. "Look at this place!" Stephen said.

Hans took a deep breath and knocked on the door. A tall butler in a black suit with tails opened the door. "May I help you, young gentlemen?"

"Are you Mr. Barnaby?" Hans asked.

"No, I'm Alfred. One moment, please," Alfred said. Then he shut the door.

Hans turned to Stephen. "One moment, please," he mimicked in his fake English accent. "I'm Alfred."

After a few moments, the door opened again. "Please, follow me," Alfred said.

Stephen and Hans looked at each other and followed him down a long ornate hall. Stephen bumped a table, and a vase wobbled, toppling over. Hans grabbed it before it hit the ground. He glared at Stephen and quickly set it back on the table. Alfred turned around, and the boys both straightened, as if nothing had happened.

The butler opened a huge carved wooden door. "Gentlemen," he said formally, and with a sweep of his hand, the boys were ushered into a library with floor-to-ceiling shelves full of books.

A gray-haired man in a tweed suit was seated at a table inside. He looked up from a pile of papers and smiled. "Yes, boys. What can I do for you?"

"You're Mr. Barnaby?" Hans asked.

Barnaby nodded. "The one and only."

"Marla sent us," Hans said.

"You are some of her Kindertransport children?" Barnaby asked.

Stephen nodded. "Yes, sir, I'm Stephen. This is Hans. We're from Germany."

"Nice to meet you," Barnaby said, extending his hand across his desk to shake theirs.

"My parents are hiding from the Nazis in their friends' attic so they won't be arrested. We're trying to get working permits for them, so they can come to England before the Nazis get them," Stephen said.

Barnaby cleared his throat, more from emotion than reluctance.

Hans stepped forward and bobbed his head. "Sir, my father owned a factory. He was killed in a concentration camp. My mother, brother, and grandmother were arrested. I don't know where they are, but there's still time to get Stephen's parents out."

"Indeed." Barnaby tapped the desk in front of him. "What would they be willing to do?"

"My father is a doctor, but he can clean stables, and my mother can do anything," Stephen said.

"A doctor willing to clean stables? Come see me, tomorrow." Barnaby looked down at his papers, but not quickly enough to avoid them seeing the emotion in his eyes. "There are always jobs for that kind of determination."

"Thank you, Mr. Barnaby. Thank you!" Stephen said.

"Tell my daughter to come see me," Barnaby said.

"Your daughter?" Stephen asked.

"Yes, Marla. I'm her father, Barnaby Kincaid."

Stephen and Hans looked at each other.

Barnaby added: "If you two need jobs, you can work as dishwashers at Percy's Tavern. That's the way I started."

"Thank you, sir. That would be wonderful," Stephen said, smiling broadly.

Alfred nodded to the boys. "Let me show you out." He opened the door.

"Goodbye, sir," Hans said, as they followed the butler out.

They walked politely down the lane from the house to the road, not saying a word.

When they shut the heavy gate, thinking they were out of sight, they yelled and jumped around. "We did it!" Hans said.

"My parents can come to England! They are saved!" Stephen yelled. They slapped each other on their backs.

"Thanks to Marla," Stephen added, "and her father."

"I didn't know she was that rich!" Hans said.

"What's she doing with us?" Stephen asked, laughing as they walked back down the road to the bus stop. "We are German heroes."

"And we are English dishwashers!" Hans said.

—⁂—

Barnaby and Alfred watched the children from the library windows. "Boundless determination," Barnaby said.

He thought of when he was a boy, growing up in Blackpool on the northwest English seacoast of Lancashire. His mother, Vivian, was a beautiful and resourceful woman with an unfortunate weakness for men of no honor. His father, Percy, was a brash, daring, and often drunken sailor.

One day, Barnaby and his mother had waved goodbye to his father. Percy had saluted back to Barnaby, blown a kiss to Vivian, and boarded his ship to India. When the ship had returned from its voyage, Vivian and Barnaby waited anxiously until the last sailor got off. When they'd demanded to know where their beloved Percy was, they were told, simply and without sympathy, that he'd disembarked at a port in India and never returned. The ship had sailed without him, and that was that. Barnaby's father was not coming home.

Barnaby and his mother had often wondered what had happened to Percy. Had he left them for something else, or had some unexplained tragedy befallen him in India? They soon lost their comfortable little cottage by the sea with the great view of the sunset, and they went to live in the back room of a boarding house.

Barnaby had been ostracized by the other children for being different, being fatherless, wearing the same clothes day after day, eating only butter sandwiches for lunch, living in a boarding house, and every other humiliation fatherless poverty brings. He'd grown up determined to never depend on anyone again, but instead of bitterness, he chose generosity.

Barnaby and the butler smiled as they watched the bold German boys determined to save their families.

"No wonder Marla loves those children," Barnaby said.

—⚏—

In the rock pit near the Bockenburg Camp, Eva flung the heavy sledgehammer down against the rocks, breaking them into small pieces of gravel. The bits of white dusty rock flew in every direction.

She struggled to raise the hammer again, but then let it drop. The rock split, and a large piece flew and hit her nose. Blood gushed from the wound. She dropped the hammer and gently touched her nose, wiping away the blood.

Grundy, seeing her stop crushing rock, swung a fist from behind and hit her on the back of her head. She fell forward onto the ground.

He kicked her. "Get up. This isn't a holiday camp."

Eva's eyes fluttered open, as she came to, bloody and dusty from the gravel. She struggled to get up, trying to bring her eyes back into focus. She got to her feet, wavering. Grundy shoved the hammer into her hands and waited as her quivering thin arms hefted the hammer over her head, and she smashed the next rock.

He passed on. When he was out of sight, Eva bent over and spit out blood.

CHAPTER 24

A CHANGE OF PLANS

(September 1939)

As the sun rose on the morning of September 1, 1939, another Kindertransport passed across the border into Holland. Inside the train, Marla sat down and leaned her head back against the seat, closing her eyes. She barely slept during the Kindertransports. She spent most of the time praying that they would cross the border safely.

That night, a small boy of five sitting across the aisle sobbed. Marla opened her eyes and motioned to him. He tentatively walked to her.

She picked him up and cuddled him on her lap. "It'll be okay," she told him. "You're going to a good place. I promise. It'll all be over, soon."

The boy sniffled, tears welling up in his eyes. "My Papa says it's just starting."

"Ah, so it seems. You know what? On one of the Kindertransports that rolled out of Germany, there was a boy named Peter, who loved the violin. He was good. I mean really good. When he played, he became a different person. The quiet boy became like a musical warrior. A violin commando." Marla smiled and looked at the boy, who had calmed down. "Do you want me to tell you about when the police officer found Peter's violin and challenged him to play?"

The boy nodded, his lower lip quivering.

"It was a Kindertransport, exactly like this," Marla said. The boy lay back and relaxed against her. His little hand reached for hers. She looked at his tiny hand in hers and gently closed her fingers around it. Then she pulled his hand to her mouth and kissed it. "Peter was eleven. His fingers were long and nimble, perfect for playing the violin."

—␣—

Peter stared at his finely trained musician's hands, now covered with cow manure stuck with straw. He sighed and returned to shoveling the muck from the barn floor in Coventry. "A clean floor shows German pride," his father had always said in the butcher shop.

Peter smiled, remembering the day he got his violin. His father, still wearing a bloody butcher's apron, had found him in front of the radio, listening to Mozart while sitting precariously on the ball.

"Peter," his father called, "I have something for you."

"What is it, Papa?" Peter asked, reluctantly pulling himself away from the seduction of the concerto.

Henry held out a violin.

Peter stood up and stared at the instrument. "Is it for me?"

"Yes, Peter, you will be a great musician, someday. You are like me; we are good at whatever we set our minds to. We don't let others tell us who we are."

Peter reached out to touch the beautiful gift his father had given him, the gift of acceptance. He knew he had his father's permission to be himself.

"Thank you, Papa," he said. "I will try to make you proud like a football player."

"You already have, Peter."

—␣—

That night, September 1, 1939, at the German Port of Wilhelmshaven, the darkness was thick. The lighted windows of the boat to America, waiting in the harbor, seemed to twinkle with the promise of a voyage away from the evil that plagued Germany's Third Reich.

Arnold, Evelyn, and Charlie, carrying their few possessions and ready to board, waited anxiously outside the metal passenger gates. Charlie, wearing a blue cap, hopped from foot to foot with anticipation of another voyage. The last one had been interrupted by his father's love and desperation.

The boat whistle blew, and Charlie cheered.

—ᙡ—

The Kindertransport whistle blew. Another train, this time led by Jules, was ready to leave the Berlin station. The parents waved goodbye from behind the fence.

Jules noticed that each Kindertransport departure seemed to be getting more chaotic and the people more desperate.

Jules, the ex-German soldier turned refugee organization worker, boarded another train filled with children. "Say your last goodbyes, children. We are about to leave."

The parents waved and cried outside the train windows, still separated by the fence. The sound of their weeping was unmistakable, like the primal sounds of animals in agony. The anguish ebbed and flowed in volume, the pain palpable. The grief of voluntarily giving their children life, while dooming themselves to certain despair, was more than any of the parents could handle.

Jules and the children waited nervously in their seats, ready to leave. The heart-wrenching faces of the mothers and fathers outside were almost unbearable.

Jules knew he would breathe more easily once the wheels moved forward on their freedom journey. It was not the kind of relief that came after crossing into Holland, but it would be a loosening of the vise that gripped his heart. Jules waited for the screech of the wheels beginning to turn, because the sounds of the lamenting families would slowly fade. Then he could focus on getting his young charges to the safe harbor of Holland.

Suddenly, a group of police officers swept into the Berlin railway station. They spread across the yard like a black tidal wave and streamed onto the train cars, boots pounding.

A police officer with beady eyes and a huge nose banged on the seats and hit the ceiling with his club. "Out! Out! Everyone out!" he shouted.

A little girl clutching a stuffed blue bunny screamed, "Mutti!"

Jules jumped up and gestured to the children. "Your parents are still waiting for you outside. Leave your bags and quickly find your parents," he said.

"We aren't going to England?" a tiny girl with brown ringlets asked.

"No. There's been a change of plans," Jules said. "We must leave the train."

"We didn't escape Hitler, did we?" asked a studious-looking boy.

"Shhh. We must focus on exiting the train and finding your parents. Please move quickly," Jules instructed.

The children, confused and scared, scrambled over the seats and pushed to get out, calling for their parents. When the parents saw the police officers boarding the train and the children streaming out, they jumped over the fence and ran to the train cars, searching in the chaos for their children. The din of the Nazi officers' shouts, the cries of the children, and the yelling of the parents sounded like the roar of a tornado bent on destruction.

—⚒—

At the Port of Wilhelmshaven, where Charlie and his parents waited for their boat out of Germany, Nazi officers swarmed over the docks. They pointed their guns at the waiting passengers.

A skinny bug-eyed Nazi officer waved his gun in the air. "Poland has been invaded! Germany is at war! No one may leave! Go home, or you will be arrested!"

Arnold, Evelyn, and Charlie stood in shock, unable to absorb the meaning of the words. The officer approached them. "Did you hear me? I said go home!"

"We are far from home. We thought we were leaving. We have nothing to go back to," Arnold explained.

The officer prodded them with a club. "I don't care about your troubles. Move along. Germany is at war! The border is sealed."

Arnold picked up their small bags filled with everything they owned. Evelyn grabbed Charlie's hand, and they walked away from the unexpected change in their escape plans.

"But Uncle Ernst is waiting for us in America. Where will we go?"

Charlie asked with the innocence of a child, who still believed his parents had the answers and could keep him safe.

"What are you waiting for?" the officer yelled at them, threatening them with his billy club.

"We don't know this town. We traveled here from Berlin to begin our journey to America," Evelyn said.

The officer pointed to an idling military truck across the street. "If you hurry, that truck over there will take you back to Berlin."

Arnold, Evelyn, and Charlie picked up their bags and ran to the truck. The officer turned to another officer and smiled.

The next morning, Marla and her group of Kindertransport children arrived in England and disembarked from the boat at Harwich Port.

Sebastian found Marla in the crowd and pulled her aside. "We received a telegram from the refugee office in Germany. Jules's train didn't leave the station last night. The police raided it and forced them to get off."

"Why?"

"Germany is at war. The borders are sealed, and Jules was arrested."

As the sun rose at the Bockenburg Camp, Eva waited in line for bread. She watched, as Grundy was distracted, and saw the man in front of her stuff his pockets with moldy bread. Nobody else saw him, and he got away with it.

Eva reached out her hand to do the same, but then she saw the long line of people who were just as hungry, waiting behind her. She pulled her hand back.

Grundy jerked the man by his shirt and threw him to the ground. He reached in the man's pockets and pulled out the stolen bread.

"A thief!" Grundy shouted for all to hear. "A menace to all humanity." He pulled his gun and shot the man who was bold enough to steal extra bits of stale bread.

Eva backed away, leaving her share of bread for someone else.

—∾—

In London, Hans and Stephen ran down the sidewalk from the hostel, pushing each other as they headed toward the bus stop. A newsboy on the corner waved a newspaper excitedly, shouting, "Paper! Paper! Get your paper!"

"Let's go straight to Mr. Barnaby's place and get the work papers for your parents!" Hans called.

"I'm ahead of you!" Stephen answered.

The newsboy yelled, "GERMANY INVADES POLAND! BORDERS SEALED! Read all about it!"

Stephen and Hans stopped and stared at each other. Their bodies went limp. When he could move again, Stephen paid the newsboy and grabbed a newspaper from the stack. He looked at the paper's headline, and then he heaved it into the air.

"I hate this world!" Stephen yelled, as the loose, fluttering pages of devastating news rained down.

—∾—

Peter shoveled the barn floor, ankle deep in cow manure, slop, and straw. Emil watched from the doorway, scowling and shaking his head in disapproval.

"Stop piddling about. You better learn to muck the barn faster, or you'll never become a farmer," Emil, the agrarian hobgoblin, admonished. "Farmers aren't much for idle time, fancy dreams, and musical nonsense."

"I don't plan on being a farmer, and I'll be leaving here soon," Peter said.

"Oh, I guess you haven't heard." Emil sighed. "Germany has invaded Poland. The borders are sealed. England may go to war. You're not going anywhere for a long time."

Peter's shovel dropped to the ground, as he stared at Emil in shock. The cows startled and mooed.

—∾—

At the Cohens' in London, Becca played under the table with her doll, Gina. She quickly moved her doll under a chair. "Hide in the wardrobe, Gina, and don't say a word, or they will take your papa away."

—⟋⟍—

In Berlin, the burned synagogue was now a temporary camp and fenced with barbed wire to keep the Jewish people in, until they could be sent to other, more established camps. It was an unholy insult to be imprisoned on the grounds of their place of worship, but for Sylvia, who had to look across the street at her old apartment and the butcher shop where she'd been so happy with her family, it was unbearably cruel. She and Baby Lilly were camped out in front of the burned synagogue, with no shelter but a crude makeshift tent, as they waited to be transported out of Berlin.

It was a cool September night, and Lilly shivered violently. Sylvia picked her up and held her inside her shirt, allowing the warmth of her body to surround the trembling baby who had a fever. She noticed a red rash on Baby Lilly's arms and face. She opened Lilly's mouth. Her baby's tongue was bright red.

Sylvia gasped. She ran up to the Nazi officers. "My baby is very sick. She has a fever and a rash."

A fat officer, with jowls that rippled when he spoke, laughed.

"I'm afraid she's going to die," Sylvia said. "I think she has scarlet fever."

"That will be one less Jew to transport," the officer said. "Don't come near us with your infected child."

Sylvia walked away crying and repeating a prayer between sobs: "Hear, O Israel, the Lord our God, the Lord is one."

CHAPTER 25

WAR

(September 1939)

It was deathly silent on the streets of London the night of September 3, 1939, when Prime Minister Neville Chamberlain gravely declared war on Germany.

Marla looked out the window of Sebastian's Bloomsbury House office at the lights of London. Sebastian stared at his hands as he twisted them nervously.

"You'd think declaring war would be loud, but it's really very quiet," Marla said, watching the emptiness of the streets as the reality of what war would mean sank in.

A newspaper on Sebastian's desk read: "ENGLAND AND FRANCE DECLARE WAR ON GERMANY."

Marla paced as they listened to the radio. Prime Minister Neville Chamberlain spoke: "It is evil things that we shall be fighting against, brute force, bad faith, injustice, suppression, and persecution, and against them I am certain that the right will prevail."

—⚏—

In Coventry, Peter pulled thin mattresses and blankets under the stairwell. Emil and Maude sat at the kitchen table, staring at the wooden radio, the only modern thing on the farm. Emil had bought it for the news, not the music. Maude turned the knobs, until they heard King George's voice.

" . . . I call upon my people at home and my peoples across the sea. I ask them to stand calm, firm, and united in this time of trial. The task will be hard. There may be dark days ahead, and war can no longer be confined to the battlefield, but we can only do the right as we see the right, and reverently commit our cause to God."

Peter tucked the last straw-filled mattress into the small crawl space under the stairs and stood staring at the radio, as if it held the answers to what was coming next.

"Don't forget the blankets, Peter. When your people bomb us, we need to be prepared," Maude demanded.

"At least France is with us," Emil said.

"We'll need more than that against such an uncivilized country." Maude sniffed.

Peter turned and climbed the stairs to the attic.

"The blankets, Peter! Don't forget the blankets!" Maude screeched in her high, grating voice.

Peter ignored her and kept walking up the stairs. Tonight, he could not tolerate the belittling bullying of Emil and Maude. He needed the silence of grief to absorb the meaning of war.

In his mind, he heard bars clang shut and lock. No one was getting out of Germany, and there was no escaping Coventry. His mother and baby sister were trapped inside Germany with Adolf Hitler, and Peter was trapped in England with Emil and Maude.

—⚬—

At Bloomsbury House, Sebastian laid his head on his desk with arms crisscrossed over his neck, like he was seeking cover in an air raid. He sighed a shuddering gasp and looked up. "It's done. We did our best. The Kindertransports from Germany are shut down. Yours was the last train across the border."

"What about the children still left there?" Marla asked.

Sebastian shook his head. "We did what we set out to do. We saved as many children as we could, almost ten thousand."

"But what about Jules?" Marla asked.

"I'm sorry. There is nothing we can do for him. It's impossible. We don't even know where he is. No one will be allowed in or out of Germany. Perhaps we can still get a few more Kindertransports out of the Netherlands, but the rail lines into Germany are shut down."

"So, it's over? We walk away?"

Sebastian nodded. "We don't have a choice. We did the best we could."

———

In the Vogners' apartment, in the designated Jewish Residential District in Dinsdorf, Eddie was hopping back and forth. Anna motioned to him. "Come on, Eddie, we need to get to the brick factory."

"But I need to go," Eddie complained.

"Eddie, the toilets don't work anymore. They turned off the water."

"Why did they do that? I need to go."

"You'll have to go in the bucket, like I told you."

"I can't do that! I can't do that!"

"I am so sorry that life is like this, but there is nothing we can do," Anna said. "When you're done, pour it in the big ditch on the perimeter."

"Maybe I will pour it on Hitler." Eddie glared at the bucket.

"That would not be good, Eddie," Anna said.

"I wish Hans was here." Eddie started crying.

Anna put her arm around her loving, trusting son, and thanked God Hans was not there.

———

Eva limped down the road at the Bockenburg Camp. A black Nazi car pulled onto the road and, without slowing down, headed right for her. She jumped out of the way and rolled to avoid being run over, then lay on the ground after the car passed.

With no one around to see her, she cried heaving sobs of sorrow, as the cold from the hard ground seeped into her soul.

———

Marla drove up to the farmhouse. Her fancy car was an incongruous sight in the Coventry countryside. Peter didn't hear the chugging sound of the car. He was pitching hay for the horses and cows.

Marla poked her head into the barn and smiled when she saw him. "Hello, Peter!"

"Miss Marla?" Peter answered.

Marla watched as he threw a pitchfork of hay to Olga, the fussy cow who mooed an incessant complaint about the cruelty of farm life. She was surprised at Peter's transformation into a strong and able-bodied farmhand. "If nothing else, the farm has made you strong."

"You are right. There is nothing else." Peter smiled. "What are you doing all the way out here?" He stuck the pitchfork into the pile of hay and wiped his hands on his pants.

"I came to apologize."

"For what?"

"For separating you and Becca, and for placing you here with Emil and Maude."

"It was the best you could do."

"Yes, it was, but sometimes, my best is not good enough. I've never forgotten the way you played that song on the train. It was the most beautiful thing I have ever heard. I'm sorry. It was wrong to place you here."

"But you're right. It's made me stronger. I am no longer the frightened little boy who rode the Kindertransport. This place and those people have hardened me."

"Ah, the Kindertransport is no more. I don't know what to do, Peter. I'm sorry. It's over. They arrested my friend Jules. The Kindertransport is done, but I will find you another place to live." Marla hugged the growing and muscled Peter. "Don't ever let go of who you are."

"My mother used to say that," Peter said, wistfully.

"She sounds like she was a wonderful mother."

"She is."

—⚊—

Eddie, Oma Greta, and Anna trudged back against the wind from the brick factory. Oma Greta, walking hunched over from back pain, coughed and scratched the rash on her arm.

"Are you okay, Oma?" Eddie asked.

"I am old, and bricks do not agree with me," Oma Greta said, smiling.

The wind blew Eddie's hat off. As he chased after it, a policeman suddenly grabbed Eddie's arm and spun him around.

"How has this one escaped? Operation T-4 calls for mercy deaths for all incurable imbeciles. He needs to come with me," the policeman shouted.

Anna grabbed Eddie's other arm. "He works at the brick factory. He's small enough to crawl in and clean out the brick kilns. No one else can do that," Anna lied.

The policeman eyed the small boy. "Perhaps he is useful."

Anna nodded.

"Keep him out of sight," the policemen said as he hurried away and left Eddie to live, thanks to the insistence of his clever mother.

—⚶—

Sylvia woke up in her makeshift tent on the front yard of the burned synagogue, cradling Baby Lilly, as the September sun rose against the Berlin skyline.

Lilly didn't move, and her skin with the red rash was blue.

"Wake up, Lilly. Wake up now. Open your . . ." Sylvia felt Lilly's cold skin.

She screamed and rocked her daughter's limp and lifeless body. "My baby is dead! You killed my sweet Lilly!"

Across the yard at the guard station, the police officer stepped out. "Shut up, over there!" he shouted. "The Brits just declared war on us!"

Sylvia cradled Baby Lilly in her arms and stared unfocused, absorbing the man's words. Then, she rose slowly and trudged across the yard, as if in a trance, searching the ground.

Near a trash pile, she bent down and picked up a jagged piece of broken windowpane from the destroyed synagogue. With one long, deep, and final slash, she sliced her arm down through her veins from her wrist to her elbow. She shook with a shiver of pain and its finality when she saw the resulting gash and the red stream of blood.

She lay down beside Baby Lilly and stroked her baby's innocent face. "My Lilly, my Becca, my Peter, my Henry, I am lost without you."

As the blood spurted from her arm and spread out on the sacred ground of the synagogue, Sylvia put her dead baby on her chest and wrapped her arms around her precious Baby Lilly, now soaked in her blood.

"England, take care of my children. They belong to you, now." Sylvia folded her hands over her little girl. Her head tilted toward the Nazi police. "And may God's revenge be swift."

CHAPTER 26

DOCTORS SAVE LIVES

(September 1939)

The windows of the Cohens' house at 16 Poppleton Circle were covered with black curtains. A gas mask lay on the table beside Becca's bed, as she thrashed around in her sleep. She cried out, "Mutti! Mutti!"

Mrs. Daniels tottered in sleepily and turned on the light. "What is it, dearie?"

Becca was crouched at the end of her bed with the covers over her head. Mrs. Daniels pulled the covers back. A disheveled, sweaty Becca peered at her with the distant eyes of horror.

"Another nasty nightmare, I suppose?" Mrs. Daniels asked.

Becca nodded.

"Let's hear it, lass," Mrs. Daniels said.

"Hitler found me. He was waiting for me under my bed. He tried to pull me under there."

"I'd like to see him try. I'm from Swansea, Wales. We're coal miners, a tough lot. Hitler wouldn't stand a chance against me." Mrs. Daniels smiled.

Becca looked up at her. "I miss my Mutti."

"Of course, you do, lass."

"But she's never coming to get me."

"That's not true. Why do you say that?" Mrs. Daniels asked.

"Because Hitler had her and Baby Lilly under my bed, too," Becca whispered.

Mrs. Daniels reached out her fleshy arms, pulled Becca to her large bosom, and hugged her. Becca clung to Mrs. Daniels's strong embrace.

Mrs. Daniels knew that beneath Becca's sassy, cheeky exterior, she was a frightened little girl, who was facing the end of everything she knew, and everything that made her who she was. As a motherless little girl, Mrs. Daniels had known that same all-consuming fear when the coal mine collapsed, trapping her father and two brothers. They'd suffocated when the mineshaft ran out of air. At fourteen, she'd moved to London to take care of other people's families because she had none.

—⁂—

The door to the Berlin attic where Stephen's parents lived opened. Clara held out a tray of pretzels and cheese, and a jug of water. "We're going to the market," she said.

"Thank you, Clara," Jacob said, taking the tray. "The food looks delicious."

Nora smiled at Clara. "Were you able to send Stephen the message?"

Clara nodded. "Yes. He's a smart boy. He'll understand." She pulled the attic door shut.

Jacob and Nora heard the door shut downstairs as Klaus and Clara left the house. They ate the pretzels and cheese.

"I wonder what happened to Sylvia and Baby Lilly," Nora said.

"I'm afraid to think of it," Jacob said.

"It's sad to think that we're the lucky ones."

Suddenly, there was a desperate pounding on the back door. "Klaus! Clara!" a woman's voice yelled. "Oh, dear God, someone, help me!"

Jacob and Nora looked at each other. Then Jacob climbed on a chair to peep out the attic window. It was Mindy, the neighbor from the house next door. She was pregnant, and blood stained her dress. "Who is it?" Nora asked.

Jacob looked out the small window, watching as Mindy headed

unsteadily back toward her house. She turned, looked up, and saw Jacob watching her. Suddenly, she clutched her stomach and fell to the ground.

"It's the neighbor from the house next door. Mindy, the pregnant one. She's in trouble!" Jacob picked up his doctor's bag.

Nora grabbed his arm. "No, Jacob! Please, it isn't safe."

"But I'm a doctor," Jacob said.

Nora nodded reluctantly.

Once outside, Jacob and Nora hurried to Mindy. She looked up at them. "Help me! Help me!" She pointed to the attic window. "Were you in . . . oh, thank God, you're here. Don't let me lose my baby! Oh, God, not my baby!"

"It'll be all right now. Don't worry, Jacob's a good doctor," Nora said. "He's delivered many babies."

"My prayers are answered," Mindy said breathlessly.

They helped Mindy into her house.

Two hours later, with Jacob and Nora's help, Mindy delivered a baby girl.

Nora wrapped a blanket around the baby and handed her to Mindy. "You're lucky. Children are such a blessing."

The door opened, and Mindy's wiry husband stood there staring at them. "What's going on?" he demanded.

Jacob was startled, but smiled. "Are you the father?"

He nodded. "What are you doing in my house? Who are you?"

"I helped deliver the baby. Congratulations, it's a girl!" Jacob said.

Mindy kissed the baby, smiling through her tears. "Look, isn't she beautiful?"

Mindy's husband stared, unable to fit what he saw into his orderly German world.

Mindy looked up at Dr. Levy. "Thank you, Doctor. You saved our lives," she gushed. Her husband, a small man, paced angrily beside Mindy, huffing with each frantic stride.

"We'll leave you alone now," Jacob said, as he and Nora slipped out the door.

Mindy's husband turned on her. "I don't know that doctor. Where did he come from?"

"I don't know. I was bleeding all over. I was in trouble," Mindy said. "But the baby—"

Her husband roughly grabbed the baby out of her hands.

"No! No!" Mindy cried, with her arms outstretched. "Be careful."

"Perhaps now you'll remember," he said, holding the baby hostage. "Where did the doctor come from?"

The baby cried the bleating sound of a newborn, able to pierce any new mother's heart. Mindy reached out for the child who was her duty to protect. Her husband held the baby at an awkward angle, threatening to drop her.

Mindy cried. Her daughter was more important than anything. "Maybe from next door, maybe Klaus's attic."

He tossed the tiny bundle to Mindy. "She is cursed." He looked out the window and nodded. "Klaus, you have betrayed Germany, and that Jew doctor has violated German law."

Back in the attic, Jacob and Nora heard footsteps coming up the stairs. Then the door flew open.

"Clara, did you—" Nora asked, as she turned around.

It was not Clara. A policeman stood in the doorway.

"Klaus and Clara have been arrested," he said. "And you will be too, for practicing medicine on non-Jews."

Across the yard, Mindy held her baby girl protectively and watched out the window of her house as Jacob and Nora were dragged from their hiding place. Stunned at the consequences of the doctor's humanity and her selfish betrayal, Mindy cried and buried her face against her new little daughter, the one she had sold her soul to keep. "God forgive me," she whispered, "and bless the Jewish people."

Her husband slid up behind her and jerked her away from the window. "Don't cry for Jews. Cry for the daughter you have contaminated."

—⚒—

In Coventry, Peter waved goodbye to Emil and Maude as they drove the mule cart into town for needed supplies. He watched them clop down the dirt road until they turned a corner and could no longer be seen. He turned and smiled. With them gone, it was finally quiet, except for the hens clucking inside the chicken house, and even that seemed unexpectedly soothing. He had come to appreciate how the hens defended their unhatched chicks.

He was headed into the quiet house when he heard Olga, the cow, loudly mooing another complaint. What's her problem now? he wondered. He stopped and sighed, his shoulders slumped, but he turned around and walked to the barn.

Olga, the bad-tempered cow he sang to in order for the milk to flow, was lying down. When Peter walked up to her, she raised her head and mooed, scolding him for not coming sooner.

He knelt down beside the persnickety beast. "What is it this time, Olga?" She mooed and strained in distress. Peter looked anxiously toward the empty road that a minute ago had been his relief, as Olga turned restlessly.

Peter heard a whoosh of water being released. He moved down the cow to check for any injuries. When he got to Olga's hind legs, he saw the head of a calf emerging.

"Oh, no!" He looked around in panic. "You had to do this now, didn't you? Just to spite me."

Olga strained again, working hard to give life to her baby. The calf's legs unfolded. Olga gave another moo and a push, but the calf was stuck. No matter how Olga strained, the calf did not move. Peter looked at his hands. He would do what he had to do to save Olga and her calf.

He got in position between the cow's back legs, reached out his nimble musician-turned-farmer hands, and grasped the calf. He set his feet, and when Olga pushed, Peter pulled until he was sweating, but nothing worked.

"Try again, Olga girl," he said to the cow. Then he sang "Schmetterling" as he tried twisting the calf with his hands again and pulling with his hay-pitching muscles. The calf finally slipped free with his turning and was born.

Peter breathed heavily as he stared at the new farm life before him.

He leaned his head back and laughed. He hollered, "A baby cow! I delivered a baby cow!"

The calf's legs were wobbly, and it rested, panting next to its mother. Olga nudged the calf, licking it clean of its afterbirth. Tears came to Peter's eyes, as he watched the once crotchety cow become a loving mother. He dropped to his knees beside the cow. "You're a mutti now!" Peter exclaimed, as he put one arm around Olga and his other around her new calf. Olga, in an unguarded moment of grateful motherhood, let him.

———⚒———

At the Bockenburg Camp, Eva was covered with thick rock dust as she worked in the gravel pit. She glanced around to make sure Grundy wasn't watching. He seemed determined to make her life miserable. She put the hammer down and wiped the sweat from her forehead, despite the coolness of the fall air.

———⚒———

Jacob and Nora shuffled off the train and were herded into the back of crowded trucks like unwanted cargo.

After traveling a great distance, the trucks stopped, and the door opened. They had arrived at Dinsdorf. The designated districts now accepted any Jewish people that Germany didn't know what to do with, since the jails and concentration camps, like Sothausen, were overflowing.

As Jacob and Nora stumbled out of the truck and onto the street, they spotted a boy throwing rocks against the curb. Nora nudged Jacob with her elbow. "Jacob, look, is that Eddie Vogner? It is! Eddie!" she called.

Eddie looked up, smiled, and waved to them, as if they were expected for dinner.

"Hey, I know you! They got you, too?" He ran and hugged them, as he jumped up and down.

"Eddie! Eddie, where's your mother?" asked Nora, smiling at his warm greeting.

"Come on, I'll show you," Eddie said, happy to see his old friends.

Eddie bounded up the stairway and burst into the small apartment, followed by Nora and Jacob. "Look who the Nazis found!" he exclaimed.

"Oh, dear God," Anna said, as she hugged Nora.

"I have good news for you, Anna. We got a letter from Stephen before they arrested us. Hans is in England," Nora said. "He is fine."

Anna and Oma Greta cried with relief. "Well, at least the children are all safe," Anna said.

"Yeah, the children are safe," Eddie said. He nodded and smiled.

Later that night, Jacob and Nora lay on a thin mattress on the floor in Anna's apartment, behind a makeshift door made out of a tattered sheet. "I worry about Klaus and Clara. They risked their lives for us," Jacob said.

"Such good people. Do you think they'll be able to get another letter to Stephen?" Nora asked.

"Klaus will find a way," Jacob said.

"How long can we last?" Nora asked, lying in the embrace of her husband, the only familiar thing that still remained of their old life.

"We can outlast the Nazis. God is on our side," Jacob said, smiling.

Nora kissed Jacob. "I would hate to see what our lives would be if God wasn't on our side."

"Well, perhaps, God could see his way to giving us a little bit better mattress." Jacob patted the dilapidated and stained pad. Nora laughed and hugged her husband.

CHAPTER 27

BAMBOO STICK

(February 1940)

In London at dusk, William Rosenberg waited in Regent's Park, by the rowboats at the Boating Lake. Waterfowl swam at their leisure despite the chilling wind, unaware of the escalating war.

A man with heavy eyebrows and yellow teeth sauntered over to William. He stomped his feet at the ducks sitting in the grass. They waddled off, quacking in fright.

"I hate ducks. They're so useless," the man commented.

"They taste good," William said.

The man nodded. "So, do you have the stuff?"

William pulled the bacon, butter, and sugar food ration books from under his jacket.

"Well, you're a regular Harrods, ain't you, mate?" The man smiled his yellow-toothed grin as he took the stolen ration books. He slipped William the money, and William took off briskly through the gardens, as if he were out for a vigorous evening stroll.

―ɯ―

Thousands of people were now crowded into many of the Nazi camps and designated areas of cities, held against their will. They were being forced to work building roads, farming, working in factories, constructing buildings, digging ditches, crushing rock, working in mills, digging coal, and even producing chemicals and armaments. The camps were nothing more than prisons that exploited the inmates' labor. Children could not work as hard as adults, but that did not stop the Nazis from trying. They did the best they could to work any child to the point of exhaustion. For many children, it proved too much, and they died trying to live in the camps. Noah ended up in a camp, but despite everything they tried, he would not die.

One day he climbed in the back of a truck supply transport that he had been loading. In this way, Noah crossed the border into Poland. He lived on the streets of Soblin. But shortly after Germany took Poland, Noah was swept up in the removal of the Jewish people and ended up in the Soblin Ghetto, on the outskirts of Poland.

The Soblin Ghetto soon had an eight-foot electric fence surrounding the incarcerated community of Jewish people, and they were forced to work for the cause of Germany. The crowded confinement brought confusion, disorder, unsanitary conditions, and a frustrated hopelessness that often led to desperate, dangerous actions.

Noah crossed his arms over his stomach and walked casually past Adler and Dirk, the policemen who guarded the gate. He could hear the hum of the electric fence, with its continuous current, instead of pulsing energy. Police were the guards at most of the camps and ghettos and felt it their duty to inflict the harshest punishments for the smallest crimes of human survival, because their jobs were to keep order at any cost.

Adler picked up a long bamboo pole used to whack prisoners under the pretense of keeping them in line. Everyone knew he loved to hit people hard with the pole and watch the red welts swell up. The wood was almost unbreakable, light, yet bendable enough to get a stinging hit on the skin. It was an amusement to him to help him pass the hours.

As Noah walked in front of him, Adler unexpectedly swung the pole and whacked him as hard as he could. A loaf of bread fell from under Noah's shirt.

"Well, look at that! Come look at this, Dirk!" he called to the short guard next to him, pointing to the bread on the ground. "This filthy little Jew is stealing food."

"They're all thieves, dirty, rotten, beggar thieves," Dirk said. His tiny pointed nose turned up in disgust. Although Noah was only ten, he was only a foot shorter than Dirk, a small man with a big Nazi chip on his shoulder.

Noah stood tall and glared defiantly. "I didn't steal it. I traded my coat for it," he said, glancing at the loaf of bread still on the ground. "I'm hungry and cold now, too. And I worked all day in the mill!"

Adler puckered his jowly face and mimicked Noah in a baby voice. "The Jew thief is hungry." He clicked his tongue in mock pity. "Such a shame. And now, he is cold, too."

"Yes, and I'm sick of this place!" Noah said, his hunger overriding his good judgment.

Adler and Dirk laughed at his foolish, youthful bravado. Dirk grabbed the bamboo pole from Adler and whacked Noah. "So, you want to get out of here, Jew boy?" Dirk asked mockingly.

Noah glared at them. The police guards looked at each other. "We're feeling generous today. Go ahead. Get out of here. We'll look the other way," Adler said. They laughed, and Adler's overhanging belly bounced up and down.

Noah shook his head. "No, you won't. You'll kill me and say I was trying to escape."

The policemen looked at each other. "We'll put our guns down. See, no guns," Adler said.

They laid their guns on the ground and held their hands up, palms out. Dirk set the pole down on the ground in a dramatic gesture. "No weapons, not even the bamboo stick. This is your chance to escape."

"No, I don't want to escape," Noah said, indignantly.

"You are very stupid," Dirk said, laughing at Noah's superiority.

Noah bent down, pretending to tie his shoe. Then he quickly scooped up two handfuls of loose dirt, threw it in their eyes, grabbed the long bamboo pole from the ground, and took off running.

The policemen screamed and rubbed their eyes and felt around for their guns. They shot wildly, but their aims were way off, spraying bullets randomly but hitting nothing.

With the pole held slightly above his shoulder, Noah ran, barely able to carry the long bamboo pole. When he reached the fence, humming with electricity, he stuck the pole into the ground as hard as he could. The pole bent a little as his small body pulled it down. Then, the pole's response to his speedy momentum flung him up into the air, sending him sailing over the eight-foot fence, one untied shoe barely missing the top wire. He didn't let go.

The end of the pole lifted, and the defiant boy became airborne as he gripped the pole. The pole dipped down on the other side, but it tangled in the wire. Noah hung for a moment, suspended in the air.

Then, in the kind of split-second decision that he had become good at, he dropped to the ground, rolling to a stop. Dazed for only a second, he jumped up, realizing he was on the other side of the fence unharmed. He took off running into the streets of Soblin. He was free, although still breadless.

In the city, the townspeople quickly identified him, with his ragged clothes and thinness, as one of the people from the ghetto. They were not used to seeing the prisoners walking around town as if on holiday, so they stared as he walked by, stunned by his brazen escape and casual saunter through town.

A big man suddenly reached out and grabbed Noah's small shoulder. "What are you doing here? Are you a Jew boy? Did you escape the fences? I'll turn you in and be a hero, so the Nazis will leave us alone."

The man's fingers dug painfully into his shoulder, and Noah bit them.

"Ow! You little vicious animal!" the man yelled. He released his grasp, and Noah tore away. The big man thundered after him.

Noah wove in and out of the crowd, finally losing the bulky man. Free of his pursuer, Noah rounded the corner and ran right into Dirk and Adler, the once-ridiculing and now completely furious policemen.

"You are stupid," Adler said, grabbing Noah by the back of the neck. He was escorted roughly back into the ghetto by the two guards, whose uniforms still showed the spray of Noah's dirt bomb.

When they passed through the gate, they pushed him to the ground.

"Try that escape trick again, and you'll be shot on sight," Adler said.

"You're barely even worth the bullet," Dirk said.

Noah knew he would have to find another way out.

—⚹—

At 16 Poppleton Circle in London, Becca, and Priscilla in her wheelchair, sat at the kitchen table. They rolled old tinfoil into balls, to turn in as scrap metal to support the war effort.

"You should hear my brother play the violin. It makes you want to dance or cry, depending on what he plays." Becca laughed. "Peter's music is going to save the Jews."

"How?"

"I don't know. That's what my papa used to say, and Papa never told a lie."

"Maybe his violin shoots out bombs." Priscilla threw tinfoil balls at Becca.

"Maybe the violin bombs make music when they fall," Becca said. They laughed, hysterically.

—⚹—

Although Poland was now occupied by Germany, the residents of the Jewish Residential District in Dinsdorf were not sent to Poland immediately. The brick factory had come to rely on their free labor, and the war effort needed bricks to build the new camps all over Poland.

In the apartment shared by the Vogners and the Levys, Eddie slept on the floor next to Oma Greta's bed. Although she had been sick for several days, there was no other place to sleep. His mother slept on the floor on the other side of Oma's bed. Nora and Jacob slept in the small makeshift bedroom.

As morning dawned, Eddie got up and tapped Greta. "Wake up, Oma! They're passing out bread and cabbage this morning, and I'm hungry. I want to go early to get some before I have to carry bricks all day."

Oma didn't respond. Eddie nudged his grandmother, whispering, "Wake up, Oma." He rubbed her cheek. "You're very cold, like an icicle."

Oma didn't move. Her mouth hung open, and her skin was drained of color and slack, its vitality gone. "Oma, Oma, wake up. It's morning," Eddie said in a singsong voice. "Why are you so cold?"

He stared at Oma. He poked her, and then grabbed his head. "Oh, no! Oh, no! Mutti, Oma is empty!" He screamed, rocking back and forth, holding his head.

Anna jumped up off the floor and tended to Oma. But it was too late. Oma was dead. She held Eddie and rocked with him. "She's gone, Eddie. She's gone."

"Where did she go? She was right here last night, in this bed."

"She's dead, Eddie. She went in peace," Anna said.

"She didn't go in peace. The Nazis killed her!" Eddie shook his head rapidly, refusing to accept that his oma would willingly leave him.

"Eddie, you must not say that!" Anna shook her finger at him. "Don't let anyone hear you say that."

"It's true," Eddie said. "She'll tell you when she comes back."

Anna put her arm around Eddie. "She's not coming back, Eddie."

"Like Papa?"

Anna nodded. "She's gone for good."

"My Oma," Eddie wailed. "I'm glad she escaped, but maybe she should have taken us with her."

—◆◆◆—

Later that day, Victor, a beefy, pompous policeman, and Michael, an ugly big-eared man with close-set eyes, came and wrapped Oma Greta in a blanket, so they wouldn't have to touch her.

Jacob, Nora, Anna, and Eddie watched them remove the pale, lifeless body of the woman who had left Poland for what she thought would be a better life, only to be returned by Hitler, and in the end died in poverty and bigotry, imprisoned in a filthy apartment.

"Typhus?" Victor asked.

Michael nodded. He shivered and made a wrinkled face of disgust. "Look at the way they live. What do you expect? They're filthy!" Michael grabbed the edge of the blanket with his dirty fingernails.

Jacob took a deep breath and drew himself up. "We don't choose to live this way. I'm a doctor, and it's almost medically impossible to stay alive in a place this overcrowded and unsanitary. Typhus is impossible to avoid when we're forced to live like filthy rats in a hole."

"You are rats. Foul, scroungy vermin, and if you keep complaining, I'll make you work double hours digging ditches," Victor said angrily. He lost his grip and dropped his side of the bundle. Oma Greta's head hit the floor, making a horrifying thud.

Anna gasped and bit her lip to stop herself from crying out, but Eddie didn't have the same restraint. His face contorted in anger. "Don't drop her! She's my Oma! She's a very nice lady."

"Shut up, you deformed clown!" Victor yelled. He would have hit Eddie, but his hands were occupied with carrying one more dead Dinsdorf inhabitant.

Nora hugged Anna. Jacob put his arm around Eddie. Victor and Michael picked Oma up from the ground and carried her out still wrapped in the blanket, but they knocked her against the doorjamb as they left, as if she were an old couch instead of a beloved grandmother.

Eddie's arms reached out for his oma, as her small blistered feet, sticking out of the blanket, disappeared from the room.

"Come back, Oma!" He looked up at his mother. "I wish people would stop dying. There's not going to be anybody left."

Victor and Michael carried Eddie's grandmother down the steps and outside. They shuffled over to the curb and, on the count of three, flung Oma Greta into the Dinsdorf street like unwanted trash.

At Bockenburg Camp, Eva waded through the marshes. The mosquitoes swarmed around her. She batted at them, slapping her skin, but nothing could keep them from biting. Soon, the cold weather would kill them, but then, she would have to fight the freezing temperatures. Eva's life had become an unending battle against man and nature.

That night, in line for soup, with red welts from the mosquito bites all over her skin, Eva scratched, tormented by the itching.

Helga pulled her arm away. "Stop it. You'll tear up your skin."

Bert ripped a piece of his shirt off the bottom and dipped it in his cup of water. He placed it gently on Eva's skin, relieving, for a second, the intensity of the bites.

Eva smiled at her father. "Thank you, Papa."

—ᴡ—

Later that day after returning from the brick factory, inside the Dinsdorf apartment, Anna divided the last chunk of bread among Eddie, Jacob, and Nora. Anna knew the tradition of sitting shiva to mourn the dead must be done. She covered the mirrors to remind them to look beyond outside appearances and focus on the good inside. There was a lot of good to reflect on in Oma Greta's life. Although they were prisoners in an overcrowded, disease-infested apartment in a Nazi-controlled neighborhood surrounded by armed guards to keep order, Anna knew the dead must be mourned. The prayers must be said. Respect for the dead must be shown, even in a makeshift prison. Maybe even more so.

—ᴡ—

After months at a work camp near Frankfurt, Charlie and his parents had been shipped without explanation to the Soblin Ghetto in Poland. They looked around at the unfamiliar neighborhood. They walked toward corpses lying in the street and stared at the stack of dead bodies awaiting disposal.

"Why are those people sleeping in the street?" Charlie asked.

Arnold put his hand on Charlie's shoulder. "They are dead, my son. They are sleeping with God now."

Charlie stopped and stared with the shocked vision of a child faced with mortality of the cruelest form. Arnold divided a small chunk of bread and handed it to Charlie, who had sores on his face and arms.

Charlie, exhausted and weak, stumbled and fell. He dropped the bread, which landed among the dead. He reached for the bread, but Arnold pulled his hand away. "Don't eat that, son."

"But I'm hungry."

"Here." Arnold handed Charlie his own share of the bread.

Charlie popped it in his mouth, as he stared at the empty shells of people. "Why do they want us to die? What did we ever do for them to hate us so much?"

"We exist, Charlie, and that's enough," Arnold said.

"Can't God see what they are doing?" the boy asked.

"Maybe God is waiting to see what we will do," Arnold said.

"That's enough now. Let's find a place to live," Evelyn said. She looked at the dead bodies lying in the street. "Looks like maybe an apartment has opened up."

"Evelyn, you shouldn't mock the dead," Arnold said.

A train whistle sounded in the distance. "I wonder what Becca and Peter are doing now," Charlie said.

CHAPTER 28

HITLER'S A MADMAN

(April/May 1940)

Many months had passed, and the military tension had increased. Adolf Hitler was determined to spread his control toward world domination. For the Kindertransport children, their lives continued to be relatively safe, but they were riddled with worry, loneliness, and uncertainty.

—⁂—

The April weather turned milder. The wind was not so sharp, the air not so heavy. The night had become restless, as the wind rustled the trees and blew through the fields around Coventry. In the farmhouse, Emil, Maude, and Peter listened to the radio.

"Reporting tonight's news on April 9, 1940, German troops invade Denmark and Norway," the radio announcer said.

Emil shook his head. "Hitler's a madman. They shouldn't prat about. Someone should just kill him." He turned to stare at Peter. "Why haven't your people turned against him? Some people don't have the courage, I guess."

Peter clenched his fists, but he held them tightly to his sides, his nails digging into his skin. He glared at Emil and Maude. "It's not about courage. It's about power. When someone controls everything you do, it can be a prison even if you aren't confined."

—∞—

One May afternoon, a lanky British man in a wool sweater followed William into a London pub, the Blue Ox Tavern. The man got a pint of ale and sauntered up to William.

"You any good at darts, lad?" he asked, taking a sip of his ale, his Adam's apple bobbing up and down.

"I'm good at everything," William said, simply, as if it was an undisputed fact.

"Can I have a go, lad? Winner buys the next ale."

"I never turn down a free ale." William handed him a dart. "The center is the bull's-eye, lad," he said, mocking the man.

"I would be honored to play with such an expert." The man smiled. "So, what's your name?"

"William." He aimed his dart.

"William what?"

"Rosenberg."

The man grabbed William's arm, and William shook him off. "Wait your turn!"

"There will be no bull's-eyes tonight. You're the one I've been looking for. You are under arrest," the man said.

"Since when is it illegal to get drunk and play darts?" William asked. "This is England, after all."

"You're an enemy alien! You're a Jerry."

"I'm a German Jew. I'm an enemy of Hitler," William said. "I was brought into your country on the Kindertransport to escape the Nazis."

"What a delightful tale. You're over sixteen, and you're German. You're an enemy alien until you can prove otherwise. Your new home is the prison on the Isle of Man."

The man handcuffed William and marched him out of the pub.

—∞—

Peter hefted a huge bag of chicken feed onto his back and set it down inside the barn. He scooped some out and entered the chicken coop behind the barn, spreading the grain out with a shake of his hand.

He lifted up the self-satisfied reddish hen with the black streak on its wing. He cupped the egg resting warmly in the nest. Then, he set the egg back down. He could not take the hen's egg. He moved down the line. Next, he picked up Henrietta, a white-feathered sassy hen known for her vicious pecking. There was no egg, so he plopped her down quickly before her beak could take another chunk out of him.

Peter laughed triumphantly. "I'm getting too fast for you, Henrietta," he said to the aggressive fowl.

Peter stooped down and picked up one of the newspapers piled in the corner. He opened the first paper and spread it on the coop floor. He looked at the next paper in the pile. Then he stared and turned it around to look at the picture on the front page.

It was William Rosenberg, Eva's thieving brother. It appeared that the boy, who had sold out his own people to get his release from the Sothausen Concentration Camp, who'd stolen Eva's Kindertransport seat, and who'd outwitted the Nazi man who threw him off the train, could not escape the English.

The May newspaper reported the Isle of Man internment was in a large stone building surrounded by barbed wire on a small island of two hundred and twenty-one square miles in the Irish Sea. The picture showed William being escorted into the massive building without a crime to his name, except being a German in England.

—∿∿—

In the street in the Dinsdorf District, Eddie chased a butterfly, the first one he had seen since leaving home. "Steal some cream for me, schmetterling! I'm hungry." He grabbed at the butterfly, his hand trapping it.

He laughed and opened his hand. The fragile butterfly was smashed.

Eddie stared at the beautiful broken wings of the schmetterling dead by his hands, and he cried.

CHAPTER 29

A TREMENDOUS BATTLE

(May/June 1940)

Hans and Stephen, thirteen years old, sat in a London school, not too far from their hostel. Stephen, Hans, and the other students watched the teacher trace the huge map of Europe. "Hitler is able to control his troops through coded communications, using mail, telephone, and telegraph. So, although we intercept his messages, we lose precious time until we can decipher them, and the Nazis have been able to stay one step ahead of us. Now, Germany has invaded Belgium, the Netherlands, and today, France. What does this mean?" she asked.

"That we're next!" Stephen said.

"Air raid drill!" someone in the hall shouted.

Hans, Stephen, and the other students scrambled to put on their gas masks, which the younger students carried in boxes around their necks. Stephen and Hans hid under their desks with their arms crisscrossed over their heads and with no room to spare.

Hans called out to Stephen. "When Hitler invaded the Netherlands, I wonder what happened to the basket baby."

"Karla Blinker is fine, I'm sure," Stephen said, hesitantly. "I hope."

—⁕—

On May 19th, in the farmhouse kitchen, Peter sat at the table with Emil and Maude and listened as the new Prime Minister, Winston Churchill, spoke on the radio. "I speak to you for the first time as Prime Minister in a solemn hour for the life of our country. A tremendous battle is raging in France. It would be foolish to disguise the gravity of the hour. It would be still more foolish to lose heart and courage."

Emil turned off the radio and snarled at Peter. "Look what your people have done!" his gravelly goblin voice sputtered.

—⧝—

In their room at the youth hostel, Stephen looked at a letter in his shaking hands. Hans sat on the bed next to him.

"It's from Klaus, again," Stephen said.

"What does he say? Are your parents okay?" Hans asked.

Stephen read the letter. "Dear Stephen, I have sad news for you. Clara and I were arrested, and our futures remain uncertain. I have since heard that your parents were arrested as well. A friend is mailing this for me. I pray it reaches you. Do not give up hope. Someday, you will all be together. Yours truly, Klaus."

Hans nodded. "This is not good news."

CHAPTER 30

HEAD FOR COVER

(September 1940)

William was released in September, several months after his imprisonment, after the authorities finally determined that he was not a national security threat to England. He was a belligerent young man with a bad attitude and a knack for stealing the shoes of the other prisoners and then trading them back to their owners for food, but that was not enough to keep him in jail.

He walked out of the prison gate with nothing but two pounds in his pocket and anger on his mind. He climbed onto the boat waiting to take him across the short expanse of sea, back to England. He squinted his eyes and threw his head back, letting the setting sun hit his face, breathing in the cool salty sea air.

William remembered a day when he was young, and he and new his friends were skipping rocks on the lake at Edelweiss Park, trying to beat their record of ten skips. The birds were screeching, squawking, and soaring over the water. His rock had skipped only six times across the glassy lake.

He'd turned around, and Eva was running toward him. He'd looked away, pretending he didn't know her, but when he'd turned back, she was standing in front of him. "William, what are you doing here? Papa's been looking for you. He needs your help in the shop."

"That's your sister?" one of his friends had asked.

William shook his head. "No," he'd said, denying his sister.

Eva had put her hands on her hips. "You're going to be in big trouble if you don't get to the shop, you zhlub!"

His friends stared at him. "You're one of them?" a boy asked.

William shook his head, but his hands trembled at his sides. Then, his friends had suddenly turned on him, beating him with their fists, and viciously kicking him.

"Dirty, lying Jew," his best friend said, "trying to trick us!" Then, he motioned to the other boys, who a few moments ago had been happily competing to see who could skip their rocks the farthest.

"Let's get out of here," the boy said. He spat on the bloody William splayed out on the ground, then turned suddenly and spat on Eva. Each of the other three boys did the same.

Eva hadn't moved from where she stood. She'd watched them run away as their spit slid down her face. She'd looked down at William and wiped the humiliating wetness from her face. "Those are your friends?" She'd bent down to help William up, but he'd pushed her hand away and slowly gotten up on his own.

"Not any more, thanks to you!" William had picked up and thrown a rock, and with the velocity of his anger, it skipped eleven times across the water.

In England, William couldn't wait to get off the boat from the Isle of Man and away from the spray of the water. When the boat docked, he almost jumped off before it stopped moving. I need a pint of ale about as fast as they can pour it, he thought. He headed toward the Black Anchor Pub, the closest tavern he could see, where he planned to blow through his two pounds.

That night, the pub's blackout curtains were pulled tightly across the windows, so no light shone through, hiding them completely from the feared threat of German planes. The radio blared music and war news. He sat at the bar on a black leather stool and ordered a glass of dark foamy ale, which he chugged down as if it was a nightly ritual. He slammed the empty glass on the bar. "Another pint!" William called to the bartender. "And fill it to the top this time!"

A burly, bearded man at the bar eyed him suspiciously. "Your accent. You're a Jerry." William glared at him, and the man glared back. "Thought so. Why don't you go back to Hitler-land?"

"Because I'm Jewish," William said. "Haven't you heard? Hitler hates Jews."

"Jews started this whole problem. England doesn't want you either," the man said.

William slowly set his ale down. "We started the problem? You are an idiot. I just got off the Isle of Man where I was imprisoned for being an enemy alien."

"Jolly good. You're a German, you can't be trusted."

William sucked in his breath. "England brought me here on the Kindertransport, but I found the same human wasteland that I left."

"Bite your tongue. England is fighting Germany, and we will win. We are far superior."

"England and Germany are the same. I was imprisoned in both countries, for just being who I am. But I have a message for you and Hitler." William planted his feet and swung at the man, connecting with his bushy face.

The bearded man staggered. Gripping the blackout curtains to stay upright, he pulled them open, exposing the light of the pub.

William turned to the bartender. "And I really need another pint."

Without missing a beat, the bartender pulled the tap and filled the glass as the bearded Englishman staggered outside, convinced of the brutality of Germans and confirmed in his hatred of Jews.

The radio blared "Fools Rush In" by Glenn Miller. William could not hear the sound of the airplane motors as they rumbled overhead. He did not hear the bombs as they fell, until the great bandleader was interrupted.

"Head for cover!" the radio announcer shouted. "Bombers reported over—" Then the radio signal was lost.

William jumped up and ran toward the door. The bomb hit the pub, its light exposed through the open curtain, and exploded before he could escape. The pub was destroyed. Nothing was left but a fireball of smoke, bricks, splintered boards, ash, and spilled ale. The German bombs could not distinguish between an Englishman and an alien enemy.

William, the boy who'd stolen his sister's seat on the Kindertransport to escape Hitler, was dead, killed in England by a German bomb. The German Blitz had begun.

CHAPTER 31

THE WORLD'S ATTENTION

(November 1940)

In the Coventry attic, Peter flopped down on the thin mattress after an uneaten dinner of fried eggs. Despite his immense hunger, he could no longer bring himself to eat the eggs of his friends the hens, their children's lives stolen by the brutality of farmers. After knowing Olga the cow, he was not sure he would look at the butcher's meat the same way again, either.

He was exhausted from the perpetual farm work. He had barely lain down when the air raid siren shrieked in the distance.

Peter picked up his violin case with the picture of his family tucked in it, and ran out of the attic. He stumbled down the stairs to the small space underneath, where he'd put mattresses and blankets. If there was one thing Peter knew, it was that Hitler would not stop until he had destroyed everything in his path, and Peter seemed to keep getting in his way.

Emil and Maude were already there, sprawled out. "We left that bit for you," Maude said to Peter, as she pointed to the only remaining tiny space back beneath the stair frame.

Peter crawled over them, cradling his dusty violin in his arms, as the sound of airplane engines roared overhead. This time, the unmusical duo did not say anything about his violin, not from any change of heart, but only from their preoccupation with impending doom. Peter's weary, and now quite strong, body shook. Hitler has found me, he thought. Perhaps I haven't escaped after all.

"Pray, and Jesus will protect you," Maude said.

"But I'm Jewish. No one protects the Jews," Peter said.

The German plane engines got louder. The high-pitched whistle of the bombs shrilled through the air. Then, an explosive burst nearby sounded as if the Earth itself had split. Another plane flew overhead. The high-pitched whistle of a bomb got louder until it was over their heads. It hit the farmhouse in a fierce explosion.

One side of the sturdy old stone farmhouse was ripped apart. The bombed structure peeled open like a rations can, revealing its contents. The only thing left standing was the stair frame, and Peter huddling underneath it.

Emil and Maude were dead, but Peter emerged, crawling on his hands and knees from under the stairs. He was covered in dirt and blood, but he was still alive and relatively unharmed. He glanced around, and then looked down at his body, as if stunned to see it was still in one piece. He wiped the blood and debris from his face in long-fingered streaks.

He turned and frantically pulled boards away, pulling up his mattress and revealing his violin. He grabbed the case and carefully wiped its cover with his sleeve. He set the case down and slowly opened it.

The violin was unharmed. He picked it up and held it aloft, like an offering to God, an acknowledgment that this was evidence that confirmed God was watching over him. Then he bent down in prayer with the bow and violin still in his hands. *I give my life to you*, he prayed.

What Peter had run from had finally caught up with him. A flash of understanding surged through his mind. A shiver ran through his body, and he knew that running wouldn't work. Staying and fighting was the only way to survive, and it was time to stand up.

He rose to his feet. The smoke from the debris swirled around him like a dust tornado. When it cleared, he saw the moon had not changed. He would live to see another day. He had survived the bombing, and he decided he would never let anyone control him again. Enough was enough. He was ready to fight back.

England was under attack in what the British press nicknamed "The

Blitz," a German word for lightning. Hitler was no longer just a Jewish problem. Germany had the world's attention, and fear was quickly spreading.

The constant barrage of bombing was in full force. The German war had arrived in the backyards of the Kindertransport children. Peter had made it through the rubble of his life at the farmhouse with a determination that something needed to be done, and now he would do it. He decided to head to London to make sure Becca was unharmed before putting his plan into action.

He walked through the bombed-out countryside with his violin, the last remnant of anything civilized. He made arrangements with the nearest farmer to take care of Olga the cow and the other animals. He said his goodbyes to his animal friends and then walked away from the farm that had imprisoned him, free to make his own decisions at last.

In the village, he hitched a ride with a soldier returning to London to report on the unbelievable destruction of Coventry. Peter's anger had outgrown his fear, and he knew what he had to do.

Marla took a deep breath and rubbed her forehead, as she paced in front of a meeting of the refugee workers at Bloomsbury House. "Hitler is on our doorstep, chasing our Kindertransport children," she said. "Their worst nightmares have caught up with them. We've waited as long as we can; now we have to move them to the countryside. Even that may not keep them safe, but at least they'll have a better chance in the country."

Sebastian stepped up beside her. "Marla's right. Everyone pull out every favor you can."

"Do whatever it takes. Beg, cajole, threaten if you have to," Marla said, "but we must help find these children places in the countryside. We've done no good if the German bombs get them now."

Later that night, Peter, covered with dust from the explosion and with nothing but his violin, and the picture of his family in his pocket, sat in the hall of Bloomsbury House. Children shouted and milled about. The phones rang, and general chaos ruled.

Marla walked into the hall with a file. "Peter? Peter, where are you?" she called out.

Peter stood up, chalky debris dust still falling from his clothes. Marla walked over to him. "Peter, I'm sorry about Emil and Maude. That must have been horrible." Marla patted Peter's arm. "Don't fret, I will find another family who will take you."

Peter held out his calloused, blistered, and bleeding hands. "No, what I need may require more than that," he said.

A small girl with a bandage on her head tottered down the hall. "Miss Marla! I need you," she cried. Marla stopped to tend to her.

Peter hurried down the hall, but he turned off when he came to the reception desk. There was so much confusion that no one noticed him when he opened the file cabinets and searched quickly through the files. He found his sister's file and memorized her London address: 16 Poppleton Circle. He stuffed the file back in the drawer and closed it. Then he picked up his violin, his only remaining possession, and hurried out the door.

Peter was no longer willing to wait for answers. He was going to find them himself. Despite the risks, he decided he preferred the London streets to the daily rigors and humiliation of English farm life. He was going to find Becca and extract her from the clutches of the English.

The next morning, Peter, in the same ragged, filthy clothes, woke up on the sidewalk outside the gate of the beautiful Cohen house at 16 Poppleton Circle. The house was intact and unharmed. He stood up.

Under the light of morning, he could see full well the beauty of the prestigious home. His idea of rescuing Becca and their living together on the streets of London, happily begging for their food each day, and exploring the city's music halls, washed away with the waterfall fountain in the middle of the circular drive.

The door to the house opened, and a girl pushed another girl in a wheelchair out the door. Peter gasped. It was nine-year-old Becca. She had grown. It shocked him to see her looking so much like a proper, wealthy English girl.

Peter hesitated, then backed up and hid in the bushes by the street. Maybe it was not the time to rescue Becca. Maybe Becca was best off where she was.

Peter took out his violin. He hadn't played it much since the Dovercourt dining room serenade. Hidden from view behind the bushes on the street, he played "God Save the King" memorized from the sheet music his mother had sent him, its lilting notes floating on the morning air.

—⧓—

"Listen, everyone. Someone's serenading us!" Priscilla yelled.

Doris, Mrs. Daniels, and Harry hurried outside to listen to the great violinist weave his notes into a musical tapestry. When the beautiful tribute to England ended, another song began. Peter's distinctive violin style played "Schmetterling."

Becca jumped up and down. She ran across the front lawn, turning excitedly every which way. "It's Peter! That's my brother!" she shouted. "Peter!"

"That can't be your brother, dear," Doris said. "Miss Marla said he's at a farm in Coventry. That's over sixty-four kilometers from here."

"No! No! He's here. I know that's Peter!" Becca said. She grabbed Mrs. Daniels's hand. "That's him, Mrs. Daniels. I know that's him. I just do."

Mrs. Daniels looked at Becca, as she ran across the lawn, searching for Peter. "Blimey, I hope you're right, lass," Mrs. Daniels said to herself. "I certainly do."

"Peter! Oh, Peter, where are you?" Becca called. A butterfly flitted around her head. She cried out, "It is Peter! It is!"

Doris turned to Mrs. Daniels. "That can't be her brother playing. Poor dear's been under a lot of stress."

"I don't know, ma'am. She seems very sure," Mrs. Daniels said.

—⧓—

Peter watched through the thick trees and bushes. Becca smiled, clapped, and danced as she ran toward the music.

The song ended, and Peter ducked out of sight, smiling. Becca was happy, and she was safer with them than with him. He would never ruin that. Now he was free to become a rebel.

—⚊⚊—

Marla was at Bloomsbury House, sorting files and cleaning up. In the background, the radio played "I'll Be Waiting for You."

I'll be waiting for you, no matter how long it takes.
I'll be waiting for you, no matter what the stakes.
I'll be waiting across the sea,
Just come home to me.
Just come home to me.

Marla heard footsteps and looked up. Peter stood in front of her. She smiled. "Peter? What are you doing here?"

"This time I came to apologize to you."

"For what?"

"For not appreciating what you did for us. Now I understand that escaping is necessary. We were the lucky ones and we got out, but I was raised to have faith in my people's destiny, and I've been thinking that maybe God is testing me. Maybe I should help myself, you know, not just stand by and accept everything. I think it's time to fight back."

"Oh, my God, you're so young," Marla said.

"I'm much older in German years," Peter said with a smile.

Marla hugged him. "Yes, you are, Peter. But there's a war. It's not safe."

"Neither was the farm in Coventry. I have no country, no home, no family."

"What about Becca?" Marla asked.

"She has another family now. A little girl soon forgets."

Marla sighed, her shoulders slumping with the weight of Peter's determination.

"What do you need me to do, Peter?"

"I need you to help me."

"If I can, I will, Peter. I owe you that. It's just that I thought I had saved you."

"You did, you did. Now, it's my turn to save others, and maybe also save a bit of myself along the way."

—ɷ—

At the Bockenburg Camp, Eva and her father pulled themselves out of the gravel pit and walked toward the barracks, along with the other prisoners. Their day of breaking rocks had ended.

"It's been so long since I've heard music. Remember how good Peter was at playing the violin?" Eva said.

"Yes, he was born with music in his soul, like you." Bert smiled.

"Sometimes, I sing in my head to keep my mind off the rocks."

Bert nodded. "Music is one thing they can't take away from us. Don't ever forget the songs."

—ɷ—

In a dimly lit London pub, the Blue Ox Tavern, Marla talked in a hushed voice to Sloan, a handsome, dark bear of a man, and Mica, a wiry man with long hair. Both were Jewish men from Germany.

"Say that again," Sloan said to Marla.

"The Kindertransport is shut down, so I need you to help me smuggle Jewish children out of Germany and Poland," Marla repeated.

Sloan took a deep gulp of his ale and shook his head. "No can do, lady."

"Why not?" Marla said. "You're a leader of—"

"I've seen a hundred like you. You're hollow, soft, a cream puff. The Resistance needs real commitment," Sloan said. "You do more harm than good."

"I've already got some money lined up." Marla smiled coyly.

Mica nodded eagerly at Sloan, who drank his ale and slammed the empty mug on the table. His big shoulders shrugged, and he slowly, reluctantly nodded.

"Good enough for me," Mica said. He reached across the table and shook Marla's hand. "Don't mind him. He doesn't like anybody."

Sloan leaned in close to Marla. "Don't get in our way, Blue Eyes. I don't like distractions, even pretty ones."

Marla stared the man down. He smiled, but he was the first one to turn away. "And one more thing," she added. "I need you to train a boy named Peter."

"Train him for what?"

"To join the Resistance," Marla said, as if it was an ordinary thing to ask.

"We don't have time or resources to train anyone," Sloan said. "Who is this boy?"

She motioned. Peter, who was waiting in the shadows, carrying his violin, walked over. He stood up as tall as he could to look older. He tried to look serious and dangerous by squinting his eyes and furrowing his eyebrows, but inside he was reciting the cuts of meat: lamb chops, rump roast, sirloin, shank.

Mica and Sloan looked him over. "He's just a lad," Mica said.

"He's already escaped Hitler in Germany and survived the bombing of his farmhouse in Coventry," Marla said.

Sloan glared at Peter, challenging him. "Why do you want to join us?"

"Because I'm tired of waiting for somebody to do something," Peter said earnestly. "Hiding in the English countryside will not save anyone but the cows, and even they want out."

Sloan smiled at Peter. He looked directly into Peter's gray eyes, searching for the weakness that surely lived inside one so young.

"Let me ask you, young, fiery lad, are you ready to suffer and give your life for the Resistance?" he asked. "Rebels die young, you know."

"What else is there to live for?" Peter said.

"Then, welcome to the Resistance," Sloan said. He reached out to shake Peter's hand, but Peter was holding his violin. "What's that?"

"The only thing I value."

"A violin? Better leave it here for safekeeping."

"Leave it here?"

"A pub owner is the one person worth trusting," Sloan said. "A violin will do you no good where we're going. If you're coming with us, the only thing you can value is the rebellion." He turned to Marla. "And one more thing, Blue Eyes, we'll need money to buy a truck." He smiled.

Peter could see that Sloan was a shrewd man. Sloan conceded to the pretty woman, but he would demand something for having the young boy forced on him. The burden of Peter was valued equally with a truck. Peter already liked the surly, but practical, bear of a man.

—⟋⟋⟍—

The next day, Marla helped the children, clutching their bags, climb onto double-decker buses outside the London school. "Everyone on board. The countryside awaits," she called.

Stephen looked at Hans. "Does this remind you of anything?"

"Dovercourt," they said together, nodding.

"London is the bombing target now. You will be safer in the countryside," Marla said.

"Tell that to Peter," Stephen said.

That night, as the sun set golden on the horizon of the English countryside, the buses pulled up at a huge estate called Pellbrooke. It was a beautiful old stone mansion resting on a hill that sloped gently to a manicured lawn, perfect for a spirited game of football.

The children streamed out of the double-decker London buses, again chased from their homes by Hitler. They were getting good at moving.

CHAPTER 32

THE WEIGHT OF THE NAZIS

(May 1941)

The Blitz lasted until May 1941, but no one in the Dinsdorf Jewish Residential District knew that. Anna, Jacob, and Nora were so removed from what was going on in the rest of the world that they believed Hans and Stephen were safe from the destructive hands of Adolf Hitler. It was the one bright spot they loved to dwell on, often playing the game, "What are the boys doing now?"

Eddie had just turned ten, but he really hadn't grown any. In some ways, he seemed smaller, as if he were turning inward, crumpling under the weight of the Nazis. With the lack of food, the intense but tedious work of loading bricks, and the constant stress, Eddie's growth was stunted.

—⁓—

Eva was fourteen, and despite the filth and hard work of the Bockenburg Camp, she was growing into a young woman and a pretty one. Late one night, she walked back to her unit from the gravel pit, having been required to stay longer than the others because Grundy had accused her of breaking her rocks too slowly.

Suddenly, he appeared as she rounded the bend. He grabbed her and pulled her to him with a hard jerk. His fingers dug into her arm, as he pressed his lips against hers. His breath smelled foul, and his forceful kiss was painful. Tired from twelve hours of hammering rocks, Eva struggled to pull away, but he was stronger and unrelenting.

His filthy hand clamped over her mouth as she let out a muffled cry. From behind, she heard footsteps.

"There you are, Eva," a voice said loudly. "The matron is looking for you. She needs to finish her count. You better hurry, or she will come' looking for you." It was her father. His voice was calm, but she could recognize anger in his eyes.

Eva pulled away, and Grundy released her as he glared at her father. She ran for the women's barracks.

Bert did not see Grundy raising the butt of the gun behind him, because he was too intent on watching Eva get safely back. When she disappeared inside, Grundy smashed the hard end of the gun into the back of Bert's head, and stomped off.

Bert lay on the hard cold ground all night.

—m—

Hans and Stephen washed dishes in the back kitchen at Percy's Tavern restaurant, one of many establishments owned by Marla's father.

"I hate our lives," Hans said, as the cook brought him a huge pan with burned-on sauce.

"Yes," Stephen agreed.

—m—

On a dark road in a Dutch forest, Sloan and Mica hid guns under the belly of a truck. The vehicle had been purchased with Marla's money, taken in exchange for Peter.

"Marla wanted us to use him," Mica said.

"He's just a kid," Sloan said. "He's had no training."

"Neither did we."

"He's a farmhand. He should be in England milking cows or something," Sloan said.

"He's smart and willing," Mica said. "The rest will come."

"If he stays alive long enough."

"Wait, you like him. That's it, isn't it? What happened to 'there's no room for emotion in a rebellion'?" Mica asked. "Listen Sloan, I like him, too, but Isha is planning the train depot bombing. There aren't many of us. We need more people. They don't know his face, and he might just surprise you."

"Not yet. He can be our runner, but here in England. Give him time to season," Sloan said.

"You like him too much, Sloan. It's affecting your judgment," Mica said, but he smiled. "Me, too."

—ᵐ—

In the morning, on her way to the Bockenburg Camp rock quarry, Eva saw her father sprawled on the ground with a lump on the back of his head.

"Papa, what are you doing here?"

"I must have stumbled," he said, letting her help him up. He looked into her beautiful young face full of worry and love, and the pain in his head seemed a small matter.

CHAPTER 33

JUST LIKE RABBIT HUNTING

(December 1941)

More than a year had passed since Peter's escape from Coventry. At the beginning of December 1941, after several weeks of traveling, he arrived in Soblin, Poland. He was fourteen.

He'd spent the previous year in England running errands and delivering messages, transporting supplies and food, and keeping tabs on Becca. He had gotten used to the sounds of bombs and the destruction of homes and businesses. It had become a way of life. The bombing had stopped in May, but he had continued to live in the underground train station and scrounge for food. He was often seen outside the London concert hall, listening to the concerts as the sounds seeped out the windows, and playing along on his imaginary violin. He had become good at surviving.

That winter, Sloan had relented and agreed to let Peter go to Poland. Sloan told Peter he would see things he might not be able to forget, and he'd do things he might not be able to forgive.

On his first reconnaissance mission, Peter saw the Soblin Ghetto from across a park, and wondered if Sloan was right. Maybe he was too soft and not the commando type, but it was too late to back out. He was committed and in enemy territory, and Hitler was still a monster.

This would be his first act of sabotage, Operation Rakete, or skyrocket. His job was to get the explosives from a mysterious, but well-connected, man named Abraham, who had been a chemist living comfortably. Then the Nazis had taken his house, shut down his lab, and prohibited him from communicating with his counterparts in the United States, who were trying to help him emigrate to be a part of a secret military project.

Abraham now lived in a Soblin sewer with his old housekeeper, Martha, who had been displaced along with him. Although she could keep a house clean and cook a hearty stew, she was not very bright and relatively unattractive. Without Abraham, she would have succumbed to the brutality of the Nazis a long time ago.

Peter made his way to the designated sewer manhole in the middle of a secluded Soblin street. He slid it open enough to climb down, as Sloan had instructed him.

As he descended the ladder into the sewer, the smell of decay and human waste assaulted his nose. Maybe Sloan was right. Maybe he wasn't the rebel soldier type. He grabbed his stomach as it contracted, and held his breath, trying hard not to retch. He hesitated, unsure if he could continue.

But then he thought of Marla, and how she'd forced Sloan and Mica to take him because he'd asked her to. He thought of Eva left behind in the hands of the Nazis, while the Kindertransport took him away to freedom, and what fate had befallen his mother and baby sister. He steeled himself, placed his sleeve over his mouth and nose, and descended into the giant Soblin sewer pipes.

Peter wandered the dark tunnel until he heard echoing voices in the distance. He turned the corner and saw two ragged, filthy people, huddled together on the side of the curved pipe. They looked like Sloan had described. Martha, a woman with few teeth and patchy hair, smiled, her eyebrows perpetually raised in surprise. Sloan, never one for subtleties, had called her a crooked-nose witch. Abraham was a tall thin man with a large head and a scraggly beard. Sloan had described him as the Ichabod Crane look-alike chemist.

Abraham motioned to Peter. "Where did you come from?" he asked, pointing a long finger at him. Peter expected Abraham's big pumpkin head, balanced on such a skinny neck, to fall off at any moment.

"London," Peter answered.

Martha ran her hand nervously through her scraggly patches of frizzy witch hair. "Who leaves London to come here?" she asked.

"I joined the Resistance," Peter said. "What are you doing here?"

"Waiting."

"You can't just sit here waiting."

"Why not? That's what we do. We're Jews," Abraham said.

"If we wait, there won't be many of us left," Peter said.

"He has a point," Abraham said to Martha.

"What do you want?" Martha demanded.

"Ah, Sloan sent me," Peter said.

"You? You're a boy." She laughed. "And you're still alive?"

Abraham raised his eyebrows and looked at Martha. "God has smiled on this one." He held out a shriveled potato. "Here, you must be hungry."

Peter reached out and reluctantly took the disgusting, moldy potato. He held it gingerly between his thumb and finger, examining it. "It's rotten."

"You're new, right?" Abraham asked, scratching his beard.

Peter nodded. "They sent me for the explosives for Operation Rakete."

"If you don't want it . . ." Martha snatched the mushy potato from Peter's hand and stuffed it in her mouth.

"Come back tomorrow. I'll have what you need," Abraham said.

Peter went back the way he came, balancing on the curved concrete edge with his sleeve over his nose and mouth.

Martha shook her head as he walked away. "I dislike that boy. He looks suspiciously like one of them."

The next day, snow flurries streaked the air. December was cold and punishing. Peter hurried along the downtown streets of Soblin to find the sewer witch, the scientist, and the promised explosives.

A crowd had gathered around the newsstand. Curious, Peter pushed his way through to the front to see what all the commotion was about. He saw that everyone was buying newspapers with the headline: "DECEMBER 11, 1941: US DECLARES WAR ON GERMANY!"

Peter slowly backed out of the panicking crowd. His hand quickly covered the smile he could not contain. He knew with the United States on Hitler's tail, it would change everything. For a moment, a tiny piece of happiness sprang up inside him.

Then he frowned and shoved the joy back down. In the chaos of the news, he noticed the bread cart next to the newsstand was left unattended. Sloan had taught him that opportunity was everything. Emotions had no place in war.

Peter looked around. His surge of confidence from the news about the United States made him bold. He reached up, grabbed a loaf of bread, and briskly walked away. When he came to the entrance of the sewer, he glanced around. When the street was empty, he opened the cover and disappeared into the sewer pipes under the city. The smell still repulsed him, but he had become used to no longer having a choice in anything, and acceptance created a tolerance for the intolerable.

Peter found Abraham and Martha in the same spot on the edge of the curved sewer pipe. "There's the young rebel who is too good for our potatoes," Martha said.

Peter held out the loaf of bread to her. "Thought you might like some bread."

Martha eyed it. "What? Did you steal it?"

Peter glanced down, ashamed. He nodded.

Martha smiled, showing the few teeth she had left. "Good! You might make it after all."

Abraham laughed. "I have your explosives, but tell Sloan to be careful when he hooks up the wires. The connectors are loose, and I don't have the tools to fix them. It's sad when science has to be used to destroy things."

"Maybe you won't have to stay down here very much longer. The United States just declared war on Germany!" Peter smiled, happy to be able to give them the news.

Abraham smiled. "We will dance when Hitler is defeated, but he has taken everything we own, and we have no other place to go."

"Me too. I need to go now. We have people to rescue," Peter said with artificial bravado. He picked up the knapsack with the explosives and marched off, like a child entering a football game, confident he can score.

"I like that boy," he heard Martha say to Abraham, as she chewed a big piece of bread. "He's going to be a good rebel, because he can blend in with them."

"I told you God likes that one."

"I thought God liked us all," Martha said.

Abraham scratched his scraggly beard and shrugged. "Ah, you know, perhaps some more than others."

In the strange echoing sounds the sewer system made, a voice reverberated against the pipes. The sound of Peter's quiet singing whispered along the foul-smelling underground space.

We are marching forward,
With God by our side.
We will not leave our path,
For He will be our guide.

When Peter passed the bread stand, he left his last coin there.

———◊———

Noah, the defiant orphan, was now twelve, but still small for his age. He peeked around a building inside the Soblin Ghetto.

He darted out and rolled under one of two gas vans waiting to be loaded. Noah unhooked the hose that delivered the poisonous exhaust into the back of the van that killed the unwilling passengers before they reached their destination.

A Nazi soldier opened the back of the van. Noah recognized him as Dirk, one of the soldiers at his escape attempt with the pole. Dirk pushed in old people, women, and children. "It's not that difficult! Get in the van!" he shouted.

Noah's grip slipped, and he dropped the hose. He looked up, and Dirk was bending down, staring at him.

Dirk grabbed his arm and pulled him out from under the van. "What are you doing, trying to escape?" He shoved Noah into the van so hard that he hit his head on the floor. Beside them, other soldiers loaded the van Noah hadn't been able to reach.

The doors shut and the locks pulled across, leaving Noah trapped among the crowd chosen for death. The people in the van clung to their loved ones. Noah sat alone in a corner.

The engine started. Inside, the van was dark as it rocked back and forth, occasionally hitting a bump. People wept and prayed. An old lady passed out from fear. A little girl with matted hair and rags for clothes cried, as her mother hugged her tightly.

"Where are we going?" the little girl asked her mother.

"Wherever God takes us," her mother said.

The two gas vans pulled off the road, into a forest near a wide muddy river in the Polish countryside. Dirk opened the back of the van; then, startled, he jumped back. The people in the back of the van stared at him.

Dirk motioned to Adler, the other driver. "Quick! Come here! They're still alive!"

Adler struggled to bend down as he looked under the van. "The hose broke!"

"It was that kid," Dirk said, pointing accusingly to Noah. "The bamboo pole kid. I should have known."

Adler opened the other van, and dead bodies fell out. The little girl screamed when she saw the cherry red color of their skin from the severe carbon monoxide poisoning. Her mother covered the little girl's mouth to stop her horrified screams. Noah looked at the bodies tumbling out on top of each other.

Dirk roughly pulled the people, arrogant enough to still be alive, out of his van. "Everyone out!"

Noah, dizzy and disoriented from the bump on his head and the rough ride, stumbled out by himself. He was almost the last one off.

"Move out!" Dirk shouted to them.

Adler and Dirk herded the people to the deep swift river, driving them to the edge. "Enter the water and don't stop!" Adler shouted.

No one moved. Dirk suddenly pulled out his gun and shot the little girl. He shoved her forcefully into the muddy swift river.

The crowd jolted and moved, walking into the cold river water until it was nearly over their heads. They cried and called for their mothers and fathers, their husbands, and their God. They held each other's hands, but they continued marching into the water.

The little girl, bloodied and missing part of her head, floated quietly down the river, carried by its current. The girl's mother wept great sobs of grief, gulping the air as she walked into the cold water. She did not stop. There were a few bubbles, and then nothing. Without her daughter, death was a welcome comfort.

Only a few more people remained on the land, waiting their turn to die. Noah slowed at the water's edge. He was dizzy from his head injury. He looked up at the nearby woods, which spun in his vision, causing more disorientation.

The mother's submerged dead body sprung unexpectedly to the surface, floating swiftly as if to catch up to her daughter. Adler and Dirk, startled by the body, turned and shot at it.

Noah startled as well, and, without thinking, turned and ran.

The Nazis shot at the escaping boy, but Noah was so little and so dizzy that he couldn't run straight. Their bullets missed his uncontrollable serpentine zigzag. He ran crookedly into the woods. Dirk ran after him, shooting indiscriminately into the trees. Adler, unused to any exertion, remained by the river.

Noah's footsteps were so light that even in the forest, he barely made a sound. He rounded a clump of trees.

Then someone grabbed him from behind. A hand covered his mouth. He disappeared into the woods, swallowed up by the trees.

Dirk could no longer see the little boy who'd had the audacity to sabotage his van. He stopped running and twisted each way, looking for Noah. He shot randomly into the woods, and then stood still, listening for the escaping sounds of the little saboteur. But the forest was quiet, giving nothing away of the young fugitive. Dirk lowered his gun and spit on the ground.

Dirk went back to the gas vans, looking over his shoulder.

"Did you get him?" Adler asked.

Dirk nodded. "Just like rabbit hunting," he lied.

They laughed and climbed into their empty vans, ready for another load of people to poison.

—⚏—

Inside the large clump of bushes, a false floor lifted up. Peter, who was carrying the knapsack that Abraham had given him, pulled the boy he'd grabbed down into the underground tunnel.

"Be quiet and follow me, if you want to live," Peter said, making his voice deep and trying to sound like a rebel who understands the danger but doesn't care. He forgot to watch where he was walking and stepped on an icy patch. His foot slipped.

He fell, and the knapsack with the explosives tumbled with him. He held the knapsack up, and his head took the brunt of the fall, hitting the edge of a tree root.

The boy watched him bounce. He leaned down. "Are you okay?"

Peter nodded, embarrassed. "Don't worry, the connectors are loose. It won't go off." He gingerly picked up the bag. He straightened up, rubbed his head, and strode off, a commando in training and lucky to be alive.

"Have you done this long?" the boy asked.

"Yes. It can be treacherous. There is danger all around," Peter said in his deep, fake rebel voice.

"Oh," the boy said. He followed Peter as they walked along a dark tunnel.

They came to a large underground cavern with many people milling around. Carbide lanterns lit the area, casting strange shadows on the walls. Mica and Sloan were almost unrecognizable in dirty camouflage rebel clothes. "Peter, you made it!" Mica said. "How'd you like the sewer?"

"I didn't. Here." He handed Mica the explosives from Abraham. "But I have better news. America's in the war now!" Peter said with a big smile.

Mica let out a yell. "Hitler's got the big guns to deal with now!"

"Finally, the Yanks have found their backbone," Sloan said. "I was wondering if they had one."

A woman stepped out from the shadows. She was the rugged rebel they called "Iron Isha," who would have been pretty if she wasn't dressed in men's clothes and covered in dirt. She wore a scarf tied tightly around her head. "Or they didn't want to be next. Either way, they're in," she said, "and that's good."

"If they crack the Nazis' new Berlin communication code, and now with the Allies on attack, we might really have a chance to win this war," Sloan said. "Or just bomb them to smithereens. That would work, too."

The boy emerged from the dark tunnel and stood up. Sloan pointed at him. "What is that?"

"Refused to be drowned," Peter said. "Can't run straight, but he's fast. He outsmarted the Nazis."

"So, you've cheated death, Little Man. Have a seat," Sloan said. He looked at Mica. "Looks like our rebellion has become a kindergarten."

Mica handed both boys a piece of bread. The younger boy tore into it like a ravenous dog. Peter looked at Mica. "The sewer stunk, and their potatoes were rotten."

"We have a cream puff on our hands, Sloan," Mica said, laughing.

"No cream puffs allowed!" Sloan shouted.

In the light of the carbide lanterns, Peter stared at the boy. "Do I know you?" Peter asked.

"No, no one knows me."

"Yes, I do." Peter paused, remembering a face he could never forget. "You're the stowaway in the luggage on the Kindertransport. I was on that train."

The boy smiled and nodded. "The Nazi kicked me off and put me in jail, but I escaped."

Sloan and Mica laughed. "He really is brave," Sloan said.

"I'm an orphaned Jew. I don't really have a choice," the boy said.

"You're wrong, son. We all have choices, and you've chosen to live or die trying," Sloan said. "What's your name?"

"Noah."

"Are you from the ghetto?" Mica asked.

Noah nodded. "Been there since I was little."

"Since you were little?" Sloan mumbled to the small twelve-year-old boy. "You know your way around it?"

"Around it, once over it, and sometimes under it," Noah said, smiling.

"Under it? Well, welcome to Operation Rakete," Sloan said, his eyebrows raised, as he put out his huge hand to shake Noah's tiny one.

———※———

At the Bockenburg Camp, Eva and her mother washed clothes in buckets. They dunked the well-worn and filthy clothes in the brackish water.

"When you were young, what did you think your life would be like?" Eva asked, as she scrubbed a bloodstain out of a pair of pants.

"I thought it would be lovely. I didn't know people could be so cruel. I guess I should have warned you," her mother said, as she dunked the clothes in the murky water.

Eva put her arm around her mother, and for once, her mother didn't pull away.

———※———

The next night, all was set for Operation Rakete. Noah led Peter, wearing his shoeshine rucksack, to a patch of bushes next to the fence outside the Soblin Ghetto. He parted the bushes, revealing a hole in the ground that led under the fence.

"You really did dig a tunnel out of the ghetto," Peter said, astonished.

"I had to do something. They took away my pole," Noah said, smiling. "With the tunnel, I could go and get bread. No one notices a kid like me gone. They can't even tell me apart from the others."

"Why did you go back?"

"Got nowhere else to go," Noah said. "I'll go first, then you throw me the rucksack, but I'm not a good catcher."

"It has an explosive device in it," Peter said, rolling his eyes. "Try to be a good catcher today, okay? 'Leave no room for failure.' My father used to say that," he said, remembering better days.

"He didn't know me," Noah said. The brave little boy looked worried, but he was prepared to do his best to survive another day.

Peter eyed the tunnel hole. "Are you sure I'm going to fit in there?"

Noah shrugged. "We'll soon see."

"Wait. You don't know?"

"Hey, it was Sloan's plan, not mine. I'm not a rebel, I'm just hungry," Noah confessed. "Just keep moving through the tunnel. Don't stop." Then, he was gone into the hidden hole in the ground.

"Thanks for the advice, from a kid who couldn't even hide in a luggage compartment!"

"I've learned a lot since then." Noah's voice was muffled, as he crawled through the tunnel, an experienced ghetto escapee.

Peter, much bigger than Noah, hesitated at the hole. He moved one way and then the other, trying to judge the right angle to avoid being wedged in an underground grave and certain death.

Noah soon popped up on the other side of the fence, moving the woodpile tied together with dried vines that covered the hole on the other side. He motioned to Peter to throw him the rucksack.

Peter hesitated. This was never going to work. He could hear the fence hum with electricity. He should never have listened to Sloan and Mica. They would be waiting for him in the truck at the park nearby, but he was about to die. What choice did he have? He was going to die sometime. It might as well be that day.

Peter gently tossed the rucksack with its small explosive device over the tall fence. Noah reached for the tumbling rucksack, caught it, and then lost his grip, bobbling it. Peter jumped down, flattening his body, covering his head with his arms, and waiting for the explosion.

Nothing happened. No explosion. He looked up. Noah grimaced and shrugged sheepishly, but held the rucksack up like a prized trophy. "Leave no room for failure!" he whispered.

It was Peter's turn to burrow under the fence into the ghetto like a desperate rodent. He stuck his head in, wiggled his shoulders, and then disappeared into the hole. He inched his way through the short tunnel under the electric fence, contemplating how his life had led him to breaking into a Nazi ghetto where he might never get out.

He could hear the hum of the electric fence above him. When the tunnel's darkness engulfed him, he panicked. He knew he should not be doing this, but it was too late to back out. He was committed. Noah was right, he had to keep moving.

He broke out in a sweat. He inched forward, wiggling his legs and pulling with his arms. Suddenly, his back wedged against the top of the tunnel. He tried to pull himself out of it, but he couldn't move. He twisted his arms to scrape the dirt ceiling, but he couldn't reach it. He couldn't move forward or backward. He was stuck in a tunnel, under an electric fence with Nazi police guards nearby. Perfect. He felt he would die in the darkness underground, alone, already buried. Maybe he should have stayed in England. Even the Coventry farm seemed like a decent place compared to an earthen tunnel tomb.

Then he thought of Olga, the cow, and her struggle to give birth. He had not given up. He'd helped Olga by twisting the stuck calf to save its life. He would not give up now. He used every muscle and twisted his body, until he finally broke free and inched on, this time not stopping until he climbed out of the hole on the other side behind the bush.

"It's bigger than you think, isn't it?" Noah asked.

"No," Peter said. He brushed off the dirt and took the rucksack from Noah. "Nice catch." They replaced the tied-together woodpile and moved casually into the ghetto yard.

Noah led him to the main station, where the police guards gathered to smoke and complain about the disgusting people living in the ghetto. Peter nodded to Noah, as he slipped Abraham's explosive creation out of the shoeshine pack.

Peter attached the detonator wires to the small explosive device that Abraham, the sewer scientist, had fashioned from TNT and wires hooked to the sometimes faulty connectors. He set the timer that would press against the wires on the connectors, creating friction, and making sparks that would ignite the TNT. He hooked the device under the guard station, and motioned for Noah to exit the area.

As they backed out, a guard grabbed Peter and Noah by the neck, stopping them. Noah looked up. It was Adler. Noah's body tensed.

Adler stared at him. "I thought Dirk killed you in the woods."

"Me? No, must have been somebody else. I'm alive," Noah said, patting himself down to prove it. He shrugged. "We all look alike." He looked quickly at the bomb underneath the guard station. It could go off at any moment.

Adler pointed to Peter. "He doesn't look like one of you."

Peter stepped forward, pulling away from Adler's grasp. Sounding disgusted, he said, "I'm not one of them. I'm Johan. My father's a policeman. I brought him some food."

"You that shoeshine boy?" Adler asked.

Peter nodded and patted his rucksack. "I'll give your boots a good polish the next time I see you, for a reduced charge."

"You need to get out of this area," Adler said to Noah.

"I'll take this boy back to the central area," Peter said.

"Who's your father?" Adler asked.

"I'll tell him to watch this one," Peter called, glancing over at the device underneath the guard station near the back fence.

Peter grabbed Noah's arm and quickly marched him away without responding. He sneered at Noah. "What are you doing in the forbidden zone? Don't you Jews know how to read?" Peter shouted. "Or are you too stupid?"

Adler smiled, but followed them for a way.

When Noah and Peter rounded the first building, Noah let out his breath. "How many minutes before it goes off?" Noah asked.

The explosives blew.

"None," Peter said. "Run."

Inside the compound, everyone's attention turned to the explosion. The policemen shouted and ran from the outlying stations to investigate.

Peter and Noah ran to the guard station, now empty. Peter pulled out a long length of thin but sturdy rope with a loop on the end from his rucksack and dropped it on the ground like he had been told. Then they turned and fled.

"What happened?" Noah asked Peter.

Peter shrugged. "The connectors were loose."

They ran behind the bush, pushed off the bundled woodpile, and crawled through the tunnel, appearing on the other side by the bushes.

"But did you see it? It worked," Peter said, as he straightened up.

—⟋⟍—

The only ones who paid any attention to Noah and Peter, as they ran, were a mother, father, and their three small boys, who watched with interest as they sprinted away. The tall gaunt mother wore a housedress that was stained and ripped under the arms. The father's two black eyes and swollen jaw told the story of an unrelenting, but losing, scuffle with authority.

Marc, seven, wore pants that were several sizes too small. Normie, five, had the bruise of a handprint across his cheek. The youngest boy was Kramden. He was three, with light brown hair, and a smile that belied the fact that he could not remember anything besides the ghetto. He had never known a toy, or music, or a playground, and had no memories outside the fence. The red marks on the boys' arms and necks pointed to vicious bedbug bites. They watched Peter and Noah run for the hidden exit.

The father gathered his desperate family and ran to the woodpile as he saw the boys appear on the other side of the fence. "This is the answer to our prayers," he said to his wife.

"But we can't make it through that hole."

"At least they will make it," he reasoned. She nodded, tears flooding her eyes with the realization that she would be saying goodbye to the children that it was her duty to protect. She was sending them to freedom with strangers.

"You there! Boys! Wait, please, stop. Help us, please," the father shouted after Peter and Noah.

—⟋⟍—

Peter looked at the truck waiting for them in the distance, and then at the ghetto, alive with chaos and confusion as planned. Hesitantly, Peter and Noah turned back to help the family.

They watched as the thin and pale father, tasting freedom for his family, sent his three boys through the tunnel under the fence. They easily made it. They were small enough and did not carry the fear of the dire consequences of their actions. They were just obeying their father.

As each boy appeared, Peter sent him to Noah to be hidden behind the bushes, out of sight of the policemen. The father stopped and listened, straining to hear. There was no howling hum emitted from the fence's electricity. The explosion had temporarily taken down the power. "There's no electricity. You must climb the fence now," he said urgently to his wife.

"Are you sure?" she asked, suspicious of the killer fence that trapped them in the ghetto.

"Listen, it's quiet."

She nodded.

"The fence is down. Go. Go. Go," the father whispered to her. "I will help you, then I will be right behind you."

She nodded. He lifted her onto the fence, and she climbed as fast as the awkward task would allow, but she was weak from hunger and constant worry. She moved slowly, breathing heavily from exertion. She had nearly reached the top when the fence's frightening hum suddenly returned. She looked down at her husband with the blank fear of death on her face, but nothing happened.

He nodded. "Keep going. You're not grounded. You'll be okay. Just jump off the fence at the top."

She reached for the last wire. She was almost over.

A shot exploded. A bullet hit her shoulder. It knocked her off balance. She grabbed the barbed wire with her hands. She cried out in pain, but flung her leg over the top of the barbed wire fence in a last-ditch effort to get to the other side. Her dress twisted around the barbed wire, so, although she had somehow made it over, she hung trapped by her clothes.

Another bullet hit her arm. She released her grip. Her dress ripped, freeing her from the wire's clutches, and she fell. On the way down, her legs tangled in the wire, ripping her skin. When her arms hit the ground, making a full circle circuit, she was electrocuted on the freedom side of the ghetto fence.

Peter could hear the sizzle and smell the burning flesh. Noah had told him that an occasional rabbit or a wayward cat or two often fell victim to the grilling of the fence, but he was not prepared for the gruesome electric death. The woman's hair and skin were singed. Burn marks appeared where the electricity entered her body, and immediately her skin bubbled into blisters and turned red.

Despite the shock of his wife's horrifying electrocution, the father only had a moment to size up the situation. "Take my children. Keep them safe," he said to Peter through the fence.

He waved to his boys, still hidden behind the bushes, but protected by Noah from witnessing the horror of their mother's death. "I love you. Remember that. I love you!" the father called to his children. "Go with them. Don't look back. We will come to you shortly. We will all be together. Go! Now!"

Frightened, the three brothers all ran toward the park after Peter and Noah, obeying their father's final command. Peter remembered when his own mother had lied to him, that she would shortly follow him to England, that they would soon be reunited in a new country. Without the lie, he wouldn't have gone, but to discover the deceit was overwhelming, and the feeling of being abandoned left a hollowness that could never be filled.

He wondered if these boys would ever be able to forgive their father. Peter knew he hadn't fully forgiven his mother until he helped Olga deliver her calf. Then, he'd understood the connection of a mother to her child and how his mother might be willing to do anything, even the unthinkable, to save her children.

The police guards' flashlight beams hit the father near the fence in the forbidden zone, as he shouted to his children. Shots rang out. The father crumpled beside his wife, dead, but on the ghetto side of the fence.

The children ran on with Peter, unaware they were orphans. They were focused only on escape from their prison, obeying their father's last words. They ran across the park and through the open market to where a farmer's truck was loaded with produce, hay, and burlap sacks.

Sloan and Mica, dressed like local farmers, sat on the front seat of the truck. They turned when they saw the children running toward them.

"What happened?" Sloan demanded.

"Went off a little early," Peter said, shrugging.

"So, the building blew up too early, and you brought me three children that I have no escape plan for? Not an overwhelming success, young rebel," Sloan said, shaking his head.

"They followed us out. The police shot their mother and father," Peter whispered to Sloan. "I couldn't leave them."

"Don't get personally involved. It makes you weak," Sloan scolded.

"Get them on the truck, now!" Mica said, glancing back at the ghetto.

Peter pulled up the burlap bags to reveal an entrance to a hollowed tunnel under the hay. He lifted Marc, Normie, and Kramden up and pushed them through the hole. He motioned to Noah, who ducked down and followed them in to the crowded spot.

Peter walked over to Sloan. "Can I drive the truck?"

Sloan shook his head. "Not today, the cab is full."

"No, it's not. There's still room. I'm a good driver. I used to drive my father's meat truck when I was little."

"We're waiting for one more. Get in the back, meat-man," Mica said.

Peter shook his head and grumbled. "Why can't he get in the back?"

The faulty connectors had sped up their departure. The flames of Operation Rakete still lit the darkening sky behind them in the ghetto. It was a bit of a risk exploding early. Although Sloan was not pleased, Peter considered it a celebration of sabotage and not bad for a new rebel boy and his young ghetto guide.

A man inside the ghetto threw the loop of the rope that Peter had left over the edge of the abandoned guardhouse. He put the other end of the rope through the loop and pulled it through. With a running start, he swung over the fence, as smoke billowed from the explosion, giving him thick cover.

The man ran from the ghetto toward them. He ran out of the smoke. It was Jules.

He climbed into the front seat of the truck next to Sloan and Mica, putting on an old farmer's shirt. He was free, but it was still a long way to England. Marla, who had become good at negotiating with Sloan, insisted that a condition for a very large sum of money he needed was to get Jules safely to England. The rebel "Iron Isha" had bribed a Nazi officer to discover Jules's location from his records in the basement of Berlin headquarters, and the rescue was planned. Soon after, both Iron Isha and her Nazi informant had been arrested at the handoff of additional records. That had ended the rebels' access to Jewish inmate locations and slowed their rescues, but Jules had been saved, and Marla would be happy.

Reluctantly, Peter crawled into the back of the truck and returned the burlap bags to their cover. Inside the truck bed, he smiled at Noah and nodded. "Operation Rakete!" he said excitedly. "Successful!" His smile fell into a sneer. "But they should have let me drive."

Much later, as the moon climbed high in the sky, the truck reached the border between Poland and Germany. Peter dug a hole through the hay. He and Noah watched as Sloan, Mica, and Jules sat in the cab of the battered truck.

The three rescued boys slept, exhausted from their daring flight from the ghetto. The fake farmers in the cab pulled their hats down low on their heads and buttoned their coats up around their necks.

At the border, the truck was stopped by a guard who stepped out in front of the security gate. "Halt! Where are you headed to in the middle of the night?" he demanded suspiciously.

"Home," Sloan said.

"Where have you been?" the guard asked.

"Delivering potatoes," Mica said.

The guard eyed them. "Let me see your papers."

Sloan, Mica, and Jules handed him their papers. He looked at them and handed them back, his eyes lingering on the truck. "You don't have any Jews hiding in there, do you?"

"No sir, just some hay and a few potatoes," Mica said casually.

The guard waved them through, and they drove across the German border.

Then the guard raised his gun and randomly shot into the truckload of hay. "Just making sure the potatoes are dead."

Once out of sight down the road, Sloan pulled the truck to a stop. Marc and Normie crawled out from under the burlap bags, seed bags, and bales of hay on the truck bed, crying. Unflappable Noah followed them with his eyes open wide, looking stunned.

Peter emerged from the hay, carrying Kramden. The boy was shot dead, the blood barely visible from the perfect hole in the side of his tiny head from the guard's random bullet.

Sloan walked over to Peter and took the lifeless boy in his arms. "He died free of the Nazis. That is more than he had before you rescued him. Emotions serve no purpose in war. We must move on and protect the other children," he said harshly, pointing to Marc and Normie, who sobbed uncontrollably as Noah tried to comfort them.

—⁓—

Noah knew how the boys felt. He'd watched his parents beaten to death for trying to protect their home on November 9, 1938. He was little and hadn't really understood, but he knew the Nazis had no right to destroy their home. His parents had stood up to the Nazis, and the retaliation was swift.

On that long-ago night, when the blood from a blow to his mother's head had splattered in the Nazi's face, Noah saw his chance and fled the house his parents had bravely refused to vacate. The Nazis hadn't even bothered to chase him. A boy his age on the street would be dead by morning, especially on that night when Nazis stalked the streets, hunting Jews. But not Noah. He had an uncanny ability to live.

He'd wandered the streets that night in a trance of shock and horror, an orphan whose last images of his parents were brutal and bloody. He couldn't even remember how he got to the orphanage, but he could remember the sausages he was fed that night. Although not much had changed with the brutality, somehow, since he'd found Peter, he didn't feel so alone. A small sliver of hope had returned. Outside the hay truck that night at the border, Noah tried to comfort the other two boys.

—⁓—

Peter nodded to Sloan. He tried desperately to separate himself from the despair and anguish he felt. The random unfairness of life always shocked Peter.

"Peter, we need to finish our business here and move on. We've got to get through to Holland, yet. Do you understand?" Sloan asked.

Peter nodded. He watched as Sloan bent down and kissed the assassinated little boy's forehead, before he gently laid Kramden in the ditch and covered him with weeds. The hardened commando still harbored compassion for those taken by unexplained cruelty, and Peter knew that it was impossible to separate emotion from war.

—❦—

Several days later, Marla paced around a bench in London's Hyde Park. Anti-aircraft guns stood behind the locked iron gates. Gunnery sergeants watched the sky through binoculars.

Sloan and Peter stepped out of the shadows with Marc and Normie, who'd escaped the ghetto, but whose price for freedom had been the lives of their mother, father, and little brother. Marla ran and hugged Peter and Sloan.

"Well, if it isn't my favorite cream puff," Sloan said, as he hugged her. Behind them was Jules, Marla's friend and German Jewish organization worker.

"Here he is, Blue Eyes," Sloan said. "Like I promised."

She ran and embraced Jules. "Jules! You finally made it! I'm so happy to see you."

Peter nodded at the kids and stepped forward. Marla saw their sleepy faces. "Oh, my goodness." She knelt down to them. "Hello, children. Come with me. Everything is going to be better now." She stood up, and Sloan and Peter were gone.

"Where did they go?" She looked at Jules. "Why are they always doing that?"

"Dramatic effect. There's one more surprise," Jules said.

Noah walked out of the shadows. Marla stared at him. Noah stared back, and she broke into a smile. "My little stowaway?"

He nodded.

"Not so little any more," she said.

"It took me awhile, but I finally made it, thanks to Peter."

"Peter?" She smiled. "Indeed. So, come, welcome to England, at last."

Jules gathered the children, picking up Normie, who was so sleepy he could barely walk.

"So, Jules, what do you plan to do in England?" Marla asked her Kindertransport friend.

"Join the British Army and fight Hitler," Jules said with a smile. "I am a good soldier with a very personal grudge."

Sloan and Peter strolled around the locked park. Peter looked at Sloan, who was smiling.

"You like her. You don't like anyone, but you like Marla," Peter said.

"No, I don't. She's demanding and annoying."

"Yes, you do. You're in love with Marla."

"There's no time for love in war, mate," Sloan said.

Peter smiled. "The war has to end, sometime, mate," he said, imitating Sloan.

"Let's see if we can speed that up." Sloan put his arm around Peter. "Do you think she likes me?" he asked, like a schoolboy.

"Who wouldn't be overwhelmed by your charms?" Peter teased.

They both laughed, as they melted into the busy pace of downtown London and a chance for a real meal before heading back to Germany.

CHAPTER 34

SPARKS FLEW

(June 1942)

Peter, who at first had resented the Kindertransport, had come to agree that his people should be saved at any cost, including family separation. He had since added sabotage, murder, and the heavy use of explosives to his list of acceptable responses to Hitler. It was war, and Peter was right in the middle of it, a soldier of the underground.

There was too much to do, and he needed recruits. While he was in England, he decided to find Hans and Stephen, the football stars who'd never minded taking a hit. He hoped they would join him.

—ɱ—

A farmer drove a donkey cart to the old Pellbrooke Mansion in the English countryside, where many of the Kindertransport children were housed.

Peter jumped out of the back of the cart. He'd been eleven when he'd ridden the Kindertransport; now he was fifteen and as tall as a man. Like his father, he had gotten his height, suddenly.

Peter pointed to the old stone mansion. "Are you sure this is it?" he asked the farmer driving the cart.

"It's hard to miss them and their football games."

"That's them. Well, I thank you then for the ride from the station."

Peter waved to the farmer. He turned and walked up the hill. "Definitely a step up from Dovercourt," he muttered to himself.

Peter ran into the boys' room in the mansion. "Any football players from Berlin in here?"

Hans and Stephen stared at him. "Peter?" Hans asked.

"The same," Peter said.

They hugged each other like lost brothers.

"You've grown," Stephen said, looking him up and down.

"We heard about Coventry. Where have you been?" Hans asked, excited to see his old friend.

"Germany and Poland. I joined the Resistance."

Eva and her father, still dusty from their day's labor at the gravel pit, sat on the ground between the barracks in the Bockenburg Camp. The sun set and night settled in. A train whistle blew in the distance.

"I wonder what the boys are doing in England," Eva thought aloud.

"They're not breaking rocks, that's for sure," Bert said.

"What about William? Do you think he ever thinks of us?"

"I think William mainly thinks about William," Bert said. He patted Eva's arm and nodded with his chin toward the shadowy ditch in front of the wall that kept the prisoners in range of the guard towers. A prisoner hunched over, crept along the side, keeping hidden in the shadows.

The prisoner turned as if calculating the distance to the ditch. Eva saw the prisoner's face. It wasn't a man. It was a woman, dressed like a man. She wore a piece of cloth tied tightly around her head. She crouched down and, under the cover of darkness, sprinted toward the ditch. When she reached it, she jumped, her long legs stretching to reach the other side. Unbelievably, she made it.

Eva wrapped her arms around her father and whispered, "She's going to make it. She's going to escape!"

Like a cat, the woman climbed the wall, somehow finding crevices to cling to. She was almost to the top, and Eva held her breath. A shot ran out from the guard tower, but it missed. The woman threw her leg over the top of the wall, but the shot had notified the other guard towers.

A barrage of bullets rained down on the woman who had the audacity to try to escape. Her body jerked as it was riddled with shots, and she fell off the wall and into the ditch. The guards returned to their posts as if nothing had happened.

Eva, horrified at the woman's murder, looked sadly at her father. "She didn't make it."

—◊—

That night, as the boys sat on their bed at the Pellbrooke Mansion, Peter leaned close to Hans and Stephen, so the others couldn't hear. "The Germans are killing all the Jews in gas chambers and then burning them up in ovens," he said.

"What? That can't be true," Hans said, shaking his head.

"Which part, that Germans would kill Jews, or the ovens?" Peter asked.

"The oven part sounds like Hansel and Gretel," Stephen said, as he shivered, knowing that it was real.

"Only this isn't a children's tale. It's real. I've seen the crematoriums at the Reinigen Camp in Lodansk, Poland. The smoke. The piles of dead bodies waiting to be burned," Peter said. "Killing us the old-fashioned way was taking too long for Hitler."

"It can't be," Hans said, shaking his head.

"It is," Peter said, nodding.

Hans hung his head, and his shoulders slumped. "Nothing seems real anymore. The Kindertransport seems so long ago."

Stephen looked at Peter. "Remember when that ugly Nazi made you play your violin?"

Peter nodded and shivered. "My fingers felt like rocks that would break if I moved them."

"I thought it was over for you," Stephen said.

They laughed.

"Have you heard anything about your family?" Peter asked.

Hans picked up a letter. "Here's the last letter I received from my mother. 'Dear Hans, I am sad to say Oma passed away of typhus. Many people in the Jewish Residential District in Dinsdorf are being deported to another camp in Poland, and I'm sure our turn will be coming soon. This will be my last letter to you. How our beautiful lives came to this point, I don't understand. Here we are, facing what will surely be the end, apart and frightened. Please know deep down in your heart how much we love you and how happy we are that your life was saved. Make the most of it. With all my love, Your Mother.'"

When Hans looked up, Peter stood next to him, his face solemn and searching. "That's why I came," Peter said.

"Why?" Hans said.

"I was angry to leave Germany. Now, I understand why our parents sent us away, to save us. But Hitler will not be stopped unless we do something. We have to stand up to him to save others."

"So, what do you want us to do?" Hans asked.

"Fight the Nazis," Peter said.

"You're kidding, right?" Hans asked, smiling.

"I've joined the rebels," Peter said.

"Jewish rebels?" Hans asked.

Peter nodded.

"Aren't you scared?" Stephen asked.

"All the time, but I'm more scared of doing nothing."

"We're going back to the hostel next week. We miss London, even with the risk of bombs, but that's about as brave as I get. I'll never set foot on German soil again," Hans said.

"I'm sorry, Peter," Stephen said. "My parents wouldn't want me to risk my life again, after all they went through to save me. I may be the only one left from my family."

"You were always so bold," Peter said, disappointedly.

"Not like you, Peter," Stephen said. "You were never afraid to be yourself."

"When did you become a fearless German hero?" Hans asked with a smile.

"I'm a late bloomer."

—∿—

A week later, inside a crop duster plane flying high over the countryside of Poland, Sloan slid the door open as the motor hummed loudly. Mica adjusted the parachute bag attached to Peter's back. "All right. We are here. Remember to pull the cord. It's as easy as that," Mica said to Peter.

Peter peered out the door. The high altitude wind whipped his face. It was a long way down.

"You'll be fine. It's actually quite a thrill," Mica said.

"Are you ready to be a famous rebel?" Sloan asked him.

Peter shook his head.

"Too late," Sloan said, as he nodded to Mica.

Mica grabbed Peter from behind and pushed him out the airplane door. Peter screamed, as the wind whipped his face. He was falling rapidly to his death, until he remembered what he was supposed to do. He pulled his ripcord, and the parachute deployed.

Mica's and Sloan's laughter could not be heard as it was lost in the wind as they fell. They landed safely near Peter, who reached the ground without any broken bones.

—◊◊◊—

Several days later, Peter returned to shine shoes on the sidewalk outside the Soblin Ghetto's electrified fence, waiting to rendezvous with Sloan and Mica.

He polished and shined Adler's shoes. He spat on the toe of one shoe with disgust, shining the shoe with a rag in his hand and revenge on his mind.

The ghetto gate opened. Peter watched as two young police officers only a few years older than him marched a pregnant mother, her young son, and a few others at gunpoint through the high grass.

"What did they do?" Peter asked Adler, pointing to the mother and boy.

"They prayed," Adler explained matter-of-factly. "Jews can't follow rules. They aren't civilized."

The officers lined the group up beside a huge ditch outside the ghetto, just a short distance from the playground behind them. The death ditch was hidden from the rest of Soblin by a grove of trees, but it was within viewing distance of the others inside the ghetto fence. It created fear in the rest of the ghetto residents if they had to watch others die.

Peter saw the boy, about eleven, reach out to hold his pregnant mother's hand. The boy glanced nervously around. Peter saw his frightened face. He stared as the boy turned around and looked back at the people watching from inside the ghetto fence. It was Charlie, Becca's friend from school. Peter was sure of it. He would never forget the face of the boy whose father had pulled him out of the train window.

Peter quickly finished shining Adler's shoes. "No charge," he said, as he put his shoeshine supplies back in his rucksack. He stood watching the unfolding scene of mass murder, unable to do anything, but unable to look away. Adler, unaffected by the killing, re-entered the ghetto gate, with nicely shined shoes.

In the field outside the ghetto, Evelyn stared down at Charlie's innocent, brave face and forced a smile. "Charlie," she said, "I think this is it, my love."

"Mutti, I'm glad I didn't go on that train. Then you would have died alone," Charlie said with the pure love of a child, one who accepted death as easily as he had accepted the unexpected retrieval from the train. "I'm glad we prayed, even if today they will kill us for it. At least God knows we didn't forget him."

"I love you, Charlie," Evelyn said. "You are the pride of Germany."

The police officers raised their guns.

"Look at me, Charlie," his mother said. "I want you to see my smile."

Charlie looked up at her smiling face and said, "I love you!"

"I love you more," his mother said. "Hold tightly to my hand."

When the young guard raised his gun to shoot, Peter saw it was Kurt, the boy who ran with the bully Wolfgang at Peter's school in Berlin.

Kurt paused. The other young guard slapped him on the back, laughing. "What's the matter, Kurt?" he said. It was Wolfgang, Peter's school tormentor. Both boys were now twenty-one years old, and hard-core murderers.

"I'm about to shoot a kid and a pregnant woman," Kurt said.

"He's not a kid. He's a Jew. You're doing him a favor," Wolfgang said.

Kurt shook his head. "I don't know. He looks like that kid from our old school."

"If you can't handle it, why did you ask for this assignment?" Wolfgang asked.

"I didn't. You volunteered us," Kurt said.

Through the fence, Arnold, Charlie's father, watched the preparation for the assassination of his family. He held his head and yelled in agony. "No!"

Peter watched as their guns mowed down Charlie, Charlie's pregnant mother, and the rest of those forced to the edge of the ditch. They fell into the ditch, disappearing in the next breath, their lives snatched in a second by swift but sure gunshots.

Wolfgang and Kurt, another chore completed, returned inside the ghetto fence. Arnold turned away from the murder pit, burying his face in his hands.

Peter stared, stunned at the coldness of the killing. "Charlie," he whispered. "They got Charlie."

As Peter remembered the moment when Charlie had disappeared from the train window and was pulled back by his father, he saw Charlie's hands grab the top of the ditch. They hadn't gotten Charlie. The fall of his mother must have pulled him down, but the bullets, unbelievably, had missed him.

Peter looked around. Wolfgang and Kurt were back inside the gates, the cold-blooded murders they had committed a few seconds ago already forgotten.

Peter ran to the grove of trees and crawled to the ditch, covered in part by the high grass. He grabbed Charlie's hands and pulled him out of the pile of dead bodies.

On the other side of the electrified fence, Arnold's mind snapped. He marched over to Wolfgang and Kurt and pointed to himself. "You killed my family!" Arnold shouted, beating his chest. "Kill me, too! I demand it!"

Kurt backed away.

Wolfgang laughed and shook his head at Arnold. "Your turn will come soon enough, and I will be glad to oblige."

"My sweet Evelyn and Charlie!" Arnold turned to the officers, sobbing. "You're a filthy, evil killing squad. You murdered my pregnant wife and son, but now you don't have the guts to kill me?" He waved his hands in the air. "God forgive me, I took him from the train!" He leaned his head back and yelled, "Forgive me, Charlie!"

Charlie turned when his father shouted his name, and watched as his father ran at full speed, throwing himself against the electrified fence. Arnold's body sizzled at every contact. The sparks flew as his soul sought the end of living in the flesh without his family. He was free to seek a final peace with those he loved—except Charlie was still alive.

Arnold convulsed, then released, and his blistered and partially charred body fell lifeless from the fence.

Wolfgang laughed and clapped. "I love this job!"

Kurt swallowed hard and nodded.

Charlie collapsed on the ground next to the ditch.

Wolfgang and Kurt, distracted by removing Arnold's electrocuted body from the street, did not see Peter pull Charlie away from the edge of the death-filled ditch. He hefted the unconscious Charlie over his shoulder, like he was a sack of chicken feed on the Coventry farm, and disappeared into the trees toward the playground.

In his death, Arnold had finally given Charlie his freedom. Kurt, meanwhile, had survived another day in the Nazi world by being the aggressor. Even as a teenager, he'd played the bully, because he was afraid if he didn't, he would be the target. No one knew his deepest secret; that his stepmother, who'd raised him, was Jewish.

Weeks later, Charlie sat in Marla's London Bloomsbury House office, hungrily eating fish and chips.

Marla smiled at him. "So, you finally made it, Charlie. You are in England now. You are safe."

"But what will I do?"

"You will stay at the Pellbrooke estate. There are other boys from Germany there."

"But what will I do?"

"You will go to school."

"No, I mean what will I do? I have no family left."

CHAPTER 35

LET THE BOY DRIVE

(August 1942)

On the outskirts of Soblin, Sloan slid into the driver's side of the truck. Peter stepped up to the window. "Can I drive? I used to drive my father's meat truck—"

"When you were little." Mica, in the passenger seat, finished the sentence for him with a smile. "We know." By now, they'd heard Peter's consistent, but unsubstantiated, meat truck delivery claims many times.

Mica looked at Sloan and shrugged. "Let the boy drive. Let's see what he can do."

Sloan looked at Peter and rolled his eyes. "Drive slowly and don't draw any attention."

Peter opened the driver's door, and Sloan the Bear scooted over to make room for the butcher's son. Peter put the truck in gear. It lurched, and the engine died.

"Your roast is going to be late, ma'am!" Mica joked. Sloan roared with laughter. Peter turned the key, grinding the gears.

"I'm not used to such a poorly maintained vehicle," Peter said, angrily. The clutch finally grabbed. The truck lurched forward onto the Polish street and headed into Soblin.

Peter pulled the truck onto the road leading past the front gate of the Soblin Ghetto.

—∿—

Outside the ghetto gates, Wolfgang and Kurt lined up and shot another group of prisoners at the ditch. One man, injured and slumping, but not dead, still stood. Wolfgang shot again, and still the man stood.

Wolfgang and Kurt walked over to the man, and Wolfgang used his old schoolboy trick of hitting his legs out from under him. The man finally fell into the ditch, and Wolfgang shot him again for good measure.

They lingered at the edge. Kurt covered his nose and mouth with his hand against the smell of the decaying bodies still piling up. "That stinks," he said.

"The ditch is almost full," Wolfgang said. "The ghetto is running out of room. That's why they're shipping them out."

—∿—

Smiling, Peter drove the truck down the street. When he saw Wolfgang and Kurt examining their fresh kills at the ditch, his eyes squinted into angry slits. Then he jerked the wheel, turned sharply, and headed on a seldom-used side road toward the death ditch.

"What are you doing?" Sloan demanded.

"I know those boys, and I owe them one," Peter said.

"No! No! Pull away! Don't do this!" Sloan shouted.

Mica pressed his hands on the dashboard. "I knew we shouldn't let him drive."

"Stop, Peter!" Sloan yelled in his booming voice. "There is no room for emotions. Personal vendettas will only detour our plans."

Peter couldn't pull away. His eyes were fixed, his face emotionless. With the power of the truck under his hands, and Wolfgang and Kurt in his sights, Peter pressed the gas pedal to the floor.

As the truck sped closer, Sloan grew quiet. "More to the right and hold her steady." Accepting the danger of his destiny had always been one of Sloan's strong suits.

The truck bounced off the road, barely missing the trees, and drove closer, narrowly missing Wolfgang and Kurt. With looks of horror very similar to those on the faces of the people they'd killed, the two Nazi boys dove into the pit of murdered, decaying bodies to avoid Peter's vengeful onslaught.

The truck's wheel rode the edge of the pit. The front right tire lost its solid ground, and, for a moment, the truck was headed into the pit, too.

Peter suddenly jerked the wheel away, and the tires finally grabbed.

The truck careened erratically back through the trees and onto the road. It merged into the traffic of the street, with other cars screeching to a stop and honking.

"You are a very bad driver!" Mica shouted.

Sloan gripped the dashboard in front of him. "That was incredibly stupid!" He paused and took a breath. "And one of the greatest rides of my life!"

"Wish I was driving a garbage truck! Would have been more terrifying to them," Peter said, his transformation into a merciless commando complete.

—ᴍ—

In the ditch, Wolfgang and Kurt yelled and screamed, clawing over the dead bodies that pulled apart with the boys' desperate struggles to get out. They emerged, crawling out at the edge of the ditch, slathered with blood and human waste, and covered with maggots.

CHAPTER 36

GOD HAS NOT FORSAKEN US

(October 1942)

The Jewish ghettos and camps were overcrowded, filled with disease and great despondency, but it was only the beginning of suffering. Soon, Jews were being shipped to death camps in crowded train cars like cattle, mostly in Poland, and mass killings became routine.

—m—

On a cold October morning, the door to the Vogners' Dinsdorf apartment swung open and slammed against the wall. Victor stomped in and read from a list held in his outstretched hands. His face had a pompous smirk, as if he enjoyed the job of announcing the latest transports. "Jacob Levy, Nora Levy, Anna Vogner, Greta Vogner, you've been selected for resettlement to the east."

"What does that mean?" Anna asked, wondering why Eddie's name was not listed.

"Means you're leaving tomorrow morning," Victor said.

Anna and Eddie stood rigid and speechless. Nora stepped up. "Greta Vogner won't be going. She died," she said.

Anna glared at Victor. "Remember the old woman you threw out on the street like a dead rat?"

Victor shrugged. "There are so many dead rats." He crossed her name off the list. "Good. Good. That will give us room for one more. Eddie Vogner. Report at six o'clock in the morning."

"But we didn't do anything wrong," Eddie said to Victor.

Victor, with his jowly cheeks and haughty face, looked at Eddie. "You were born a moron, isn't that enough?"

———m———

Bert paced outside the barracks in the Bockenburg Camp. His wife, and Eva, fifteen, walked over to him. Distraught, Eva rushed to Bert and clung to him.

"What's wrong?" Bert asked anxiously.

Helga waved her hand. "Eva and I are being deported tomorrow morning at six," she said, as if the shocking news was routinely expected.

Bert collapsed against the wall, all energy gone from his body. "Oh, no. It has come. Then I will go, too."

"But, Papa, they say these camps are even worse than ours," Eva said.

"There's nothing worse than losing you," Bert said.

Helga clicked her tongue. "I'm so glad William is safe," she said, pointedly.

Eva's eyes narrowed, and her mouth pinched into a circle. The years of being second best erupted. "You! You are a horrible mother! To love one child more than another must be wrong before God!"

Helga slapped Eva across the face. "How dare you speak to me of God? He has forsaken us a long time ago. I never wanted to have you in the first place!"

Eva gasped. "You would have done me a favor," she said, evenly.

Helga raised her arm again to hit Eva, but Bert grabbed her arm. "No! No more. You will no longer torment this child."

She lowered her hand, and Bert let go. "God has not forsaken us. He is testing us. We must show our faith and believe in Him and the goodness that still lives somewhere inside all people," he said.

Helga's rage rose until she could no longer contain it. "Faith? How can you be so stupid? What kind of a man accepts a child that is not his? Tell her!"

Bert shook his head.

"Then I will tell her!" Helga hissed. She turned to face Eva, gritting her teeth, almost spitting. "A German police officer forced himself on me years ago. Your beloved Bert is not your father!"

Eva's body jerked, as if she had been hit by a bullet straight to her heart. Bert raised his hand to stop Helga from talking, anger seeping from every pore.

"No more! I said, no more! You have turned against those who love you the most! The Nazis have surely won!" Bert reached out for Eva and hugged her tightly. "Forgive me, my little mouse. I should have spoken up for you a long time ago."

Eva's face filled with the horror of a hidden truth revealed. "Is it true, what she said? I am one of . . . them? I am not yours?" Her eyes filled with tears.

"Do not listen to her bitterness. You are my daughter, although you may not be my blood."

A sob from the depths of the child's soul erupted with the discovery that what little support and dignity she had was crumbling. Bert pulled her chin up gently until she had to look directly into his eyes, as she still gasped for breath between her cries. "Listen to me, my little mouse, you are something greater than blood. You are my heart and my soul. I was afraid, if you knew, you would not love me back, so I let Helga control me. That will not happen again. I ask your forgiveness."

"You will always be my sweet Papa," Eva said. "I don't want to die."

"Remember, my child, as long as there is life, there is hope," Bert said. He kissed her repeatedly. "I will go with you to face whatever the next camp brings."

Helga glared and turned her back on them both.

—⁓—

Early the next morning, Anna, Nora, and Jacob stood in line on the Dinsdorf street, as Victor checked his official deportation list. A line of transport trucks idled nearby.

"Where's Eddie?" Jacob whispered to Anna.

"I don't know. I've looked everywhere," Anna said.

"What are you going to do?" Nora asked Anna.

"I don't know. I'm scared. Here or there our fate will probably be the same," Anna said. "But I can't face either without my son."

"Next! Name?" Victor shouted at them.

"Jacob Levy and Nora Levy," Jacob announced.

"Oh, yes, the lice doctor," Victor said, checking his list. He pointed to the waiting truck. "Wait over there for transport. Step aside."

Anna, not knowing what to do, stepped forward. "I'm Anna Vogner. I forgot something. I need to go back."

"No. You need nothing," Victor said. "Where is Eddie Vogner?"

"He's here somewhere," Anna lied, searching frantically for Eddie.

"Wait over there for transport. Step aside," he said.

The processing of transports continued. Anna, Nora, and Jacob waited beside the trucks, wondering nervously what would happen to Eddie if he was left behind without anyone to look after him. Anna also wondered how she would survive without Eddie.

—ɷ—

Inside the apartment, Eddie hid in a dumbwaiter, wrapping his small uncoordinated body into the small space. Scrunched up like an accordion, he rocked his head back and forth. "Scared. Scared. Scared," he muttered to himself.

Footsteps entered the apartment. Eddie whispered almost breathlessly. "Dead. Dead. Dead."

It was Michael, the guard who resembled a complaining rodent. He stomped around, searching the apartment, his mouth twitching.

Eddie held his breath, and his face turned red. His head still bobbed. He strained, listening for Michael's footsteps, his eyes opening wide.

Michael looked in every room. He stopped.

Eddie grabbed his head, forcing it to stop moving. All was quiet.

Michael took one last look around the small apartment and left.

—ɷ—

Outside, the trucks were opened, ready to be loaded. Jacob helped Nora and Anna climb into the truck.

Suddenly, Eddie ran out of the apartment building and into the street toward them, his arms and legs flapping. "Wait for me! I changed my mind. I want to go!"

Victor raised his rifle and aimed it at him, not recognizing the running, flopping boy as Eddie. "Halt! You are not authorized!"

Jacob lurched, grabbed the rifle, and pulled it down. Eddie awkwardly jumped up and flung himself into the truck.

Victor kicked Jacob and jerked the gun free from his grasp. The gun exploded, shooting Jacob, ripping his stomach open. His intestines hung out like spongy springs. He was propelled back and fell to the ground dead, not far from the other dead bodies waiting for pickup beside the curb.

Victor stared at Eddie. "Oh, it's you, the moron."

A man shoved the door closed, and the truck sputtered and took off.

Nora and Anna sat shaking with terrified sorrow. Eddie's hands flopped, and he screamed as he rocked back and forth. "I'm sorry! I'm sorry! I'm a moron! Poor Dr. Levy!"

Anna and Nora hugged Eddie as they sobbed.

"Dr. Levy won't be coming back, right?" Eddie asked.

Nora nodded between grief-filled gasps.

"Is he like Oma Greta?" Eddie asked.

Anna nodded.

"Oh, no! Oh, no! Not again!" Eddie pulled at his hair. "I wish Hans and Stephen and Otto were here. I'm not good at this."

The truck with Anna, Nora, and Eddie drove along in the long line of trucks. The ones that went straight on an old dirt road were headed to the train station. The other line of trucks took a right, leading into a heavily wooded forest where the people riding in them would be lined up and shot, their bodies falling into a ditch until it filled with corpses. Then the Nazis would throw some dirt over it and dig another ditch.

Eddie's truck rocked to a stop. The door opened, and fresh air blew in, allowing the stale, sorrowful air to finally escape. Eddie peeked out.

"It's a train! We are going somewhere!" he said. "Maybe we are going home!"

As they were pulled out of the truck, the police suddenly jerked Nora away and pushed her into another group heading to a different train. Anna and Eddie's group were herded toward a train on another platform.

"Nora!" Anna screamed. "Nora! Grab my hand!"

Nora strained to get back to them, but the police, almost shoulder to shoulder, prevented her from reaching Anna and Eddie. She jumped up and down, trying to see them over the police, as tears streamed down her face. Suddenly, complete fear replaced the sadness.

"Anna?" Nora yelled. "Help me!"

Anna, being pulled in the other direction, grabbed onto Eddie's arm and struggled to get to Nora. "Nora! I love you!"

Realizing she could not force her way through the Nazi barricade of police, Nora jumped up one more time. "May God go with you!" she yelled, suddenly completely alone after the death of her husband a short time before, and now the separation from her best friend. She was empty. There was nothing left. She succumbed to the pushing police and the surging crowd and was swept along with her grief in a sea of deportees.

Anna gripped Eddie's arm as they were pushed into the center of the group. Anna's response could not be heard over the rumbling of the approaching train, taking them to their uncertain destination.

An empty deportation train pulled into the station in Munich, ready to load the people being transferred from the overcrowded Bockenburg Camp.

Grundy, the Nazi guard, pushed Bert as he helped Helga into the train, but she pulled away from him. Bert lifted Eva into the dark train.

"Danke, Papa," Eva said. He climbed in after her. More than eighty people were crammed into their train car.

The deportation trains were now a common sight. They rumbled through the German and Polish cities and the countryside, where local people went about their lives, mostly ignoring the trains filled with people barreling toward the death camps.

Inside the train car, Anna and Eddie were barely able to breathe. They took turns sucking fresh air through the slats in the wall.

The train slowed and pulled closer to the station. It was Anna's turn to breathe, and she looked through the slats. She saw an old man driving a wagon pulled by a mule.

She yelled to him. "Where are we?"

The old man slashed his finger across his throat. Eddie watched Anna's ashen, horrified face when she turned around.

"What did he say?" Eddie said.

"He didn't say anything," Anna responded.

As nighttime crept around the train, it barely made a difference inside the almost pitch-black rail car. Several people had died. Their bodies were carefully laid in the corner, waiting for proper funerals that would never come. There was crying, moaning, and audible prayers, but there was nothing else that could be done for the dead. At a stop to load more people into the already crowded train, Anna heard that they were being taken to the Mengele Ghetto, just inside Poland, until it was decided which camp could process them the quickest.

Eddie peered through the barbed wire twisted around the train's small window. He pointed at the moon. "Look, Mutti. Look at the Nazis' moon."

"No, Eddie. No one has power over the moon," Anna said.

"Then that's where I want to live," Eddie said.

Anna put her arm around Eddie and sang "The Sleepy Moon." Eddie rested his head on his mother's shoulder. She always made things seem better and had kept him safe, refusing to put him in an institution when he was little. Eddie quietly sang along with her, remembering the old days before he knew about death.

The Moon. The Moon.
The big sleepy Moon says goodnight to you.
He'll see you soon.
Close your eyes, make believe and
Float away on the tune
Of the big sleepy Moon.

The Moon. The Moon.

—ᴡ—

With freshly counterfeited documents, Sloan, Mica, and Peter drove the truck from Poland into Germany. They were traveling under the pretense that Peter was their nephew, and they were returning from the funeral of his father, who'd died in a dire farming accident involving a cow. Peter had added that detail.

The lies fooled the border police guards. The gates lifted, and the three ill-equipped, but determined, commandos drove into enemy territory.

When they entered Berlin, Peter thought he was going to throw up, afraid that at any moment someone would recognize him as the frightened little boy who'd run away from Germany on the train years ago.

They drove to Edelweiss Park. From inside the truck, they stared at the Berlin Nazi headquarters, the old police station where Peter had begged for his father's release. It was the target of their next operation: Extermination of the Rats. Peter eagerly looked forward to the explosion. On a limited budget, very little expertise, and logistical problems, their operations were mostly run on defiance, determination, sheer guts, and risky maneuvers.

The Resistance rebels had to employ relatively primitive resources. The petrol bomb, or as some called it, the Molotov Cocktail, was one. It was a simple device consisting of a bottle filled with combustible liquid, usually gasoline, and a rag soaked in fuel stuffed in the bottle's neck for its fuse.

Sloan looked at Peter. "They are moving all the records soon. This is our only chance. We will go down to the basement where the records are kept, get what we're looking for, and get out." Peter nodded. "When we are out, we will throw a petrol bomb into their offices in the other side of the building to demonstrate our resistance, and boom!"

"It is very dangerous, but for Isha, we must do it!" Mica said.

"We will rendezvous at the old synagogue tonight to celebrate the elimination of the Nazi rats. And one last thing." Sloan paused to look at Peter. "You will be the one stealing the records."

Peter shook his head. "Me? I thought you said it was dangerous."

"Yes, but you will be dressed as a Nazi," Mica said.

"No! No! No!" Peter threw up his hands.

Sloan smiled and nodded slowly. "Yes! Yes! Yes!" He laughed and nudged Mica, who shared in his enjoyment of Peter's reluctance.

"Me?" Peter asked.

"We need to get inside. They know us, but you look like one of them," Mica reasoned.

"I am gravely insulted," Peter protested.

"You are the bravest young rebel who has ever lived," Mica said. "Children will read about you in the history books."

"Be bold," Sloan said. "This is your chance to do something."

"I'll do it, but don't ever tell anyone I dressed as a Nazi. This is stupid. If I'm risking my life, it should be a big rebellion," Peter said, gesturing with his hands. "Aufstand!"

"Small acts of sabotage create fear. Fear makes them second-guess themselves. That causes mistakes, and mistakes can kill," Sloan said.

"But I'm talking about big, incapacitating sabotage. I'm talking about blowing up a death camp. Let the Nazis know that we're not afraid of them, that we can strike from within and kill the killers. Make them live in fear. That would really make them second-guess themselves."

"Who are you?" Sloan asked. He turned to Mica and shrugged his shoulders. "Who is he?" His eyes opened wide, and he stared exaggeratedly at Peter. "I thought you were a violin player," Sloan said, pretending to play the violin.

"Violinists are fearless," Peter countered. "Have you ever tried to play Mozart?"

"Listen, maestro, today our goal is to find out where they took Isha and blow up a few offices. That is enough for now," Mica said, smiling. "Then we will consider your big rebellion."

—∿—

Peter was barely sixteen, but tall and serious, and looked much older in his Nazi uniform, a size too big. He marched up to the old Berlin police station next to Edelweiss Park. The building had been turned into the city's Nazi headquarters. He mimicked the stomping of Karl Radley, who had forced them out of school when he was eleven. Peter would never forget Radley's cruel vigor and the sound of his boots hitting the floor.

Peter caught a glimpse of himself in the window wearing a mask of Nazi power, and he shivered. Mica and Sloan were right; he did look like one of them.

Peter walked through the lobby unnoticed, but as he opened the door to go into the basement, a Nazi commandant grabbed his arm. "Where are you going?"

Peter turned around to face Karl Radley, his old nemesis.

Peter had heard that Radley's cruelty and ruthlessness had allowed him to rise in the ranks and become a commandant. But now he was standing in front of him. Peter couldn't speak. His mouth was dry. His tongue was thick. No words would form. Would Radley recognize him?

"You must be new. That is the cleaning supplies closet," Radley said, laughing at him.

Peter coughed, and his tense body relaxed. His tongue finally found the ability to form words. "Oh, yes, of course. I was distracted."

Radley looked intently at him. "I just arrived from Poland, but I have not seen you before. What is your name?"

Peter paused. His name. What was his name? He hadn't thought that would come up.

"Johan Bruno," he said, invoking the code name from *A Tale of Two Cities*, and his favorite German Shepherd, unjustly killed despite his canine innocence.

"Well, Officer Bruno, learn your way around here. We have important things to do, like win a war," Radley said, as he walked away. "Supply closets will not help us do that."

Peter closed the closet door. He waited until Radley turned the corner, then opened the door next to the closet and hurried down the stairs.

The basement was filled with file cabinets and shelves of files. Peter didn't know where to begin. He searched the files, which were sorted by last name.

The door to the basement opened. A clerk carrying a file came down the stairs.

"I didn't know anyone was down here," he said, surprised. "Who authorized you?"

"Commandant Radley ordered me to find a file," Peter said.

"Radley? Well, don't forget to put it back."

"Of course," Peter said, nodding.

The clerk took out a key from around his neck and unlocked a file cabinet. He removed some files and set them on top of the cabinet. As he locked the cabinet, one of the files fell between the two cabinets.

"If this war goes much longer, we're going to need more file cabinets," the clerk said. "I'll be glad when we move them all to a better location." He took the files and went back upstairs. Peter sighed. He knew he had to hurry. He knew what would happen if he was found out. He flipped through them until he found Iron Isha's file. As a prominent rebel, she was marked as high profile.

Peter opened it and quickly read the documents. The news was not good. Iron Isha had been killed at the Bockenburg Camp near Munich, gunned down as she tried to escape over the wall. They were too late to save her.

Peter checked the stairs. No one was coming. He figured, as long as he was here, he would look for his mother and sister.

He searched through the other cabinets, but he could not find them. Maybe, he thought, they don't have files because they weren't arrested. Maybe they're in hiding somewhere or safely in another country. Maybe.

The door at the top of the stairs opened. He noticed the file wedged between the two cabinets, accidentally left there by the clerk. Peter picked it up. He stared at the pages inside that were filled with intricate grids of numbers and letters. If it had been in a locked cabinet, he figured it might be worth something.

He took the pages and stuffed them under his Nazi uniform shirt in the waist of his pants, along with Iron Isha's file. He hurried up the stairs, passing the clerk coming down.

He was sweating as he took a deep breath, opened the door, and stepped into the hall to the main reception room. He was nervous. The hardest part was always getting out. He felt the Nazi uniform was getting tighter, cutting off his circulation, and he could barely breathe. He was on his way through the lobby and was almost out. He could see the door.

"Bruno!" Radley called, but Peter didn't recognize his name and didn't stop. "Bruno!" the commandant called again. "Officer Bruno!" The commandant reached out and grabbed Peter's arm.

Peter realized Radley was talking to him. He was trapped. He reluctantly turned around, afraid he would be recognized this time.

"Yes, sir?" Peter said, in a barely audible voice.

"I need you to deliver these to the train office immediately." Radley held out a folder stuffed with papers. "Confirm the cargo invoices. The shipments must not stop."

Peter's hand shook as he reached out to take the papers. "Yes, Commandant Radley. I will deliver them right away." He took the papers and turned quickly toward the door, as if eager to complete his assignment.

He was almost out. He reached for the doorknob.

"Bruno?" Radley called out.

Peter turned back. "Yes, sir?"

"How did you know my name?"

Peter stared, not knowing what to say. He cleared his throat. "Everyone knows you, Commandant."

Radley smiled and nodded, filled with his own arrogance.

Peter waited until he was outside and a block away before he looked at the folder in his shaking hand. The invoices Radley had given him were from the train scheduling department, invoiced payments for the trains carrying Jewish prisoners. He opened it up. It was the charges for a list of Jewish prisoners deported from the Bockenburg work camp the day before, to the Reinigen Camp in Lodansk, Poland.

He scanned the list until he saw Eva Rosenberg, Bert Rosenberg, and Helga Rosenberg. He stared unbelievingly at the names, until he finally accepted their reality. His beautiful Eva had been sent to Reinigen, meaning cleansing, a place known for the cruelest torture and almost certain death. He had seen the camp and witnessed its atrocities from the cover of a farmer's house nearby.

He crumpled the paper in his hand. Breathing heavily, trying to control the surge of anger, he raised his face to the sky. Then, he smoothed out the papers that held Eva's name, folded them, and put them in his shirt, along with the other papers. Eva, his beautiful Eva, was alive, but being shipped like cargo to a death camp. All Peter was doing was blowing up a small Nazi building, a minor irritant to the unstoppable Nazi machine.

Inside Eva's swaying train car, without fresh air and no bathroom facilities, it had become unbearably foul. Eva clung to Bert.

"Papa, the smell, I'm sick. There's no air," Eva said.

"Sing," Bert said.

"Sing?" Eva shook her head. "No, I can't. I can't even breathe."

Bert took her face in his hands. "Yes, you can. You are the bravest girl I've ever known."

"Do you think God can still hear me?" she whispered, with tears in her eyes. "Papa, am I still Jewish?"

"You are a strong and faithful Jew, and God smiles on you," Bert said.

Eva sang:

Hear, O Israel
Our prayer has begun.
The Lord is our God.
The Lord is one.

The other passengers sang quietly with the beautiful young woman. Helga stood with her arms crossed, her lips pursed as if to make sure no prayer escaped, as the train rumbled unsteadily along the tracks.

The wind blew the clouds across the sky as the moon peeked out. Peter, wearing a Nazi uniform, walked the streets of his old neighborhood in Berlin. He would wait for the huge explosion at Nazi headquarters. Then he would meet Sloan and Mica at the burned synagogue across the street from the only home he had ever known, except for Coventry, which he did not see as a home, but rather as a place of temporary incarceration. His childhood had been spent on that block in Berlin. His memories of home were here. He could still remember the foul sickening odor of the fire as it demolished the holy place, his synagogue. The sun had gone down and the wind had kicked up.

—⁓—

Sloan readied a petrol bomb outside Nazi headquarters. He held up the deadly liquid-filled bottle with the rag poking out. "I'm looking forward to some fireworks."

Mica took his box of matches from his pocket and lit one. Before he could light the rag, the wind blew the match out. Mica lit another one, and a gust blew it out.

"You can't light a simple rag?" Sloan asked impatiently.

"Not in this gale. We should have waited for a calmer night," Mica said.

"Commandos wait for nothing. Light it again. Pretend it's a Hanukkah candle."

Mica smiled. He lit the match and cupped his hand around the flame to protect it from the wind. The match stayed lit, and he moved it slowly toward the rag.

"Hurry up, Mica, they're going to see the match," Sloan warned.

Mica's protective hands brought the burning match to within an inch of the rag. Sloan rolled his eyes and stuck the rag into the small flame. Not being saturated enough in gasoline, it was slow to ignite. Precious seconds ticked by as Sloan heaved the bottle with the burning rag toward the office window of Nazi headquarters.

It somersaulted in the air. The bottle broke the window, smashing against the floor inside as planned, but there was no ignition. The fuse had been extinguished on its wayward tumble.

Unaware of the kink in their plan, Sloan and Mica waited, expecting an explosion, but all they heard was heavy breathing and the pounding of Nazi boots. Then they were quickly surrounded by officers, with guns pointed at them.

—∿—

In his old Berlin neighborhood, Peter strolled by the red-and-green garbage trucks parked in neat rows, the same trucks where he used to climb in and pretend to drive when he was younger. He stopped and looked at the cabs that had seemed so impossibly high when he was little. The simple dreams of childhood faded when faced with the reality of life's brutal messages. He still had the urge to pull himself into the garbage truck's cab and start its powerful engine, but he didn't. He had more important things to do. It was not the night for childhood fantasies.

He walked on, past 435 Edelweiss Street where Herr Frank and Bruno the dog used to live, until he came face to face with his childhood block awash with memories. A shiver went through Peter when he saw the remains of his burned synagogue across the street and what looked like an abandoned camp on its grounds.

He crossed the street and stopped outside his family's old butcher shop, which had become a shoe repair shop. He looked up to see a light on in the apartment above the shop, his family's apartment, his family's home.

Peter remembered the day his father told him he would grow up to take over the butcher shop, and how his heart had stopped with the realization that he had no other choices. As he looked at his old neighborhood, he knew he would give anything to have his father back in the clean shop with the orderly meat, even if that meant he was destined to do the same.

Footsteps snapped behind him. "Guten tag. Have you heard the good news?" a police officer asked him.

"No," Peter said. "I'm off duty. I've been looking for my dog. What has happened?"

"Tonight, we can celebrate. Two rebels have been captured."

Peter couldn't breathe for a second. "Who are they?" he asked, his heart pounding with fear.

"Notorious rebel leaders. The man they call the Bear, and Mica the Murderer. Both are wanted enemies of Germany."

"Ah, excellent," Peter said, as sweat beaded up on his forehead, despite the chilly evening wind.

"It's been a long time coming. It's a glorious day for Germany! The Resistance has suffered an irrecoverable blow," the officer said.

Peter whistled, pretending to be searching for his dog, then casually asked, "How did it happen that they captured these criminals?"

"They tried to blow up headquarters."

"Tried? Surely, they were not successful."

"There was a gasoline spill in an office, but no fire. They are as dumb as straw. Dummkopfs!" the officer said, laughing.

Peter swallowed hard. It felt like he had a mouthful of Maude's unforgiving porridge caught in his throat. It wouldn't go up or down. "Were the rebel leaders arrested?"

"Yes.

"Good . . . how will they be punished?"

"I hear that tomorrow morning they will hang the rebels by their necks in Edelweiss Park."

"That is unusual."

"They will be made an example, so all can see that we do not take rebels lightly."

Peter swallowed hard, trying to find some air to breathe. "I won't miss it," he said, forcing the words through clenched teeth. "Well, I've got to go. Loin roast tonight. My dog will have to come home on his own. Auf Wiedersehen."

"Auf Wiedersehen."

Peter looked back at his home, stolen by the Nazis. He remembered the look of utter helplessness on his father's face as the Nazis had pulled him out their apartment door. No man, even one with good legs, was strong enough to stand up to the power of Hitler, not even the rabbi.

He looked at the burned shell of the synagogue across the street. Surely, God would allow retribution for the destruction of this sacred place.

Peter was alone, young, and new to this rebellion, but he knew there was no one else to do it. It would be up to him to land a blow against the Nazis and rescue Sloan and Mica from hanging.

He hurried down the sidewalk, glancing up at Herr Frank's, and the real Bruno's, old apartment. Herr Frank had been a coward in life, and, maybe, a coward in death, too. Peter also realized he had been a good man, a man trapped in the evil of his time, and he had not been strong enough to pull away from it.

When Peter turned the corner, he saw there was still a commotion around the broken window of headquarters. Instead of turning away, he found himself striding toward the scene of his friends' capture. After all, he was still dressed in a Nazi uniform.

Peter managed to maneuver his way to the broken window.

He stared at the building. His petrol bomb had failed. It was his fault, but he couldn't try again, because Sloan and Mica were being held there now. He would not let it go. Someday, he would finish the job.

Peter disappeared into the Berlin night, carrying the heavy burden of his mistake. He'd let Sloan and Mica down. Mistakes could kill. He would make his plan, and tomorrow, before the hanging, he would carry out his rescue. His father had always told him: If you work hard, you can make your own luck. Peter was going to need some luck, but this time, he would not act like a child. He would not be careless. It was time to grow up and be a man, fighting for his people and his friends.

The clouds covered the moon, and the windy night grew dark. Peter strode off into the darkness with Iron Isha's death notation, the death-train invoice list, and a strange grid of letters and numbers that were so important they'd been locked up, still hidden inside his shirt, tucked in the waist of his pants.

CHAPTER 37

THE END OF THE LINE

(October 1942)

Eva's deportation train pulled up to the Reinigen Camp in Lodansk, Poland, and stopped. It was the end of the line. The tracks ended abruptly at the entrance gate.

The moon shone brightly above the barbed wire fences. The Nazi guards, wearing skull and crossbones insignias on their shirts, stood in watchtowers holding guns at the ready, in case some defenseless prisoner should decide to risk freedom for certain death.

Brick buildings stood in rows along cobblestone streets. The ordinariness of the buildings fooled the arriving inmates at first, but starvation, torture, and death awaited them inside. There was nothing ordinary about the Reinigen Camp.

Police guards and dogs were outside the fences, ready for the train's arrival. When the train opened, soldiers pulled people out of the cars at the camp's front gate. The dead, who had been so carefully cared for on the train, were dragged out and roughly stacked like wood on top of each other.

A woman held her limp dead baby still wrapped in a blanket. She wept in sorrow for the child, who had never had a chance to live, and in gratitude, that the child had been spared from the horrors of the world. A Nazi officer ripped the baby from her arms and tossed it onto the pile of dead bodies. She wailed.

Bert reached up and helped Eva down. He held his arms out for Helga, but she pushed them aside. Nazi officers shouted orders as German Shepherds barked and snarled, straining at their leashes, trained to rip flesh on command.

The people stumbled and looked around. A police officer, swinging a billy club, motioned to them. "Men to the right! Women and children to the left!" the guard yelled to the traumatized new arrivals.

"Where are we?" Helga asked. "What is this place?"

"I don't know, but it's not good," Bert said.

The sick and sad people, exhausted from the train trip, shuffled around, separating reluctantly from loved ones. Eva clutched her father. "No, Papa. I can't leave you. Please, Papa. Tell them we have to be together. Please, Papa."

"Eva, we must do what they say," he said, gently.

"Papa, I can't live without you. You're the only one who's ever loved me. I can't breathe without you!" Eva said.

"You have my love with you. You won't be alone. And you have God. Do not throw away your hope. It may be the only thing that will keep you alive."

Eva nodded, her chin quivering with emotion, trying so hard to be brave for the father who had given her the strength to accept herself when her mother hadn't. He was a father whose blood did not run through her veins, but his love ran through her heart.

"Move along!" the policeman yelled.

Bert, still holding Eva, didn't move fast enough. The guard hit him with the butt of his gun. Bert let go of Eva's hands. She held them out to him.

As he moved away from her, she whispered. "Papa. I love you. Thank you for being my one true papa."

"I love you, too. You are my sweet joy," Bert said, as tears ran down his cheeks. It was the first time Eva had ever seen her father cry, and it was more frightening than anything else she'd seen.

The crowded line of women and children swept Eva along like a riptide of fear. Helga slogged determinedly ahead without looking back. She moved easily away from them, as if this destination had been what she was waiting for to finally get her freedom from them.

The camp's reception and prisoner processing building still had a line outside. Helga swayed, almost fainting from the lack of food and air on the train. Eva ran to her and held her up.

Inmate matrons were prisoners but worked as guards, keeping the other inmates in line. One matron was tall and fairly thick, in contrast to the extreme thinness of everyone else, which attested to the extra perks she was given for her betrayal of her people. She held her hands out. "Stop. What's wrong with her?"

"Nothing. She's just tired. It was a long train ride," Eva said.

"I really can't allow—"

"She's a very good seamstress. The best in Berlin. You can't even see her stitches. If you need anything, she—"

"What about you? Are you strong?" the matron interrupted, with a slight nod.

"I've got the strength of two women in me," Eva answered, struggling to hold up her mother to prove her claim.

The matron almost smiled. Smiles, unless in ridicule, were rarely seen at Reinigen. Happiness vanished for all who entered. "Go on in, Little Hercules, but remember where you are. Even the toughest don't survive here."

Eva helped Helga walk into the building, as they were herded along, roughly pulled and pushed by the policemen.

Another inmate matron shaved their heads. When Eva's long beautiful hair hit the floor, she cried.

"What are you crying for? Your hair is the least of your problems," the matron scolded.

"It's all I had left of who I used to be," Eva said.

"You're a bald prisoner, now," the matron said, as she shuffled them along to the showers. "Welcome to Reinigen. I'm Ramona. You'll be seeing a lot of me."

In the showers there was a pause, then a whoosh. Water burst out of the nozzles. That day they would be clean, not dead, but there were no promises beyond that.

The women were given ill-fitting dresses and shoes taken from the suitcases of former prisoners, their last possessions stripped from them with their dignity and freedom in an unrelenting vengeance. Eva looked at her shoes. One was black and two sizes bigger than the other one, which was brown and too small. The men, still separated from the women, wore faded blue and gray-striped pants and jackets.

Another inmate matron grabbed Eva's small pale arm and twisted her forearm up. Before Eva knew what was happening, the matron pressed down a metal stamp of needles, punching an entire serial number proceeded by an "R" onto her arm.

Eva screamed and bit her lip as soon as the sound escaped. She watched the blood ooze in the unexpectedly violent punctures of the tattoo on her arm. The matron, with a look of disapproval on her face, callously rubbed blue ink into the wound until Eva could see the outline of an "R" followed by her new identification numbers.

Eva stared at the letter and serial numbers with tears streaming down her flushed face. "What does this mean?"

"It means you're a number now," the matron said without emotion. "That identifies you when you die."

The inmates were led to their barracks, long buildings in rows. The women and men were taken to separate buildings. The living quarters had dirt floors, no windows, no insulation from heat or cold, no bathroom, only a bucket or a barrel outside the door. One light bulb hung down near the door.

Thirty-six wooden bunk beds with triple tiers lined the walls and ran down the center. Six people slept on each wooden plank. They had meager covers, no pillows, and no mattresses.

Eva helped her mother into the bunk. "Did you see the railroad tracks? They ended here. There is no leaving this place."

"There never is," Helga answered.

Eva gave her mother her ration of bread, and watery soup, made with rotten vegetables and a trace of fatty meat. The one heating stove in the middle of the barracks went out.

Eva lay down in the bunk next to her mother. It would be the last night she was allowed to stay in the women's barracks. The next day she would be transferred to the kinderlager, the children's barracks, to help with the children in the overcrowded housing. That night, her first night in hell, she stared at the bottom of the bunk above her. Written in Yiddish graffiti was: "NO ONE GETS OUT OF HERE ALIVE."

—⚊—

In London, at 16 Poppleton Circle, Becca sat up in her bed, crying. Mrs. Daniels passed her room and heard her sniffling. She slipped into her room.

"What's the matter, Becca? What's wrong?"

"My mother and Baby Lilly."

Mrs. Daniels nodded and sat beside Becca, trying to comfort the poor girl. "You miss them. I know."

Becca shook her head. "It's not that."

"What is it, then?" Mrs. Daniels asked, patting her back.

"I can't remember their faces anymore," Becca said, whispering her horrifying confession.

Mrs. Daniels put her big wobbling arms around the sassy little refugee and hugged her tightly. "Not to worry, my little lass. God watches over all of us."

"I don't think God can see us anymore."

Over Becca's shoulder, the tough lady from Swansea closed her eyes, and a tear squeezed out. "No, no, he sees you for sure."

CHAPTER 38

THE VIOLIN WOLF

(October 1942)

Peter walked the streets of Berlin until the sunrise lit the horizon. He knew his plan was risky, but doing nothing was certain failure. He would do it. He would do something, and if God was with him, it would work.

Still wearing the stolen and uncomfortable Nazi uniform, he hurried to the back of his father's old butcher shop. After he made sure no one was looking, he dug in the dirt under the back steps. He uncovered the old dented tin box he'd buried there after the Nazis attacked when he was eleven. He opened the top. The ball and jacks, the yo-yo, and the meat cleaver wrapped in a cloth were still there, waiting for him to return.

He put the ball, jacks, and yo-yo in his pockets. He opened the wrapped meat cleaver and sharpened the blade on a stone, scraping it until it sparked, then wrapped it back up like a package of meat. His plan was in motion.

He walked the two blocks to his favorite parking lot filled with neat rows of red-and-green garbage trucks. He could hear the orchestra of strings in Edelweiss Park warming up as they competed against the hammering of the workers hastily finishing the hanging platform. He had to time his rescue perfectly, or it would be sure death for all of them.

Peter casually made his way to the office with its pegboard of truck keys. He tried to pry open the window like he had when he was younger. It was locked. He looked around, pulled out his meat cleaver still wrapped, and slammed the handle against the window, breaking it. He hated the sound of breaking glass. It reminded him of the night his childhood had died inside the wardrobe. Disobedience was sometimes born of necessity, it had to be done; too much was at risk. He knocked the jagged pieces of glass into the office, then carefully reached in and lifted a key off the hook on the first row of the pegboard.

He opened the door of a truck in the front row with the key and pulled himself up into it. He set the wrapped meat cleaver on the seat next to him, added the jacks, balls, and yo-yo from his pockets, and was ready to drive.

Peter gripped the huge wheel, like he had when he was little. It felt so much smaller in his big hands. He bounced on the seat, and his head hit the ceiling. He grabbed his head and laughed. He took a deep breath and turned the key. The engine sputtered, but didn't start.

He sat back in the big seat. If God loved the Jews, sometimes things needed to go their way. This was a good time to start. Now was a good time to prove his faith. He gripped the cold key and turned it again. It sputtered and turned over. He was really going to do it. He was going to drive a garbage truck. He wished Eva was there to see him. He moved the gearshift. The truck jerked forward, then shook, until Peter got it in the right gear and it lurched onto the street. It was different to actually drive it. He was a good driver; the truck was just unpredictable.

Peter drove the truck slowly toward Edelweiss Park and waited. When the time came, he pulled the lever and could hear the back opening as he drove into the park.

The two nooses swayed as a crowd of people milled around the makeshift hanging platform, as if it were a celebration. The orchestra waited in their seats on the bandstand at the edge of the park, the same bandstand Peter had often dreamed of playing on as a child.

Officers on horses patrolled the area. Commandant Radley stood beside his horse, whose breath snorted from his huge nostrils.

"Bring out the prisoners!" Radley ordered.

The strings of the orchestra played music, as Sloan and Mica were marched onto the hanging deck with their hands tied behind their backs.

The music was cut short, and the officers placed the nooses around the men's necks.

Peter drove the garbage truck to the bandstand near the edge of the park and paused. He opened the door and leaned out toward the orchestra, pulling himself up into full arrogant Nazi entitlement. "I need to borrow a violin on behalf of the Third Reich."

A small mouse of a man held his violin aloft, so used to taking Nazi orders he did not even question the absurdity of the request from an officer driving a garbage truck.

Radley swung up onto the saddle of his powerful horse to give the orders to hang. He raised his arm and pointed dramatically at Sloan and Mica. "They are Jewish rebels and traitors to Germany! They must suffer! They must die!" he shouted to the crowd that had gathered to watch the rebels die. When the clapping and cheering died down, Radley dramatically raised his hand in a Hitler salute, "Heil Hitler!" He was clearly enjoying the moment.

"Heil Hitler!" the crowd responded in unison and with passion.

"Ready?" he shouted.

The officers on the platform nodded. "Yes, Commandant!" they yelled back in unison, poised like point dogs on a hunt, waiting for the order to open the trapdoors in the floor and leave the two rebels swinging by their necks. However, Radley's dramatic arrogance gave Peter the few crucial moments he needed to implement his rescue plan.

Peter tucked the violin, an old familiar friend, under his chin, and immediately relaxed. He felt the sweet resistance of the strings as he loudly played the violin, like he had at the farm when angry at his swollen farmhand fingers. He purposely and defiantly screeched out a savage wolf song.

When his violin howled, the horses stampeded through the park, bucking off their riders, including Radley, ready to give the brutal command to hang. Chaos erupted.

Peter respectfully handed the violin back to its owner. He quickly nodded a graceful musician's bow and ducked back into the truck.

He bumped over the curb and onto the park lawn's expanse, the diesel engine chugging closer to the hanging platform.

Commandant Radley, dazed and unexpectedly dethroned from his horse, limped rapidly toward the offending garbage truck. He looked up and saw Peter driving the renegade truck. "Bruno? Johan Bruno? What are you doing?" he shouted. "Halt!"

Peter did not halt.

"Johan Bruno! Exit the refuse vehicle! Schnell!" The commandant saw the determination in Peter's defiant gray eyes, and he raised his gun.

Peter grabbed his yo-yo from his pocket and leaned out the window, he flung the yo-yo at the commandant. It wrapped around the commandant's gun like it was the Vogners' old porch post.

Radley's shot went into the air, and Peter pulled the gun back, wrapped tightly in the yo-yo string. Peter smiled. It's all in the spin and the snap back, he thought.

Radley's errant gunshot brought the other officers running. Bullets pinged off the huge metal garbage truck like it was a tank. Peter picked up his father's meat cleaver and gripped it in his hand. It was up to him. If he failed, it would be a crushing blow to the rebel movement. Be bold, he thought. It was time to be his father's son.

As he approached the hanging platform, Sloan and Mica, with the nooses around their necks, recognized it was Peter heading straight for them in a giant garbage truck. Mica looked at Sloan. "Look! It's Peter! I'd say that boy's been worth the trouble."

"We'll soon see what the rebel lad is made of," Sloan said, smiling.

"Ziehen! Ziehen! Pull! Pull!" The commandant's shouts were muffled amongst the loud chaos.

The confused officers looked at each other. "What did he say?" one officer asked. The delay allowed Peter to drive closer.

The marauding young commando leaned out the window, steering with his foot like he had practiced as a young boy.

Radley screamed, "Pull! Pull!" He gestured wildly to the officers on the hanging platform.

The officers shrugged and pulled the lever. The trapdoors opened just as Peter drove by and slashed the ropes above the heads of Sloan and Mica in one swipe, like it was a beef shoulder. He ducked back inside the safety of the metal garbage tank, breathing heavily.

Sloan and Mica were released from the platform with nooses and rope tails still attached. They fell through the open trapdoors and landed hard on the ground below, stunned but unharmed.

Peter hollered like he had as a make-believe driver and stepped on the brake, pulling the truck to a stop. A bullet hit the hood. Peter motioned to the back as Sloan and Mica looked up.

Limping from the fall, with their hands still tied behind their backs, Sloan and Mica awkwardly threw themselves into the back of the truck's open trash receptacle.

The crowd in the park scattered as fast as they could, running from the renegade garbage truck, as shots were fired. A bullet hit the back of the open receptacle. Sloan and Mica were lying low, and the bullet ricocheted away. The gawkers in the park who had come to watch a hanging dove for cover.

Peter drove the huge truck out of the park, still dodging bullets from the officers running after them. He pulled onto the road. Radley's gun, with the yo-yo still wrapped around it, lay on the floor of the truck, out of reach.

A Nazi car squealed around the corner and pulled in behind the truck. In the rear view mirror, Peter saw a hand with a gun extend from the car window. He reached across to the seat, grabbed the jacks, and threw them into the street behind him.

The driver shot a few rounds while trying to avoid the jacks. The car screeched and swerved, until it spun out of control and crashed into a lamppost.

The man with the gun climbed out the car window and ran along the road, but Peter's garbage truck soon outdistanced him.

He drove the truck a few blocks and slowed to a stop. Sloan and Mica rolled out of the back, and Peter pulled them into the cab. He took the cleaver and cut through the ropes tying their hands.

"Called it a little close, didn't you, mate?" Sloan asked.

"No, perfectly timed," Peter responded. "I'm a good driver and a very good butcher." He made the meat-slicing motion that he'd used to cut the hanging rope.

Peter moved into the lineup of all the trucks beginning their trash pickups and was lost among the parade of garbage trucks. Although the Nazis were right on his trail by then, there were too many red-and-green trucks going in every direction to find him. The getaway garbage truck blended in with the regulated schedule of garbage men and the flowing life of the city. The urban camouflage was complete, and Peter sped away, driving a garbage truck in a daring and dangerous rescue. It wasn't as fun as he had imagined as a boy, not without Eva.

Before he made his first turn, he glanced back. The hastily built hanging podium was empty. There would be no hanging of Jewish rebels that day. He kissed his fingers and tapped them on the steering wheel.

"So, did you get it?" Mica asked, always focused on the mission.

"Not now," Peter said. "I'm driving."

"I know; that's why I asked. I might not live much longer. Did you get Isha's location?" Mica insisted. "Please tell me we didn't do all this for nothing."

Peter stared at the road and slowly shook his head. He couldn't look at Mica. "I'm sorry, Mica. She was killed at the Bockenburg Camp, trying to escape. I'm so sorry."

Mica grabbed his head. "I'll kill every last one of those murderers with my bare hands. I swear I will," he vowed quietly.

"She was important to you?" Peter asked quietly.

"She was my sister," Mica choked out.

"Sister?" Peter said. "I didn't know. I'm sorry, Mica."

Sloan put his arm around Mica.

With shaking hands, Peter reached into his shirt. He pulled out Iron Isha's arrest file, the train invoice, and the grid of numbers and letters, and gave them to Sloan.

Sloan, eager for the distraction from Isha's death, examined the papers. "Do you know what this is?" he asked, quietly, almost whispering. His hands were shaking.

"What?"

"What is it?" Mica demanded, hearing the excitement in Sloan's voice.

"You might not have to kill all of them with your bare hands. I think he found the new Berlin communication code," Sloan said, smiling.

"What does that mean?" Peter asked.

"If we give this to the right people, it could help end the war," Mica said stoically. "And kill the Nazis that killed my sister."

"So, I did good? Right, Sloan?"

"You didn't even know what it was," Sloan grumped.

"You did good." Mica managed. "Real good."

"We will see," Sloan said. They both slapped Peter on the back, as he drove the truck past his old school. "But I have one question. Who is Johan Bruno?"

CHAPTER 39

DON'T THINK OF THEM AS PEOPLE

(May 1943)

Eddie and Anna were still at the Mengele Ghetto when the word came down from Nazi headquarters in Berlin that most of the prisoners there were to be moved to the Reinigen Camp, where the facilities allowed a faster process of elimination, with large gas chambers, more ovens, and quicker deaths. The mass murders were not fast enough for Hitler, so Anna and Eddie were shoved into another train car and shipped out without warning.

Once inside the suffocating train car, Eddie wet his pants. He looked at his mother. "I'm glad Hans is not here. He would not like it."

His mother hugged him. "You are the bravest boy in all of Germany."

"Braver than Hans?"

His mother nodded. Eddie smiled, despite his wet crotch and the overwhelming stench of urine.

—〰—

Eva had been at the Reinigen Camp for several months. Each time a train pulled up and unloaded its human cargo, she felt compelled to watch, as if witnessing such a cruel and inhuman act would confirm that it was real.

One day, Eva, wearing a strip of an old dress as a scarf to cover her butchered short hair, watched as a new female prisoner entered the inspection point, holding the hands of two children. The little girl looked about six. Her long brown hair was matted and twisted. Her brother was about twelve, a tall boy with sad eyes.

The cruel Nazi greeter of new inmates stopped them. "Only one child allowed," he snapped, enjoying the emotional abuse inflicted on the Jewish prisoners.

The mother hesitated for a second, and then dropped the girl's hand. Without looking back, the woman continued through the checkpoint with the boy. He craned his neck to find his sister. With tears streaming down his face, he waved.

The crowd surged around the loving brother and the decisive mother, swallowing them up in the chaos. The mother never looked back, and the girl did not see that both her mother and brother were herded into the middle line, the killing line. She stood lost, uncertain of what to do.

Another policeman motioned to her. "Where's your mother?" he demanded.

Eva ran over from her observation post and grabbed the girl's arm. "Our mothers are right up there. We got separated from them." She pointed into the crowd, hiding the arm with the tattoo, so they would not know she had already been processed. "Look, there they are."

Eva nudged the girl past the policeman, before he could say anything, and the next train car of arrivals needed his attention.

Eva put her arm around the girl. "I saw what happened."

The girl stared at Eva with wide, vacant eyes, still trying to absorb her mother's betrayal.

"Come on, their rules are intended to break us down," Eva whispered. "We're all on our own in here anyway. What's your name?"

"Lory."

"I'm Eva."

Eva led Lory to the reception building, where the prisoners were processed. There was still a long line. Lory looked around. "I don't see my mother."

"I will stay with you," Eva said. "Stay in the left line."

—ɯ—

If Eva had returned to her usual post, she would have seen Eddie and Anna emerge from one of the back cars. They shuffled along with the crowd, until they reached the death-determining policeman.

"Men to the right, women and children to the left," he said, pushing Eddie to the right.

"But he's a child," Anna said, grabbing Eddie's arm. She held on tightly.

"Doesn't look like a human child to me. How did he make it this far? To the right! Do as I say!" The guard pointed to Anna. "You, to the middle line."

Anna didn't let go of Eddie. "No, he's my son. We have to stay together."

The policeman nodded to two others, who quickly came over and pulled at Anna's tight grip on Eddie. Anna wouldn't release her grasp.

"Let go of my Mutti!" Eddie yelled.

A policeman drew his gun and pointed it at Eddie's head. "Release him, or we will no longer have a problem," he threatened Anna.

Anna quickly let go of Eddie, but she remained beside him.

"Is he going to shoot me?" Eddie whispered to Anna, as if the guard couldn't hear.

"No, no, Eddie, I have to go in a different line. I'll find you later. Do what they say. It'll be okay. I'll find you, I promise," Anna said. "Eddie, God gave me two beautiful, smart sons."

"Am I one of them?" Eddie asked innocently.

"Yes, Eddie, you definitely are."

"And I'm the bravest."

"There is no one braver," Anna said, and meant it.

The guard pointed for Anna to go. "Middle line! Middle line to the showers!" Anna nodded and turned away from Eddie. The middle line led to a building with a flat roof and a tall smokestack.

Eddie walked past Dr. Braun, a solemn-faced man with dull eyes looking out of small, round rimless glasses. Next to the doctor, a young policeman gave orders, as Eddie watched his mother advance in the crowded middle line. He soon lost sight of her.

He stood, undecided, in front of the doctor and the policeman. The doctor glanced at Eddie with disdain, as Eddie's hands flopped in front of him. "Hi, I'm Eddie."

"Showers for him," Dr. Braun said, "middle line!"

"Good. Showers." Eddie clapped and let out his strange squeaking cheer. "My Mutti's going there."

The young policeman with the clipboard beside Dr. Braun heard Eddie's voice and suddenly turned around to look. It was Otto, who was now twenty-two years old.

Otto pulled Eddie aside. "Eddie?" he whispered.

Eddie, still fixated on looking for his mother, watched as the middle group walked down a long street to the brick building with the tall square smokestack that had flames rising from it.

"Eddie!" Otto said quietly again.

Eddie glanced at Otto. "Otto? Hi!" Eddie said, excitedly. "They brought you here, too?"

A short distance away, Dr. Braun pointed to Eddie and shouted. "I said showers for the idiot!"

Eddie looked at Dr. Braun. "I'm not an idiot. My mother has two smart sons."

Dr. Braun rolled his eyes. "Middle line," he said, jerking his head.

"I need a shower. Good, thank you. That train was dirty and smelly."

Otto stepped up to the doctor. "What about your medical experiments? This one might be useful to you."

Dr. Braun looked at Eddie, studying him. "Perhaps. Yes, okay," he said, nodding.

Otto's shoulders relaxed. He walked over and leaned in to Eddie and whispered, "Stay to the right."

Eddie shook his head. "No, I want a shower, too."

"It's okay, Eddie. Stay to the right."

Eddie shook his head. "No, I need a shower."

"Do what I say, Eddie!" Otto ordered under his breath.

"Okay, Otto, okay." Eddie said, finally giving in to his old friend.

Otto walked backward with Eddie, still directing other people to the lines. "Stay in line!" Otto yelled to the crowd. He turned to Eddie. "Where's the rest of your family?"

"Hans is in England. He took a train. Not like our train, I hope. My Vati and Oma are dead. They are not coming back. They left Oma on the street. And my Mutti . . ." Eddie pointed to the gas chambers. "She's taking a shower." He frowned. "I wish I could."

Otto's eyes opened wide with horror. "Stay to the right, Eddie," he said gruffly, pointing. "Do it for me!"

"Okay, Otto." Eddie nodded and merged into the right line.

Otto hurried down the middle line, searching the faces as he passed until he got to a building with a sign over the door: "To the bath and disinfecting rooms. Cleanliness brings freedom, and one louse may kill you." Otto did not get there in time to see Anna descend into the cellar.

—m—

Two policemen ushered Anna and the others into a giant shower room. Eric was older, tall, with a rigid stride. "You must get disinfected and take a shower! You must give up any valuables and get undressed! Schnell!" he ordered.

The policeman named Borg was a small mouse of a man. Although stone-faced, he had beads of sweat running down the side of his ashen face as he stood watching the prisoners enter.

The women undressed and hung their clothes on numbered hooks to be retrieved after their shower. Then, they waited in the whitewashed room with its showerheads and pillars and concrete floors.

Eric checked the lock on the steel gas chamber door. "Borg, it's your first day. You do it."

Borg shook his head and wrinkled his rodent face. "That's okay. I don't—"

"Throw the pellets down the air shaft," Eric ordered. "It's not so bad after the first time."

The women and children stood naked in the gas chamber, stripped of their clothes and their dignity, never suspecting their fate would rain down on them in a spray of poisonous gas.

Borg hurried to the place where the air shaft opened. He took a deep, halting breath and threw the Zyklon-B pellets down. He stood back, bracing for what would happen next.

—◊◊◊—

Anna looked around. No water came out of the showerheads. They were fake. The holes in the hollow pillars let out the hissing gas. The bitter almond smell was overwhelming. It was hard to breathe. She felt the air sting her throat and fill her nostrils with hydrogen cyanide. In those few seconds, Anna realized that death was upon her, and there was nothing she could do to save herself or Eddie.

"Eddie! Oh, dear God! No!" Anna screamed, realizing full well what it would mean for him. "Eddie!"

The people inside the chamber with her screamed, howled, and prayed. Anna jerked with involuntary convulsions as the poison took over. She closed her eyes. "Eddie. Hans," she mumbled as she slumped to the cold concrete floor. The heart-wrenching screams and cries inside the chamber finally ended, their prayers unanswered.

—◊◊◊—

Borg watched through the peephole in the door at the huddled cherry-red bodies. He quickly turned and walked back to the air shafts. He stumbled through the door to the outside, directly behind where he had dropped the poison and murdered a room full of people. He leaned against the building, sucking in the cold fresh air. Sweat streamed down his face. He wiped the constant dripping from his nose and coughed.

Eric opened the door and followed him out. "Had the same reaction my first time."

"How do you stand it?" Borg asked.

"You'll get used to it, and a tall glass of vodka helps," Eric said, laughing. He slapped Borg on the back.

Borg took a huge breath, but he nodded. He wiped his eyes and looked up at Eric. "Did you hear some of them praying?"

Eric shook his head. "No. After a while you block out the sounds, so you don't think of them as people."

As fast as the policemen could usher them into the gas chambers, other inmates were forced to load the bodies into the ovens and burn all remnants of the gruesome violence. No one, not even a child, was beyond the horrifying fate of the crematorium, as it puffed its smoke, creating foul-smelling air.

—⟋⟍—

The next day, Eddie, with his head shaved and wearing baggy striped pants and a shirt, walked up to Eric and Borg outside the crematorium. Eddie pointed. "Where is my mother? She's been taking a shower for a long time. She should be clean by now."

"I don't know, boy. Move on," Borg said.

Eric pointed to the smoke. "Say Auf Wiedersehen. She is smoke by now," he said, laughing and showing his yellow teeth.

Eddie didn't understand, but he stared at the strange smoky sky. "The sky is smoking." He walked on as he twisted his head to continue looking up at the sky. "That is not good."

"How is that one still alive?" Borg asked.

Eric laughed and shrugged as the sky puffed foul death-smoke. The one thing the Nazis hadn't counted on was the smell of burning human flesh. The stench seeped over the camp like a foul fog, a constant reminder that souls had been sacrificed.

—⟋⟍—

Smoke came out of the chimneys as the red sun went down behind London's skyline. Peter, hidden behind the bushes outside the Cohens' house, watched as Becca played croquet on the well-manicured lawn. Priscilla wheeled up next to a ball and whacked it with her mallet.

Mrs. Daniels emerged from the house with small cucumber sandwiches for the girls. Assured that Becca was still safe, Peter turned away and walked off, ready to plan another underground plot to stop Hitler.

CHAPTER 40

HATE IS HARD TO KILL

(May 1943)

Ramona, the inmate matron, led Eva into the warehouse the Jewish people called "Kanada," which symbolized their dreams of a place with great wealth and freedom. In it, mounds of clothes, shoes, suitcases, and other belongings were piled thirty feet high, a Matterhorn of stolen possessions. Huge baskets overflowed with eyeglasses, combs, brushes, and wedding rings.

"This is the sorting warehouse. It's not hard. You sort things into piles," Ramona explained. "The valuable things are sent back to Germany."

"Why?"

"To be sold. It pays for the trains that bring us here," Ramona said matter-of-factly, as she searched the side pockets of a suitcase.

"Why do you do their dirty work? You're one of us," Eva said. "I think that—"

"Don't think," Ramona interrupted. "Just try to survive. Thinking always causes problems."

"But if you survive, how can you live?" Eva asked.

A Nazi officer walked in. Ramona stood straight, her face scrunching up into a wrinkled, bitter snarl. "Get to work! This isn't a holiday!" she shouted at Eva.

A rat ran out from the piles. Eva didn't even flinch. She kicked it away. She pulled down a suitcase, opened it, and scavenged through the possessions of her fellow prisoners. Vermin and loss of privacy were the least of her problems now.

—⁓—

Stephen and Hans dressed, choosing their day's clean folded clothes from their drawers. Then they boarded the London city bus to go to their jobs as dishwashers at Percy's Tavern.

—⁓—

Peter rolled under Commandant Karl Radley's big black car, which Peter had watched until Radley went into the headquarters building. He attached a crude homemade bomb to the undercarriage and rolled out. He had learned a few things from his friend Abraham, the Ichabod-looking scientist. Peter stood up and strolled away without looking back.

A short time later, Radley emerged from his meetings, walking in his fast-paced stride with his driver hurrying to keep up. Radley flipped his gloves in the palm of his other hand, as he passed two police officers standing nearby. They were too busy talking to notice the arrogant commandant or appreciate his incessant need for power. Radley stopped suddenly and turned toward the two officers. The driver opened Radley's door, went around the car, and got in.

Radley's turned-up nose flared. He took his gloves and slapped the two officers across their faces. "Salute when I walk by you!" he yelled.

The driver started the car. It exploded in a fuel-induced ball of flames.

Peter eagerly looked back to see his final revenge fulfilled against the abhorrent commandant. Instead, he saw Radley rise from the ground where he had taken cover, shaken, but very much alive, and Peter realized it was harder to kill hate than he thought.

—⁓—

At the Reinigen Camp yard, Eva and Lory sat beside Helga. Eva smiled. "Look what I found." Eva opened her hand to show them a candy bar. She divided it into three pieces, handing one piece to Lory.

Lory looked at the rich dark chocolate. "Where did you get the sweet?" she asked, awestruck.

"Hidden in a suitcase pocket," Eva whispered.

"I've forgotten what chocolate tastes like," Lory said, as she shoved hers into her mouth. Eva held out a piece to her mother as she raised her other hand to eat hers. Her mother hit her hands, and both pieces of chocolate fell on the hard dusty ground.

"Don't eat that. You stole it from your people," Helga said. "If they catch us, they will kill us."

"They're going to kill us anyway, and I think we should have it rather than a Nazi."

"I will not die over chocolate. It's not dignified," Helga scoffed.

Lory snatched the dusty pieces of chocolate off the ground and tossed them into her mouth. "My people would want me to have it," she said, as she chewed the sweet chocolate.

Helga had not eaten adequate food for a long time, and what little hair she had was falling out. The once plump woman was now very thin. She turned and marched off. Suddenly dizzy from her explosive rage and the smell of chocolate, she collapsed.

The guard pointed his gun at Helga. "Get up! Schnell!"

Eva ran to her side. The guards paused.

"Mutti, get up! You must get up!"

"I can't," Helga said.

"Then prepare to die a very undignified death," Eva whispered angrily.

Helga glared at her but rose slowly. Eva helped her to the camp infirmary. It was contradictory to all logic for the Nazis to have an infirmary at a place where they routinely killed people, but nothing at Reinigen was logical. It served their purposes to use patients for their unsanctioned medical experimentation, and to hide their cruelty to the outside world by pretending to give medical care.

Hans and Stephen practiced football kicks in the hostel yard. "What do you think happened to Eva?" Stephen asked.

"She's probably bossing Hitler around," Hans said, "like she did us."

"Remember when she wanted to attack the Nazi and save the librarian?" Stephen asked, as he side-kicked the ball.

They looked at each other.

"She's probably dead," Stephen said, sadly.

Hans nodded and sighed, and ran after the ball.

CHAPTER 41

THE FINAL SHOWERS

(July 1943)

Shortly after their arrival many months before, Eva had been moved, along with Lory, into the kinderlager in order to supervise the younger ones. The children's barracks were separated from Dr. Braun's medical camp by two rows of barbed wire.

The trains unloaded cars of new prisoners each day, and the ovens dumped out the remains of prisoners each night. It was a constant factory of death, and no one was spared the fear that their turn was next. There were almost eighty thousand prisoners at Reinigen Camp. Sometimes family members didn't see each other for months, even years, if they stayed alive that long. Sometimes they never saw them again once they entered the camp.

Eva looked forward to the occasional glimpses of her father. He was looking older and so much thinner. Sometimes, she barely recognized him, because so many of the inmates looked alike: dressed the same, skeleton-thin, and bald.

It wasn't until sixteen-year-old Eva was on her way to work that she finally saw Eddie as he stumbled out of the medical building. She barely recognized the pale-faced mute with a zombie walk and an overwhelming sadness, as if his emotions had been emptied, as the perpetually enthusiastic Eddie.

Eva waved her arms, trying to get his attention without the policeman noticing. She whispered, "Eddie? Eddie? Is that you?"

Eddie jerked forward. He stared right at her but didn't respond.

"Eddie, it's me, Eva, Hans's friend from Berlin. What did they do to you?"

Dr. Braun walked out and steered Eddie back into the building.

"No," Eddie said, almost unintelligibly to Dr. Braun. Eddie tried to twist away from him. "No, it hurts. I need my Mutti. Where is she? She said she would find me."

Dr. Braun nodded to his medical assistant, a pinched-faced man with a disapproving snarl, wearing glasses and dressed in a white lab coat. The sour assistant, whose face resembled a dried apple, roughly pulled Eddie back into the medical building, as Dr. Braun hurried out of the camp.

Ramona grabbed Eva and pulled her into the barracks. "Do you know that boy?"

"I used to," Eva said.

"What's wrong with him?"

"I think his joy has been extracted."

—⚈—

Otto, who worked in the processing building most of the time, had not seen Eddie again after the first day when he saved his life, and he did not know that Eva and her family were there, either. He assumed Eddie had been spared a horrifying death and to seek him out would have been dangerous for both of them.

That morning, Otto turned toward the medical building and walked into the medical office to collect reports. He stopped abruptly when he saw Eddie twitching violently, strapped to a table, and screaming as electrical probes shocked him.

"Unstrap him, immediately!" Otto said, trying to control his anger.

"I just got him hooked up again," the assistant grumbled.

"I am to escort him to the infirmary."

The assistant unhooked the wobbling Eddie from the electrical probes. Otto quickly helped Eddie, who was shuffling like an old man, walk out of the building.

Otto maneuvered Eddie, his legs almost dragging, across the medical camp, by supporting him under the arms. "Eddie. It's Otto. Do you remember me?"

Eddie looked at him, as drool spilled out of his mouth, and blood dripped from his nose and ears.

"It's me. Otto. I'm so sorry, Eddie. Come with me." Otto helped Eddie walk across the yard. A bucket tumbled toward them. Otto stretched out his foot to prevent it from hitting Eddie. He kicked the bucket like a football, and it spun rapidly away.

"Otto?"

"That's right, Eddie. I'm sorry they hurt you. I'm so sorry, but it's okay now, I'll find your mother for you," Otto said.

Eddie eyes lit up. He finally understood. "Mutti? Thank you, Otto."

They reached the door to the gas chambers.

"Go on in, it'll be okay," Otto said.

Eddie wobbled and leaned on Otto. "You are my best friend."

"That's right, Eddie. That's right," Otto said, holding the door.

Eddie walked into the crowded chamber. Otto walked in after him.

"You're going to take a shower too?" Eddie asked.

"Yes, Eddie. I'm very dirty."

The door shut and locked.

The gas whooshed out for those destined for death.

In the crowded chaos of the death herd, no one noticed or even cared about the handsome ex-football player turned Nazi policeman and death camp guard, or the kind, adoring young man whose innocence was not the least of the things that had been taken from him. All Otto and Eddie had were each other, two unlikely comrades as they waited to die, their final escape from the control of the Nazis.

CHAPTER 42

THE DULL GRAY OF DEATH

(January 1944)

One winter morning at a nearly empty Regents Park in London, Hans and Stephen played football. The cold rain had frozen on the lawn, and the ball made a crunching sound as it hit the icy blades of grass.

"What if they never come back for us? What if they all die?" Stephen asked.

They kicked the ball back and forth down the field. "We'll have each other. We will always stay together," Hans answered.

"That's all we have now, anyway," Stephen said.

"Last night, I dreamed Eddie was sitting on the moon, watching us play football and cheering. He seemed so happy," Hans said.

Bert waited, as the children walked by from the camp kinderlager. Eva spied him.

"Papa?"

Bert motioned to her and slipped a round object into her hand. He smiled. "Happy birthday, my little mouse."

"It's my birthday?" Eva said.

Bert nodded. "Best day of my life."

"How can you say that, Papa?"

"I believe good things, unexpected wonders, can come from imperfect situations."

Eva smiled. "Thank you, Papa. Thank you for saying that. I love you."

Bert blew her a kiss.

Eva moved on, following the line of children. She towered above the heads of most. She was almost eighteen now. To lighten her own load, Ramona had put Eva in charge of the kinderlager, but unlike Ramona, Eva was not cruel. The children looked up to her like a big sister.

Eva clutched the orange. In winter this was an obvious sign of eternal optimism, an orange blossom of hope. She quickly slipped it in the pocket of her baggy work dress. To be found with such a precious item would surely be death, but when death was a daily companion, it didn't seem such a huge risk.

That night, after everyone was asleep in the kinderlager barracks, with Lory, seven, on one side of her and Inge, a ten-year-old skeleton of a girl on the other, snoring softly, Eva pulled out the orange and smelled it. She rubbed her hands over it and kissed it.

The sweet, almost forgotten smell of the orange awakened Inge. She sniffed. "Is that really an orange?"

"Yes, isn't it beautiful?" Eva said.

Lory turned over and stared at the orange. It really wasn't even a very good orange. It was wrinkled and no longer firm. It had lost its sweet tenderness a long time ago. It was just an orange peel, containing what used to be the promise of a fragrant fruit.

"Did you find that in the warehouse?" Lory asked.

"No, it's from my father," Eva whispered.

"You still have a father?" Inge asked, more amazed. Eva nodded.

"Can I have a piece of it?" Inge held out her thin hand, so pale it showed the blue veins through her skin.

Eva shook her head. "It's a birthday present. I want to make it last, maybe tomorrow."

Eva clutched the orange to her chest and fell asleep. The precious birthday orange remained unpeeled.

"Happy birthday, Eva," Inge said, as she lay awake next to her, too hungry to go to sleep.

The next morning, Ramona entered the kinderlager barracks and prodded Eva, Lory, and Inge with a billy club. "Get up, lazy girls! Roll call! Appell!" She moved on to jab the other children.

Eva stirred. Inge, lying next to her, was stiff and colorless. Eva nudged her as Lory scooted away from her.

"Inge's dead. She never woke up," Lory said, whispering the horror of the quiet death that took Inge away without a sound, right beside them as they slept.

Eva nodded. "Drag her out to roll call, or they will hold us outside for hours. Today, even the air is frozen."

Lory and Eva struggled to carry their dead friend outside the kinderlager barracks. They carefully laid her on the snowy ground, next to them, to be counted. When Ramona ended roll call, she yelled, "Dump that dead one in the new ditch, and get to work!" She turned on her heels and left.

Eva looked down at the pale, lifeless Inge. She pulled the shriveled orange out of her pocket and placed it in Inge's cold hand, an offering too late to change the course of death. Eva wept, surprised there were any tears left.

The other inmate matrons picked up Inge and threw her in the newly dug ditch not too far outside the camp. Eva's birthday gift from her father fell from Inge's lifeless hand and landed in the ditch, a bright orange contrast against the dull gray of death at Reinigen Camp.

CHAPTER 43

PRESS FORWARD ON ALL FRONTS

(June 1944)

At the Cohens' house on 16 Poppleton Circle, Becca, twelve, and Priscilla, fourteen, shared a chocolate bar in tiny bites to make the precious, dark, rationed sweetness last longer. Doris and Harry sat on the couch. Mrs. Daniels turned the knob on the radio, her flabby arms swinging.

"D-Day, June 6, 1944, marks the end of Hitler's domination, as Allied Forces invade Normandy, France, and push for Western Europe's liberation," the radio announcer said, solemnly, but with a lilt of hope.

They cheered. Becca danced around and spun Priscilla in her chair.

"We have far to go, but let us pray this is the end of Hitler's invasions. If we can press forward on all fronts," the radio announcer said, "victory may be near."

"Rumor has it that the Allied Forces have broken the Berlin code. If that is true, it won't be long," Harry said.

"Not a moment too soon, aye," Mrs. Daniels said.

"No turning back now," Harry said. "Kill all the Germans!"

Becca stopped dancing. Her joy disappeared.

—⚊—

Peter, Mica, and Sloan ate stale bread in the underground room beneath the forest outside Soblin. "I'm telling you, now is the time to sneak inside the camp and blow it up. Things aren't going well for Hitler. He is distracted by failure, since some incredibly brilliant commando cracked his undecipherable Berlin code, and the Allies are serving him defeats. If we strike now, his power will crumble even more. If we don't strike now, they will kill everyone in the camps out of fear of the Allied Forces invasion," Peter reasoned.

"How did you become such a reckless aggressor?" Mica asked.

"I learned from a farmer I once knew," Peter answered. "Strike when they are weak and never relent."

"What you are asking is certain suicide," Sloan said.

"Let me ask, are you ready to suffer and give your life for the Resistance?" Peter asked, repeating the question Sloan had asked him at the English pub. "Rebels die young, you know."

Sloan smiled and turned to Mica. "Well?"

"If you two are dead, there is no need for me to live. I'm in," Mica answered.

"Young rebel, we are in agreement. Plan your big, incapacitating sabotage of a death camp and say your prayers."

"Which one will it be?" Mica asked.

"Reinigen, at Lodansk," Peter said, choosing the camp where Eva was imprisoned, if she was still alive.

"So, it is decided; we shall die together," Sloan the Bear said. "I wish we had some ale. A big fat barrel of it."

"There will be plenty of time for that when Hitler concedes defeat," Peter said.

"I hope your actions are as bold as your words, foolish rebel meat-man," Sloan said.

Mica looked at Peter. "Then a big rebellion it is."

Peter nodded and smiled.

"It was nice knowing you both," Sloan joked.

CHAPTER 44

BE BOLD

(January 1945)

Sloan, Mica, and Peter carefully mapped the Reinigen Camp so each building was clearly identified. They visited several times to get the visual lay of the camp at Lodansk. To infiltrate the camp and blow up the buildings, they would have to know it by heart.

Before she was arrested, Iron Isha had spoken to two people who had escaped Reinigen in an old potato wagon used to carry the corpses from the camp and dump them in ditches. She'd quizzed them for days as she helped them cross the border into safety. She'd recorded the smallest details of the camp, including even the shaft where the poison pellets went down into the gas chamber. Peter used those notes to add detail to his map. He knew every inch of the Reinigen Camp.

At their last reconnaissance mission, Peter, staring at the vast and secure camp from a safe distance away at a farmer's barn, thought that Eva might still be captive at the prison. If she wasn't there, if he was too late, it would be too heavy to bear. Each camp explosion would be a personal tribute to his old friend, Eva, and to the fact that without the Kindertransport this would certainly have been his fate as well, or worse.

———

Peter went to get the scarce explosive material by visiting his Soblin sewer explosive expert. He also wanted to learn how to make a better petrol bomb; the botched Berlin Headquarters attack still weighed heavy on his mind.

In the sewer, hearing that Martha had died from dysentery was surprisingly painful. Peter could see that Abraham was crushingly lonely for his housekeeper, who had become his unofficial wartime sewer wife. Abraham said he could no longer obtain the ingredients to make the clever bombs he had always concocted.

"These are my last bombs, since my supplier was discovered by the Nazis and shot. I only have some simple explosives left," he said.

He showed Peter how to make a rudimentary bomb from TNT hidden in a hollow pine log as a camouflage casing. "I call these pine bombs," Abraham said, and he gave Peter the bundle of TNT. "You'll have to find the logs yourself. They are scarce in my neighborhood."

"What will you do now?" Peter asked.

"I will die a free man, here in the pipe," Abraham said. "That's more than I can say for most."

"Freedom is worth any price," Peter said, as he hugged the old scientist.

Abraham nodded with a slight bow. "May God guide your feet."

Peter looked down at his boots as he walked away. He would miss his odd, but determined, sewer friends.

—◊—

Sloan, Mica, and Peter rendezvoused in Lodansk on January 16, 1945, a cold day with icicles hanging from the eaves of the rooftops. Their plan was to go into the Reinigen camp at night, so people would be asleep in the barracks. They would blow up all the other buildings without danger to the prisoners, because prisoners were restricted to the barracks and the medical building, the only buildings the rebels would spare from demolition.

The frigid air chilled them through to their bones. The frozen ground crunched under Peter's boots as he looked through the binoculars at the camp in the distance, like he had several times before. His hot breath vaporized into the cold air. He was hidden at a safe range in a barn a short distance from Lars's farmhouse.

Lars, a Polish pig farmer and a devout Christian willing to risk his family's lives to help the Jewish Resistance, was the opposite of Emil, the troll farmer. Lars was a compassionate man, whose soft lilting voice soothed his animals and gave confidence to anyone bold enough to attempt the supreme sabotage of destroying a Nazi death camp.

Peter was now eighteen. He had grown taller than his father, and was head to head with Sloan the Bear. He had filled out and was lean and muscular from his years with the underground. He was a handsome young man and a poster boy for a rugged, daring rebel. Sloan and Mica looked him up and down with weary eyes and saw Peter's good looks as a problem. "You're too much of a pretty boy for a prisoner, too much muscle, too well groomed," Sloan said. "You'll be spotted right away."

"You look mighty well fed yourselves," Peter pointed out.

"But he makes a good Nazi. Even Karl Radley fell for it," Mica observed, smiling.

"Oh, no! No! No! No! I'm not doing that again!"

"Oh, yeah, you are," Sloan said. He pulled out the Nazi officer uniform Peter had worn before. This time he filled it out.

"Bruno? Johan Bruno? Exit the refuse vehicle! Schnell!" Sloan said, laughing as he imitated Commandant Radley when he'd seen Peter driving the garbage truck.

Peter shook his head. "No! No!"

"This was your idea, the big sabotage, the big rescue," Mica said. "Be bold, you said."

"You can't back out now, rebel boy," Sloan said. "Your destiny awaits, Johan Bruno!" They laughed.

Lars gently nudged the pigs with a stick to make his way through their pen. "Come on, men, let's go inside until dark. The moon will be full tonight, and you haven't tasted my wife's paczki."

Inside the small but cozy farmhouse, Lars's wife made them coffee and paczki, a deep-fried, flattened, round dough. It reminded Peter of the pastries his family had eaten on Sunday nights, when he was a child. Sloan, Mica, and Peter sat at the kitchen table and set up explosive devices inside hollowed-out, split wood that looked exactly like the logs the Nazis used to fire up the crematorium and other furnaces at the camp.

Peter also assembled two petrol bombs. He modified his usual bomb, eliminating the fuse. This time he made the petrol bombs out of sulfuric acid, sugar, and potassium chlorate like Abraham had shown him. "This will ignite on impact. It doesn't need a rag fuse. I've found some people don't know how to light a fuse." He looked meaningfully at Mica.

Mica picked up a piece of his paczki and threw it at Peter. It hit his arm and landed on the table. Peter picked it up and popped it in his mouth. "Don't waste the paczki."

They laughed, and Peter continued to make the bombs that would free the Reinigen prisoners. They would be prepared for anything and accept nothing but total destruction of the Nazi camp.

"Don't forget to tighten the connectors this time, boy," Sloan teased. Mica and Sloan laughed, heartily.

Peter rolled his eyes. "Who saved you from the hanging noose? You ungrateful renegades!"

"The meat man," Sloan said, "in a dustbin lorry!"

Sloan and Mica laughed.

"But who taught you to be a heartless rebel?" Mica reminded him.

"Two old washed-up commandos," Peter said, as he spread a map on the table. "Now, let's look at the map one more time. We leave the barracks and medical buildings alone. We explode the gas chambers and crematorium first. I will personally see to that. We check the warehouse to make sure only Nazis are in it, and then, systematically, we eliminate them all. Sloan, you take these buildings, Mica these, and I will take these." Peter pointed to the buildings on the intricate homemade map.

"You have taken the most dangerous for yourself," Sloan pointed out.

"It was my idea," Peter said.

"You are either very stupid, very brave, or a little touched in the head," Sloan said.

"I'm with you, aren't I?" Peter teased.

"Our goal is complete annihilation," Mica said gravely. "You realize if it doesn't work, it will surely be our deaths."

"I cannot think of anyone else I would rather die with," Peter said.

The humor evaporated from the room. Sloan pointed to Peter. "If I am ever lucky enough to be a father, I hope I have a son like you, who is not afraid to attempt big things."

Peter hugged Sloan. "You are the closest thing to a father I have had since I was eleven." Then he hugged Mica. "We will do this together."

Mica put his hands on Peter and Sloan's shoulders. "Whether we are successful or not tonight, my friends, together we will make history. We will do something great. We will fight the Nazis, and one way or the other, free our people."

"Tonight, we fight for God," Peter said. They raised their coffee mugs in salute to their revolt.

Late that night, a light snow fell. The moon shone brightly, casting its white light like a lunar lantern on their daring deed. Peter was dressed as the fake Nazi. Mica and Sloan were dressed like prisoners in baggy striped pants and shirts Lars's wife had sewn to hide their healthy thickness. They headed to the entrance of the camp in a farm wagon driven by Lars, a Christian pig farmer with a sense of justice.

Peter got out from the front of the wagon. Radley's old gun, the one Peter had retrieved with the yo-yo, was in Peter's holster, but bullets were nearly impossible to get. The gun was only for show. A large leather pouch strapped across his shoulder rested at his side. He usually used it for carrying important papers or packages, but that night, it contained two petrol bombs as backup. "Leave no room for failure," he whispered to the others.

Then Peter motioned to Sloan and Mica in the back of the wagon and raised his voice. "Out! Schnell! Schnell, you Jew scum! Carry the farmer's wood for my fire; it is cold tonight."

Mica and Sloan got out, heads hanging as they shuffled toward the camp's entrance, carrying armloads of split logs with explosives nestled securely inside.

Peter shouted at the police guards. "Open the gate!"

And remarkably, the gates opened.

They moved through the entrance, carrying the armloads of small logs filled with bombs. The gate clanged shut. They were in, but without complete success, there was no way out. They had to destroy the camp and kill, or run off, all the Nazi guards, or they would be trapped inside and killed as Jewish rebels, the worst kind of prisoners. In his head, Peter recited the cuts of meat, as the Kindertransport boy who escaped Germany, returned, and infiltrated a death camp dressed as a Nazi officer.

Lars drove nervously away to wait inside the farmhouse with his wife for the camp's fireworks show and an end to their unwelcome neighbors that was long overdue. Soon, they hoped their country would be returned to the good people of Poland.

Peter marched Sloan and Mica, carrying the small but powerful explosives, disguised as logs, through the dark camp. Once out of sight, they divided the matches and pine bombs, each taking four bombs.

"It is time," Sloan said.

"May God guide our feet," Peter said, repeating Abraham's last words to him.

They turned to go. A flashlight shone on Mica and Sloan. A German Shepherd growled and pulled at his leash beside the big man holding the flashlight. Mica and Sloan quickly turned their faces away from the light.

"What are you doing here? You will be shot for leaving your barracks!" the man shouted.

Peter set his four log bombs down in the snow and stepped out from the shadows. "They are my responsibility. I will escort them back." He crossed into the beam of the flashlight and stood face to face with Karl Radley.

Peter froze. Radley was the Commandant at Reinigen Camp? The unexpected confrontation with his Nazi enemy would put a huge kink in their bomb plot.

"Bruno? You worthless scum. You owe me a hanging," Radley said, as he pulled his gun and aimed it at them, his hands shaking slightly. "Tonight, I have you trapped, and this time I will not miss."

Sloan and Mica turned, still holding their logs, and faced Radley.

Radley stared. "Ah, your rebel friends. A bonus."

Sloan whispered out of the side of his mouth in Yiddish: "On the count of three, rush him. He can't kill all of us."

Peter grabbed the pine bombs from the ground.

"One," Sloan said.

Without waiting for Sloan's count to finish, Peter hit the vicious dog and charged toward Radley.

Sloan and Mica, only a second behind him, caught Radley off guard, but he fired, as he ran backwards trying to avoid the unexpected commando onslaught. The shot missed them, but alerted the police guards. Bullets riddled the ground around them.

"Run!" Sloan commanded. They stopped their attack and sprinted into the darkness of the camp and the cover of the camp's many buildings. Radley shot repeatedly, but the darkness and their swift flight prevented a hit.

"Traitors!" Radley yelled, shooting randomly at them. "Attention! Jew rebels are among us! The traitors are here! Kill them on sight." The three commandos could hear his murderous orders as they hid behind the water tanks.

"You don't understand what 'count to three' means?" Sloan scolded Peter.

"Three was too long." Peter put his pine bombs in his leather pouch, along with the matches. "Take the opportunity, you taught me that."

Sloan breathed heavily. "This was a shorter rebellion than I anticipated."

Peter shook his head. "We are not done. There is still fight in us."

"You are like a cat with an unrealistic notion of the size of the dog," Sloan said.

"You were a good teacher," Peter said.

"Don't blame me. If we are to do this, we must do it quickly. They won't be far behind us," Mica said.

"Get done what we can before we die," Sloan said.

"We will not die today," Peter said. "We will take down the big dog."

Sloan smiled. Peter's confidence helped him collect his shattered bravado. "Let's go."

They took off in different directions to execute their schedule of demolishing buildings and to strike a blow against Hitler for Reinigen and all Jewish people.

—⚊—

Karl Radley gestured excitedly to the officers summoned by his shouting, Eric among them. "I tell you, it's Johan Bruno, the traitor of Germany, who freed Sloan the Bear and Mica the Murderer. They are all here!" Radley said excitedly.

"Here in Lodansk?" Eric asked.

Radley nodded. "Here, inside the compound."

"Then they are trapped like rats. We will find them and kill them, and we will be the talk of Germany," Eric bragged.

Borg ran up to the group. "Commandant, on the teletype there are reports that Allied Forces have crossed the border and are headed this way," he said, breathing heavily.

Stunned for a moment, Radley grimaced, and he paced like a man used to giving orders. He shouted, "Send all the children to the gas chambers! And march all those who are able out of camp. Stop for nothing. Evacuate and shoot whoever refuses. No one will take this camp. The rest must hunt down and kill those worthless rebels at any cost! They will not humiliate me again!"

—⚊—

A short time later in the kinderlager barracks, Ramona burst through the door, letting the frigid night air blow into the already frosty, unheated building. She stood stiffly in front of the children, staring straight ahead, not willing to look them in the eyes. She cleared her throat. "All kinder are to report to the showers, now!"

She turned on her heels and strutted out. The door banged shut.

The children stared. The inevitable had finally come on the dark wings of night, and all hope evaporated into the frosty air. There was muffled crying and moaning at the realization that death had at last come calling, and they were being forced to answer.

Eva was still in the children's barracks, and as the oldest, she was responsible for them. She was extremely thin, and her hair was jagged, dirty, and matted. In spite of that, she was still a beautiful girl. She lay in her bunk and thought about her childhood. She wished she'd been able to take that ride with Peter in the garbage truck.

She closed her eyes and curled up in a ball, contemplating which would be worse, to be shot in the cold barracks or to die in the showers. Either way, death was a certainty. She decided to stay and be shot. She would refuse to go. It would be her last defiance, her last stand.

Three shrill warbling whistles broke through the silence of the night, like Peter's call she remembered from her school days. She opened her eyes and sat up. She listened, her ears straining for the sound of Peter's distinctive call, but everything was quiet.

She shook her head. She had crazily misheard a train whistle, or she was hallucinating from lack of food and complete exhaustion. Perhaps her mind had finally snapped. It could not be possible; it could not be Peter. He was in England. The memory of Peter and her life before her arrest, however, gave her the courage to get up and face her fate. She would not abandon the children who depended on her in their last moments.

CHAPTER 45

A HEART'S LIBERATION

(January 1945)

In the kinderlager, Ramona led Eva and the other children from their barracks.

"They're going to kill us," Eva said.

Ramona nodded, but looked away.

"How can you do this?" Eva asked.

"Dark days call for dark choices," Ramona answered.

Eva and the children lined up outside the gas chambers, as they had seen so many others do. Ramona leaned in and whispered to Eva, who stood at the head of the line. "Take deep breaths; you'll die faster."

Eva stared and nodded. "Now you want to help me?"

The three commandos could wait no longer. Radley was implementing his kill orders. Guards were beginning to round up the inmates for a death march out of the camp. A line of children waited at the front of the gas chambers, which would make their sabotage more dangerous, but it was time. If the rebels didn't act, their bold mission would be jeopardized.

Peter stood outside the officers' building. He could explode it quickly because no inmates were ever allowed there. He pulled the thin fake end off a pine bomb. It was not on securely after Peter had thrown them on the ground when Radley surprised them. He lifted up the fuse.

If ever there was a time for God to be watching, it was then, thought Peter. It was at that crucial moment when his daring rebellion needed intervention for his people, God's chosen people. Right then was the moment when life could change, when the advantage could go to the Jewish people.

Peter took out a match and lit it. The fuse sizzled and finally caught. Then it went out. He lit another match and touched the fuse, but the match extinguished. He lit another, and it again sputtered into flame, then went out. He was wasting precious matches. He felt the fuse. It was completely soaked from setting it down in the snow earlier.

He quickly took out another pine bomb. He hesitated, overwhelmed with what he had done. Now he would not have enough bombs to blow up all his targets. Even with the two petrol bombs still in his pouch, it would not be enough explosives.

Nazi officers, shouting orders, ran through the camp. An officer ran past Peter and stopped. "Open the gas chambers! The children are waiting! Commandant Radley's orders!"

Peter slammed the pine bomb against the officer's head. The officer slid to the ground. He quickly lit another pine bomb, a dry one, and threw it into the officers' building. It exploded. Peter cheered, as if he were watching Stephen and Hans at a football game at Dovercourt.

Across the camp, the reception building suddenly exploded in flames. Sloan had hit his target. Peter carried the remaining three pine bombs, although one fuse was too wet to light, and ran to the gas chambers.

He saw the children waiting their turn in line to be killed. This was a problem. He could not destroy the gas chambers if the children were there. The line of children was so long that from where he approached, he could not see the children in the front. So Peter did not see Eva huddled with a group of children near the gas chamber's entrance, determined to be the first to die, to show the children courage.

Peter walked up to the children waiting at the back of the line.

"You must leave, kinder. I am not a Nazi. I am a rebel. Today, you will be free!" Peter said. "Run to the barracks."

The children, thinking it to be a trick, moved slowly away from the Nazi. They had been fooled before. The idea of freedom was no longer something they could understand, and rebellion and rescue were as foreign as warmth and comfort. To hear these words from a Nazi was certainly a lie.

The children at the back of the line didn't listen to Peter the Nazi's words. They remained in line, waiting for the command to enter the gas chamber. That cold, strange night, they had accepted their final fate and were in line to die. Nothing could scare them anymore.

Peter knew time was crucial, and his last three targets were still standing. He decided he would run and blow up the crematorium and the warehouse. When he could find Sloan and Mica, who were not dressed as the enemy, he would get them to rescue the children. Peter planned to come back to blow up the gas chamber. He could not risk it with the children in line.

He ran toward the crematorium. The gas chamber would have to wait until last, and he hoped the chaos would prevent anyone from carrying out the order.

—⚏—

Bert, searching for Eva, ran up to the empty kinderlager barracks. In the background, the guards' stand and camp entrance exploded. He saw the burning skyline of buildings and looked around frantically. He saw the children waiting to go into the gas chamber.

He ran and grabbed Eva at the front of the line, and hugged her.

"What's going on?" Eva asked.

"I don't know, but you must run and hide! We have been spared," Bert said, barely able to catch his breath. "They say the rebels are here."

"You mean we are to disobey orders?" Eva asked, unbelievingly.

"Yes, emphatically," Bert said, nodding.

"What about you, Papa?"

"I'm going to check on your mother. Take the children back to the barracks. Don't worry, I'll find you," Bert said.

Eva motioned to the other children. "We are saved for today. Follow me!" she shouted, and remarkably, they followed.

—⚏—

Peter had studied the map and knew the camp well. He soon reached the crematorium. Since his first bomb had a wet fuse, and he'd had to use a second to blow up the Nazi officers' building, he only had two remaining usable bombs and the two petrol bombs. He still had the warehouse they called Kanada as one of his targets. He would blow up the crematorium and come back later for the gas chamber when there were no children by it. Hopefully, the wet fuse would be dry enough by then and take the match, he thought.

He lit a pine bomb and tossed it into the crematorium. The building where so many people had burned was being incinerated by a Jewish butcher's son. There was something near justice in that rebellious act, and Peter could feel the joy of destroying evil fill his soul. He felt more powerful and fearless with each explosion across the camp.

—⟵⟫⟶—

Eva led the children toward the barracks. Several police guards were gathering people for the death march. "Line up. The camp is being evacuated. Anyone refusing will be killed!" a policeman by the barracks ordered.

She motioned to the other children, and they changed direction. "Go quickly. We will hide in Kanada," she said quietly. She ran into the warehouse, followed by all the other children whose new acts of defiance made them shake with fear.

The children hid, squeezed behind the huge mountain of suitcases at the warehouse. Ramona opened the door. She saw Eva pull the smallest child back behind the suitcases.

A Nazi officer entered right behind Ramona with a gun pointed at her head. "We will march them all out of here. No one is to be left if they can walk. I need all inmates outside immediately," he said.

Ramona hesitated, and then nodded.

"That means you."

"Me?" Ramona asked.

"You didn't really think you would be spared, did you? All clear in here?"

Ramona hesitated. "All clear," she lied. Only when she was faced with her own death did she finally take an action on the side of her people.

———ᗱᗱ———

Looking for Helga, Bert hurried boldly up the steps of the camp infirmary, a place he had not been allowed to enter.

Suddenly, he was jerked from behind and pulled back down the stairs. He was herded into a thick line of thousands of prisoners being led on foot out of the camp by the remaining well-armed guards. The Nazis had to get rid of the evidence of their evil. If they just killed the prisoners, the bodies would tell the world of their crimes. The inmates had to be removed completely to leave no proof of the Nazis' inhumane and torturous prison.

Bert turned to a man next to him. "What's going on?"

"The rebels are here. They are throwing explosives. One is even dressed as a Nazi. The commandant is evacuating all prisoners."

Bert turned. "Eva," he whispered to himself, "stay hidden."

The Nazi officers drove a seemingly unending line of more than twenty thousand prisoners on a death march out of the camp and through the snow into the Polish countryside. It would have been more, but the increased gas chamber loads had significantly reduced the number of inmates in recent months. The Nazis were efficient at killing.

On the death march, some inmates had no shoes. One inmate dropped dead before even getting out of sight of the camp. The rest just stepped around him, callously conditioned to accept sudden death.

Bert and another inmate stopped to move the dead man to keep him from being trampled. Eric and Borg saw the line pause and stomped over.

"What is the problem?" Eric demanded. They parted the inmates and saw Bert picking up the dead man. He was so thin he didn't weigh much, but was cumbersome in his lifeless lankiness.

"Keep moving, or you'll end up like him," Borg shouted with the uncaring voice of the Nazi he had been trained to be. But he trailed off at the end, uncertain of his conviction.

The line moved slowly around them. Eric and Borg picked up the dead man and tossed him to the side, out of the path, not with sympathy but with efficiency.

Borg grimaced. He looked at the line of prisoners stretching as far as he could see. "Where are we going?" he asked Eric, cold and weary, walking beside him.

Eric pointed ahead. "It doesn't matter. We will go until they tell us to stop."

"Who will tell us to stop?" Borg asked, finally questioning the madness. "It is only us." He looked around and shook his head. "But it won't be me, anymore." He took off running across the field.

Eric, unused to anyone questioning the Nazis, stared after him. Then, the fog of confusion lifted, and his Nazi sensibilities clicked in. He pulled out his gun, aimed it at the fleeing Borg, and shot. Borg, at last on his way to his own freedom and finally giving in to a long simmering rejection of his murderous people and his own actions, stumbled and fell face down in the snow. He was dead at the hands of his own people, for disobeying a Nazi command.

"I hate cowards," Eric muttered, as he continued moving forward with the death march of prisoners.

Bert realized the murder of one of their own revealed how desperate and weak the Nazis had become, and he knew his time for escape was now.

A herd of slow-moving cows, a few yards away, watched the Reinigen camp death march pass by, as they nudged the frozen ground looking for any surviving grass stubble. Bert reached down quickly and scooped up several ice-covered stones. The frozen rocks burned cold in his hands.

He glanced around. The Nazi guards were still focused on the unmanageable job of marching the line of people as far away as possible from the rebellion and the advancing Allied military forces. Bert maneuvered to the outside of the huge line by shuffling behind people and sliding over, avoiding any attention. He watched as they marched closer to the herd of cows, who casually accepted the Nazi intrusion through their frozen field.

Bert bounced the rocks in his hand, listening to them click together.

He raised his hand to throw them, but a black-and-white cow raised her head and mooed loudly. Bert pulled his arm down. The cow bobbed its head back down, pushing the snow with her cold nose, looking for something to eat.

Bert took the quiet cow moment and heaved the stones into the bushes at the opposite side of the long marching line. The police guards turned and fired where the rocks landed. The prisoners all ducked as bullets riddled the empty frozen bush.

While the guards were distracted, Bert slipped out of the death line and dove into the herd of cows on the other side. The Nazi police turned back around, after they realized it was just a leafless bush they had riddled with bullets. The cows mooed.

"Hurry up! Move out! We've got a long way to go!" Eric shouted.

The miles of prisoners trudged on, leaving Bert hiding among the mooing, hungry herd. The cows ignored him and went about their bovine business of chewing what little frozen grass they could find. Bert could still see the camp in the distance, smoke rising from the rebel explosions, but he waited there, until the remaining line of inmates filed out of sight.

Bert left his cow cover and headed back to camp. For years, he'd dreamed of escaping Reinigen. Now, when it was finally possible, he was returning back to camp for Eva, and Helga, still in the infirmary, if there was enough of her left to save.

—◊◊◊—

The door to the Reinigen Camp warehouse swung open. Quick, heavy footsteps sounded as someone searched the room, stopping beside the suitcases. The children huddled in fear as the footsteps came toward them. Eva looked up, ready to defend their moment of freedom.

The footsteps rounded the corner. It was Bert.

"Papa!" Eva cried.

"Oh, Eva, my princess, I've found you. I was so scared when I saw the barracks were empty. Come out, children. The rebels are here. The camp has been emptied. We will be free!" Bert said.

The children emerged from behind the suitcases. Booted steps sounded behind Bert.

A young Nazi officer loomed over them. The camp had not been emptied of all Nazis. Just when freedom seemed so certain, they would be killed amongst the stolen last possessions of their people.

The Nazi officer stared at Eva. He trilled three high-pitched whistles. Then he smiled, and his whole face changed. It was Peter.

"Eva, it's me, Peter. I have come to set you free," he said matter-of-factly.

Eva stood very still, her mouth hanging open. "Peter? It was your whistles I heard!"

"Yes," he said, at last coming face to face with the girl he had dreamed of for so many years. "I hoped you were still here. I hoped you could hear me."

She looked him up and down. "Peter! You're a man," she said. "What are you doing in a Nazi uniform?"

"It is the best way for a rebel to hide. We're blowing up the camp," Peter said. "The Allied Forces are only a few days away."

"A rebel in a Nazi uniform?" Eva asked. He smiled and nodded.

She looked at Bert. "Peter's a rebel, Papa!"

Bert walked over, put his arms around Peter, and buried his face, wet with tears, in his shoulder. "Peter, your father was right. You were destined to save the Jews!"

Peter smiled. "I left my violin at home this time, Herr Rosenberg. Explosives seemed more effective."

Eva laughed, ran to Peter, and hugged him. "Thank you, Peter!"

The children crept out from around the piles with looks of horror, as they watched Eva hugging a Nazi officer.

"He is not a Nazi, children. It is only his disguise. He is one of us," Bert reassured the children, as his daughter looked up at the handsome boy of her childhood.

"So, we are free?" she asked, as if the idea was unbelievable, and the words had a hard time forming in her mouth.

Peter nodded. "Today is the Nazis' last day at Reinigen."

The children cheered.

"Have you seen my mother and sister?" Peter asked haltingly.

"No," Eva said sadly, shaking her head.

Peter looked at Bert. "The Levys or Vogners?"

"I have not seen them," Bert said.

"I saw Eddie, but they had done terrible things to him. There wasn't any Eddie left," Eva said.

"So many are gone," Bert said. "They marched everybody who could walk out of camp."

"We need to vacate this building. Get all the children out. Send them to the barracks or the medical clinic. All other buildings will be destroyed."

Eva hurried to the door, then stopped, and turned back. "Have you seen Stephen and Hans?"

"They are living in London and are the same as you remember."

Eva sighed and smiled. "Tell them I'm sorry I missed the train."

Peter nodded. "I will."

"You were safe in England. Why did you come back?" Eva asked.

He looked at her and shrugged. "I had to do something."

She smiled, and tears ran down her face. "Peter," she called to him, "will you find me after the war?"

"Well, I still owe you a ride in a garbage truck, and believe me, it's worth it." He smiled at the thin, haggard girl who still looked beautiful to him. "Unless you have plans, I'll find you after I blow up the rest of this prison and get out of this Nazi uniform."

She smiled and laughed. "I have no other plans."

Peter nodded to Bert, standing beside Eva. "Nice to see you again, Herr Rosenberg."

"It's my pleasure, son," Bert said, with tears in his eyes. "You're strong like your father, a very brave soldier."

"Thank you, sir."

Eva turned to the kids. "You heard the handsome rebel. Run to the barracks and wait," she said. "We will all be free again!"

"What does free mean?" a young boy asked another boy.

"It means food," an older boy said.

Eva and Bert followed the children out.

—⋙—

Peter smiled. He hadn't been this happy since his father had given him his violin, when life seemed so simple, and Hitler wasn't killing Jews. He sighed, but this was no time to be nostalgic.

When everyone was out, he reached into his pouch and got the last good pine bomb. He lit the fuse, tossed it into the pile of stolen belongings, and ran through the door just before Kanada exploded, blowing away the remnants of so many destroyed lives.

As Peter ran out, he knocked into a frail old man scurrying away, disoriented from the confusion of the random explosions. The old man fell to the ground. Peter stopped and reached out his hand to help him up, but the old man covered his head with his skeleton-thin arms. "Please, no! Don't kill me!"

Peter looked at the man's outstretched arm and then his own uniform. "I am not a Nazi. It is just a camouflage to hide behind. I am blowing up the buildings. I am Jewish, and I am here to set you free."

The old man squinted his eyes. "What took you so long?"

—⚒—

Although weak from hunger and exhaustion, the children hurried to the kinderlager barracks.

Bert hugged Eva, as they headed toward the infirmary. "You're so cold," Eva said.

"They marched us out of here, but I escaped. The Allied Forces must be getting very close to risk such an evacuation of so many thousands."

Eva kissed him on the cheek. "Oh, Papa, God gave me exactly the right father, but where are we going to go? What are we going to do?"

"We will go home and demand our lives back," Bert said. "Let's tell your mother about the rebels and Peter. I can't wait to see her face when she hears the little maestro turned into a commando." They laughed and hugged each other, filled with a joy they hadn't felt for years, a joy of possibilities, a joy of tomorrows.

—⚒—

The Nazi guards were gone, evacuated by orders or fleeing from fear. A few prisoners wandered around, disoriented. A woman curled up on the ground, with her hands over her head, and lay frozen in her act of fear.

Peter returned again to the last target on his assignment list, the one he'd skipped when the children would not leave: the gas chambers. However, he only had the pine bomb with the bad fuse and two petrol bombs in his leather pouch. One way or the other, he had to make them work. It looked from the chaos of the camp and the number of buildings burning that this bold endeavor was successful after all. The gas chamber could not remain standing. Its destruction was crucial to the success of their mission, to Peter's personal vengeance, and as a symbol of their liberation.

Peter entered the building to make sure it was empty. To kill one of his own people from carelessness would be unforgivable.

"Anyone here?" Peter shouted. "Please go to the barracks where you will be safe. This building will be exploded immediately."

He entered the gas chamber, a chilling room of emptiness, and he could feel the cold fear and dread of what had taken place there. The pegs for clothing were bare; for many months, the killing had gone on without any pretense.

Boots clicked on the bare concrete floor.

"You have forgotten one thing, Bruno." Radley stepped from behind a pillar. "Me. You will not run away this time. You will die, like all your people, at the hand of a superior race." He pointed his pistol at Peter.

His death would come at the hands of his old enemy, Peter thought. But until his last breath, he would still fight. He remembered Abraham's last words: May God guide your feet.

Peter leaped into the air, mimicking the football side-kicks of Hans and Stephen that he had watched every afternoon at Dovercourt. He kicked his leg out, hitting Radley's knee. The gun went off, the bullet embedding itself in the wall. Radley went down, and the gun skidded across the room.

Peter picked up the gun. "Hitler's days are through," he said, as he walked toward Radley. He aimed the gun at him, thinking it was finally the end.

With his heart beating fast, Peter pulled the trigger, but he heard nothing but a hollow click. The gun was empty, its shells spent on Radley's previous attempts to murder him.

Radley got up, his injured knee preventing him from fully extending his leg. He limped toward Peter, pulling a dagger from his belt. "I will kill you myself. You are nothing but a Jew boy."

The dagger sliced toward Peter. Peter blocked it with his forearm, but the dagger grazed him in retreat and blood ran from the slash line.

Radley laughed. "You are inferior, Bruno!"

Peter took a deep breath and pulled up his slashed arm. He shook his head. "My name is not Bruno. I am Peter Weinberg. My father was Henry Weinberg, and he served with honor in the Great War."

"You are the weak little violin player?" Radley asked, with disdain and surprise. He stabbed the dagger at Peter, but Peter danced away.

"No, I am the great Jewish rebel who plays the violin, and you are my enemy."

"I hated your smug, no-good father." Radley swung the dagger again. Peter quickly backed away, forcing himself off balance, and he fell. Radley hovered over him.

"I remember when I slapped that arrogant sister of yours," Radley said, as he slashed the dagger down toward Peter's chest.

"I remember, too," Peter said. Using Wolfgang's schoolboy leg sweep, he suddenly jerked and spun around, kicking Radley's legs and buckling his injured knee. Peter jumped up and threw his fist with every ounce of anger in him, hitting Radley in the face.

Radley crashed down, with his dagger still in his hand. His head hit the floor.

"That's for Becca," Peter said. "Nazis should keep their mouths shut."

He grabbed the failed pine bomb from his pouch and stood up. He touched the fuse. It was slightly damp. He lit the last match and held it up to the uncooperative fuse, and this time it lit.

He threw it on the floor, which startled Radley, who was dazed after his head had hit the concrete floor. Radley threw the dagger at Peter.

But Peter ducked, wheeled around, and ran out of the chamber.

"Now you are running away. That's all you Jews do!" Radley shouted.

The pine bomb sizzled, sputtered, and went out. Radley threw back his head and laughed. "See, you can't kill me! You are a shame to your shabby, undignified family!"

Peter pulled the heavy door shut and locked it, the lock that prevented any escape by the inmates.

Peter could hear Radley's laughter, but no explosion. Leave no room for failure, Peter thought, and he smiled. He ran to the room the map identified as the place where they dropped the pellets to release the gas. He took out the petrol bombs from his pouch.

"And this is for my father!" Peter yelled as he threw the petrol bombs down the hole and into the pillar in the chamber where Radley was trapped.

Then Peter ran faster than he had ever run in his life, as the Mozart tune he had so often struggled with played in his head. He jumped out the back door, as the gas chamber, with Radley in it, exploded behind him, the petrol bombs finally igniting the reluctant pine bomb.

Peter was thrown into the air. He hit the ground hard. A little dazed from the blast, he scrambled up and ran away from the burning building as the heat from the explosion propelled him forward, like the anger still surging through him.

A woman with sores on her arms, whose one eye was almost swollen shut, pointed to Peter as he escaped the flames of the burning gas chambers. "Look, there is still one Nazi left."

The old man whom Peter had run into earlier shook his head. "He is not a Nazi. He is a rebel, the greatest rebel of all, a Jewish one. He just blew up the gas chambers. God is surely with that one."

Sick prisoners lay in beds at the camp infirmary, but no one attended them. The medical personnel had been the first to leave after the terrifying initial explosion.

Eva and Bert sat beside Helga. "Mutti, it's over," Eva said. "It's finally over. The end has come."

"The rebels are here, and you won't believe it, but Peter Weinberg is one of them!" Bert said. "And the Allied Forces aren't far behind."

"Peter Weinberg? Impossible," Helga said. She rolled over, and her gown opened. There were scars all over her stomach and infected open sores.

"What have they done to you?" Eva gasped.

"The Nazis know no bounds," Helga said. "I learned that a long time ago."

Eva patted her mother's arm. "You feel hot, Mutti."

Helga looked at Eva. "Don't worry about me. Always worrying about me." Her hand wavered to Bert. "So like your father." She looked at Eva. "You should have gone to England."

Eva reached out and held her mother's shaky hand. Helga sighed, as if her attempt at an apology had taken everything out of her. She shuddered, closed her eyes, and passed away.

Eva laid her head down on her hand clasping tightly to her mother's. Bert gently closed Helga's eyelids and kissed her forehead. "She's free now, too," he said.

—m—

That night the homemade bombs ended the reign of Nazi terror at Reinigen. Although they were weak and exhausted, and some were near death, the realization of freedom brought the remaining prisoners jubilance. For the first time, the children laughed, talked, and rested in the yard where they used to stand still for hours at roll call. The busy camp had been emptied of Nazis. The prisoners who were left gathered in the street between the barracks, sharing what little food they could find. It was slowly sinking in for the Reinigen Camp inmates that freedom was near.

Eva, and Peter, who had taken off the Nazi uniform and bandaged his injured arm, held their hands out to warm themselves at a fire in an open barrel by the barracks.

"I actually feel warm," Eva said. "I had forgotten what it felt like. Things have changed so much since we were children."

"I know. I think I might be better at football than I thought."

"Are you going to play?" Eva asked, surprised.

"No, too dangerous." Peter smiled. "Music is my game."

She smiled at Peter. "You still play the violin?"

"I've been sort of busy lately," he said. "A pub in England is holding it for me. It's a long story. Why don't you come to England with me and see Hans, Stephen, and Becca?"

Eva laughed. "Do you know how many times I have dreamed of that? How is my favorite little spitfire?"

"She is a proper English girl with fancy black, shiny shoes." Peter laughed. "And she plays croquet on the lawn."

"I cannot wait to see her, and Hans and Stephen," Eva said. "I dreamed of your lives each night as I lay in my bunk, and knowing you escaped gave me hope. I have to take my father home and see if there is still a place for him there, but I will come as soon as I can. Will you ever come back to Germany to live?"

"I will always love Germany, but I cannot live there anymore. It has betrayed us. I will find my mother and Lilly and bring them to London. Germany is no longer my home."

"I understand." Eva rested her head on Peter's shoulder. "You've changed, Peter, and yet, you are the same."

"Is this night really almost over?"

The sun reached the horizon, emitting its hazy half circle of illumination. Peter looked at the lighting horizon as morning emerged. "The night is dark, until the sunrise," he said.

Eva sang quietly, and the children stared with their mouths open, for some of them had never heard music before.

The night is dark until the sunrise.
Your heart is lonely until I answer your cries.
Your path is steep and filled with stone,
But I will walk beside you.
You are not alone,
Although the heavy pain you carry is your own,
You are not alone.
You are not alone.
I am God. Follow the way I have shown, and
I will help you find your way home.

When Eva finished singing, she looked over and across the field. Shadows moved there in a long line. It was the death march inmates returning to camp on their own. The Nazi police guards had deserted them when they saw the entire camp burning, and saw no end to the march. Abandoned by the Nazis who fled for their lives, the inmates, with nowhere else to go, returned to camp, the only shelter they knew.

Peter leaned down and kissed Eva gently on the cheek. He pointed to the returning inmates. "Look what your singing can do."

Peter knew it was not the time to linger on personal joys, and a prison camp was not a place for a romance. He was more concerned about getting Eva to safety and moving on to his next mission. He hoped there would be time for love later.

"I will never forget tonight, but I cannot stay. Take your father and the children to the farmhouse down the road and wait for the Allied Forces to arrive. I will see you again," he said.

"Where will I find you?"

"Leave word with Becca. She lives at 16 Poppleton Circle in London."

"I could come?"

"If you wanted to," Peter said.

"We really are free?"

Peter nodded. Eva smiled at him and wrapped her arms around him. He knew at that moment that the risk of the big rebellion had been worth it. He could feel her heart beat against him, and he wished that night would never end, but the sun was already up. It was time to go. Peter knew that to be a part of the Resistance, he must give up everything. This he'd promised he would do for his people and for God.

Peter, the commando, walked through the blown-open front gate and waved to Sloan and Mica, waiting for him on the train tracks that had brought Eva and so many others to that nightmarish place. He turned back, trilled his whistle three times, and then was gone.

Several weeks later, Peter looked up at the orange sunrise spreading its morning brilliance over the Nazi headquarters in Berlin. The Allied Forces were taking back the countries Hitler had invaded, but there was still work to do. As long as there were Nazis somewhere, Peter was determined to finish what he started. He realized his father was right. Wars were started by people in offices and ended by soldiers on the front lines. Peter was a soldier, just like his father.

Sloan, Mica, and Peter huddled in the bushes.

"There is too much wind," Mica pointed out. "We should not proceed."

"I'm not too fond of that hanging platform," Sloan said.

"The wind does not matter any more," Peter said. "I told you, I am an explosives expert. These are like the ones I used at the gas chamber, they do not require a match."

Peter grabbed two petrol bombs, scored vertically to ensure breakage and no need of a fuse. He pulled his arm back to throw the bottles, but stopped. He handed one to Sloan and one to Mica. "You do the honors. I owe you."

Sloan and Mica threw the bottles. The bombs crashed through Nazi windows and exploded on contact.

The Nazi headquarters lit up the block like a bonfire. Peter smiled.

Sloan gave his deep bear laugh. "Retribution tastes so sweet, huh, fearless rebel?" he asked as they hurried away. "Do you have a dustbin lorry waiting for us?"

"Next time, I'll just let them hang you."

"There won't be a next time," Sloan said. "The war is almost over. Now we need to get out of here. There are still Nazis in Berlin."

CHAPTER 46

VICTORY

(May 1945)

Four months later, on May 7, 1945, the church bells rang in England announcing victory in Europe. Traffic barely moved, and horns honked in a spontaneous celebration.

People cheered all over London. Some people wore paper hats and waved noisemakers. They hugged and kissed total strangers, and they danced with abandon in the streets of Piccadilly Circus. Great relief swept over England. The fear was gone. The burden of war was finally lifted from the people, and their hearts' joy was unbounded.

Hans and Stephen ran into the street from their hostel. "What's going on?" Stephen shouted to a man passing by.

"Germany has surrendered!" the man yelled back.

The perpetually dark streetlights flickered and glowed brilliantly, lighting up the streets for the first time since war was declared. Searchlights joyously crisscrossed the night sky, lighting up the darkness, signaling safe skies to the people of England.

The war with Germany had ended. The joy of victory spread throughout England. The Kindertransport children's nightmares were finally over.

—⚙—

At Bloomsbury House, Sebastian watched, from his office window, the boisterous celebrating in the streets. As quiet and serious as the declaration of war had been, it was as loud and as rambunctious when victory was announced. Tears were in Sebastian's eyes as he watched the chaotic merriment of loved ones and strangers, dancing and shouting in the streets. He put his palms flat on the windowpane.

"May the great name of God be exalted!" he whispered. Tears ran down the face of the burly, unflappable man who'd fought to save the children from Hitler.

Marla walked into his office and gently put her hand on his arm. "We did it."

"Indeed. Quite remarkable, actually. What will you do now?" Sebastian asked.

"Same as you, try to help the children find their families. But tonight, I'm going to find a handsome rebel and see if he can dance."

"Sloan?"

Marla smiled. "Maybe. What about you?"

"I'm going to go find my pretty Jewish wife, who has put up with me all these Kindertransport years, and drink wine. Finally, we have something to celebrate."

In the London streets that night, Stephen danced with a pretty girl in a swirling blue skirt.

A beautiful girl with brightly painted red nails grabbed Hans and kissed him, then skipped off into the jubilant crowd.

"Who was that girl that just kissed you?" Stephen asked.

"I don't know who the dame was!" Hans said, imitating Humphrey Bogart's voice in the movie *Casablanca*. "But who cares? She kissed me!" He laughed loudly, a boisterous laugh that could only erupt from the freedom of victory. "I really like this end-of-the-war stuff!"

"Yes, we'll have to do this again," Stephen said.

"No, no, no, one war is enough for me," Hans said.

"Oh, it'll happen again, but who will be the Jews next time?" Stephen asked.

"I'm not thinking about that right now. All I know is Hitler's dead, and we kicked Germany's tail," Hans said.

Stephen twirled the pretty girl in the blue skirt around again. Hans grabbed another girl walking by. Both boys danced with an abandon they had not felt since long before they'd boarded the Kindertransport and fled their homes and everything they loved.

—ᴍ—

In the London pub, The Blue Ox, the blackout curtains were opened. A relaxed Sloan and Mica, both smiling, looked very handsome. Sloan's dark demeanor was gone. He was no longer a bear.

Sloan, Mica, and Marla, now twenty-seven years old, celebrated inside with Peter. All except Peter clinked pint glasses of dark foamy ale. "Here's to the end of the war and to Hitler's suicide!" Mica said. "The cowardly wretch."

"I would have been happy to do it for him," Sloan said.

"Here's to the kinder who will live to tell their stories!" Marla said.

They looked at Peter.

"Don't look at me, I want to forget," Peter said, quietly, as he let out a heavy sigh. He leaned back in his chair with his shoulders relaxed. "I just want to find my family and get my life back."

Marla picked up her glass and lifted it high into the air. "Here's to Peter getting his life back."

"And that pretty girl from the camp," Mica teased.

"To the best young commando, but the worst driver!" Sloan said.

"Unless he's driving a dustbin lorry, and we're about to lose our necks!" Mica corrected.

"I'm a good driver!" Peter challenged.

They laughed, and all except Peter raised their glasses, downing their ale. Peter stood up. "There is something I need to do."

He picked up his violin from the bartender. "Thank you for taking care of my violin," he said to the barkeep.

Then, with a short salute to his rebel friends, Peter left the pub.

"He reminds me of me," Sloan said.

"Only good looking and kind," Mica teased.

Sloan laughed. "Another round of ale. The war is over! We can begin to live again." He looked at Marla. "I hope you've got some shillings on you, Blue Eyes, because this could be an expensive tab."

Marla smiled. "I think we'll be all right. My father owns this tavern."

Sloan lifted his empty glass. "Now, there's a man I can respect, and you are a woman I can love."

Marla laughed and hugged him.

"Another round!" Mica said.

"And keep them coming!" Sloan yelled.

—⚹—

As Peter hurried through the crowded and joyous streets with his violin, he passed a pub where the radio blared "I'll Be Waiting for You."

I'll be waiting for you
No matter how long it takes.
I'll be waiting for you
No matter what the stakes.
I'll be waiting across the sea,
Just come home to me.
Just come home to me.

He hesitated at the door, listening to the song. It always reminded him of Eva. He had received a message from Jules, who had joined the British Army, telling him that Eva and her father were back home in Berlin.

Peter had paid his debt to his people in Germany, but it was no longer his home. He had to get Becca. Together, they would find his mother and sister, and bring them to London.

—⚹—

At the Cohens' house on 16 Poppleton Circle, the family celebrated the end of the war. The lights were all on, and they drank tea with milk and ate empire biscuits. Harry and Mrs. Daniels had a small glass of brandy.

Outside the house, hidden by the bushes, Peter took the violin out of his case. He caressed it like a long-lost friend, familiar but uncertain. He placed it underneath his chin. The violin felt so much smaller in his large hands.

Under the faint light of a sliver of a yellow moon, the lone violinist played. The music started out softly and grew in volume.

Inside the house, Becca heard the music and put her biscuit down, unsure of what she heard. She ran to Mrs. Daniels, grabbed her hands, and pulled her up. "Mrs. Daniels. Get up. It's him! It's Peter! He's come for me!"

Mrs. Daniels struggled to get up out of the chair. "Then run to him, Becca! The war is over, and we are all free!"

Becca took off running to the front of the house. Mrs. Daniels shouted to Harry, Doris, and Priscilla, who were listening to the radio. "The violin serenader is back! Peter has come for her!"

Harry, Doris pushing Priscilla, and Mrs. Daniels ran to the front lawn after Becca.

The violin played the lilting tune of "With God By Our Side" that filled the air with the clear and sure notes that only Peter could play.

"Becca, is it Peter?" Priscilla shouted.

"Yes, yes, I know it's him. I feel him," Becca yelled. "He's here."

Peter sang.

We are marching forward, with God by our side.
We will not leave our path, for He will be our guide.

Becca ran down the lawn toward the music. "Peter? Peter?"

Peter stepped out from behind the shadowy bushes, at last revealing himself.

"Blimey!" Mrs. Daniels exclaimed.

"Peter!" Becca screamed.

"It is him! Becca was right! Peter has come for her," Priscilla said.

Peter dipped and swayed with the notes, as he walked up the lawn to Becca, playing his violin with a vigor he had not felt in years. He sang.

Hold my hand, lift our voices
In prayer across the land.
For we have made our choices
And together we will stand.

Peter's music blossomed against the cool night air. He was back, and Becca ran to him, dancing around him. He turned to her each time she circled him, and·their homecoming was the melody of their hearts together again.

When his song ended, Becca threw herself into his arms. "Peter! I knew you would come for me!"

Peter hugged her with one strong arm, and with the other he held the violin. "I never forgot you, not even for a minute."

The war was over. Although it had taken so many things from them, their apartment, their butcher shop, their father, their childhood, and even their country, they still rejoiced, because they had survived. They had found each other, at last, and Hitler had not won.

CHAPTER 47

LOST AND FOUND

(June 1945)

A few days later, at the London Red Cross office, lists of the survivors were taped to the windows. People crowded around to read the lists, hoping their loved ones, by some miracle, might have made it through.

Hans and Stephen fought their way to the windows. Hans pushed Stephen in front of him. "You go first," he said.

Stephen stepped forward and quickly read the long list. None of his family was on it. He moved to another list. His family wasn't there either. He moved to another, and then stared. His mother's name, Nora Levy, was on the last list.

He blinked and looked again. He reached out and touched her name, as if to make sure it was real. "Nora Levy," Stephen said in a faraway whisper, as if he couldn't believe it. He turned to Hans. "She's alive! She made it. I am not a hopeless orphan anymore!"

They hugged each other. There was quiet relief and an unburdening of the weight that had sat on Stephen's young shoulders for seven years. It was a hesitant celebration.

"Now, your turn," Stephen said.

Hans stepped forward. He searched the lists, jostled by the surging, anxious, and often weeping crowd. He couldn't find anyone on the list. He turned and shrugged. Stephen walked up and searched, too. Not one member of Hans's family was listed.

Hans shook his head.

"No one is left, not even Eddie," he said, accepting his greatest fear, a final reality. What Hans had feared all these years was true. They weren't ever coming back. There would be no promised reunion for Hans.

———m———

Eva, extremely thin, but stylish in a wide-shouldered dress cinched in at her tiny waist, waited with her father on the porch of their old house in Berlin. Her hair, somewhat grown out, had a slight curl.

She and her father watched as Olga, a chubby version of her younger self, and her parents hurriedly moved their things out of Eva's house. Two American servicemen, with guns and broad grins, supervised.

As they left, Eva held out her hand to Olga, who stared at Eva's thin, outstretched hand.

"The war may be over, but that doesn't mean people feel differently," Olga said, as she turned and walked away. It was Olga's turn to be displaced with nowhere to go.

"I don't believe that. Germany is as much mine as it is yours. You'll see. Germany will rise again!" Eva shouted after her.

Bert reached over and put his arm around her and smiled. "I should have let you hit her the night they took our house." They laughed together like the old days.

That night they wandered their old house. Many of their possessions were missing, but it was filled with so many memories. They remembered a time when life wasn't perfect, but the horrors of the camps were unknown. They marveled at everything they had taken for granted: the running water in the kitchen, the comfort of their bathroom, and electricity at their demand. It was all overwhelming, and they basked in their victory.

"We made it, Papa. We're home," Eva said. They sat at the kitchen table eating apple strudel and drinking hot cocoa, tasting each flavor and savoring the luxury on their tongues.

"We are, indeed. Didn't I tell you we would?"

"Yes, you did. I wish Mother could see that we made it back home," Eva said.

"She can, and maybe now she can see how much we loved her."

"I wonder where William is," Eva said.

"We will try and find him in England."

Eva set her cup in its saucer and it teetered. "Can we go to England?" she asked excitedly.

Bert smiled. "Yes, we will go and visit Peter, and find out what has happened to our William, as soon as things settle down."

Eva clapped and kissed her father's cheek. "Do you know how much I love you, my dear, sweet Papa?"

He kissed her back. "Yes, because I love you the same."

"You look tired. Do you want me to help you to bed?"

"Yes, my little mouse. That huge soft bed is calling me."

With her arms around him, she helped him up the stairs to his old bedroom, hijacked by Olga's family, but returned to them by God, who looks after his people.

That night, as Bert and Eva slept in their family home with the memories of better times swirling around them, and the nearly forgotten warmth and comfort of beds beneath them, Bert's heart finally gave out. He had survived the "Night of Broken Glass," the Bockenburg camp, the Nazi killing camp, and the death march, but at home in Germany, Bert faced death on his own terms. His heart decided it had had enough.

Bert never woke up, and Eva was left alone to find her way.

—⚬—

A few days later in London, an old hunched woman limped to the hostel. Her clothes hung loosely on her thin frame, as if nothing was left of her but the bones. Holding onto the side of the house for support, she slowly knocked on the door.

Stephen opened the door. "Hello, can I help you?"

The old woman grabbed Stephen with thin scarred hands and pulled him to her in a hug. "Stephen! I have dreamed of this moment," the woman said in German.

"Mother?" Stephen said, recognizing the voice from a long-ago memory, but not the words or her appearance. "Is that you?"

The old woman nodded and smiled, showing missing teeth under her split lip. It was Nora. "You look so handsome. So English."

Stephen stood stiffly, staring at her. The young, beautiful mother he remembered was gone. Standing before him was a weathered, bent old woman with patches of hair missing. Only the light in her eyes remained the same. He searched her face. Hitler had taken his mother's beauty, but she had somehow held on to her soul.

"I'm sorry, but I don't speak very much German anymore," Stephen said.

"I said you look so handsome, so English," Nora said, speaking in English. She stroked his face. "My little boy, finally, we are together. I dreamed of this since I waved goodbye at the Kindertransport."

Stephen smiled. His heart warmed to the sound of her voice, like a dream almost forgotten, but so much time had passed. "I'm not a little boy anymore," he said, gently.

Nora nodded. "I can see that. You have become a man without me."

Stephen reached out and held Nora's scarred hand. "What happened to you?"

"Some things are best left unsaid. We will leave for America in a week," Nora said, matter-of-factly. "They are finally allowing us in."

"I don't want to go to America. I want to stay here," Stephen said. "I don't want to start over again."

"You are my son. You'll do what I say," Nora said.

"I've been on my own for seven years," Stephen said.

"You lived in England in safety, while we suffered."

"Yes, but we suffered, too."

"Shame on you. You should be grateful the Kindertransport took you out of Germany! You were the lucky ones," Nora said. "You have no right to compare your life to the horrors those other children suffered, like Eddie and Eva."

"Eddie?" Stephen's eyes teared up. "Eddie's gone."

Nora's face of stone, hiding suffering and unspeakable horrors, cracked, and a tear ran down her cheek. "Anna?"

"She's gone, too. Hans has no one left."

"But you and Hans are here," Nora said. "Do you understand?"

"Yes. I'm sorry. It's been so long."

"We survived Hitler. We'll survive this, too. We can survive anything," Nora said. "We will decide together where we will live."

"What about Hans? I won't leave him."

"He will live with us, wherever we decide to be. I promised Anna. Now invite me in. I'm about ready to faint."

Stephen smiled and opened the door. Nora, battered from Hitler's war, walked into her son's life again.

On the steps outside the Cohen house, Harry, Doris, Mrs. Daniels, Priscilla, and Becca watched with anticipation, as Peter silently read the telegram from the Red Cross that had just been delivered.

"WE REGRET TO NOTIFY YOU THAT SYLVIA AND LILLY WEINBERG DIED ON THE GROUNDS OF A TEMPORARY CAMP AT 404 EDELWEISS STREET IN SEPTEMBER 1939."

His mother and sister were dead. They had died across the street from their home and shop, on the grounds of the burned-out synagogue, only nine months after he and Becca left on the Kindertransport, he thought.

Peter's body shook. The brave commando, who had faced every fear, did not want to see this, the end of Becca's hope. He had no choice.

He took a breath. He looked at Becca and sadly shook his head. "They didn't make it."

Becca cried out. "Hitler won after all!" She looked at Peter. "We are lost, Peter! We are sunk!" She ran into his embrace. The telegram from the Red Cross, announcing the end of their dreams, fluttered to the ground.

Peter held the sister he had missed so much, his annoying, bossy, chatterbox sister, who was his connection to his past, his family, and his memories.

He took a deep, shaky breath. "We are not lost, Becca. We have each other, and nothing will ever separate us again. I will walk beside you, and I will stand and die with you, but never again will we be lost."

Across the wide expanse of lawn at 16 Poppleton Circle, Eva, free from Germany at last, ran toward her rescuer and her favorite little spitfire. It was time to live again.

EPILOGUE

After the war, Peter returned to his violin and the solace of his music, to heal. He studied at a London music conservatory and spent his days basking in the challenge of conquering the elusive Mozart.

One night, a crowd of people, in their finest suits and dresses, filed into the London concert hall to listen to Peter play. His night had come. He was no longer outside listening, he was inside playing.

Backstage, a nervous Peter adjusted the violin strings, and a fear overtook him. He knew the King and the Prime Minister were in the audience. The emotions of the night were too powerful. He felt he did not deserve the victory, when so many others were lost.

Then he thought of the day his father had given him the violin. It seemed so long ago, in a world where the atrocities of Hitler were not possible, at a time when his father's gift had allowed him to dream of such a night. His father would have expected nothing less. Silently, Peter recited the cuts of meat in his mind: loin, shoulder, porterhouse, rack, and shank.

He took a breath of this new world, and with fear and defiance, he walked out onto the stage as the crowd erupted into applause. He stood transfixed as he gazed at the packed concert hall filled with people who had come to hear him play, and his gratitude flooded over him.

He saw Eva and Becca hugging each other. Peter barely recognized Sloan and Mica in their unlikely suits, as they applauded with a thunderous force. Marla sat between them, beaming at Peter. Hans, Stephen, Charlie, and Noah waved to their friend. There were two empty seats near the middle, because Sebastian's wife was in labor. His little boy, who would be named Peter, would be born on the night of Peter's concert debut.

The time flew by as Peter concentrated on each note, filling the hall with his music and his emotions, just like he had at the Dovercourt mess hall. That night he fought with Mozart again, and Peter won this time.

Peter bowed to the King in the royal box. He nodded to the Prime Minister next to him. He tapped his heart with his bow and then pointed to Becca and Eva.

Then he took a breath and began his finale. It was the music he'd silently practiced in the farm attic, his secret message to Becca and his tribute to the people of England, who gave him this sanctuary. Peter, the butcher's son, played the British national anthem, "God Save the King."

The music reverberated from his violin and his heart. He played it in gratitude for all of England, the country that had given him and the other Kindertransport children refuge when most of the world had turned away. Escape on the Kindertransport was necessary, he had come to believe; giving up was not.

When he finished, the people in the audience rose to their feet as the hall shook with thunderous applause. Peter, the violin commando, graciously bowed his musician's acceptance, knowing that to survive and live with love and appreciation was the greatest victory of all.